# THE ESCORT TO THE GRAVE

# G.T. WALKER

GT WALKER

THE ESCORT TO THE GRAVE

**Copyright © G.T.Walker 2022**

G.T. Walker has asserted his right to be identified as the author of this work in accordance with the Copyright, Designs and Patents Act 1988.

This novel is a work of fiction. Names and characters are the product of the author's imagination and any resemblance to actual persons, living or dead, is entirely coincidental.

This book is sold subject to condition that it shall not, by way of trade or otherwise, be lent, resold, hired out, or otherwise circulated without the publisher's (G.T. Walker) prior consent in any form of binding or cover other than that in which it is published and without a similar condition, including this condition, being imposed on the subsequent purchaser.

ISBN number: 9798824704921

GT WALKER

## Contact Information

Email: gtwalkerbooks@hotmail.com

Facebook: www.facebook.com/gtwalkerbooks/

Instagram: www.instagram.com/gtwalkerbooks/

Newsletter:

https://dashboard.mailerlite.com/forms/26131/52738049431308202/share

GT WALKER

# THE ESCORT TO THE GRAVE

**For Clare, Nathan and Gracie xxx**

GT WALKER

# THE ESCORT TO THE GRAVE

Contents

THE ESCORT TO THE GRAVE ................................ 1
Copyright © G.T.Walker 2022 ............................... 3
Contact Information ................................................ 5
For Clare, Nathan and Gracie xxx ........................ 7
The Dialogue of Gwyn ap Nudd ......................... 13
**Prologue** ............................................................... 15
**Chapter 1** ............................................................. 27
**Chapter 2** ............................................................. 37
**Chapter 3** ............................................................. 42
**Chapter 4** ............................................................. 47
**Chapter 5** ............................................................. 57
**Chapter 6** ............................................................. 63
**Chapter 7** ............................................................. 66
**Chapter 8** ............................................................. 73
**Chapter 9** ............................................................. 77
**Chapter 10** ........................................................... 86
**Chapter 11** ........................................................... 92
**Chapter 12** ........................................................... 98
**Chapter 13** ......................................................... 111
**Chapter 14** ......................................................... 115
**Chapter 15** ......................................................... 124
**Chapter 16** ......................................................... 127
**Chapter 17** ......................................................... 131
**Chapter 18** ......................................................... 138
**Chapter 19** ......................................................... 145

| | |
|---|---|
| Chapter 20 | 152 |
| Chapter 21 | 161 |
| Chapter 22 | 168 |
| Chapter 23 | 184 |
| Chapter 24 | 194 |
| Chapter 25 | 201 |
| Chapter 26 | 207 |
| Chapter 27 | 215 |
| Chapter 28 | 222 |
| Chapter 29 | 227 |
| Chapter 30 | 232 |
| Chapter 31 | 240 |
| Chapter 32 | 248 |
| Chapter 33 | 254 |
| Chapter 34 | 265 |
| Chapter 35 | 271 |
| Chapter 36 | 280 |
| Chapter 37 | 288 |
| Chapter 38 | 304 |
| Chapter 39 | 308 |
| Chapter 40 | 313 |
| Chapter 41 | 316 |
| Chapter 42 | 324 |
| Chapter 43 | 333 |
| Chapter 44 | 347 |
| Chapter 45 | 351 |
| Chapter 46 | 357 |

| | |
|---|---|
| **Chapter 47** | 361 |
| **Chapter 48** | 365 |
| **Chapter 49** | 368 |
| **Chapter 50** | 371 |
| **Chapter 51** | 379 |
| **Chapter 52** | 384 |
| **Chapter 53** | 387 |
| **Chapter 54** | 398 |
| **Chapter 55** | 400 |
| **Chapter 56** | 403 |
| **Chapter 57** | 408 |
| **Chapter 58** | 418 |
| **Chapter 59** | 422 |
| **Chapter 60** | 429 |
| **Epilogue** | 435 |
| **Note from the Author** | 450 |
| **Acknowledgements** | 453 |
| **Contact Information** | 455 |

# THE ESCORT TO THE GRAVE

*"I have been, I have been, where the soldiers of Britain were slain.*

*From the east to the north, I am the escort to the grave.*

*I have been, I have been, where the soldiers of Britain were slain.*

*From the east to the south, I am alive, they in death."*

**The Dialogue of Gwyn ap Nudd
The Black Book of Carmarthen.**

GT WALKER

# Prologue

## 6th September 2012

Ever since the very first one all those years ago, I have wondered if they felt remorse. As they drew their last breaths, knowing it was the end, did they ever regret their actions? Now I know.

My body is shutting down. My hands and arms are numb. I can't feel my legs and no matter how much I try to lift my head, my cheek stays stuck to the dash. I still feel the warm blood pouring from it, cooling as it tracks down my face and neck. The pain that moments ago hurt so much is fading away. My eyes are stuck open, and I try desperately to move them, or even to just blink, but I can't do that either. The tickling feeling I had from spit and blood bubbles popping on my lips has gone. My vision is darkening and closing in as I begin to lose focus. I can barely see straight ahead. The end is coming. I regret so much.

I can just make out Jane across from me. Her head is against the steering wheel and her face is a bloody mess. She whimpers as she looks at me, and whispers something I can't hear over the mangled, screaming engine, but I can see her mouth the words.

'I'm sorry.'

Even the foul smell has gone, that acrid stench of spilled petrol and oily fumes has somehow dissipated. All I have left is the disgusting taste of copper in my mouth, and now the pulsing in my head, in rhythm with my racing heart, is fading too. The blood is slowing. There can't be much longer.

The car door cranks open, and my body is pulled back into the seat. Another pulse of warmth leaves my head as hands caress my soaked face. Fingers find my neck, searching for signs of life. I hear a familiar voice calling my name, yet it sounds so far away. A hand pulls my chin sideways, and he is in my line of sight. It is Eddie, my wonderful Eddie. He is here to save me, but it's too late. He is crying and looking at me with those big beautiful eyes, brimming with tears.

'I can't live without you,' I see him say.

I try to tell him it will be ok, but my lips do not move. He cannot hear me.

'I'll always be with you,' I try to say back. 'Now go help her. Help her end this.'

His lips come to mine, then he drops his head and leaves. He thinks I am already dead, but I still see Jane in the driver's seat as her door pulls open. She screams out, and my head rocks side to side as he lifts her from the car.

My Eddie. He will save her, and I hope she will tell him everything.

My vision breaks completely and is now a kaleidoscope of dark, jagged shapes. The pain softens and I can't hear the squeal from the engine anymore. A buzzing sound rings in my ears as the most brilliant colour of white comes. It is not intrusive or worrying. It is peaceful and enveloping.

I think of my Eddie. I worry for him. I think of all the time I have spent with him. The laughing of good times and the crying in bad. The joking, the teasing, the petty arguments, and the making up afterward. If I had listened and told him my secrets, then maybe this wouldn't have happened. Maybe she was right.

I think of Jane. How alone she must have felt to do this. I hope Eddie saves her, and she tells him everything. She deserves a chance to make things right.

The tinny, buzzing sound in my ears softens. Now there is only silence.

The choke of the blood, oil and smoke eases.

The white light fades and everything turns black.

# 10th September 2012

*'The hours, and even days, following the birth of her baby, a new mother can find herself dangerously running on adrenaline. A mother's need to rest is more important than unnecessary worry over a sleeping infant.'*

Sarah remembered reading this from the birth of her first daughter, Jennifer, eight years ago. That first time, she would sit in a daze with a permanent smile etched on her face next to the baby's cot, as her own mother, Mary, was on hand to welcome anyone and everyone through the doors to coo over the new arrival. The excitement Mary protruded becoming a grandmother for the first time made her own job so easy. She would sit and smile and nod at the questions, and Mary would fill in the rest. Back then, David was always on hand to muck in when she needed him too, full of enthusiasm, fussing over her as most first-time dads would.

Maybe that's why it was different this time around. Because it was her second baby. Maybe everyone tunes out and acts differently if it's your second, or third, or fourth. Maybe they only act that way if it's new to you.

*Who am I kidding? It's because my mother died and he's never here.*

She had received visitors the first two days this time around as well, of course. David's assistant Victoria came by with a hamper she had thoughtfully made up herself, full of newborn washing and feeding necessities. A lovely gift, to be fair. Business associates and flunkies of David made up the rest of the visitors, obvious attempts to impress the up-and-coming MP by showering his wife with gifts and compliments. Sarah was not lost to the amazing coincidence, since David had left for London yesterday, the leeches were nowhere to be seen.

Now Sarah sat alone in her living room, the ticking of the mantle clock her only company. Upstairs, Ana, the housemaid/nanny, had put the baby down for the evening in her nursery and was now busy bathing eldest daughter Jennifer. Sarah took a sip of her green tea, her mother's favourite, wishing she were here more than ever. She would no doubt bustle around cleaning up after everyone or leading the conversation about how the baby had her grandfather's eyes and, thank the lord, her mother's lashes.

*If only Mam had told someone she felt ill sooner. Diagnosis and treatment could have started straight away. We would have paid privately for the best doctors money could buy.*

The ring of the doorbell jolted her enough to spill her tea into her saucer. It was a harsh buzzing sound more fitting to a prison secure unit than a rural country house but was just one of many changes on her original list when buying the property five years ago they had just not got around to sorting out. Placing the cup and saucer back down on the side table, she checked her silk pyjamas over for any spill. The saucer had done its job. She peered over at the clock above the fireplace. 8.30 pm.

*Who would call so late?*

Sarah opened her mouth to call Ana, catching the sound before it left, as she remembered she was busy bathing Jennifer. Rising slowly from the settee, Sarah used one hand to push off the armrest as the other cradled under her stomach. Letting out a low groan as she straightened, the stitches and padding tape pulled at her tender skin. She took the best part of a minute to get to the hallway, stopping at the living room doorframe to peer around it. The inner door was open, allowing Sarah a limited view out onto the courtyard through the clear glass panels to the side of the oak front door. The courtyard was in darkness, the motion sensors on the coach lanterns on either side of the door failing to switch them on.

*How long did I take to get to the door? The lights stay on for at least five minutes.*

Lifting her winter coat from the hanger behind the porch door, she took care not to over-stretch as she reached her arms into it. With one hand on the latch, and with a final peek through the glass panel, she unlocked the door and inched it open. Picking up on her movements, the coach lights illuminated the courtyard. A cold gust whipped up and forced her to wrap her arms tight around herself.

No visitors. A delivery.

Resting at her feet was a large wooden crate around three feet by two feet. It looked as old as it looked delicate. Each side had a rope handle and what looked like straw sticking out through the gaps in the wood. No note. Her immediate thought was David had ordered more stock for his vintage wine or whisky collections, maybe celebrating the birth of his daughter by purchasing something to sit in the cellar and not see the light of day or touch a person's lips forever and a day.

*He just loves to show off his money.*

She scratched at the crown of her head, scrunching her long red hair into a further mess.

*The delivery driver left without a signature.*

Sarah scanned the empty courtyard and gardens beyond. The perimeter wall lights illuminated much of the grassy area, yet there were plenty of hiding places amongst the shadows of the trees and shrubs. The huge wrought-iron gates at the bottom of the graveled entrance road were closed, and only then did she realise she hadn't opened them from the porch switch for anyone to enter, anyway. They automatically closed after a visitor had entered, and alarmed with a rather obnoxious sounder if stuck open for any length of time. She stood in silence, her cold exhaled breaths her only company before they drifted off into the night. Whoever had left the box was long gone. She strained to listen out for a vehicle driving away on the country road outside the property grounds but heard only rustling from the bushes over towards the double garage. Common at this time of evening in September, a fox or rabbit out exploring early as the sun had set just over an hour ago. Then she remembered Ana had spotted a rat over there when she was in the hospital. Sarah hated rats. It sent a tremor through her shoulders and up the back of her neck. She contemplated calling Ana again, instead deciding to get the crate inside as quickly as possible. Stepping back from the delivery, she gave her chin a rub as she weighed up her options. The night sky was clear, yet her back ached from the plunging temperatures and the battle wounds from a few days' past.

Giving the crate a small push with her foot, it moved easily enough, giving her the confidence to lift it herself. It was relatively shallow, around eighteen inches deep, so she needed to squat a rather unladylike position, taking a grip of both ropes and straightening her back to allow her legs to do the work. Contrary to her initial analysis, the weight surprised her. Squeaking as she straightened up, she cursed herself for not seeking help, then cursed her husband for the inconvenience some more. Through heavy, ragged breaths, she waddled back through the front door, the rough wood rubbing against her neat belly as she kicked it shut behind her.

Sarah dropped the crate onto the coffee table in the living room, sweating from the effort. She blew out an exhausting breath, taking a staggering step back to assess the delivery. In the soft, warm lighting, she could make out every blemish from the aged timber. The crate looked at least a hundred years old, but then again, she was no expert. Nailed shut, rather than screwed down, gave another indicator of its age she had learned from one antique show or another. Turning it a full 360 degrees, checking for a stamped mark or return address, Sarah found no clue to the contents. She rubbed at her chin again as she pondered her next move. David's hand tools, untouched for years, were over in the garage. No way was she going over there tonight. She could send Ana, but that wouldn't be fair either, considering the monster rats could easily gobble her up as well. Then she remembered the touch-up tin of paint the decorators had left behind after finishing the nursery and the flathead screwdriver used to open the lid accompanying it. She had stored them under the stairs. Retrieving the screwdriver, she diverted to the kitchen for the wooden steak mallet hanging next to the pans above the island countertop.

It took the best part of an hour to open the case with her make-shift tools. It turned into a mini-project she was unwilling to give up. Flashes of the old Sarah shone through: tenacious, head-strong and stubborn. She couldn't say why she persevered. David's purchases had never interested her before, and if she actually thought the crate held bottles of whatever vintage he was attempting to show off to his business chums, she would have dumped it at the porch door until he or Ana moved it elsewhere. But something was calling to her to open the case, waiting for her to free it. She worked away, her delicate condition forgotten as she hammered and prised away at the gaps in the wood, pulling and scraping with her well-manicured nails and forgetting all about the poor table surface getting destroyed beneath it, scratch by scratch. With determined and steely grit, she concentrated on getting it open any which way. An almighty mess ensued, splinters of wood and straw all over her pyjamas, the coffee table, and the designer rug below.

At one point, Ana poked her head down the stairs to tell Sarah her eldest was ready for bed, only to be shooed away with sore and grazed hands from a sweaty and dusty Sarah. Eventually, the last of the nails gave, groaning as the rest of the lid came free. Placing it aside, Sarah reached into the crate, her hand hitting something firm beneath the thin layer of straw covering it. Scattering it side to side, the majority spilled out onto the table below. A musty smell of dust and age hit her nose, confirming her suspicion it hadn't seen the light of day in quite some time. Staring back at Sarah was a beautiful wooden box, a miniature chest, rich brown in colour. At the centre of the lid, black and gold inlays made up an intricate circular design of a tree, the top half the foliage, the bottom half the tangled roots. At the centre of the trunk, sat an interlacing triangular symbol she guessed as Celtic. Surrounding the lid, more gold inlays of vines and leaves worked around the border. It was amazing workmanship, the deep black grains highlighted by the well-oiled rosewood. Tilting the box up revealed a large brass clasp central to where the lid met the body, decorated with the same strange triangular symbol as the lid. It held a keyhole, locked in position, and after heaving the box from the crate onto the settee, Sarah searched the rest of the straw for a key, making even more mess of her surroundings. She pulled out the last of the straw from the crate. It was empty now.

No key.

Sarah deflated audibly, lips vibrating from the exhaled air as she took in the surrounding mess. Dropping to her knees, she finally remembered her condition with a grimace as the stitches and dressings pulled again. She picked up the straw, dumping it back into the case. Then something caught her eye under the coffee table.

A folded note, the paper the same golden colour as the straw. In her haste to find a key, she had completely missed it. She grabbed the paper, rising to sit back on the settee as she opened it. Recoiling in shock, her hand covered her mouth, and her eyes filled as she recognised the beautiful handwriting of her dead mother.

*My darling Elinor. I am sorry I never got to meet you, but it was my time to go. You will grow up to do the most wondrous things. Your sisters will show you the way, and she will deliver your key when you are ready. ~Nana~*

Sarah shook her head, eyes letting go a stream of tears down both cheeks as she read and re-read the note with shaking hands. Finally, her arms crossed in front of her belly as she pursed forwards, her gut twisting in a knot of hurt as she let herself cry in silence.

*I miss you so much, Mam.*

After a few minutes, she wiped the tears from her face with the sleeve of her pyjamas as she calmed back down, trying her best to make sense of it. She read the note again. *Sisters? Elinor only has one. What does she mean? Who will deliver a key? What's so special about a damn box she has to wait for the key?*

A sudden realisation dawned on Sarah, her mouth dropping open as she shook her head in disbelief. Her mother died ten months ago, and she never knew the baby's name would be Elinor.

Because she never knew Sarah was pregnant.

# GT WALKER

# THE ESCORT TO THE GRAVE

*In 2019, the Brecon Mountain Rescue Team assisted with over one hundred reports of missing persons in the Brecon Beacons National Park.*

*All were recovered alive, within six hours of the alarm being raised.*

*Except one.*

GT WALKER

# Chapter 1

### 17th August 2019 - Saturday morning

'What's wrong with the dog?' Jenny asked, directing the question to both her mum and sister, as she peered back from the passenger seat to the boot of the family Range Rover. Through the mesh guards, black and white Border Collie Bandit paced back and fore, whining each time he changed direction.

'He's upset about something Mammy.' Ellie said, her face squished into the squares of the mesh. 'What is it boy?'

Sarah craned her neck to get a look at them in the rear-view mirror. 'He's just excited to get out for a stroll. Now turn around in your seat please Ellie, you shouldn't be leaning out of it like that.' She took her foot off the accelerator, allowing the car to slow as the limit reduced from 60 to 30 miles per hour. The A470 trunk road is the main link from the South to North Wales running through the popular Brecon Beacons national park, and following a spate of motorcycle accidents, coupled with the increasing popularity with the hobby hikers, the local council had recently changed the limit around the base of the tourist attraction of the Pen-y-fan mountain. All too often, the emergency services attended the scene to deal with a road traffic collision.

The Morrison family made the short trip from their country retreat in the village of Pontsticill to the mountain most Saturday mornings through the warmer months of

Spring through Summer, and with the colder months on their way and the girls back to school in a couple of weeks, it would likely be the last opportunity for Sarah to climb the mountain with her girls this year. It had been a family ritual to hike the mountain for several years, due mostly to Sarah's enthusiasm for it, and to keep the tradition going as Jenny got older, she was having to nag far more frequently.

After having second born Ellie almost seven years ago, her competitive running days were over, but the habit of keeping herself in prime shape stayed. No way was she allowing the other school-run mums to gossip about how 'her best days were behind her' or 'she was letting herself go'. Weekdays during school term, she regularly spent her lonely hours hitting the gym, pounding the treadmill or catching a spin class. But her weekends were for spending quality time with her girls. Her husband David used to come on their hikes regularly, and the girls loved his company back then, but Sarah knew the truth of it. Nothing pleased him more than to be papped as the happy family man. It was the main reason he was so popular amongst his voters. It had been some months since he'd come along. As an ambitious MP climbing the political ladder, his weekends were fast becoming clogged up by the job. This weekend, same as the last three, he was staying in London to work. There was unrest in the party, and he was busy preparing for the reshuffle he'd predicted. When it came, he would no doubt expect a front bench role.

Sarah indicated on approach to the Storey Arms car park and slowed, ready to turn in. Run by the local council, the Storey Arms is an outdoor activity centre used predominantly by surrounding schools and charities. It sits at the base of the Pen-y-fan Mountain, the highest peak in the Brecon Beacons that in recent years has become a magnet for hikers.

The dog whined a hurtful pitch again, making Sarah screw her face with a wince. 'Enough Bandit,' she shouted as she pulled in to the first available space she could find. Crunching gravel under the tyres as they came to a stop, she killed the engine quickly. 'What's got into you?' Once out of the vehicle, the three of them made their way around to the boot together. Jenny held Bandit's lead, and although the dog rarely left Ellie's side, Sarah warned them to be ready in case the dog bolted. Ellie stood back a step. On opening the boot, Bandit sat in silence. Beneath him, a puddle of urine was soaking through the carpet to the spare tyre well. Sarah rolled her eyes. Just last week she'd had the jeep valeted.

'Out Bandit!' She spoke in her best commanding voice, pointing to the floor. The dog stayed put, his eyes moving to Ellie as he dropped his head instead. The eldest two women turned to Ellie with an expecting look. She may only be six years old, but if Bandit was to listen to anyone, it would be her. She spotted the look from her mother and sister, and walked to the dog, placing her hand just where he liked it, under his muzzle. The dog's mouth opened and his enormous tongue dropped out, panting heavily, his eyes holding on hers.

'Are you coming, Bandit?'

His whine told her no. He dropped to lay his head on his front paws.

'Maybe he's sick Mammy? I don't want to leave him.'

Sarah's hands met her hips, a confused expression donning her face. 'I don't think he's sick, honey. Remember when we had to take him to the vets that time? He just lies on his side when he's not well.'

Jenny saw the opportunity. 'I'll stay with him. Keep your phone with you and I'll ring you if I need you to come back down. Oh, and can you leave a fiver?' She nodded in the direction of the burger van. 'The smell of onions is making my belly rumble.'

Sarah gave her a skeptical look. 'This is probably going to be the last chance we have of climbing the mountain this year. I'd like to do it together, as a family.'

It was the fifteen-year-old's turn to roll her eyes. She was better at it than her mother. 'We must have been up there ten, twelve times this year, Mam. Besides, we haven't climbed it as a family for ages. We've got Dad to thank for that.'

'You know he'd be here if he could,' Sarah replied, unsure why she said it. It was far from the truth, and she knew the girls knew it too. Sure enough, another expert eye roll from Jenny ensued. Sarah conceded and tossed her the car keys.

'You're not eating that rubbish,' she said, pointing a thumb toward the breakfast van. 'Come on Ellie, Bandit will be fine. We'll be up and down in no time.'

They held hands as they crossed the single file path and the bridge spanning the mountain stream at the base of the climb. Sarah started her timer on her Apple watch, and they were off. Ellie gave a last look back toward the car. She could see Bandit's face peering back through the rear window.

As a seasoned walker, Ellie kept up with her mother easily. Occasionally, they would turn to face back down the way they came to admire the view. Today was a perfect day for photographers making the climb. The skies were clear, save for the odd white flutter, and the sun was threatening a hot August day in the Welsh countryside.

They saw several early risers who were making their way back down. Customary nods exchanged as they passed. They reached the summit and Sarah stopped her watch at just a little over one hour twenty. Not a record by any stretch, but her calorie count read a pleasing five-seventy-five. She would upload the info to her fitness app later.

Ellie sat at her favourite grassy mound on the east side of the peak and pulled her water bottle from her backpack. She

# THE ESCORT TO THE GRAVE

panted beneath the morning sun, but not uncomfortably. She was used to these hikes now, it being her second year of joining in. Her once noodle legs from last year were now wiry with muscle and sinew. She was easily the fittest in her class, even fitter than Freddie Jones, and he played football four times a week.

Sarah stood next to her and drank from her own bottle, scanning the surrounding mountains. The scenery never failed to impress, no matter how many times she made the journey to the top. She removed her camera from her backpack and took a few shots of the surrounding valleys, taking care not to get too close to the steep drops. In the distance, a farmer and his sheepdogs were busy rounding up his flock from a field. Sarah gave Ellie a call to come look and pointed them out. Ellie was always looking for new tricks to teach Bandit, and it amazed her how farmers could just whistle and make their dogs go left, or go right, or lie down or come.

A group of soldiers, in their camouflage gear, sat on the west side of the summit on what looked like huge backpacks you could fit a wardrobe in, drinking from canteens. Not an unusual sight, as the British Army often used the range of mountains for training. The British Special Forces even used them for their selection processes. The Brecon Beacons National Park held a highly respected reputation, even with the elite and super fit. One soldier, dressed in a short sleeve green tee shirt, stood over the others. He was getting some attention from a group of tourists, probably quizzing him on what they were up to, but he appeared to be engaging with them pleasantly enough.

Another group of tourists were crouching around the cairn, a series of concentric stones winding up and around a central cist, a stone box protruding from the top currently holding the National Trust sign and logo, with the mountain height of 886m displayed. It was a must for any visitor to the summit to have a photo taken with the cist, and at busy periods, a queue thirty deep would form for the opportunity. Sarah would demand one with the kids for each visit.

A teenage boy with a blue baseball cap was taking a photo of the group, getting a playful ribbing from them for his clumsiness with the camera. They appeared to be an extended family. Sarah had to think about the strong, confident accents, settling on Canadian. There were two sets of middle-aged men and women, two teenagers of around sixteen, a younger boy and girl around ten, and two ladies, oddly wrapped in long, red hooded shawls. One of them appeared to be around Sarah's age of forty. Although they had their hoods up, she could see she had brown curly hair. The other lady must have been at least ninety years old, her hair protruding from her hood as white as chalk. Her deep wrinkled face and hunch made Sarah wonder if she would climb these mountains anywhere close to her age. The two ladies stood off to the side of the Cairn, probably not wanting to lose their footing on the rising angle of the cobbled stones toward the middle.

Sarah dropped her own camera to her chest, relying on the neck strap to take the weight, and walked over to the boy taking the photo. She offered her services for the lad to join his family, which he accepted. As teenagers do, he sprawled across the front of the cairn, blocking the plaque from view, but a sharp clip at the back of the head from his mother had him moving again. Sarah took the snap and gave the camera back to the lad, who said his thanks.

The group broke up and the teenager's mother approached. As she did, Sarah's gaze followed the two hooded ladies as they ambled over toward Ellie. The older lady struggled with a limp and she hung onto the younger woman's arm, and Sarah found herself equally impressed and confused by how she had made the climb in such a tender state. As the two women reached and engaged with her, Ellie rose to her feet with a smile.

*Great manners, I've taught her well.*

# THE ESCORT TO THE GRAVE

The younger lady stroked Ellie's red hair, giving it a gentle flick over her shoulder. Her hair had always been a hot topic for discussion with strangers. When Sarah was Ellie's age, her matching ginger locks were equally striking, although back then the subject of harsh and constant ridicule from the boys in her class. Made of stern stuff, she could deal with the bullying from an early age. Her daughter, however, was far more sensitive than the young girl she remembered being, and she'd been thankful such a trend had changed since her own school days. Sarah would consider it a quiet day if she didn't receive at least five compliments on the colour of her daughter's hair. Her blue eyes made it the rarest of combinations, 0.17% chance, in fact, and Sarah never missed an opportunity to throw the statistic into idle conversation.

The younger woman crouched down and whispered something into her ear. Ellie's face lit up and she let out a proper belly laugh. The woman pointed to the small container she was carrying, gesturing to it as she spoke. Ellie's eyes widened as she gazed at the pot. Sarah frowned. From where she was standing, the pot had all the resemblance of an urn. The older woman looked pained as she hunched even closer to look into Ellie's eyes, then rose smiling and nodded to the other woman.

'Thanks for the photo. My son is useless with it but insists on being the family photographer.' The woman held out her hand. 'I'm Marie.'

Sarah turned to greet the woman. 'Sarah. Pleased to meet you. Canadian?'

'I'm impressed. We normally get called Americans in the UK. We're on vacation for a family wedding in Cardiff and were told to check out the Brecon Beacons. I'm so glad we did. We have our sights back home, of course, but this is certainly up there.' Her head panned left and right, a huge smile on her face.

'Yes, it's pretty special, isn't it?' Sarah replied. 'Talking of special, the older lady with you must be pretty fit to walk all this way at her age?'

'Oh, those ladies aren't with us,' Marie said. 'I think they're Irish or Scottish. I'm not sure which. They were up here before us.'

Sarah turned back to Ellie, who was deep in conversation with the women. They leaned over her, taking turns to speak. The elderly woman took Ellie's hand in hers and placed her other hand on top. Ellie smiled ear to ear as she looked at her caressed hand then back to the woman's face. An icy shiver ran up Sarah's back to her neck.

'Uh, it was lovely to meet you, but I better get back to my daughter. Enjoy the rest of your stay,' Sarah said, off and moving before the Canadian woman could respond.

Sarah hurried over to the ladies and slapped on her best fake smile. It was a talent she had learned many years ago when she started dating David at college. He was always in the company of some right pretentious idiots, and she was the expert in giving the impression she was enjoying herself every time.

The women flanked Ellie on either side. As Sarah approached, they turned to greet her, and her gut knotted as she noticed Ellie holding hands with the tall brunette lady. The fake smile long forgotten, a growing frown took its place. She opened her mouth to speak, but the old woman beat her to it, stepping in front of her with a wide, toothy grin on her face.

'Your daughter is perfect, Mrs. Morrison,' she said with a thick Scottish accent. 'Full of imagination with an inquisitive mind.'

The tall lady spoke next, a different accent, Irish. 'She will do wondrous things with her sisters.'

Sarah's face fell slack. *Wondrous things with her sisters.*

The old woman held out her hand. Sarah's gaze followed as the woman turned it over, revealing a solid gold object filling her palm. She gave it to Sarah. It was as heavy as a paperweight and the most impressive thing she had ever seen. One side of the huge coin had a pointed triangular shape made up of three intertwined, continuous arcs. The other side had an image of a tree, the top half detailed with blooms of leaves and flowers, the bottom half of soil and root. As Sarah turned the piece in her hand, the sunlight reflected the yellow tones laced with stunningly intricate details of orange she recognised as Celtic gold.

*She had seen these images before.*

Mesmerised by the piece, she ran her fingers over each raised portion of the images, doe-eyed as the astonishing piece gleamed back at her. She had so many questions. It took a full minute before she could pull her eyes away and back to the old woman. The moment she looked up, she knew answering them would be impossible. The old woman's eyes had glossed over, like there was no longer anyone behind them. Her mouth hung open, the jaw muscles letting go of any tension there. She fell forward to Sarah, who instinctively dropped the medallion and caught the woman under the arms. She weighed very little, yet Sarah went down with her, turning her body in a delicate move to ensure the lady would land on her back. Laying her down, she moved her hand to the nape of her neck, gently lowering her head the last few inches.

Sarah cried out for help in a state of panic. The Canadian woman whose name Sarah had already forgotten responded first, closely followed by the lead soldier, who dropped to his knees next to her. He pulled a mobile phone from his pocket to dial 999.

'What's her name?' Sarah shouted as a crowd gathered around, expecting a response from behind her. She lowered her ear to the woman's mouth, feeling and hearing nothing.

'Hey, what's her name?' she called again.

When no response came a second time, Sarah turned back towards the other woman. The colour drained from her face as she realised the woman had disappeared.

And so had her daughter.

## Chapter 2

Ramping the speed up to nine miles per hour, Detective Constable Lauren Price focused on the whirring sound of the treadmill rollers responding with it. Her personal best at this pace was a shade under twenty-four minutes, and the way she was feeling she would beat that today. She was breaking all kinds of personal bests this morning. Eighteen pull-ups. Finally hitting a hundred kilos on her deadlift record, a full ten kilos over her previous best. Not bad for a 5ft 3in woman weighing just over half that herself. Today was starting out a good day.

The treadmill faced the far wall of the station gymnasium, but with eight-foot mirrors adorning them throughout, Price had a vantage of the entire room behind her. As one of the largest and busiest stations in the South Wales valleys, the exercise equipment found in the gymnasium at Merthyr Tydfil police station rivalled many private facilities littered around the borough. Contrary to the fact, she had never seen more than three people in here at the same time. Such was the state of the force these days. You'd find more officers in the queue for Gregg's bakery than you would a state-of-the-art gym like this.

The double doors burst open on their hinges, the pull handles on the reverse side hitting the walls behind them with a violent thud. Detective Chief Inspector John Hibbard glided in, hands still held out in front of him to announce his dramatic and amazing arrival. For some unknown reason, he felt the need to puff out his chest as he strutted past the throng of empty machines, as if informing them of their redundancy in sculpting his magnificent frame. Price would have laughed at the machismo if it hadn't looked so pathetic.

Scanning the room, looking left and right, he made his way towards her with a cocksure walk. He ran his hands through his dark grey, crew cut hair that matched the three-piece suit he wore. Stepping onto the empty treadmill to Price's left, he dropped his elbow onto the control panel, allowing his six-foot-two inch frame to lower until his eye-line matched hers. He gave a lasting stare, an invitation to look across, but she held firm, concentrating on the invisible road ahead. Eventually, she gave, glancing across to his reflection to see the wry smirk he held as he waited. He was a relatively handsome man, his chiselled jaw covered with designer peppered stubble, and he clearly looked after himself, well-manicured hands and year-round tan. He always wore perfectly fitted suits, clearly tailored and not taken directly from the rail.

It was as far as she could go with the compliments. His physical attributes were heavily let down by his emotional and mental ones, though she held reservations they were merely a show of bluster, bravado, cheap and unnecessary attempts to remind the masses who was boss for the sheer sake of it. The DCI had several nicknames, and was the butt of many jokes through the station, and although some were below the belt, she wouldn't mind betting he was completely aware and secretly enjoyed the patter the small folk made for their king. His narcissistic ego had her wondering if he'd even started some stories himself. The thought of it made her want to vomit.

During her time as a uniformed police constable, she had heard the second hand rumours of his womanising, and warned by other officers against joining his team, and even the department. When she had pressed the storytellers for evidence, however, there seemed to be none. They had heard this and that, from a friend of a friend. But it had to be true. Ironic outlooks, considering the business they were in. She had hit back with the old phrased cliché 'I'll speak as I find.' After all, the force had clamped down on such things in recent years and she doubted many were stupid enough to cross the line anymore. This wasn't the eighties. And then, that first day a few weeks ago when welcomed into and introduced to his team, when she had shaken his hand for the first time, those small hairs at the back of her neck stood tall. Like someone had gently blown a breath across them, sharpening her senses into fight-or-flight mode. She was weary. She recalled someone telling her, 'there's no smoke without fire.' Clichés everywhere.

He continued to stare, leaning on the treadmill, waiting. Price could take no more and conceded. No way would she beat twenty-four minutes now. Reducing the speed to three miles per hour, her hands hit her hips as she slowed to walking pace and looked across at Hibbard's smug, victorious grin.

'Something I can do for you, Sir?' she asked, with a tone normally reserved for an annoying sibling. Grabbing her towel from the control panel handle, she wiped down her sweaty face. She hit the stop button, grabbed her water bottle, allowing the last of the conveyor momentum to carry her and drop her off the back of the treadmill.

'We'll have to go for a ten miler sometime, Price.' Hibbard said. 'Although I have to warn you, I'm pretty damn fit.'

*You'd never keep up,* she thought as she continued to wipe the beads of sweat away. A spark in his eye told her he was waiting for such a response, giving him the opportunity to counter with another ridiculous line. *Not a chance.* She took a long drink from her bottle, then wiped the excess from her lips with the back of her hand. She tried again. 'You need something?'

Another wry smirk. 'When's the last time you trekked up Pen-y-fan mountain Price?'

'Couple of months, maybe. I've climbed it a few times.'

'So you know it pretty well.' Hibbard said. 'That's good. I imagine we'll be up and down a few times over the course of the weekend. I'd ask Jenkins to assist, but he's too busy stuffing his face and being a fat slob.' He chuckled at his own joke and frowned when Price didn't join him.

'What's happened on Pen-y-fan that requires Major Crime to attend?' she asked, taking another gulp from the bottle. 'And why is South Wales Police involved? Isn't Pen-y-fan under Dyfed Powys' remit?'

'Suspicious death and abduction of a minor.' Hibbard replied. 'Six-year-old girl missing, presumed taken. Merthyr resident. Turns out the ACC is a friend of the parents.' Making quotation marks with his fingers, he continued, 'He kindly offered our services because we have more resources.' Looking around himself, he double checked no one was eavesdropping.

Assistant Chief Constable Julian Bentley had one hell of a reputation. Over the years, he'd snaked his way through the ranks to the third highest position in the South Wales Police force and was renowned for ruling with an iron fist. He also loved the high-profile nature of the Major Crime Investigation department, enjoying nothing more than sticking his nose in to steal plaudits, air time and notoriety that went with a major case.

'How could the ACC do that?' Price asked. 'Getting involved with a case over the border for a mate?'

'Because of who his mate is. Made a special request to the Chief Constable, and when the Chief found out who the parents are, she jumped at it.'

'Who are they?'

'David and Sarah Morrison.' Hibbard gave her a moment to connect.

'The MP David Morrison?'

Hibbard nodded with vigorous enthusiasm. 'I'm the Senior Investigation Officer for the case, but this one's important, so I'm coming out into the field. You're with me.'

Price nodded. 'The kidnappers killed someone during the incident?'

'The suspicious death is one of the suspected kidnappers.' Hibbard replied. 'Get your hiking boots ready. We leave in thirty minutes.'

# Chapter 3

Price had to hide the smile on her face as she hiked the mountain, the twist in her stomach telling her she should feel guilty for it. It was a glorious day from a weather viewpoint, a gentle hint of a cool breeze preventing an uncomfortable climb in the afternoon heat. The sun was past its high-point, but would continue its glare for hours before falling behind the westerly peaks. She had made this journey many times before, at least into double figures, but this was the first time she had done so without the continuous interruptions when the mountain was open to the public. The mountain had become ridiculously busy in recent years. It was necessary to pull to one side on narrow parts of the path for people passing or to have picture takers stopping abruptly ahead, taking up the whole path without a thought for those coming up behind. Now all she had to deal with was the company she was in, her DCI a running commentary as he battled to keep up with her pace. With his mental capacity not yet reaching adolescence, he was clearly struggling to allow himself to be beaten to the summit by a female. He had even picked up into a mocking canter fifty yards out, assuring his victory and actually fist pumped in celebration. Arriving at the top, Price couldn't help but scan the stunning landscape, taking in the splendid endless view of the surrounding peaks and troughs of the Beacons. The clear sky painted the richest of palettes on the scenery below. 'Carved from God's own hand,' her father would have said, and while she had lost her faith in recent years, it was hard to argue with such analysis.

# THE ESCORT TO THE GRAVE

The summit was bustling with activity. Paper suits scavenged on hands and knees as they searched the vast gravel and grassy areas. Price walked to the National Trust plaque nestled atop the stones circling up to it. It read the same as it had done every other time she had been up there.

PEN Y FAN 886m.

*Hell of a long way up just to kidnap a child.*

Turning a slow 360 degrees, Price attempted to put herself in the kidnapper's place. How could they possibly get from here without being seen? Over twenty witnesses, albeit preoccupied with the chaos of attempting to save a life, but no one saw them take the girl? Steep gradients fell in three directions from the summit, and would have undoubtedly led to serious injury if they had gone over any of them. Narrow paths to the north, east and back the way they came from the south, led gradually to further peaks, and if the mother's claim she worked on the old woman for barely a minute was true, then spotting them would have been straightforward enough. Below the steep drop to the west was the pretty Llyn Cwm Llwch Lake, where the Mountain Rescue team were busy searching that very moment, like brightly coloured ants scouring for food. It would have taken an age for the kidnapper to get her down there. Nothing appeared to add up.

Laughter pulled her attention. Two of the forensics team were talking to Hibbard. He was no doubt filling them in on one of his self-absorbed exploits or making one of his many dad jokes. The older blonde woman was Deborah King. Completely brilliant Forensic Coordinator, yet for all her brains and out of the box thinking, often found completely void of any common sense. A complete scatterbrain in the real world, yet here she was, leading the South Wales Police Forensics department. She was so enthralled with Hibbard she may as well have clung onto his leg like a frustrated poodle, her reactions to his punch lines a laugh so over the top it made Price screw up her face. She even placed her hand on Hibbard's chest as she chuckled away. Her young apprentice, Price recognised from some of the basic forensic training classes she had attended, but couldn't put a name to the face. She stood off to her tutor's side, hiding an uncomfortable grimace from the flirty pair. As she approached, the young forensic officer straightening up at the welcoming interruption. Price gave her a nod, then cocked an eyebrow toward Hibbard. He returned a wide grin.

*Dear God, he thinks I'm jealous.*

'Sorry to interrupt, Ms. King,' Price said. 'But I was hoping to get an update on the dead body lying behind you.' She glanced at Hibbard again, the grin still plastered over his face.

Deborah King took her cue, her cheeks flushing with embarrassment. Or was she just smitten? It was hard to tell. She turned back to the body and reached down to lift the privacy sheet. The dead woman stared straight up, her lifeless eyes unresponsive to the sudden burst of sunlight. The skin on her face pulled so taut on her cheekbones it looked shrink-wrapped, mottled with blue and purple bruising from the decomposition process already underway.

'We're still waiting on the helicopter to get her down from here.' Deborah said. 'I need to get her on the table for the pathologist to identify a cause of death, but she appears at least ninety years old. They'll carry out a full examination, but I'm guessing her body just gave out, her time to move on.'

Price looked back the way they came, thinking of the climb she and Hibbard had just endured to reach the top. As fit as she was, she had been out of breath herself, her heart racing in her chest during the final push. Hardly a walk in the park. Hibbard had even requested she join him in place of Jenkins, on account of him having doubts he'd make the summit in one piece. So what was this woman doing here at her age? She looked down at her body again. Her sunken eye sockets and stretched lips set an eerie, sinister smile. The look of a woman holding the answer to a secret, before moving on to the next place.

Hibbard stepped in. 'What have you found regarding the accomplice? Any idea on the route she took back down?'

'The team has been searching for two hours now, Detective. The ground is just too hard for footprints and even if it was softer, there were a dozen soldiers and equal amounts of tourists trampling the immediate area to search for the girl. You could pull in a team of Native American trackers and I'd bet they'd be walking in circles.'

Taking a knee next to the woman's body, Price held back the urge to reach out and close her eyes. Not that she would have been able to. The rigor mortis stage was well underway, and the first body part to stiffen up was always the eyelids. She took out a glove and snapped it on. The woman's burgundy velvet cloak was lying open from inspection, and she couldn't help but admire it. Even through the synthetics of her latex glove, she could feel the quality of the smooth fabric. Pulling it back around the woman's body, as though to protect her modesty, the chest plate of her gown revealed an intricate triangular pattern stitched in gold thread.

'It's a Triquetra.' Deborah said, answering the question she'd yet to ask. 'A relatively common symbol. You'll find them pretty much everywhere in Celtic folklore. Including on the offering she gave to the abductee's mother.' She gestured with a nod of the head towards the nearby slope. Price obliged by following her gaze, stopping as she saw the object glistening in the grass. A crime scene bollard, shaped like a miniature traffic cone, stood next to it.

'An offering?' she asked?

'Seems so to me.' Deborah replied. 'She gives the mother a gold pendant, then her accomplice takes her daughter? Sounds exactly like an offering.'

Price pondered Deborah's analysis as she bent down over the gold medal. She turned to her as she pointed down at it. Deborah nodded her approval for inspection. She lifted and turned it over in her hand.

Deborah continued. 'The Tree of Life. Another mystical emblem in many religions. The Celts worshipped trees so much they thought of them as ancestors, and the gatekeepers to the Otherworld.'

Price stood to face her again, the pendant still in her hand. 'How do you know all this?'

'I don't get out much.' Deborah replied, glancing at Hibbard as she spoke. She looked him up and down invitingly. He caught the look.

Price's eyes rolled almost audibly. 'Did they get any prints from it?'

'Yep. They're running them now. I doubt anything will come up, though. She's just a little old lady.'

'A little old lady who abducts young children.' Hibbard added, with a hint of annoyance.

Deborah looked to her feet. 'Yes. Yes, it appears so. Apologies.'

'Can you call us when you're done with the autopsy, please?' Hibbard asked, not waiting for his answer. He started back down the slope.

'Let's go, Price,' he said. 'We've got some interviews to conduct.'

# Chapter 4

Staring down into the shadows, only the continuous roar and the fresh mist coating his face gave away what was below. Centuries of persistence from the water had carved the rocks into steep columns on both sides that glowed in the moonlight, echoing a constant rumble that made thinking difficult. The same question came to mind, though. Same one as always.

*How long would it take them to find my body down there?*

During the warmer spring and summer months, the streams beneath the towering Pontsarn Viaduct were brimming with sunbathing families, playing ball games and swimming in the shallow rock pools. The popularity of the area with the local communities made children's laughter the common sound during the daytimes in the school holidays. Yet unknown to most who came here for their fun and games, two hundred yards to the south, the stream dropped off to create a waterfall that, until the late nineties, was fully accessible. Nowadays, a galvanised fence littered with yellow warning signs surrounded the area. For years, locals had campaigned for the falls to be closed off to the public, only to be rejected by the council time after time. The residents knew better, of course, and it took a twelve-year-old boy impressing his friends tombstoning from the top to force the council's hand. The Blue Pool was so named for its glass like appearance, the water settling from a white froth beneath the falls to a stunning and picturesque lagoon as it waited patiently to continue its journey down the valley. But beneath the calm surface, deceiving, conflicting currents churned and folded continuously, meaning it was several hours before his body resurfaced. It was pure luck it had emerged at all, bloated and bruised from the best part of a day tumbling and pounding in the depths. It added another, more sinister dimension to the falls, with the boy's body so discoloured and broken when it had finally surfaced, the locals renamed it the Dead pool. Eddie remembered the case. He had only joined the force the previous year.

*Days. It would take days to find me.*

Stumbling back to the boulder, Eddie grabbed for the open bottle perched there and knocked it to the grassy floor. He dropped to his knees with a squelch, mumbling indecipherable curses as he scrambled to save the contents. At the third attempt, he slumped back onto the rock in a seated position and surveyed the mess. Clumps of wet mud, forever damp from the waterfall mists, held firm to his denim covered knees, and he scooped them away with his hands, flicking the majority to his side.

He took another pull from the bottle, trying to recall how long he had been coming here. At least six years, almost seven, ever since the drinking started. Ever since she was taken from him.

Beyond the galvanised fence and the cover of the foliage lining it, a car raced over the bridge, pulling his attention. Windows down, the ground thumped vibrations of bass, the driver barely slowing as he took the bend and blasted off up the hill. As the noise of the oversized exhaust faded into the night, Eddie pulled a last swig of the bottle before dropping it to the muddy grass at his feet. He pushed off the boulder, puffing out his chest and lifting his chin like an Olympic diver preparing for his final round jump. He thought of where he needed to be and what he had lost. No one would miss him. He would be a burden when they found his body, of course, and he hoped whoever did could handle it. Not young kids, though, or someone in the wrong frame of mind, like him. That would be the worst. Maybe a dog walker, or a council worker, or environmental health. They've seen all sorts. Someone strong enough to recover from the ordeal of seeing a body floating at the water's edge.

He steadied himself and closed his eyes, breathing out a final breath, when her blood-stained face came to him again, blank eyes open, mouth slack.

'I need to be with you,' he said, as he stepped toward the drop.

He picked up the pace, ready for the last two steps. Yet just as before, so many times before, those last two steps never came. An immense burst of constricting pain crushed in on his chest, buckling him to his knees short of the edge. Huge jolts of pressure smashed into his shoulders, forcing his body backwards. He let out a low growl as the momentum twisted his knees with sharp pain, as if someone had shot them out from under him. He laid there a moment, his back soaked through. A gap in the dark clouds allowed the moon to stare down at him, to pass judgement at the coward who couldn't do it, yet again.

*Fucking pussy.*

Climbing to his feet, he pulled at his filthy shirt to free it from his back and took one last look down into the shadows. Working his way back along the overgrown path, he picked up the two coach bolts he had removed, then climbed through the fence. Realigning the upright steel slats, he threaded the bolts in place and reattached the nuts hand tight the other side. It would be pointless dogging them up. He'd be back to try again in a day or two. The first time he had come here, he'd failed to get through the fence, but returned with two pairs of adjustable wrenches. They were likely still in the bushes around here somewhere, all rusted solid, testament to just how long he'd been trying, and failing, to end his misery. He took one last look toward the falls, before turning to make his way up the hill towards home.

Eddie's meagre two-bedroom flat sat above the Pant village convenience store and the shopkeeper, Sam, doubled as the flat's owner. The two had built up a friendship over the last few years that started with Eddie's frequent visits to purchase cigarettes as he drank next door in the pub. Sam had three children, at the time young enough not to complain about sharing a single bedroom above the shop. That would have soon changed, however, and following a chance conversation with Eddie regarding the rising prices of decent houses in the area, found the perfect solution in swapping homes, so Sam and his family could enjoy the space they deserved. The house he had shared with Gwen had sat empty for almost a year since the accident, Eddie unable to spend any time there. For all the wonderful memories they had made, the candlelit dinners, the endless hours snuggled up on the sofa in front of the fire, it was their last moment, away from the house, that continued to plague him. A constant tapping at his mind, over and over, unrelenting. Every happy moment clouded over by his last of her. His grief, he had been told since, would ease with time. But that was the problem with grief. It was different for everyone. No one-size-fits-all. No text book answers to his problems, no matter how much the experts with the letters after their names liked to think so.

And it was the curse he endured, his sickening gift he received that fateful night almost seven years ago, refusing to give him the peace. Neither the peace to move on, nor the peace to end it. He was in his own version of purgatory, or maybe it was hell. It was too hard to tell either way.

Blocking her out had been his only refuge, the bottom of a bottle his hiding place, the self-destruction that followed a by-product he couldn't escape. He had floated from couch to couch until the solution presented itself. It had taken some convincing, Sam and his wife Farah at first unwilling to take advantage of such a generous offer, but he had insisted. After all, it was perfect for him, too. Living above the shop, everything he needed would be within arm's reach downstairs or on the other end of the phone, in one of the many takeaways littered around the town. They had eventually agreed, everyone was happy, and although Eddie could never part with the house by selling it, found an answer in Sam becoming warden over the property and his possessions.

A separate doorway sandwiched between the shop front and the neighbouring Miners Arms led up to the apartment, and as Eddie approached, he could see a rowdy group of five or six men crowded around the entrance, pint glasses and cigarettes in hand. The sun had long gone down behind the houses, but the air still held some warmth. A tall bald man with both arms sleeved in tattoos was animatingly telling the group of his exploits on the rugby field that very afternoon. He'd gotten into an altercation with his opposite number, and obviously he'd come out on top and got a red card for his troubles. The group listened in awe, hanging off his every word.

Another man was busy urinating over Eddie's front step. He was shorter, around Eddie's height of five foot eleven, and had a sly, rat featured face, with a long hook of a nose and eyes far too close together to be trusted. They were so engrossed in the bald man's story, none of the group saw the inebriated man staggering towards them. Ambling straight through the middle of the group was enough to stop the storyteller, puzzled eyes moving to the muddied drunkard. Eddie stopped, waiting patiently behind the urinating man, as the rest of the group looked on in confusion. The man zipped his fly, jolting backwards as he turned from the door to be confronted by a new face. A mud caked one.

'Last time I checked, the Miners had working toilets, boy. Any reason you needed to piss all over my front door?'

Eddie knew what followed. His strategic position had him at an advantage, and he had already split a path through the group as he walked through it. It was an invitation the bald-headed storyteller couldn't help but take. He rushed through the gap, pushing his friends to each side as he moved. An easy target and a chance to show his mates what he could really do. His confidence was misplaced.

'What are you going to do about it, you scruffy fat twa...'

Eddie's head whipped and smashed into the storyteller's nose. The audible crack of skull on nasal bone as the latter gave way shocked everyone but him. They all watched, mouths gaping like hooked fish as the man went down, blood pouring over both sides of his wrecked face. Eddie had never heard a man of his size cry like a baby before, testament to the precision of the strike. He almost felt sorry for him, the pain being so obvious. Turning back to the urinator, the man promptly withered away from the doorway on jellied legs. Pulling his key from his jeans pocket, Eddie turned back to the group. They were all ears, mouths still catching flies, apart from the big man, of course, who continued to whimper in a heap on the pavement.

'Before you go thinking of repercussions, I suggest you go ask in the Miners who lives above the shop. They'll soon tell you to leave it well alone.'

Eddie was confident there'd be no more of it. As he sat back on his torn sofa, he dropped two ice cubes into his glass and used the rest of the bag to prevent any swelling to his head. It would probably bruise, but that was ok. The landlord of the Miner's Arms, Stephen 'Stretch' Lewis, knew how handy he was, growing up as a frustrated teenager fighting out of the boxing gym where Stretch had been one of the senior guys taking him under his wing. He might not look the part anymore, but he had lost little speed. The element of surprise proved his secret weapon. Get the first one in hard and fast to put them on the back foot, or in most cases, their arse. It was quiet out front now. No doubt Stretch had warned them off, told them to chalk it up to experience, and sent them on their way with their tails between their legs.

The ice cubes in the glass cracked and fizzed as he poured in the whisky. On the mantelpiece, the lone framed photograph stared back disapprovingly, Gwen's eyes boring a hole into his heartbroken chest. She would have given him a right rollicking over that one. It was the only item he could bear, a photo of the two of them the day he had asked her to be his wife. She stared straight ahead, her perfect teeth showing through her wide smile as Eddie kissed at her cheek. Better times. Holding the tears back, he lifted his glass, a toast to the dead. Then a refill to toast the living. And then another for those somewhere in between.

At some point, his head fell back as he drifted unconscious. The dream came again.

*He was back at the hospital, having finally pulled himself from the morgue to make his way through the winding corridors of the Intensive Care Unit. Inside the ward, Peter held Jane's hand at her bedside, an array of tubes and monitors surrounding her as Eddie held his head in his hands in the waiting area outside. A cork bulletin board faced him, pinned with leaflets advertising bereavement counselling and support groups. It was an eerie place, ICU. Not like other wards in the hospital. The smells were familiar, strong disinfectant and stale body odour, but it was the noise, or rather the lack of it, making it different. Staff kept communication to a minimum as they went about their business, conversations carried out in hushed tones. No laughing. No joking. The commanding sounds* throughout the ward always the pinging noises from the heart monitors and ventilators. They governed the ward, ruled over it, commanding the workers into action should they ever change tone.

The sound of the monitors was faint here, barely heard from the corridor. Eddie sat folded forwards, his hands behind his head, pulling it toward his knees. With his eyes closed, all he could see was Gwen's bloodied face, devoid of life, enveloped by death. He had lost the only thing he cared about.

A distinct sound came, rising in volume. A clacking of heels on hard floor, getting louder as they approached. Then the sound stopped, a body brushing against his as it sat beside him. Eddie's hands pulled away, his head rising to greet the new arrival, giving him a view of the newcomer's long shapely legs crossing over each other as she sat. A hot twisting knot burned in his belly, rising through his chest, forcing him to sit further upright. He sat back in his seat and turned to face his companion. The woman stared back at Eddie with electric blue eyes, sharp crystals of ice piercing through from the dark liner surrounding them. There was a fierce strength in them that pulled him in, holding him in his moment of grief, momentarily turning it to something else entirely.

Anger.

She pulled away a loose lock of her glossy black hair hanging pencil straight over her pale, unblemished face, tucking it behind her ear. Her cherry red lips pinched together, and with a deep sigh, she shook her head in frustration.

'My condolences Mr. Venter.' The woman said. She spoke with an Eastern European accent, in close to perfect English. 'The sudden death of loved ones is difficult for the mind to process. It makes mourning them even harder, like you expect them to walk back through the door at any moment.'

# THE ESCORT TO THE GRAVE

*Eddie turned to the entrance doors he had trudged through hours ago. No one walked through. Fluttering needles stabbed at his stomach as he remembered his wife, lying alone and dead in the same building.*

*'It is different when expecting death. The mind has already finished the shock process and passed into acceptance stage.' She tutted and shook her head again. 'So much easier.' She reversed her crossed legs and laid a hand on his forearm. Eddie turned back to her.*

*'I came tonight to welcome someone into the world, Mr. Venter. There is a family upstairs celebrating with overwhelming joy and relief their baby is safe in their arms. I came to meet her. Then I saw you, Mr. Venter, watching your wife's body being wheeled into the hospital morgue. So I came here first, to tell you something very important.'*

*The woman grabbed Eddie firmly by the chin, her red nails digging into his cheeks as she turned his face to hers. Her eyes narrowed as she pulled closer, searching his face. When she spoke, the words spat through her pristine white teeth.*

*'It was not her time, Mr. Venter. Your wife died saving another not deserving of pity. That other lies in bed with a second chance because of your wife. She will recover and live when your wife has died. She will bask in the sunshine while your wife lies in the cold. She will laugh in good company as your wife rots alone. It is an injustice, Mr. Venter.'*

*Her hand squeezed tighter, her nails digging deeper, accentuating the importance of what she was saying. Her eyes searched his, then relaxed as she smiled. She had found what she was looking for.*

*'You will do wondrous things together, Mr. Venter. When the girl is ready, you will find each other, and you will do the most wondrous things.'*

Eddie's body uncoiled as he released from the dream. Surrounded by the darkness of his living room, he pressed a button on his mobile phone, illuminating it. The clock on the home screen read 02.38 am. From the mantelpiece, Gwen continued to look down disapprovingly. He had fallen asleep with his drink in hand, the contents now soaking through his shirt and lap. His head thumped a painful tune, a cocktail of alcohol and head butts and misery the primary culprits. A loud groan escaped as he rose from the settee. He took a moment to ponder the dream he had had so many times, as his hand went to the fresh scratches on his cheeks, spotting with blood.

Who was she? Why does she continue to invade his dream and tell him these things?

A flame of resentment burned within. A churning retch at the pit of his stomach. A knot of guilt. It was only a dream, but the feeling was there. In his darkest hour, when he had lost the woman he loved so much, he'd allowed the grief to be forgotten, even for a moment. He'd allowed her to part blame on his wife's friend, *his* friend, a woman who'd almost lost her own life in the crash. But mostly, he felt the anger with himself for thinking, for some unfathomable reason, the woman in his dream had a point.

# Chapter 5

## Sunday

A knock at the door interrupted Detective Superintendent Peter Enfield's call with ACC Bentley. He'd been updating him on the lack of progress being made with the search on the mountain when DCI Hibbard stuck his head in. He waved him in as he wrapped up the call. Hibbard sat across from his desk and waited.

'Yes, Sir, of course. I'll update you as soon as we have any more information. Yes, I know how important this is, Sir. We're doing everything we can. We'll find her. Thank you, Sir.'

Blowing out a huge breath, an attempt to exhale the stress away, Enfield replaced the receiver. What Hibbard said next ramped the stress up a notch instead.

'David Morrison just turned up at reception, causing a scene. He's even got his lawyer and a PA with him. PC Harris on the front desk took the brunt of it. I've calmed him down somewhat, but he's demanding to speak to you. I've sent Harris home for the rest of his shift. Poor bugger looked ready to cry.'

Peter resigned back into his seat, hoping it would swallow him up. He should be so lucky. Why did the missing girl have to be the daughter of the most influential MP the South Wales valleys had ever seen? Her father, David Morrison, was a front runner to gain a high ministerial role soon, likely to head up one of the high profile Government departments. Some even labelled him a prime minister in the making, such was his popularity amongst the party. And even more so, by the people he represented in his constituency. There wasn't a day his face didn't appear in the Welsh newspapers. He was ambitious, smart, and a man of the people. He came from a working class background: his father was a miner, a lifetime working in the pits, his mother, a schoolteacher. He was one of them. If anyone knew what the will of the people was, it was David Morrison, MP. The valleys were proud of him; he was putting them back on the map and the press lapped it up.

Finding his daughter kidnapped, they would lap up as well.

The MP had been in London yesterday during the incident. Enfield groaned when he heard Morrison wouldn't be present for the initial witness interviews with his wife and eldest daughter. If he were there, then he could have heard everything first hand and vent his anger all in one hit, saving everyone precious time and sanity. Instead, he would now put on a show.

Enfield nodded for Hibbard to show him through. Before he could reach the door, David Morrison burst in, followed by his entourage. The door flung back on its hinges, hitting the rubber stop and rebounding with juddering force. The three arrivals strutted in, their noses high in the air, matching looks of distaste on their faces. Hibbard jumped to one side to avoid getting trampled on. The officer he had left in their company in the corridor waiting area had obviously crumbled under the pressure and let them through. David Morrison took the seat previously occupied by Hibbard without waiting for the offer. Opening his suit jacket as he sat, revealing a matching waistcoat, he crossed his legs and laced his hands in his lap. His mousy hair was perfectly parted to the side. Immaculately presented, and perfectly relaxed, for someone with a missing child. His lawyer glided over to the left corner, his briefcase held in front of him with two hands defensively. Morrison's personal assistant flanked to the right, armed with her notepad and pen. Enfield thought of an old eighties cartoon he once saw, where a white angel and red devil, the voices of reason, were influencing a decision maker as they sat on his shoulders. Only in this case, both wore red horns and pitchforks at the ready.

'Where's my daughter Enfield?' Morrison sneered. 'Twenty-four hours she's been missing and you're sat hiding behind your desk.'

'I've got every available person up that mountain searching for her, Mr. Morrison. There are teams of Mountain Rescue and the army scanning every inch of the beacons for her as we speak. They've covered miles of rough terrain and worked around the clock.' Enfield spoke with a confidence in his team, even if he wasn't feeling it.

Morrison jabbed a finger, speaking through clenched teeth. 'It's not good enough, Enfield. This shower of shit you call a department couldn't find water if it fell out of a boat. I want answers.'

'Two police helicopters were out all afternoon yesterday and are back up there today. Traffic stops set up on every road leading north and south of the mountain. Every available officer is carrying out door-to-door enquiries. I'd say we're doing our best under the circumstances.' Enfield leaned forward, resting his elbows on his desk. The last day's events had taken its toll. Dark shadows surrounded his eyes. His shoulders sagged with fatigue, matching the drawn look on his face. He spoke with a tone of added empathy now. 'I assure you, Mr. Morrison, we are doing everything we can. We still don't know how the woman took your daughter without anyone noticing.'

Morrison was on the back foot now. His wife was one of those people. A clever shift of focus from Enfield. The lawyer noticed it in time, interjecting to gain the high ground once more.

'Mr. Morrison's daughter has now been missing for twenty-four hours, Detective Superintendent Enfield,' the lawyer said, clearly using his full title to broadcast where the buck stopped. 'He will not wait another twenty-four. It is no secret the first forty-eight hours of a kidnapping are the most important. Mr. Morrison has spent the night consoling his distraught wife and daughter, and had the grace to give you the time to do your job. You have failed to do that Det Supt Enfield. First thing tomorrow morning, Mr. Morrison will call his own press conference.'

Enfield's eyes were back on Morrison. He spoke sternly this time. 'Don't do it, Mr. Morrison. We don't know the motives yet. If it's fuelled by your high profile for the purpose of extortion, and the press gets hold of it before the kidnappers get in touch, they might panic. The press has been told enough to be on the lookout for a six-year-old girl with a middle-aged woman. Once they know it's your daughter, this stands to get very messy indeed.'

Morrison saw through it. His face took on a red hue as he stood from his chair, dropping his hands to the desk in front of him. He leaned closer. 'All you're interested in is saving face, Enfield. My daughter is with a stranger scared out of her mind somewhere and all you can think of is your pension. You're a joke. I'll see to it this is the last case you ever work on.' He turned on his heels like a soldier making an about turn. His lawyer and PA scurried after him, fearful of being left behind. Pulling the door closed as he left, Hibbard screwed his face apologetically toward Enfield, who responded with a worn out nod of the head as the door closed.

Hibbard caught up with Morrison as he walked through the automatic doors of the station reception. He called after

# THE ESCORT TO THE GRAVE

the MP, grabbing him by the crook of the arm and instantly regretting it. Morrison gave his own arm a look like a bird had just shat there, then turned to his lawyer. 'Give us a minute please, Patrick.' He looked at his PA and nodded towards the car. 'You too.' Both of them gave Hibbard an annoyed look, like they had somewhere important to be, but silently obeyed. Morrison waited until they were out of earshot before turning back to him.

'We've known each other for a long time, John.' Morrison said. 'But let me be frank. If you don't find my daughter soon, I'm going to bury Enfield and his department with it.'

'We're doing everything we can, David. Enfield's right. If you go to the press now, you may never see her again.'

'And if we wait, I may never see her again.' Morrison said. He walked to the side of the building, looking around for witnesses before taking a cigarette packet from his jacket pocket. He lit one up, pocketing the pack without offering. Hibbard had no idea he even smoked. From his demeanour, he suspected few others did either.

'Enfield was right about one thing, John. The kidnappers have taken my daughter because of my high profile. They'll demand a ransom. But they wouldn't dare hurt the child of a high ranking MP, so we have an opportunity here.' He stuck a finger into Hibbard's chest. 'You will report everything to me, and I mean everything, and I will play nice for now. Informing the press will be *my* decision at the time *I* choose. They'll expose Enfield's failings to find my daughter. If you do as I say, I'll see to it once he takes the fall you end up in his seat. You're aware of my close relationship with ACC Bentley. Well, it's just the tip of the iceberg. I've also got the ear of the Chief Constable. We're both patrons of the same charities, and over the past twelve months we've been getting rather friendly indeed. Between the two of them, they'll influence the board to appoint you as Enfield's

61

replacement on my recommendation alone. Then you can rebuild his shambolic team as you see fit.'

Hibbard stared back, slack-jawed, unsure what he was hearing, yet found himself nodding his head in acknowledgement. Morrison took a last pull of his cigarette, tilting his head to the sky as he exhaled the smoke.

'I want to know everything Enfield does from now on. And if I find out you've kept anything from me, you'll crash and burn with him.' He dropped the butt to the floor, stubbing it out under his expensive leather brogues.

'Now get and find my fucking daughter.'

# Chapter 6

## Monday

'So you had the dream again?' Wendy Bickerton-Smith MD said, pushing her glasses back to the top of her head as a makeshift hair band. She closed her eyes, rubbing her face with her palm like she was washing with an invisible flannel. Maybe when she opened them again, he would have vanished into thin air. She cracked an eye open. Nope, no such luck. He was still there, and she would have to listen to his sarky answers a little longer. Her trickiest client, Eddie Venter, lay slumped in the chair across from her. His mop of unkempt, greasy brown hair pointed out in all directions, as if attempting to escape the warped mind they clung to. He made little attempt to hide his paunch beneath the two sizes too small shirt he had clearly bought at a healthier time, and from its appearance, clearly slept in last night. He looked ready to fall asleep if she would let him. On his lap, Wendy's five-year-old Pomeranian Mossy lay stretched out in his own display of laziness. He also desperately needed a pruning, its fluffy pom-pom of orange and white hair hiding any features indicating he was a dog. Eddie was Mossy's favourite client. He made a beeline for Eddie as soon as he sat down, a far cry from their first meeting, when Eddie almost crushed the dog and he wouldn't stop yapping at him.

'I take it you'd been drinking prior to it?'

'Your powers of deduction are impressive doc.' Eddie said. 'You'd make a great private investigator.'

'I'm not sarcastic enough, Eddie.' she replied. 'Plus, I don't think I could handle the massive wages that go with it.'

Eddie laughed at that. 'You do pretty well with the sarcasm. You'd just need to dress a bit more formal.'

She smirked as she looked down at her immaculate tweed business suit, her fingers working at her silk neckerchief. It was important to give off a professional aura at all times in front of clients, no matter how well she had got to know them. A mantra she had held for years. A couple of months ago she had misplaced her favourite lapel brooch, the eighteen carat spider one with rubies for eyes and black onyx as the abdomen, and hadn't had time to find it before her first client of the day arrived. She had sat there for the full hour, feeling naked as the day she was born, not really paying any attention to what she was hearing. Luckily, she had found it soon after, before the need to cancel the next appointment. Yes, there was always a need for professional appearances.

Wendy wasn't sure if it was a coincidence, or if Eddie had clocked her making observations on his attire. She made a mental note to be more discreet in the future.

'Did the woman appear this time?'

Eddie nodded.

'How did you feel when you woke?'

Eddie made a huffing sound as he exhaled. They had gone over this a thousand times. 'Same as always. Wracked with guilt.'

'She's your subconscious testing you, Eddie. The guilt you feel is your mind tormenting you into thinking you should have done more to protect Gwen. Ever wonder why she flirts with you? Why the pain eases for a moment? While your brain remains sharp, the majority of the time it has moments where the posterior cortical hot zone displays your emotions as images. It is your subconscious telling you it isn't your fault. It is telling you to forgive yourself, Eddie.

# THE ESCORT TO THE GRAVE

Your mind is trying to heal, but your dreams are fooling you.'

It was Eddie's turn to rub his face. 'Great, I'll book in for a lobotomy as soon as we're done here.'

'Let's talk about the crash?'

Eddie's leg vibrated. Saved by the bell. Mossy jumped to attention. Wendy heard the phone and rolled her eyes as he pulled it from his pocket to check the caller. It was Peter Enfield. 'I need to take this, Doc. Same time next week?'

Wendy checked her watch. They still had fifteen minutes of the session left. She stood from her chair, pulling her jacket down at the waist, a defeated look on her face. 'Why do you keep coming here, Eddie? What do you get from it?'

'Free coffee.' He answered the phone as he rose from his chair, making his way to the door. 'Hey Pete, everything ok?'

'One more thing, Mr. Venter.' Wendy said. She always meant business when she used his surname. Looking back, Eddie pulled the phone away from his ear.

'She won't leave the dream until you forgive yourself, Mr. Venter.'

# Chapter 7

Any other day, Eddie would laugh at the suggestion he hike to the top of a Welsh mountain. Physical exertion wasn't exactly one of his hobbies of late. Yet he could hardly say no. It was for an old friend, and he needed him.

Sitting across the paper-strewn desk, slouched in his leather office chair, was Detective Superintendent Peter Enfield, head of the Major Crime Investigation Team in South Wales Police, his usual towering presence replaced by a sorrow look of defeat. The events of the last few days appeared to have taken its toll. Little sleep and endless phone calls had no doubt added a new grey hair here and there, as well as deeper creases of worry lines in his aged face. He was under enormous pressure for answers that, at the moment, he couldn't provide. And nor could his team. Not for the first time, of course. Tricky cases can take time to solve, and he had seen his fair share of those over the years. But nothing this high profile. Nothing involving a Government employee. That stuff normally happened in the big smoke of London.

It was the reason he had asked Eddie to his country cottage in the rural village of Pontsticill on this late summer morning. He needed *something*.

As Peter's fingers moved from pinching the bridge of his nose to rubbing his temples, Eddie's eyes moved to the window over Peter's shoulder and to a bird in the distance, maybe a Kestrel or even a Red Kite, circling high above the woodlands surrounding the reservoir. Its movement was idyllic, with such little effort to keep it afloat. Without warning, the bird tucked its wings, dove hard and disappeared from view, probably taking its spoils of a young rabbit or field mouse. Eddie imagined he was the mouse, one minute exploring the long grass for a seed or berry, the next having his innards pulled out as he's eaten alive. Funny how life can change so quickly.

His attention fell back to his friend slumped in his annex office chair. Grey chest hair peeked out from his unbuttoned shirt, and a dark shadow was forming beneath his chin. He sold the story of an exhausted man, his normally freshly shaven and tanned glow giving way to a grey and unhealthy complexion.

A knock at the door had Peter adjusting his posture, bolting upright as if caught napping. The handle jolted three times before the latch finally freed from the receiver and the door eased open. Eddie kept his eyes trained on Peter, who now held a weary and unconvincing smile for his wife as she wheeled herself into the room. Across her adapted lap tray she had a large pot of coffee, Peter's favourite mug with the SWP emblem, and another holding Eddie's tea. She took her time approaching, wheeling next to Eddie, and placed the tray on the desk. Neither man offered to help, all too aware of such dangers. They gave up trying years ago. Through her stubbornness, Jane refused to allow anyone to treat her differently. Sensing the importance of the meeting, Jane took Eddie's hand, pulled herself closer to peck at his cheek, then turned a well-practiced 180 to head back out the door. She took a small crook from her wheelchair pannier, wrapped it around the door handle, and pulled it closed behind her.

'What's going on Pete? I've been coming to this house for years, but this has to be the first time you've pulled me straight in here?'

Peter looked around the annex office, weighing up his words carefully, then back to Eddie. 'I need your help with this case, Ed.'

It wasn't uncommon for police forces across the US to use private investigators. However, it was a rarer relationship in the UK. In May 2018, a damning report found the Metropolitan police in London had paid vast amounts of taxpayer's money to private contractors for their services. The tabloids got wind of it and stirred the hornet's nest, stoking a raging fire of public uproar. *'What the hell are we paying the police for if they're just subbing the work out elsewhere?'* was the flavour of the day.

Following the report, pressure mounted from the Home Office for the forces across the UK to cut ties with investigators, regardless of their effectiveness. Luckily for Peter, his own Chief Constable also saw the value in using them from time to time. They could often get information or speak with people the public servants couldn't get near. She saw the value in that, and as a bit of a rule breaker in the past herself, had defended the use of them and allowed her senior officers to use them sparingly and quietly.

She wouldn't be so forthcoming if she knew Eddie Venter, and certainly not if she knew his methods.

For now, Peter and his counterparts still had the green light to use them, and he only ever went to one. He was forever in debt to Eddie, ever since pulling Jane from her car all those years ago. And he got results. Peter never quite knew how, but he got them.

'I've helped with your cases plenty of times, Pete. When your guys have missed something or screwed something up. So what's different this time? Why the secrecy?'

Peter swivelled the chair to look out at the view behind him. A group of kayakers were making their way from one side of the calm reservoir waters to the other, their smooth and laboured strokes of their paddles a polar opposite of how Peter's mind whirred in its box. He stood and walked over to his wall display of momentos from his time in the force. The thirty-year service medal hung gallantly in its customised frame next to the personalised baton inscribed with the force's thanks for his tenure. Above it was Peter's pride and joy, an A3 size frame holding his OBE and photo of the Queen pinning it to his chest.

He took a deep breath. 'You might have heard Saturday morning the six-year-old daughter of MP David Morrison disappeared from the top of Pen-y-fan mountain. Two women appear to have plotted and taken her from under Mrs. Morrison's nose. The Chief Constable, at the request of Assistant Chief Constable Bentley, approved our services to the Morrisons and to Dyfed Powys Police. The Super for Dyfed Powys didn't put up much of a fight. He knows the press will be all over it when they find out who the missing girl is, and now I have the enviable task of finding her. All our resources have teamed up with Mountain Rescue and been working day and night searching for her since. They are combing every blade of grass, and the divers have dragged the nearby lake. They're confident she's no longer on the mountain.'

'How the hell do two women kidnap a kid off the top of a mountain?' Eddie asked.

Peter sighed, dropping to sit on the leather settee beneath the display. He'd asked himself the same question a thousand times. 'One of the women collapsed and died in Sarah Morrison's arms. During the distraction, the other woman took her daughter. We have over twenty witnesses at the summit and none of them saw her take off with the girl. Morrison's high profile will have the press all over this one. They'll demand answers I simply don't have yet. All we've got is a mash-up of contradicting witness statements, and a photo his wife took at the summit on a tourist's phone. The suspects are in the shot, but their faces have blurred out. We're running out of time, and we've got nothing.'

'Tell me about Morrison.'

'He's pally with the Chief Constable and the ACC, so he's holding off any damning statements to the press for now, but if this drags out any longer, he'll put friendship aside and throw the department in the gutter. He's already making threats. The Chief won't like that one bit. She'll lean on Bentley to pick a scapegoat and with me in charge of the department, well, no prizes for guessing who's for the chopping block.'

Eddie stood from his chair and walked around the desk to the window. The view from here was indeed spectacular. The kayakers were on the far side of the water now, and the resettled surface gave a mirror-like reflection of the hills and forestry beyond it. Behind the plush green valleys, Eddie could make out the tip of the Pen-y-fan mountain.

'Spending retirement here with Jane sounds like bliss, Pete. You've done your time. Ever thought of that?'

'I always thought I'd retire on my own terms. Isn't that what everyone deserves?'

'Suppose. But why involve me on this one? You're asking for trouble. Such a high-profile case, nothing good can come of it. They'll hang you out to dry.'

Enfield's shoulders slumped as he looked to his lap for the answer. 'I have my reasons, Ed. And I need to know if I'm chasing a dead body, in case I need a head start in the aftermath when we find her. I need you... to do... your thing.'

And there it was, his thing. Made to sound like a cheap and easy parlour trick. A sleight of hand, a misdirection to captivate and amaze some two bit magician's audience, before allowing them to become engrossed and invested in the next.

The night of the crash had changed everything. He had lost the woman he shared his life with. The woman to share his intimate moments, his dreams, his ambitions. Just like he'd lost the ability to share hers. A journey ahead of sharing moments belonging just to them, taken away by one heartbreaking moment.

# THE ESCORT TO THE GRAVE

And replaced with a curse. A curse since causing him to implode, self-destruct into the shell of the man he once was. Following the crash, he hit the bottle to shield the pain. His anger festered and intensified, fueled by the alcohol, until eventually boiling over. He made mistakes and then some. Punches were thrown, and a career was lost.

In recent years, rumours of his newfound and unexplainable ability, apparently gained following that fateful night, were dismissed as ridiculous by those who heard them. Nevertheless, he had his followers, a number who had crossed paths with him as he worked a case and praised him as nothing less than a miracle worker after experiencing it firsthand. Skeptics turned open-minded, calling him blessed. Whispers continued, reputations grew, stories were exaggerated. Some saw him as a laughing stock. Others, an enigma. Those closest to him, like Peter, after seeing what it took from him, agreed it was a curse. Either way, it didn't stop people from turning to him for help, unable to ignore the unusual ability he offered. And now Peter was here, asking for his help once more, knowing what it would do to him.

But something was off. Eddie had never seen him like this. Peter Enfield was always a cool customer under pressure, but this one had got to him big time. It wasn't the high profile of it. There was something else. He wanted to help his close friend, but he was right when he said nothing good could come of his involvement.

'I have to say no, Pete.'

Peter looked back up, his eyes defeated. He opened a desk drawer, pulling a bottle of Penderyn single malt and two glasses. He poured a generous drop in each. 'Then I'm done Ed. I can't see how I'll get out of this one.' He swallowed the contents in one, sucking air in through his teeth at the burn.

Eddie's eyes narrowed. He couldn't put his finger on it. But his friend was in trouble.

'Are you telling me everything?'

'Everything I can,' Peter said.

Eddie took a moment. He swirled the amber liquid around the glass as if it would offer some tea leaf advice. Eventually, he looked back at his friend, raised the glass up and knocked it back. The whisky was good and did the trick. 'I'll need to see the report and the interview notes from the wife before I go up there. I'd normally request a meeting with her, but I'm guessing that's out of the question for the same reason we're meeting here instead of at the station. If the press finds out you've used an ex-copper turned nut-job on this one, you're finished.'

Peter cringed at the words, nut-job. His face contorted into a mass of wrinkles and his hand met his forehead again to rub away the ache there. 'I just need to know if I'm looking for a dead body, Ed, but be discreet. The trails leading up have been reopened to the public, but no doubt there'll be some reporters looking for a story. Hibbard is running the case as Senior Investigation Officer. I've told him I want you to take a look. He voiced his opinions, but he's promised to keep quiet. Just don't wind him up. A copy of the report is on the table. You can take it with you.'

'Didn't the Rescue or CID teams find anything when they first attended? No trail or direction what-so-ever?' Eddie asked, opening the report. 'Did the dogs pick up a scent?'

'The dogs refused to go up,' Peter replied. 'Wouldn't even leave the car park at the bottom.'

Eddie's ears pricked at this. His eyes lit a fire as he closed the report and came back around the table.

'Funny thing is,' Peter said, 'the Morrison's have a Border Collie they take on their hikes too. And guess what?'

'It refused to go up,' Eddie replied.

## Chapter 8

Following his meeting at the Enfield cottage, Eddie drove the short distance back to his favourite cafe in the neighbouring village of Cefn Coed. It wasn't much to look at from the outside. Pebble dash exterior walls tagged with graffiti and single glazed windows with net curtains unwashed since the turn of the millennium. Above the door, a double-sided sign still read Dai's Plaice, a throwback to the good old days when the business operated as a fish and chip shop. The deeds had changed hands twice since then, and the mysterious Dai in question had passed away in 2012, but the sign remained like a birthmark. A small plaque with a two star hygiene rating, a fact the owner Debbie felt obliged to mention on several occasions was down to paperwork issues the day of the inspection, lay propped in the side window.

If the outside of the building wasn't particularly inviting, the inside fared little better. Decade old floral paper lined the walls, nicotine yellow and torn at the edges. Six by four picture frames filled with old black and white photos of the nearby viaduct, canals and old station house covered the roughest spots, attempting to give the room some much needed character. Their colourless nature instead, making the décor even more grim.

When he took his breakfast, Eddie rarely ate elsewhere. Debbie's teenage daughter Katie was leaning on the counter as he entered, checking the quality of her nail polish. She jumped to attention at the sound of his entrance, perking up at the thought of something to do. Eddie took his favourite table toward the back of the near empty room, facing the door, and waited for her to bring his tea, ordering his usual full English to accompany it when she did.

It was quiet for a Monday morning, an hour too early for the hangover brigade, an hour too late for the highway workers. The only other diners were an elderly couple he'd seen here many times before, sitting side by side at their booth, enjoying their shared rounds of toast. Eddie took the opportunity, opening the folder and glossed over the formalities of the summary page, making a mental note of the interviewing officer's names at the top.

DCI John Hibbard

DC Lauren Price

He moved straight to the meaty parts, the witness statements.

The breakfast arrived at his table and Eddie pushed the folder to one side, leaving it open for him to look through as he smothered the food with ketchup. He proceeded in systematically demolishing his plate, occasionally glancing to the side to continue working through the report.

A squad of twelve soldiers from 160th Infantry Brigade had been on exercise from Brecon Barracks at the summit. Eddie flipped back to the first page of the report and saw the staff sergeant had called in and got clearance to assist the Mountain Rescue team for eighteen hours straight following the girl going missing. As he sipped his tea, he gave an approving nod. Fair play to them. The same staff sergeant worked on the deceased for twenty minutes after Mrs. Morrison abandoned the CPR process to search for her daughter's whereabouts.

Eddie shovelled a fork of sausage and beans into his mouth and washed it down with more tea. Through the grubby window, he spotted two familiar faces crossing the road towards the cafe door. He chuckled quietly to himself. Katie was back in her spot at the counter, jumping to attention again at some fresh customers, then grimaced as a tall, muscular man walked in, his nose packed full with gauze and covered with a protective splint. A neck brace propped his chin high, like some child on his tippy toes reaching over a fence to see where his ball had landed. The whole top half of his face was purple and black. A shorter man walked in behind him, his eyes still too close together for Eddie's liking, closing the door behind him. He made toward a table, but stopped mid-stride as he spotted Eddie sitting at the back of the room, scooping a mouthful of his breakfast up with a slice of toast. Eddie stared him down as he chewed, lifting his mug up for a loud, dramatic swig. The tall man recoiled when he realised who was there, horror etched on his face as he backed up toward the door. His friend followed suit, both men stumbling into each other as they scurried to get out. As they darted across the road, they looked over their shoulders for any pursuer. Katie frowned as she watched them go, then turned and raised an eyebrow in Eddie's direction. Eddie responded with a shrug, then turned his attention back to his breakfast and the incident report.

The Canadian family had given up their cameras as evidence following the kidnapping. They had twelve photos at the summit, all blown up and labeled with unique identity numbers. Eddie scanned through them and found two had the suspects in view. Both photos were unclear, the first out of focus due to their distance from the camera, the second taken of their backs only. Eddie took his time over the second photo. The women wore red velvet robes.

Next, he pulled the photo of the old woman's body, double checking Katie wasn't close by to catch sight of it. She was still unidentified, and no reports made of any missing persons matching her description had come in. The pathologist estimated her at ninety years of age. *How the hell did she get up the mountain?* Toxicology came back clean. Likely cause of death - Cardiac arrest.

*Indicating the kidnapping was opportunist rather than premeditated.*

What he couldn't get his head around was how the woman could get away with the girl without being seen. In three directions, with just a sixty-second window, spotting them would have been easy enough, and the drop off to the west had also proven a bust. Mrs. Morrison was adamant she took her eyes off her daughter for no longer than a minute and erupted in interview at the suggestion she was mistaken. Eddie weighed up the possibility of foul play from the family, unable to come up with a strong motive. He dismissed the idea for the time being, although it paid to keep an open mind. These incidents happen, but he thought best to keep the notion to himself for now. Pete wouldn't appreciate it if he even mentioned it anyway, so he'd readdress it later if warranted. What he needed to do first was to get up there.

And then there was the dog, refusing to leave the car. This was the reason eldest daughter Jennifer had stayed at the bottom rather than hike up. Her statement mentioned the dog refusing to settle the entire time she was with it, and on Sarah Morrison returning to the car without her youngest daughter, had continued to act erratically. The investigation wouldn't waste any time on the dog, but Eddie knew better. He'd known them to act like that before. And when they did, it always seemed to lead to one outcome. A dead body.

*The dog could sense it.*

Eddie used his last piece of toast to mop up the baked bean juice from his plate and finished his tea. Paying for his meal, he said his goodbyes to Katie and checked the time. Just after ten. One more stop to make at home to change clothes and then it was time for a hike up a mountain. Time to find out where they went.

## Chapter 9

There had been uproar at the Storey Arms car park over the course of the weekend, with the mountain above it closed off to the public. Hundreds of cars had been turned away, some having travelled considerable distances, and the officers with the enviable task of redirecting them had certainly earned their wages over the last two days. Issuing vague explanations of a major incident had irritated the inconvenienced visitors considerably. Tempers had flared regardless. There had even been arrest warnings given to a group who ignored the closure, parking a mile down the road to trudge through dense thickets of shrubs and bushes before rejoining the main path to the top. Caught around halfway up and sent back the way they came with their tails between their legs, they reluctantly coughed up their details and promised not to return.

Now reopened to the public, the tourists had returned in their droves. By the time Eddie pulled his battered 2006 Ford Focus in, there were few spaces remaining. He was gob-smacked just how many people appeared not to work on Monday mornings, and it baffled him this amount of people could consider hiking to the top of a mountain a reasonable pastime.

His balding tyres squealed on the tarmac as he maneuvered in. Two uniformed officers and two plain-clothes detectives stood at the burger van as he drove past them and into a space at the corner of the car park. At the high-pitched sound, one of the plain clothes, a tall athletic man he'd dealt with on many an occasion, spotted the car, his eyes following it all the way to its resting place.

Climbing out, he looked up to the long winding path running up the hill, getting smaller and smaller until disappearing into the distance. A steady stream of hikers along its route moved in both directions. Closing his eyes, he took in a deep breath through his nose, then exhaled through his mouth, the air catching in his throat as it left. A harsh, guttural sound followed he successfully coughed to clear, as he leaned over the side of the car to spit out a disgusting black and red tar-like-mix of mucus and blood.

*Started already.* He wiped his mouth with his sleeve. *And not even close to the body.* Rounding the car to the boot, he found his water bottle and took a mouth full. He'd barely swallowed before it was bone dry again. An ache pulled at his stomach even though he'd filled it not an hour before. Not a hungry ache, more of a warning, a gut feeling telling him to get back in the car, leave, and forget Peter had ever asked him to come here. There was a darkness here he hadn't felt before, certainly not from this distance, telling him this differed from the others.

*Maybe I should leave. Nothing good will come of this. Not for me. Not for Peter.* But he couldn't. He'd promised him an answer. Although he had a strange feeling, he already knew it. *No wonder the dogs wouldn't leave the car park.*

Locking the car, he made his way towards the burger van. He didn't recognise the two uniforms, but guessed they were part of the MisPer team or recently relieved of sentry duty. The two plain clothes were definitely Major Crime. He hadn't seen the young woman before and assumed she was a recent addition to the team. Eddie guessed twenty four at the most. She wore a thick bobble hat, a green all weather jacket, black sports leggings and well-worn hiking trainers. She held a polystyrene cup in both hands, blowing at it to cool it enough for a sip. No doubt she'd just got down from the mountain top and the weather at the summit had been rather different to the mild conditions down here.

# THE ESCORT TO THE GRAVE

It was a simple mistake to make for inexperienced climbers. The mountain was a relatively easy climb for most, but the speed at which the weather can change can be deceiving, and only a fool would make the climb ill prepared. Eddie was one of those people. He looked down at himself. His scruffy, stained hoodie, jeans and trainers combo didn't exactly look the part. His sporty days of owning waterproofs and climbing boots well behind him, he decided he'd at least return to the car for his jacket before going up.

The man with her he'd had many an altercation with over the years, even when they were colleagues themselves. Detective Chief Inspector John Hibbard made no effort to hide his delight when the force gave Eddie the heave-ho. They were both sergeants back then, Hibbard climbing rank to Inspector shortly after, the role many had thought destined for Eddie. Now as a DCI, Hibbard was running the investigation team looking into the Morrison disappearance, answering to Detective Superintendent Enfield. He stood with his back to Eddie, wearing combat style trousers and a blue puffer jacket.

Eddie had hoped not to be spotted so soon, but conceded his car turned heads for the wrong reasons. With its array of dents, it resembled a reggae steel drum more than a car, but with its squealing brakes and balding tyres, couldn't say it was guilty of playing a similar tune. He could, of course, just crossed the road and started the climb, but he couldn't help himself. Neither hungry nor thirsty following his visit to the cafe, he pulled some loose change from his jeans pocket and headed over to the van. It sat on a patch of loose gravel, and from fifteen feet away, the group heard the crunch under-foot and turned to see the scruffy overweight man approach. Eddie ignored the glare from Hibbard, purposely circling around the four to the far end of the burger van to order a tea with two sugars. The simple move caused all four to shift their positions and quieten down as they watched him order. It reminded him of an Attenborough wildlife documentary he'd seen a while back, where a lone lioness ambitiously stalked a group of wildebeest, looking for the weak spot for an attack. Every time she moved position, so would the wildebeest to keep the predator at their sharp ends.

He noticed the woman's eyes working between him and Hibbard. Eddie took his drink, thanking the van owner as he rummaged through his loose change.

'What are you doing here, Venter?' Hibbard said. 'Don't tell me you're walking up there for the scenery. And blokes like you are rather shy of fitness.' He chuckled at his own insult, looking from face to face of his colleagues for back up. The two uniforms smirked their approval.

'You know why I'm here, Hibbard.' Eddie replied, keeping his attention on the pile of coins in his hand. 'Your commanding officer already told you. If you were any good at what you do, then I wouldn't have to do what I do.'

Hibbard looked Eddie up and down, then shook his head, clearly annoyed by his presence. 'You're a mess Venter. Try not to have a coronary on your way up. Mountain Rescue are a little busy at the moment. Why are you so out of shape, anyway?'

Eddie smirked as he pulled a pound coin from his hand, payment for his tea. 'Because, Jonathan old chap, every time I solve one of your cases, I get paid in tokens for this burger van.' The coin clicked as he pressed it to the countertop.

His eyes met Hibbard's furious glare as he waited for the inevitable. Eventually, Hibbard could take no more and his eyes shifted to the coin on the counter, checking its authenticity.

The van owner chuckled as she swiped the pound coin from the counter. Eddie snorted as he made off, leaving a volcanic Hibbard behind. His young partner, Eddie guessed as the DC Price from the interview notes, lowered her head to avoid her own smirk being seen by her furious DCI.

*So much for being discreet.*

He returned to the car and took out his summer rain coat, hoping it would do. Out of sight, he tipped the remainder of his tea out and tossed the polystyrene cup into the waste bin under the information board. He crossed onto the path and looked up at the mountain ahead of him.

The climb was hardly vigorous. For the most part, the gradient was shallow and the path easy under foot. The mountain was popular with people of all age, shape and size, and today was no exception. A mild summer breeze took the edge off the heat of the overhead sun as it cast its spell over the splendid valleys below, and the tourists were out in force to get their share of the fresh air.

Although he had put on so much weight from recent years of neglecting himself, it wasn't his physical issues causing him to rest so often. He passed numerous groups descending as he made his way up, receiving more than one concerned look or comment from them as he did. Around half way up, the shortness of breath started far earlier and further out than times before. A memory came to him, of the first body, shortly before setting up as a Private Investigator. Asked by a friend of a friend to investigate her brother's sudden disappearance, he'd reluctantly agreed. The police had paid little attention. The man was an adult, with no dependents or history of mental illness. Probably gone on holiday, they'd told her. But she knew better. She'd asked for Eddie's help after hearing his own tragic story of losing his wife in a car crash from a friend in the force, and the mysterious rumour of how he'd found her that came with it. Eddie found her brother in twelve hours. Sitting inside his car in the garage he'd began renting at a remote lockup since the previous week. He'd run a knife up both arms, from wrist to elbow, and bled out. The smell, barely two days old, was still confined to the tomb of the car. The police would have found him eventually, he supposed. On approach to the garage, Eddie had found himself short of breath, almost to the point of passing out. Dizzy spells overpowered him, followed by hot flushes and cold fever like shivers. And then, just before he had lifted the shutters and found the body, he had seen him. Sitting there, alone, crying. He had lifted the knife, twisting it in his hands as he spoke.

'I miss you Mike,' he'd said. 'I've tried, but I can't do no more.'

And then he'd dug the knife in and up his arms, watching in horror as the blood emptied onto his lap. Eddie lifted the roller door, confirming his findings. The drained corpse still sat upright in the driver's seat.

Following that first case, he had spent days wracking his brain on what was happening to him, concluding somehow, for some unknown reason, he was experiencing some of the dying man's symptoms for himself. The shortness of breath as the man anxiously dug the knife in, the cold and the dizziness as he bled out. And following those shared feelings, hit with the burdening vision of what the man had done to himself.

In the aftermath, the police had investigated how he had suspiciously happened across the body. Eddie had explained his hiring by his client and found a rental agreement for the garage at the deceased's address. He left out the other parts. When he'd finally been able to speak with his client, the deceased's sister, he told her everything. In her grief, a weight lifted, knowing her brother's last moments were thinking of Mike, the boyfriend he'd lost the previous year, to cancer. The man he loved so much, and couldn't live without. She had cried and smiled and actually thanked Eddie. And Eddie had waited until he was alone before he cried some more.

And that had been the start of it.

# THE ESCORT TO THE GRAVE

Close to the summit, a burning sensation rose in his throat like it was filling with boiling honey from his belly up. Sharp pains stabbed at his lungs with an intensity he hadn't felt before. More powerful. More extreme. Harsher. He pulled up on a large rock and took in a drink from his water bottle to quench it. He had to get there. He'd come all this way. Soldiering on, he staggered the last hundred yards to the top, sweat pumping from his pores,

And then it was there, just as he expected. He dropped to his knees as the rancid stench filled his nose and scorched the hair from his nostrils. Closing his heavy eyes, he concentrated on his breathing until he could finally bear the foul odour. A couple in their twenties, noticing his struggle, came across to help. The man dropped a hand onto Eddie's shoulder, calling to him in a muffled voice. Something about medical assistance. It was only then Eddie realised he was at the summit, and from his blurred vision, he could just make out the stone cairn. The man shared a concerned look with his girlfriend, until Eddie found his hand, patted it and nodded between heavy, deep breaths.

'I'm ok. I'm ok. Just unfit, that's all. Thanks for your concern.'

'No worries. Just take your time fella,' the man replied before starting back down the mountain. His girlfriend cast a worried glance back before following.

At times, he wondered how others couldn't possibly smell it. They had removed the body Saturday afternoon, but to Eddie, it was as if they left her where she fell, a weekend of uncompromising sunlight roasting her body as it rotted. The putrid stench of decomposing flesh was unbearable. Pushing to his feet, he continued to regulate his breathing between sips of water. He wiped away the sweat at his brow as the double vision settled, allowing him his first proper look around. Amateur photographers pointed ridiculously long cameras here and there in all directions, taking in the scenery. Couples and families patiently queued towards the central cairn plaque. Other less well behaved kids ran around chasing each other. Two chavvy looking blokes in tracksuit bottoms and baseball caps sat off to the North side with refreshing cans of cider in hand Eddie would have accepted if they offered him one.

Although any evidence had been removed, Eddie closed his eyes and could see the spot the woman had died in. The body was long gone, but to Eddie, she was still there. The climbers in attendance were oblivious, feet stomping over the area without care or knowledge a corpse lay beneath them just forty-eight hours ago. Eddie sat this time, crossing his legs beneath him. He relaxed as much as he could, continuing to control his long, labored breaths. The noise at the summit lowered, like an invisible switch turned down. The happy screams of children chasing each other muffled to silence, then the rising sound of something else took its place.

Shouting, arguing, crying.

Eddie opened his eyes. He scanned left and right, turning back to look over his shoulder. A large group of people huddled in one spot, their attention on the floor at the centre of the group. Some wore camouflaged clothing. To one side, a man and woman were consoling a teenage girl, clearly upset at what she was witnessing.

Eddie stood and stepped closer to the group, craning his neck as he walked around them for a better look. Through the mass of onlookers, he could see Sarah Morrison, her shoulders pumping furiously like pistons as she carried out CPR. An army officer knelt beside her, shouting directions to another of his troop behind him to call the emergency services. Sarah was bravely taking the lead, counting out loud and desperately pressing down on the woman's chest. Eddie circled the group, ignoring them now, looking for something else.

Another spike of pain stung at his chest, taking his breath yet again. He collapsed to one knee as his vision fogged once more. Running out of time, he frantically scanned in all directions. A red blur to the east pulled his attention behind the chaos, getting smaller and smaller as it went. He narrowed his eyes, a desperate attempt to sharpen the red blur into focus. Details came, a red cloak wrapped around a figure walking away from the confusion. He fought off the dizziness, but darkness was coming. More detail. More figures further along the pathway, waiting to receive them. A taller figure, a black indistinct mass. Two smaller bulks of white haze at its side. *Animals?* Desperate for more, he concentrated hard, narrowing his eyes, willing them into focus. Then the red figure stopped, turning back to him with a broad smile, her green eyes shining through the locks of hair poking out from her hood and in front of her face. She carried something in her arms that dangled either side of her. He focused more, eyes straining and burning with effort. And then, just before the darkness took him and he passed out, he saw her. Arms and legs and red hair flopping loosely as the woman turned and carried her tiny, limp body away.

It was Ellie Morrison.

# Chapter 10

Price pondered the best way to approach the subject. The car journey back to the station, for the most part, had been in silence. Hibbard was still bruising from his showdown with Eddie and had met any attempts of small talk from the DC with one-word, mumbled answers. The first few miles he was gripping the steering wheel of his black BMW with whitened knuckles like he was trying to break it off. Price sat cramped into the leather racing style passenger seat, occasionally throwing a sideways glance.

As they pulled into the police station car park, she decided to go for it.

'So what's the story with you and that PI?' she asked.

Hibbard snarled a response under his breath she couldn't make out, giving her a look like she'd just slapped his mother. Deep lines creased into his forehead and he clamped his jaw vice tight. Then, as quickly as the rage came, it left again. He breathed out a deep sigh, allowing his shoulders to relax with it.

'Venter is a liability, always has been. He was one of us before he hit the bottle and went nuts.' Hibbard shook his head as he pulled into his parking space and cut the engine. The leather of his seat squeaked beneath him as he turned toward her.

'Venter was a good detective, but always a bit rogue. His approach to work was erratic. He had his own way of doing things, and the team liked him, but to me, he was irresponsible and unprofessional. We clashed often. Enfield was our DCI back then, and he let him get away with it all. I

# THE ESCORT TO THE GRAVE

hated Enfield for that. I put it down to the fact Enfield and Venter's wives were mates, until the crash, that is.'

'What crash?' Price asked. 'What happened?'

Hibbard continued, 'Their wives were in a bad RTC together. Venter was the first on the scene. In short, he saved Enfield's wife instead of his own. Rumours are he had to choose which one to work on, and ended up letting his own wife die. He never came back to work again. Went completely off the rails, drinking, fighting, got done for assault. Not even Enfield could save him, as much as he tried. Now he pretends he's some sort of Private Investigator to hide the fact he's just a full-blown alcoholic.'

Price shook her head, exhaling loudly. 'Poor guy, imagine having to live with that.'

'Don't feel too sorry for him,' Hibbard said. 'Like I said, he's a liability. Just because he fools Enfield with his spooky supernatural bullshit, doesn't mean we should all believe it.'

Price raised an eyebrow. 'Supernatural what now?'

'He told the investigators it was the reason he was first on the scene of the accident. Like he knew it was going to happen.' He waved his hands above his head mockingly. 'Some sort of premonition. Since then, he's been in self-destruct mode, drinking to oblivion. Eventually, he started picking up a bit of private work, missing persons, shit like that. Got some lucky results. Then he started following leads on some of our cases, offering advice and fooling Enfield with it all. He's used him on several cases in the last few years, like some other departments through the borough. Under the radar mostly.'

'Hang on.' Price said, sitting upright in her seat. 'If the Super has been using a drunk PI on cases, claiming to use some sort of spiritual intervention, how come he doesn't get his arse kicked for it?'

'Because he gets results.' Hibbard replied. 'I don't know how he does it, but Venter has solved some tricky cases for the force. Ever hear about that pensioner a couple of years back getting killed on his own allotment? The special needs kid that used to help him found covered in his blood down the road?'

Price rubbed at her chin. 'Yeah, I remember. Didn't it turn out the old guy's neighbour did it?'

'Neighbour on the allotment. An argument over a boundary fence, of all things. It was a complete mess. The special needs kid couldn't speak a word. His prints were all over the body and the shovel. Had no alibi. Looked open and shut.'

'What happened?'

'Venter happened. Got called in to look at it, and led us straight to the neighbor. Fucking idiot still had his bloodstained clothes in his garage. The Chief Constable got a big slap on the back from the media for that one. But word got to ACC Bentley about Venter. He told Enfield he can use him as long as he stays in the shadows, but the moment he screws up, the shit sticks with him. If the press ever found out the department was using ghostbusters, the ACC would bury Enfield.'

Hibbard turned back in his seat, looking out the windscreen toward the station. His eyes glazed over, then narrowed, an idea sparking somewhere between them.

'Get to know him, Price.'

'Excuse me?' she replied.

'Venter. Get to know him.' Hibbard looked across to her again, eyes alive with excitement. 'Enfield is using him on this case and we'll be seeing more of him before it's over. I want to know how he finds out the information he does. Who he turns to, where he goes. If he thinks you need his help with it, he'll open up to you.'

Price responded with a grimace. 'I hope you're not implying…'

'Don't be ridiculous.' Hibbard replied. 'Stay professional. This is a good opportunity. We can kill a few birds here. It's an excuse to keep an eye on him, find out what he knows, and his methods of doing so. This case is turning into a non-starter, and we're running out of time. Anything we can get from Venter will put us back in the game. Plus, it'll be a good step for you, and if we find the girl alive, I'll make sure you get your fair share of the recognition afterwards.'

Price sighed dejectedly. When she joined the force, she had her own aspirations, to become a detective, rise through the ranks, be a role model for other women to look up to, make a difference. Never for a moment did she think that would entail underhand tactics. Was it naïve on her part? To think success directly resulted from hard, honest work? She thought of the Chief Constable, a woman who must have seen some serious discrimination and adversity in her time. A policewoman in eighties South Wales who worked all the way to the top job, the first in the country to do so. She was a perfect role model, wasn't she? What resistance did she have to overcome from her superiors? What support did she get from her family? Did the Chief Constable go through what she was being asked? She wondered what decisions and sacrifices she must have made to get there herself.

Price dropped her head in a final moment of reflection. 'I'll do it', she said, then pulled the door handle and stepped out of the car before Hibbard had a chance to respond.

Back at her desk, Price fired up the Police National Computer and tapped in Eddie Venter's details. The system pulled his record up instantly, the most recent offences listed toward the top and running in reverse chronological order. She pulled herself forward until her elbows rested on the desk, turning the monitor an inch toward the wall to avoid the roaming eyes of the open plan office.

A nice collection of drunk and disorderly arrests over the last few years. And one earlier assault with intent to resist arrest.

Leaning back in her chair, she linked her hands behind her head as she pondered it. Hibbard hadn't mentioned he'd assaulted a copper. No wonder the force kicked him out. It wouldn't be the first altercation between two police officers, though, and she wondered how they hadn't swept it under the carpet like so many others before. It was how the force preferred to deal with things, to keep everything negative away from the media. The age old saying 'there's no such thing as bad publicity' simply didn't apply to the police. The victim must have made a formal complaint. Enfield couldn't have protected him. As for the following drunk and disorderly charges, they told a tragic story of what followed. A man falling into a pit of despair. She wondered how alone he must have felt. Nowhere to turn. No-one to help. An overwhelming sense of abandonment.

Picking up her mobile phone, she scrolled through her phone book and pressed call. 'Hey Mam, you ok?'

'Who is this?' the other person asked.

'Who do you think? It's Lauren. You know, your only daughter?'

'Oh I'm sorry. I forgot I had one. You see, *my* daughter promised when she got her fancy new detective job she was going to phone me every night. That she'd still have time to come and visit. But *my* daughter hasn't phoned me for the last two nights and hasn't been round in a fortnight.'

Price rolled her eyes. 'Sorry Mam. I've been busy with a case. But I promise I'll be round tomorrow. Do you need me to pick up any shopping? Milk or bread?'

Her mother sighed. 'I'm not old Lauren. I'm still capable of getting the shopping in.'

'I know. I just… never mind.'

'What is it, Lauren? What's wrong?'

Price pinched at the bridge of her nose, squeezing her eyes shut. 'It's nothing. Just miss you, that's all. I'm sorry. I'll make more effort, I promise. I know how lonely you get.'

'It doesn't just sound like me who's lonely. You know the funny thing? Neither of us would be if you phoned and visited more often.'

'Point taken. I'll see you tomorrow ok?'

'Ok honey. Love you. Oh, and Lauren? I'm proud of you.'

'Really? Even after… you know… everything?'

'Of course. And if your father could see you now, he would be too.'

'Do you really think that?' Price asked.

There was a silent pause from the other end. 'I do. He may not have been very good at showing it, but I know he was. See you tomorrow, honey. I'll make cheesecake.'

Price put the phone down on the table, closed down the computer and sat until the screen blanked. Her face reflected back in the monitor. Tears welled in her eyes and she fought to keep them from falling, using her sleeve to blot them as they threatened to cascade down her cheeks. She closed her eyes again, and her father's face filled her mind.

She'd sacrificed plenty for her career. She wondered if it was all worth it.

# Chapter 11

## Tuesday

The press conference was packed, every chair and standing room space filled. Representatives for every conceivable network, newspaper and online publication were present. Reserved for the big boys, the main broadcast reporters filled the front three rows. The BBC had even sent their famous political correspondent Heidi Ellenburg, a firm favourite of David Morrison. She had always reported on him favourably. Her empty chair sat at the centre of the front row, directly in line of sight of the top table seating. Once the initial statement from the Senior Investigating Officer and plea from David Morrison were complete, she would undoubtedly be first to get a couple of questions in. Ellenburg was the envy of the room, the woman everyone here wanted to be. She stood off to one corner, her junior assistant holding up a mirror as she made sure her face and hair were perfect.

In the adjoining holding room, DCI Hibbard discussed the process with the Morrisons. The MP would be familiar with the incessant sounds and flashes from the photographers fighting to get the perfect shot, but it would undoubtedly prove overwhelming for his wife. Hibbard had concerns she would even hold up and get through the press conference at all, and couldn't understand David's insistence she attend. Appearing completely spaced out, she stared at the floor a few feet ahead of her, probably down to the Cipramil and Prozac prescribed to her that her husband had been quick enough to divulge about. Hibbard had offered to get a uniformed officer to sit with her while David conducted the plea alone, but he insisted on his wife being at his side. 'If the kidnappers see how crippled she is, they may reconsider', he had said. Nothing to do with showing the world what a supportive husband and concerned father he was.

The media manager rapped at the door, indicating it was time. Hibbard led the way, followed by David, who made a show of gripping his wife by both shoulders as they lumbered out onto the top table platform. Clicks and flashes bombarded the couple as they took their seats. David pulled Sarah's chair, lowering her to it with care. He kissed her on the cheek, then sat next to her with his fingers laced into hers with a show of perfect solidarity. Hibbard spoke first, thanking everyone for attending at such short notice. He knew there was nowhere the bloodsuckers would rather be. This was headline news. Front page stuff. He ran through the known facts, reading from a pre-written statement. He took his time, purposely going into as much detail as possible. From experience, the more he could tell the press straight from the off, the less inclined they'd be to shout out their loaded questions afterwards. It was tough for the parents to hear such detailed statements, but it was nothing to having journalists attempting to shock with gory unforgiving questions and complete lack of compassion.

David Morrison captivated his audience as ever. He spoke clearly, but with tremendous emotion in his voice, silencing the room. He paid tribute to the wonderful woman sitting next to him, to his eldest daughter at home, and to his youngest, cruelly taken by her kidnappers. At her mention, Sarah broke. Her head met her hands, and she shook uncontrollably. The room lit up with yet more flashes and clicks getting the money shot. Pulling her in close, David begged the kidnappers they return their daughter unharmed. Brimming eyes met the broadcast camera as he spoke, calling out to the millions watching throughout the UK and the rest of the world.

Eddie reached for the remote and switched off his television. He knocked back the last of his drink, the harsh scotch burning his throat as it slid down. He thought of the girl's limp body, arms and legs swaying as the woman carried her away. The woman turning to smile back at him, goading him to follow, knowing he couldn't.

This was his curse.

He played back those moments from the mountain, tumbling over and over like an ocean wave wiping him out. But where the shock of a wave would hit, jarring the senses into hypersensitivity, the vision had smothered him in a blanket of claustrophobic darkness. The vision had been more powerful, more precise, than any other he had seen before. Until it wasn't. He had tried to follow them, to see where they headed, to see if she was alive. And then she had seen him, the woman carrying her. Engaged him and stopped him.

That, at least, had never happened before.

The smell at the summit, the repugnant decay of flesh, burning his nostril hairs with its foul stench, he would never get used to. He had smelled it so many times on these cases now. That sickening odour of a dead body, amplified by his curse. But was it the girl or the old woman? He had seen her lifeless body carried away to the east, limp and lifeless, but could he be sure? For what purpose would the woman carry away her dead body?

His vibrating phone on his coffee table pulled him from his trance.

'Did you watch it?' Peter Enfield asked.

'Hell of a performance. He plays the worried father well.'

'Quite. Two days ago, I convinced David Morrison not to hold a press conference. I genuinely believed as long as the public were in the dark about the whole thing, the girl would be safe from harm. He's not a stupid man though, Ed. When I conceded this morning we should go ahead with it, he knew what I was implying.'

'It's not your fault, Pete.' Eddie said.

'Do you think she's dead though, Ed? Really? I mean, why would they go to all that trouble just to kill her?' Peter asked.

'I don't know Pete. All I know is what I saw. You sent me up there, remember? Would you have preferred not to know? Would you prefer the entire force were chasing their tails?'

'I guess not.' Peter replied. 'But if she is dead, I have to find her, and the woman who took her too.'

'And like I told you, she carried her body away to the east, toward the Tal-y-bont valley. A woman her size wouldn't have been able to carry her long on her own, especially heading toward more mountain peaks. What I can't work out is how she got away without being seen.'

'I've got teams running through there right now from both directions. But it's a vast area. Are you absolutely sure they went that way?'

The woman's face flooded his mind again. Her big green eyes peeking through her brown locks hanging over them. The warm, welcoming smile she gave him before he passed out. 'I'm sure.'

At the other end of the phone, Peter sighed. 'Sometimes I wish you'd never told me about that gift of yours.'

Eddie refilled his glass with the last of the bottle. 'It's no gift. It's a noose around my neck, tightening every time. I'm sick of it Pete. I'm sick of not knowing what's going on, then suddenly knowing too much. There's no in-between. I'm plagued with knowing things without being able to prove it. Do you have any idea how it feels? Trying to convince people without having a scrap of evidence? Everyone thinking you're crazy? Everyone thinking you're in on it?'

'I don't think you're crazy, Ed. You know that. You've helped us a great deal the last few years.'

'What did you tell David Morrison? Please tell me he doesn't know about me?'

'I didn't need to tell him. He already knows who you are. Straight out asked me if I had you involved. When I agreed on the press conference, he knew I had some fresh evidence or leads. Safe to say he hit the roof. Have you dealt with him before?'

Eddie thought about it for a moment. 'No. First impression, the guy's a prick, Pete. He'll try his best to ruin you off the back of this. You should have denied it.'

'I'm tired of lying, Ed. I've put Jane through so much. That girl going missing has made me just want to stop it all. Maybe you were right about my retirement. I might not have a choice after all this, anyway. The guy *is* a prick, first class, but he's a father too. Put yourself in his shoes. You can understand his frustration when he finds out the police force tasked with finding his daughter turns to alternative methods. It reeks of incompetence.'

'I warned you not to get me involved in this. He's going to turn this into a circus.'

'I'd defend your methods if I have to, Eddie. I've always believed in your gift.'

'For the last time, it's not a bloody gift.' Eddie said. 'We've discussed this too many times. I'm being punished.' He knocked back the last of the whisky, sucking air through his teeth at the aftertaste.

'You saved Jane's life Ed, don't ever forget that. I never will. Whatever happens in the future, just know this. I'll always be grateful you were there that night to save my wife.'

*And let my own wife die,* Eddie thought.

# Chapter 12

Richard Evans sat at the broad oak kitchen table reading the paper and drinking his tea as his wife Margaret cooked breakfast at the Auger. Sounds of crackling eggs, bacon and sausage on the stove had Jack Russell Archie licking his lips at Richard's feet. Aromas of a busy farmhouse kitchen filled the air as Margaret had finished the last of the guest's breakfasts before starting on her husbands, who had just returned from his first round of tending to the cattle.

The country life in the Upper Aber village was all Richard had ever known. He had been born and raised here, and from an early age, thrown into the world of farming. His father Ryland had taught him to drive tractors by nine, shear sheep by ten, and by twelve he was more than proficient in the processing of lamb, swine and poultry. His old man often made comments such as 'he was born to be a farmer' or 'it's in your blood.' By his teenage years, Richard realised what he really meant. He will take over this farm and have no choice about it. He resented the place, but grew to accept and eventually love it, and until recently, at fifty years of age, couldn't imagine life without it. The last few weeks, however, he had been contemplating the future. With two grown-up girls living in Cardiff, he had no one to pass the farm on down to, and he'd be damned if he would trust that clown of a farmhand to run things as Richard got old and watched the profits wither away.

Besides, the farming business was getting more cutthroat than ever. Fifteen years ago, he was supplying every butcher in every nearby town with his quality product, but the arrival of the supermarket chains with their ridiculous bargains and non-existent profit margins slowly squeezed the customers from them. The butchers survived at first with the loyalty of their regulars, but everyone has a price, and month after month, Richard lost a client as the butchers closed their doors. He still sold his cattle and lamb to the abattoir at Dowlais, but again, the price he would get for a carcass in the nineties and noughties was almost double what he would get now. It was the swine that kept him afloat, his being one of few farms around the south and mid-Wales valleys specialising in more than one breed of pig. He had turned to butchering them himself, seriously difficult and labour intensive work, selling directly to the restaurants and cutting out the middle man. It had been a decision that saw them continue to turn over a small profit, and keep the wolves from the door.

Their saving grace turned out to be something he'd never been fond of. They hadn't bothered with computers when the girls were growing up, but after they had both left for University ten years ago, Margaret had learned to use it, at first just to keep in touch with them online. She taught Richard the basics, although he refused to email the girls. To him, it wasn't personal enough. It was a phone call or nothing. Eventually he started 'surfing the web' as Margaret would call it, and joined farming forums where like-minded and troubled people vented their frustrations at the government for their lack of help in their community. Soon afterwards, Margaret hit on an idea and set up a website for the farm meats, game birds and her signature jarred condiments. Maggie's Jams was born, and she even knocked up sticky labels for the jars. They had sold well, and for a time they were comfortable again. But the farming business is like no other. All it takes is a vital piece of equipment to fail, and with no more support from the bank, you're on your own to find a solution.

Five years ago, she had finally convinced Richard to convert the barn next to the farmhouse into a shower block and flatten the next field to accommodate caravans and tent pitches. She had researched online about it and how so many farmers were doing it to subsidise their income. Margaret had even knocked up a business plan, and eventually he'd agreed to gamble the last of their contingency money on it. They had power outlets installed and built camp fires complete with log seating to give the city folk that authentic 'at one with nature' experience. Richard built nature trails through the outer edges of the farmland, littered with fairy lights for the younger visitors. They advertised online, and it was a relative success, with most pitches filled through the warmer months as the tourists travelled in to explore the surrounding National Park. The front lounge of the farmhouse became the guest dining room. It was big enough for six tables and Margaret took pride in serving up her full English breakfasts using the meats and eggs reared from the farm. The long winter months in Wales, however, were crippling, and they found themselves barely surviving through the New Year. They had gambled so much money on the venture, barely enjoyed the fruits of their labour, and the margins only continued to get tighter.

Unknown to Margaret, lady luck had finally come calling three years ago. Richard answered a forum post online seeking a South/Mid/West Wales farmer with butchery skills. Discreet cash in hand payments, with large potential earnings for the right candidate. It sounded perfect to pick up some much needed work. It wasn't uncommon for farmers or butchers to be employed for private contracts. Plenty of people held small holdings throughout the valleys with a handful of pigs or sheep. Some raised them purposely to feed the family, and required a slaughterer and butcher to process the animals and do the dirty work, the dispatching and portioning. It was just what he needed to save the farm. Contact details exchanged, it didn't take long for a phone call to come in. A car full of men arrived, speaking in whispers or some sort of coded dialect barely recognisable as English. They wore leather jackets and had some sort of competition going on to see who could wear the most ridiculous looking gold chains around their necks, and each of them wore more rings on their fingers than they had fingers. Richard had realised he was in trouble at this point. The last thing you want is to be in the pocket of these types of people, but saying no might have got him in further trouble. Then the man in the expensive suit got out of the car, and for some reason, he struck more fear into him than all the other men combined. He said nothing, just stared Richard down until he could take no more and looked away. They inspected the pig barn and Richard's slaughter and butchery tables, and, looking to the man in suit for authorisation, explained what they required from him and what his role would be. Leaving five grand in cash as a good will gesture, they thanked Richard for the tour and asked if he would be interested in making more money than he could count. Something told him by this point he had little option. Probably the handgun he saw the one who stayed with the car holding. On condition he operated alone and told no-one, they left a mobile phone and told him they would be in touch.

The first time the phone rang was at dead of night. He remembered it like it was yesterday; shooting out of bed to get to it before waking Margaret. He had primed her in advance he'd promised to train up some farmhands on delivering calves and piglets, to not arouse suspicion of a late night call. With just an hour to prepare, he rushed to set up, before two men in a white van arrived with his first job and an envelope containing another five grand in used twenty-pound notes. He recalled the internal panic he had felt at seeing they had also turned up with hand guns, and made no attempt to hide them from view. He had jabbered on until one of them told him to be quiet. Other than to ask where to take the van, the men were silent, no small talk.

And when those rear doors opened, the shock at what he had seen. That first package, heavily wrapped in black plastic, the undeniable shape of it. They had pulled it out by the feet, allowing it to drop to the dirt with a thud, then dragged it through to Richard's draining table and hoisted it on. It took an age to process, and the men regularly checked their watches with yawns of impatience. He wasn't, after all, butchering and portioning a carcass for sale. This was for disposal, so intricate knife work wasn't necessary, but he imagined he would have dealt with it far easier than he did that first time. The two men watched with enthusiasm as he worked, sawing, cutting, draining, portioning with experience. Explaining what he did as he went along, like he was training up a couple of apprentices, helped with his overwhelming need to cry. The men never spoke back, never asked questions, just watched intently. Then he had used the bandsaw and mincer, feeding the portions through one at a time. He had to stop twice to vomit and had to muster everything he had not to stop for a third time when feeding in the head. The machine had caught on the skull, and he had to remove it by hand and crack it into smaller chunks with a lump hammer before re-feeding it. The men had enjoyed that, giggling to each other as Richard doubled up and retched as it cracked apart. It was a combination of the smell, along with the sound the blades made as they hit a piece of bone or gristle. They were familiar sounds and smells of course, no different to any other time, but knowing what he was processing transformed them into a whole new level of intensity. Once minced, he added it to a barrel of pig feed ready to be dished up in the morning.

Pleased with the process, the men didn't seem particularly bothered with his clean-up methods. It was, after all, slaughter equipment, and would always be messy. That first one had taken a good couple of hours, but after the next one, and the next one after that, Richard had become almost as efficient as he was butchering swine.

# THE ESCORT TO THE GRAVE

Over time, the men relaxed around him. The guns stayed hidden, but they never spoke. Then one day, two different men turned up. They looked tough and mean. One felt it necessary to point his gun toward Richard, and he did indeed shit himself, only for the other man to shout at his companion in the weird slang they used. Then they opened the back doors to the van and Richard shit himself some more. The package was much smaller than the others he had dealt with, half the size, in fact. It was obvious what he was dealing with and tried to explain to the men it was not part of the deal, but the barrel of the gun pressed against his forehead changed his mind, and he realised he had made a big mistake and was in for the long haul. Again, the men stayed to watch, guns in hand, as Richard sawed, cut, drained, portioned, minced. He received twelve grand and another mobile phone afterward. Two minutes after the men had left, it had rung, and the voice on the other end informed him from then on the packages would be the smaller ones, he would receive eight thousand for each one, and in the early hours of the first day of every month, they required his services.

Richard didn't tell the voice on the phone something stirred in him that last time. For some reason, the initial fear had subsided when he started cutting. He had enjoyed himself.

The packages kept coming and Richard kept feeding his pigs. They devoured the food with an enthusiastic greed he hadn't seen before, and the days following, when their feed had turned bland again, they would pout like grumpy teenagers. The voice on the phone sounded pleased with his work, and again, the men started leaving as soon as they dropped off the packages. It was at this point Richard began to take risks, risks worth taking, photographing and videoing each one for his personal gratification. They would kill him if they found out, but it had been years since he and Margaret had enjoyed any pleasure together, and so he had created the videos for himself to enjoy. He wasn't harming anyone; he wasn't some sicko. Anyway, they were already dead.

Then two weeks ago, he received the devastating call informing him they had delivered his last package. They were shutting down the operation, something about lying low, the product no longer being available. The phone and his butchery equipment needed disposing of. He should have felt relief, but he had become hooked, obsessed even. He did nothing with the equipment, leaving it in situ hoping they would change their minds. Then he thought of the guns, the seriousness of the men delivering the parcels, of what they were capable of. Would they tie up loose ends? Surely they wouldn't have phoned him first if that was their intention. But could he be sure?

Time to sell up while he still could.

It surprised Richard to get the online valuation of £750,000 for the farm. He had happened across a site offering 'free valuations in minutes' only to find it took over twenty to input all the details. The state of British farming at the moment he had expected far less, but he guessed at one hundred and twenty acres, the algorithm considered it good value for money. Following the estimated valuation hitting his inbox, agents bombarded him with messages, eager to get the farm on their portfolios. Adding his mobile phone number to the website had been a mistake and after three days of calls requesting they attend to take pictures of the farm, he switched the phone off in case Margaret got suspicious. He was running out of time to tell her of his plans to sell up and get from there. At the secrecy of it all, it would undoubtedly upset her he didn't feel the need to include her in the planning. She was part of the farm too, having spent all of her married life there.

The fact was, he didn't really care what she thought. It was his family farm. The sale had to happen with or without her blessing. The first of the agents were booked in to attend in two days, and he had no intentions of cancelling. If she came on board with the idea, he would take her with him, and if she didn't, then he would simply walk away. She was a good wife and an exceptional mother to his two children, but he just didn't love her anymore. If it came to that, the girls would rally around her, calling him all sorts of terrible things. But he didn't care. They were the ones who left in search of a better life. Besides, he'd done a lot worse things over the last few years.

He couldn't put a reason on why he resented Margaret. It was the little things seemed to frustrate him the most, like the way she always cleaned and moved his wellies from the back door and onto the stand beneath the coat hangers. Or the way she would change her voice all posh when answering the phone, changing it back again when she realised it was someone she knew. Or the way she always said sorry every time he raised his voice, like an automatic response instead of taking the time to find out what she had done wrong. What he did know was when he started to resent her. It was after he was spending more and more time in the evenings locked away in the study, exploring those forums. Who knew there was such a big world out there? And the things the people in the chat rooms would talk about doing and the pictures he would see; he became obsessed.

As Margaret approached with his breakfast, Richard closed the paper, folding it in half and tossing it to the empty spot on the table to his left. The TV on the worktop played some sort of press conference of parents looking for a missing child in the Beacons. Richard grabbed the remote and switched it off. He liked to eat with some peace and quiet. Margaret placed the plate delicately in front of him and backed away, her face creased up, waiting for the backlash.

It took a few seconds to register. 'For crying out loud, you've done it again. What's wrong with you? How many times have I got to remind you I hate crispy bacon?' Richard's knuckles drained of colour, as if he somehow squeezed the blood from them up to his face. 'How come you can cook five types of egg for the guests but can only seem to cremate my bacon?'

'I... I'm sorry, love. It was the press conference on the telly. The girl missing in the Beacons. I took my eye off the pan. Here, let me take it back and make you some fresh.' Margaret reached for the plate, only to be blocked by Richard's forearm. He picked it up from the table and lowered it to Archie, who didn't need a second invite and dove in greedily.

'I haven't got time to wait for you to ruin a second lot. The pigs need feeding ready for processing tomorrow. At least they'll get full bellies this morning, even if it is their last supper.'

Margaret lowered her head as Richard barged past, heading for the back door. The only sounds came from Archie wolfing down the last of the eggs and licking the plate clean. Retrieving his wellies from the stand, Richard slammed the door behind him. He heard something fall off the wall the other side, probably that ghastly oil painting Margaret felt obliged to buy from old Mrs. Williams, after she had rudely and without request, painted the farmhouse from the layby on the main road. *Good*, Richard thought. *I hope it's broken.*

He marched his way towards the swine feed dispensers across from the farmhouse. The mix of wheat, barley and high protein soyas didn't seem to give off any odours in the barrels, but Richard swore when mounted closer to the barn, the pigs played up something awful. Ever since they had a taste for the special ingredient mixed with it, their treat on the first day of every month, that is. Placing the first bucket under the dispenser, he knocked the tap open before something caught his eye. From here, Richard could see all the way back up to the farm entrance, a large single gate with old cobble stone pillars either side. They always kept the gate open during the day. Pedestrians passed through regularly, as there were public footpaths running from the lane outside the grounds in many spots. Homemade signs advertising Margaret's jams, hen and duck eggs propped up at the pillars.

Standing at the entrance was a woman dressed in a long black gown, her hood drawn up, shadowing the top half of her face, her full red lips glistening underneath. Sat prone either side of her, like two royal guards standing to attention, were two albino wolfhounds, impressive looking creatures with pure white coats, and deep black eyes. The red tips of their ears looked like they'd been dipped in blood.

And they were staring at him.

Richard stood from the dispenser, allowing himself a better view of his visitors. The woman stood tall in an elegant pose, her hands at her hips. Despite the flowing cloak, he could make out an hour-glass figure, a hint of a long dark leg peeking out from beneath the shawl to a pair of heels. No-one dressed like that in the countryside. A worrying thought hit him. An estate agent. Chancing her luck by turning up unannounced, hoping to get a foot in at the door and first dibs at getting the property on her books. But why the dogs? He was about to call out, tell her to be on her way, when he felt a rapping at his feet, and turned back to find the bucket overflowing with pig feed. Dropping to one knee, he turned off the dispenser tap, pulling a second bucket closer to scoop up the overflow.

When he looked back to the farmhouse entrance, the woman and her dogs were gone.

Drawing off more buckets of feed, he loaded them into the back compartment of his four-wheeler Kawasaki Mule and rode through the north field to the slaughter barn. It was necessary to keep the speed down due to the unstable load in the back, but around a hundred metres out, he could hear the panicked squeals over the rumble of the four wheeler's engine. He broke hard, a little too hard, hitting his chest on the steering wheel. The buckets lost part of their load into the flat bed of the vehicle. He cursed loudly, before focusing back on the noise from the barn. Even from this distance, he couldn't help but grimace at the high-pitched screams piercing his ears. An icy shiver ran up his back and his hand rubbed at his neck to meet it. The feed buckets forgotten now, he slammed his foot down to get to the barn. The Mule lurched forward as he struck his back against the cabin. A sharp pain shot down his left arm, sending him into a bubbling rage. He raced to the barn entrance; the Mule skidding to a halt at the gravel driveway. The door was open. He never left it open. There was someone in there.

The noise was horrendous. He'd heard it before, of course, but not from these pigs. He'd been around swine long enough to know they only ever make that sound once. He'd read about it. How pigs can sense it. Right before slaughter, moments from death.

Killing the engine, Richard grabbed his shovel from the rear compartment and scrambled to the barn entrance, then thought better of it and slowed to a creep. He wished he'd brought the shotgun. Or Archie at least, but he was too busy eating his burnt fill back at the kitchen. Useless lump. If there were foxes in there, he'd never get them with a shovel. But the door was open. His mind somersaulted, trying to make sense of it.

Peering around the open door, he caught sight of the first pen of pigs. They had slept here overnight, to be fed and watered, ready for tomorrow. Richard did this with all of his batches. It settled them into the environment, kept them relaxed before being led behind the plastic curtains at the back, one at a time, to be processed. It saved many a struggle to get them into position if they were happy to be led there.

# THE ESCORT TO THE GRAVE

Now they were climbing over each other to get away from something at the far side of the barn. The smaller boars struggled under the power of the fatter ones.

Richard edged further in. There were eight pens in the barn, four to the left, four to the right, with a central walkway running right up the middle, making tending to them easier. A fine dusting of straw littered the floor he cleaned out every week. The lighting was poor at the far end of the barn, his inspection lamps normally turned off until required, but who or whatever was in there needed removing or he'd end up losing swine. He crept forwards from pen to pen, the screeching and crashing into the steel framework making his brain hurt. Moving past the last of them, he tiptoed to the translucent plastic curtain drawn across the slaughter area. Behind it, a shape formed, a person maybe, waiting in the shadows. He reached out to it with an unsure hand, catching at the cold synthetic material and pulling to the side hard.

And then they were there.

Sitting atop the steel butchery table was the woman he saw at the farm gates. Her piercing blue eyes narrowed to compliment her accusing sneer. She wore the black robe he saw earlier, a gold three pointed emblem stitched into the breast. Her hood was pulled back, revealing long, silky black hair falling over her shoulders. To the side of the table, her two hounds sat on their haunches, staring up at the man with hunger in their eyes. The woman uncrossed her legs, jumped down from the table and walked towards Richard, backing him up until he hit the cold frame of the last pen. She stopped mere inches from his face. Her eyes sparkled as they swallowed Richard in. Attempts to swallow away the dry sensation in his mouth failed.

All at once, the pigs fell quiet. No squealing, no panicking, no crashing. Richard held off the urge to turn around and check what was happening, keeping his bulging eyes on hers. Another shiver shot between his shoulder blades and up his neck as his anger turned to fear.

'Hello Mr. Evans,' the woman said, her strong Eastern European accent commanding authority. She looked back to the tables, the mincer and the band-saw. 'You have been a busy man.'

Richard did everything he could to speak, but his muscles, the involuntary ones that dealt with such things, had stopped working. He just stood blank-faced, mouth open, unable to respond.

She ran a hand up his shaking chest, over his racing heart and to his neck, her hand gripping around the back of it, nails digging for purchase. Her unnerving smirk turned his face an ashen colour. The woman looked deep into his bulging eyes, reading the fear, then to his trembling lips. She kissed him then, hard, burying her tongue deep into his mouth.

Instead of euphoria, he saw only immense horror and torture as his body trembled in terror. His bladder opened, a puddle of urine forming from his trouser leg on the ground below. The woman smiled as she looked down to it, waiting for him to finish, then let go of his neck, releasing him to crumple to the piss soaked ground beneath him.

Then she spoke once more as she looked around at the equipment behind her. 'The wage of sin is death, Mr. Evans. And it is time for you to pay.'

## Chapter 13

Opening the huge barn doors, Richard pushed them right back on their hinges. Loose build ups of hay around the base resisted, forcing him to put his shoulder into them the last few feet. He slouched to the back of the barn, feet dragging beneath him as if made of concrete, pulling clumps of straw along the way. Starting with the furthest pens, he slid out the locking bolts and opened the gates, allowing the pigs to follow their noses to the troughs outside. For such weighty animals, they could really pick up the pace if it meant getting an extra few mouthfuls over their competitors. As each pen emptied, he worked forwards, opening two pens at a time until all the hogs were jostling for the best positions at their dining table across the field.

The tears fell uncontested from Richard's face, his eyes throbbing a dull pain from the horrors in his head pushing to escape, but he made no effort to relieve it. He shuffled back to the barn doors, and leaving them wide open, took the Mule the brief trip across the fields back to the vehicle garage next to the farmhouse. Through the kitchen window, Margaret watched as her husband dismounted the four-wheeler and ambled past, his shoulders slumped into a posture a stiff breeze would have no problem knocking over. Opening the back door, Margaret called to her husband as he headed toward the vehicle shed. Jack Russell Archie followed to the door, lowered his head with a whimper, then turned on his haunches into the safety of the farmhouse.

'Everything ok, honey?' Margaret asked.

Richard stopped in his tracks, keeping his back to his wife. 'Yes,' was all that came back.

'I'm sorry about breakfast this morning. I didn't see you take any lunch out with you either. You must be starving by now. I'll make up some sarnies for you. I've made a lovely fresh loaf and I'll cut it doorstop thick just how you like it. Cheese and Branston, your fave. And I'll do a bit of extras with it. Make it a proper Ploughman's lunch. How does that sound?'

Richard lowered his head. 'Ok,' he said.

'I'll bring it up to the barn in about half an hour. By about four o'clock, yeah? And a flask of tea. Sound good?'

'Stay away from the barn,' he mumbled in a flat, monotone voice. 'I'll come back for them in a bit.' He continued on to the vehicle shed without looking back.

Firing up the forked loader tractor, he picked up the vehicle fuel tank he kept at the back of the garage. Reversing out from the barn, he smashed the back end into the side of the Mule, lifting it onto two wheels and denting the roll cage before it resettled back on all four wheels. Keeping the fuel tank low on the forks, Richard drove out of the farmhouse entrance, crossing the road to the first of the wheat fields opposite, in its final stages of maturity before next week's harvest. The three quarter full tank sloshed wildly as the tractor crashed its way through to the centre of the field, but the wide forks kept it in place. Stopping at the centre, surrounded by chest high maize, he rounded to the tank, opening the tap lever a quarter turn. The unmistakable potent stink of petrol filled the air as a steady stream of the flammable liquid poured from the tap. Richard climbed back into the tractor cab to continue on.

He crossed the second crop field, divided from the first by a simple low stone wall fire break with a gap wide enough for machinery to pass, and reached the perimeter fence of the hay field holding the slaughter barn. Without slowing, Richard lifted the petrol tank high on the forks, out of harm's way, allowing the front tyres and grill of the tractor to take the brunt of the wire stock fence. It was no match for the powerful machine, the steel wire and wooden posts tangling beneath the wheels and dragging along behind. Richard paid no attention, rounding the many bales of hay formed throughout the field and the lone oak tree at the centre, all the while the hazardous fuel continuing to pour from its spout. Reaching the barn, he drove the tank inside, climbed out of the tractor, and shut off the tap. He knocked at the tank; the sound telling him there was still enough inside.

Trudging back out of the barn, he looked back down across the fields towards the farmhouse. He thought of his wife now, what she would think when she learned the truth. What the girls would say. It didn't matter now. All that mattered was making amends. This was his chance. The woman had shown him. He sobbed as he lumbered back in through the barn doors, shoulders slumped as he lethargically pulled them shut behind him. The emotion flowed from him now, pitiful moans between wild cries as the realisation of what came next dawned. He opened the fuel tank tap full, the downward pressure of the volume inside enough to force the liquid out in a pure, uninterrupted stream, hitting the barn floor with a loud splash eight feet from where it started. The powerful odour filled the barn as Richard shuffled small steps into the centre of the noxious pool. With trembling hands, he pulled his gold plated zippo lighter from his pocket, his most prized possession the girls had bought him years ago. He fell to his knees, ignoring the soaking his lower half was getting as he lifted the lighter. A tired, horrified face stared back at him in the brass reflection. He read the engraved letters one last time. 'To the best dad in the world. Happy Birthday love Kate and Carys xxx.'

They wouldn't think that soon.

His thoughts went to the other children. Frigid, lifeless bodies, lying there on the freezing steel table. Their skin all grey and blue, eyes clouded and blank, nothing behind them. So cold. The woman showed him what needed to be done. He had to warm them, bring them back, and beg forgiveness. Then he would be pardoned. Their faces flashed in front of him again, life in them now, as they cried for his help. Their teeth chattered and lips turned blue as they pulled themselves into bear hugs and begged for warmth. Then they spoke, stammering words through shaking mouths. 'Help us, please, we're so cold.'

He flicked the wheel. Flint connected and sparked. An almighty *whump* filled the barn. Then, unimaginable pain.

Across the field, their bellies filled, the pigs wandered aimlessly, paying no attention as the barn went up. Tentacles of black smoke bellowed through every available opening, meeting and joining force above the barn roof into one enormous cloud. A trail of fire snaked its way out from beneath the doors and into the first layer of dry grass outside.

Beneath the massive oak sat at the centre of the field, the woman in the black cloak leaned against the trunk. With each hand, she stroked the heads of her hounds sat either side of her, as they watched the barn intently. A ragtag group of crows sat in the branches above, cawing their excitement as the first flames rose high above the barn, into the early evening sky.

## Chapter 14

With a quick rap on the glass, she tried the handle and, low and behold, as she suspected, the door was unlocked. She stepped through into the hallway of the mid terraced home, mumbling under her breath. Stomach rumbling aromas of roasting vegetables and meat filled the air. From the kitchen at the rear of the house, her mother held a tray with an oven mitt, basting a chicken with its juices before reinserting it into the oven. She wiped her hands in a tea towel as she called out.

'Well, if it's not my long, lost daughter, come to visit her mama all the way from the other side of town. What a privilege.'

'Your expertise in sarcasm is matched only by your inability to remember to keep your front door locked,' Price replied. 'Will you ever listen?'

'You know, when you were a young girl, we didn't even have to keep our front doors closed.'

Price walked through to the kitchen, giving her mother a kiss on the cheek. 'Change the record, mother. Those days are long gone. It's a different time now. You have to be more careful.'

'Sorry mam,' her mother said in a mocking voice.

'You'll be sorry if some arsehole comes in and takes your purse and car keys.'

'Watch your language in this house, Lauren.'

Price looked over her mother's shoulder. Bubbling pots of potatoes, cabbage and broccoli filled the hob. 'Are you feeding the street today or what?'

'Next door and Trevor at number four. He'll only eat a roast dinner these days, and his home help only comes twice a week. I've got a full chicken in. Thought me and you could sit and eat together, like we used to. I've got homemade roasties in and Yorkshire puddings as well.'

'Mam, I can't stay long. I'm, um, meeting someone.'

Her mother looked her up and down. 'Right, I see. Thought you were a bit dressed up just to come and see your mother. Who is he then?'

Price rolled her eyes. 'It's not like that, Mam. It's just a work thing.'

'And too much work will kill you,' she said, turning her back. 'Just ask your father.'

'That was a brain haemorrhage, Mam.'

'From too much work, Lauren.'

They stood in stalemate, just the noises of bubbling pans filling the silence. They'd had this conversation so many times before, Price thought it would eventually make her own brain bleed. Her eyes went to her feet. 'I miss him.'

'Me too honey, me too.'

She continued to kick at her feet. 'Mam? Did you mean what you said? On the phone yesterday?'

'That he would have been proud of you? Every word. Now, come here.'

She took her daughter into an embrace, and although she was a good six inches shorter and thirty years older, the girl melted into her arms like a toddler with a scraped knee again.

'You might not have been on speaking terms for his last few years, but that doesn't mean he didn't talk about you. You were always at the front of his mind, Lauren. It was just unfortunate you took after him in your stubbornness, otherwise one of you may have decided life is too short.'

Price buried her head into her mother's shoulder. 'I regret it every day, Mam.'

'I'm sure you do. And I'm sure your father does, too. Be kind and compassionate to one another, forgiving each other, just as in Christ God forgave you.'

'Ephesians four, thirty-two,' Price said.

'Not bad, for an atheist,' her mother replied.

Price lifted her head from her mother's shoulder, breaking the embrace, a damp patch now where her cheek had been. They both laughed as she wiped her face. 'Sorry Mam.' She looked up at the palm crucifix pinned to the kitchen wall. 'You know what, I haven't got to go for a bit. I think I could manage a couple of roasties after all.'

---

Deceiving was the word that came to mind describing the Miner's Arms Tavern. The outside of the building gave the impression of a reasonably well maintained and welcoming pub. Smoke fumes from the busy village road had done little to affect the brilliant white colour of the hardy external wall, unless it had received a recent paint job, and all the pub name lettering above the door was present and spelled correctly. To the right of the front door, where the pavement tapered four feet wider than the left, sat a small café style aluminium table with two matching chairs. Chain links ran from a leg of each of them to a low level eyelet bolted at the corner of the wall. Standing at the doorway, a pensioner with a deep creased, leathery face, in a cream and brown trouser/shirt/cardigan combo smoked a cigarette, flicking the ash toward his own suede loafers without care. The warm late afternoon breeze refused to carry away his exhaled smoke, offering it back the way it came to fill the foyer behind him with a fousty haze. As Price approached, the man leaned ever so slightly to one side, leaving little room to pass. Shuffling in sideways, her face pinched together, the bitter scent of stale sweat mixing with the second hand tobacco too much to ignore.

The glass foyer door slammed shut behind her, announcing her arrival. Faces littered around the open plan U shaped lounge frowned back. The counter top of the bar straight in front of her matched the shape of the room, wrapping right around so the bar workers, of which there appeared to be none at the moment, could see all corners of the lounge. The wood panels beneath the counter looked tired and scuffed, matching the twenty-year-old threadbare paisley carpet, the pattern hardly recognizable in the busiest spots. Bench seats followed around the nicotine stained perimeter walls, facing toward the bar, with a collection of no-two-the-same tables and chairs in front of them. For an early Tuesday evening, the pub was busy, most of the patrons appearing to be on day release from the local care home. Some sat in groups around tables, others alone with their thoughts and newspapers and screwed up betting slips. The regulars. Seven days a week, no doubt.

If the smell in the foyer was bad, it fared little better here. The smoke persisted, but there was also a predominant stink of stale beer that was, at least, attempting to counteract the reek of foul body odour. Backed up by a faint whiff of vomit, as if a patch had been recently cleaned up somewhere, Price made a conscious effort not to hold her nose as she wandered to the empty bar. As she got there, she made the mistake of leaning on a service mat, instantly regretting it from the damp patch soaking through at her elbow. *That would be the stale beer smell then. Nice one, cheers.*

'Help you, Miss?' a voice from the corner behind her said. A short, stocky man in his fifties, sat at a table with a half full pint of bitter in front of him. He was bald, the top of his head smooth with closely shaven, dark stubble around the back and sides. It matched his huge dark eyebrows and moustache, apart from the amber nicotine stain at its middle. He faced the television, but she could see his nose was bent out of shape, like it had a million stories to tell. His shoulders and chest were broad, like they belonged to an ex bodybuilder who'd finally lost the battle to father time, inevitably covering his once loved muscle with the dreaded dad bod. A lit cigarette balanced precariously between his lips as he fingered a remote control for the television. Finding the channel he wanted, he walked to the back of the room and into the bar, closing the counter hatch behind him and back down to Price. He leaned on a long handled beer pump, a deadpan expression on his face.

'Um maybe.' She looked around at the faces in the room. 'I'm looking for someone who lives next door. The shop worker told me he may be in here. Name's Eddie Venter.'

The barman pouted his lips as he shook his head quickly. *A little too quickly.* 'Haven't seen Eddie in a long time. Think he drinks up the Social these days. Maybe you should try up there.'

Price gave a nod as she had another look around at the surrounding faces peering back.

'So if there's nothing else?' the man asked. 'If I see Eddie, I'll let him know you were looking for him.'

'But I haven't told you who I am yet?' Price replied.

He leaned closer, a wide grin on his face. She could smell the cigarettes and beer on his breath. 'I may not know your name, officer, but I certainly know who you are.'

A wry smile rose on Price's face. She liked him. 'Thanks for your time.' She was halfway to the door when a voice called out.

'What can I do for you, Detective?'

Eddie slouched alone in a chair with his back to her, at the far corner of the lounge, facing a second television. On the table in front of him sat a half full pint of cider and an empty shot glass. Above him, a grey mare aptly named Fifty Shades romped home at the 6.15 at Kempton. He made a frustrated 'umph' sound as he screwed up the yellow slip in front of him. Price glanced back to the barman, who reciprocated the wry smile she had given him earlier. She wandered over, sitting without invite on the cushioned bench seat across from him, sliding on her bum until the table was in front of her.

'Drink?' Eddie asked?

'Wouldn't mind a cider myself.' She replied.

Eddie peeked over his shoulder. The barman grabbed a pint glass and drew one off. If she had asked for a half, she imagined he would have had to get down on his knees and find a glass at the back of the shelf where they gathered an inch of dust, or maybe just filled a pint up halfway.

Eddie picked up his glass and finished it off. He held it up over his head. Without looking over, the barman nodded his acknowledgement and grabbed a second empty. *Alcoholic telepathy. Impressive.*

'Don't mind Stretch,' Eddie said. 'Your lot like to wander in stirring trouble from time to time, and Stretch gets awful protective over his regulars. The thought of losing money would have him pulling his hair out, if he had any.'

'No need for that,' Stretch shouted over.

'So what do you want, Detective Constable Price?'

'How do you know who I am?'

'Lucky guess.'

She thought about it. 'Well, if I had to guess, you saw me with DCI Hibbard at the bottom of the mountain, and you've probably been through the interview notes for Mrs. Morrison and her daughter, then assumed we were one and the same.'

Stretch rounded the bar, two pints in hand. He carelessly plonked them down on the hardwood table, allowing both glasses to lose the top half inch of its contents. Price shifted away from the spill. Eddie didn't move. Stretch made no apology. Eddie offered no thanks.

*They're on a mutual level of understanding this pair.*

Price surveyed the table with a grimace. As the spillage crept closer towards her, she looked left and right for a coaster on the neighbouring tables. They lay empty. Stretch returned to the table with a shot glass filled with a clear liquid, setting it down in front of Eddie, who duly lifted it and knocked it back.

'Do you always drink with a chaser, Mr. Venter?'

'Only when I'm trying to forget something. And it's Eddie. Now care to tell me why you're in the biggest dive in Merthyr looking for me?'

'No need for that.' Stretch shouted.

'I've heard a lot of stories about you, Mr. Venter. There're a lot of rumours flying around the station.'

'Ah yes, the apple women,' Eddie interrupted. 'I guarantee none of the gossips have a clue what they're talking about.'

'Well, either way, I think we can help each other. We could combine our efforts. Compare notes, whatever you want to call it. I know you've been asked to find the Morrison girl. Well, so have I. I'm sure there's information you haven't come across yet, and vice versa. Maybe we actually have a chance to find her alive if we get our heads together.'

Eddie picked up his pint and took a drink. When he put the glass back down, the top half had disappeared. He wiped the spill from his chin with his sleeve. Price kept a passive expression, but inside, she was mortified. *I think I'm going to regret this.*

'Did the king of self-obsession put you up to this?' asked Eddie.

'The who?'

'I'll make it easy for you. Go back and tell Hibbard if he's after information, then he should grow a pair of balls and come get it himself. Instead, he sends you to do his dirty work, the big shit-house.'

*Was it that obvious?* 'He didn't send me, Mr. Venter.' Price lied. 'I just want to find her. And I've looked you up. All the cases you've solved. I think we can help each other.'

'I only find dead bodies.' Eddie said. 'So you're wasting your time, Detective. I don't think you're going to find that girl alive.' He gulped the second half of the pint down, holding the glass aloft once more.

'How are you so sure?'

'Call it a hunch.'

'I've heard about your hunches too, Mr. Venter, and I know it was you that told Detective Superintendent Enfield she was taken due east from the mountain. Well, this afternoon the search party found the girl's backpack close to the Fan-y-big summit, a couple of miles from where the woman took her. Guess which direction?'

Eddie nodded, his eyes narrowing as he thought it over.

'How did you know? Really?' Price asked. 'What did we miss?'

Eddie didn't answer.

'Look,' Price said, leaning forward onto her elbows, trying her best to avoid the wet spots on the table. 'You've a hell of a reputation for getting results. You even have the confidence of the Super, for Christ's sake.'

'Peter's an old friend who helps me pay the bills now and then.'

'Detective Superintendent Enfield is in charge of South Wales Major Crime Investigation Team and uses a paranormal investigator on his biggest cases,' she spat.

A number of faces turned at her outburst.

'I'm no ghost hunter, Detective. Now piss off and leave me alone.'

Price stood to leave, pinching her face into a distasteful look. 'The recent evidence suggests there's something more sinister than a random kidnapping here. You know it and I know it. What I don't know is why you're reluctant to keep going until we find her. Why you're scared. Or do you just not care? I guess you're more like Hibbard than you know. He doesn't seem to give a shit about finding her alive, either. I guess I'll just have to figure it out myself.' She shuffled from behind the table and made for the door, thanking Stretch as she passed. Outside, the night had closed in, a strong breeze sending a curious shiver up her back, although she suspected it had something to do with the disgust she felt at her own manipulative behaviour. She pulled up the collar on her denim jacket, an attempt to keep the shudder away.

The door opened behind her.

'What recent evidence?' Eddie asked.

'The Canadian lad.' she said. 'He took a video at the summit. Didn't tell anyone in case they found his stash of porn videos on his phone. He must have had a guilt trip and handed it over this morning. There's footage of the women on there.'

'Show it to me.' Eddie said.

# Chapter 15

At twenty-five years of age, Darren Lewis was considered relatively young for a crew manager, yet that was where he found himself, albeit in a temporary capacity, since his colleague, Steve Jones, had put his back out two weeks ago. Convinced to step into the role by his Station Manager, who bolstered his ego somewhat stating he had the potential to rise through the ranks quickly if he continued to display the commitment and attitude he had in his six years in the Mid and West Fire Service so far, he'd accepted with enthusiasm. Crickhowell Fire Station sits on the A40 main road, between the rural towns of Brecon and Abergavenny, and as was the case with most through the county, was a retained, unmanned station.

Darren's alerter sounded just as he was plating up his chilli-con-carne. Knowing what came next, his girlfriend Tracy lifted a solitary eyebrow as she sat at the kitchen table. She tilted her head, jutting out her cheek for him to kiss, then he was off and running. She would eat alone tonight. Their house was a stone's throw from the station and he was rarely second to open up, normally getting a couple of minutes head start on the other firefighters who lived further afield. Tonight was no different, as he darted down and around the corner to the empty station forecourt.

Grabbing the printout from the control room, he heard the unmistakable screech of tyres on tarmac outside. Cars mounted the pavement haphazardly, doors slamming shut as the team filed in to suit up.

Driver Brian Foster fired up the appliance, and the information fed through to their Mobile Data Terminal on

## THE ESCORT TO THE GRAVE

the centre console of the dashboard. Nine times out of ten, the team would be dealing with an RTC, a road traffic collision, due to the endless winding B-roads the surrounding valleys were so popular with the motorcycling community for. The MDT, however, was directing them to the Aber village, just south of Tal-y-bont, twenty minutes away, a picturesque, quaint village. Sitting in the passenger seat, Darren relayed the information to the rest of the team as Brian made progress along the A40.

'Looks like grass fires in the fields behind a farm. No hydrants in the vicinity. Control is sending the nearest bowser from Newport, and a support team is heading in from Brecon. Station Manager is en route in his 4x4. Call received from the farm owner. Her husband left to tend to their stock this afternoon, and she hasn't seen him since. We may have a rescue on our hands, guys.' The team in the back of the cab shared a look as they dressed. They had dealt with many grass fires before, but rarely involving rescues. They added extra risk. Darren sensed their nerves. 'Don't panic, we can't do much until the bowser gets there, and by then the Station Manager will be on site.'

They made their way along the B4558 through the village of Llangynidr, into Aber Village. Foster expertly negotiating the narrow lanes as the sun began to hide behind the surrounding mountains. As late afternoon turned to evening, the flashing of the engine light bar turned everything blue as they raced to the farm. The wide windscreen of the engine gave Brian and Darren a panoramic view as they advanced forward, and as they made the final approach, orange hues peeked over the hillside that looked more man made than natural. Darkness had descended quicker than normal, helped on by the black smoke filling the skies over the valley. Straightening up from the last bend, they met their target. Darren's mouth dropped open, followed by the rest of the men. Ahead, the farmhouse sat a cold grey tombstone as the entire hillside behind, acre upon acre of it, raged a sea of all-consuming flames.

## Chapter 16

Eddie led the way as they trudged up the narrow staircase to his first-floor flat above the shop. Bare wooden treads and scuffed paintwork gave Price a forewarning of what was to come. He opened the door to a room resembling its very own crime scene. Clothes littered the floor. A Pot Noodle container with a fork sticking out sat amongst a selection of dirty glasses and tumblers filling the surface of the coffee table in front of a torn black leather settee.

'I don't get many visitors.'

Price nodded towards the coffee table. 'Are you kidding? It looks like you've had one hell of a party.'

'Smart arse.' Eddie gestured to the settee. 'Take a seat. Want a drink?'

'Only if it's in one of those delightful looking glasses you've got there.' She leaned closer to inspect them. 'My god. That one's growing a mushroom. And what's the funky smell?'

'Alright already.' Eddie said, disappearing through the door to the kitchen. Price sat at the edge of the settee, one cheek on, one cheek off, afraid it would swallow her up if she committed to it. Crumbs of something lived here and there across the surface. Next door, cabinet doors slammed shut and glasses thudded on the counter. Price took in her surroundings. The place was filthy, un-cared for, in a sad, depressing way. The way people hiding their pain do so by hiding themselves from the world outside. No reason to keep it clean if you're all alone. No-one else will see it. All alone, no-one holds you to task. No-one opens the curtains and floods the room with sunlight, and tells you to take each day as it comes and keep moving forward.

A single photo frame sat upon the mantelpiece. The young woman looked directly at the camera. Eddie sat beside her, his nose touching her cheek and his eyes closed. They were both laughing, mouths wide and teeth on show, sharing a moment just for them. In a way only people in love really do.

Returning from the kitchen, Eddie looked to Price, then the photo, then back to Price. 'My wife,' he said, handing her drink over.

'She's beautiful,' Price replied. 'I'm sorry.'

'Tell me about the video.' Eddie said, changing the subject as he dropped back onto the settee, ignoring the scraps of food littering it. The settee groaned as it welcomed him in.

Price looked at the tall discoloured glass, half filled with whisky handed to her and set it down on the coffee table. She took her phone from her jacket pocket and flicked through to find what she was looking for. The video began playing, and she handed the phone over.

The boy was hardly a professional videographer. The camera panned left, then right a number of times as the youngster recorded himself in the ever popular selfie mode, with the view behind him as he reached the top. Eventually, the poor visuals settled, replaced by an equally annoying re-enactment of Rocky Balboa hitting the top step of the museum, as the young lad jumped up and down at the summit humming an over-enthusiastic rendition of the famous tune. Again, the screen turned frantic as the lad bounced from toe to toe, shadow boxing. Eddie rolled his eyes and gulped down his glass, wishing he'd brought in the bottle. The Canadian drawl faded as Eddie spotted the women. The boy's face filled two-thirds of the screen, but there they were. Behind him, kneeling on the harsh surface of the cobbled stones surrounded the cairn, were the two robed women. They looked entranced, deep in ritual, unperturbed by the arrival of the Canadians. Eddie couldn't hear them, the only sound that of the boy speaking to the camera, but surmised from their mouth symmetry they were speaking the same words.

'They're chanting.' Eddie said. 'They're facing the centre of the mound and mouthing the same thing.'

He stood up as the video ended. 'Is that all you have of them?'

'That's it.' Price replied.

'It *was* premeditated.' Eddie said. He walked around the coffee table, pacing back and forth. His thumb met his mouth as he chewed away at the nail. 'They were planning it all along. They knew the Morrison kid was going to be there to take her. It was personal.'

Price's eyes widened. 'How can you be so sure?'

'Watch it again, the chanting. It's a ritual, like they were making an offering or something. The Morrison woman said they gave her that coin, right? The old one who croaked it, yeah?'

'It's not a coin. It's some sort of token.'

'But she gave it to her. It was a payment, Price. She gave her the token for her daughter. Then they took her. They needed the girl. And it had to be her.' Eddie turned to the photo on the mantel. His wife stared back, this time with an approving grin.

'But one of them died.' Price countered. She rose from the settee as she pocketed the phone.

He started pacing around the room again. 'Hell of a coincidence though, right? It's almost like they planned it. Getting that girl off the mountain without being seen was nothing short of magic. And what are all the best magicians good at? Misdirection.' He made a gesture with his hands. 'Look at this while we do this.'

'Are you suggesting the woman died on purpose? The autopsy reports suggest a heart attack, Eddie. No foreign substances in the bloodstream. No signs of foul play. No one can commit suicide with a heart attack.'

Eddie spoke with a new found fervor, a heated intensity. 'They were chanting at the cairn. They were paying a lot of attention to it. Like an homage. I felt it when I was up there, a dark presence. The air was thick with it.'

Price raised an eyebrow, giving him a look he didn't like. It was why he kept things like that to himself. People would think he was crazy. They did anyway, of course, and while he didn't give two shits what anyone thought of him, he wasn't particularly fond of fuelling the fire. 'Look, you might have heard stories about me, but ever since...' Eddie looked at the photo, '... well, for a long time...'

Price continued to stare.

'Look, they need this girl in particular,' Eddie said. 'Now we just need to find out why.'

## Chapter 17

### Wednesday

It was an important day for Mark Winters. Pen-y-fan mountain had been closed to the public over the weekend after an incident involving a young girl being abducted from the top. And apparently, someone had died in the struggle. Crazy stuff. It was why he decided to get here earlier than normal and avoid the crowds. There was even a news van setting up at the Storey Arms car park when he'd arrived, and no doubt they'd be spending the day interviewing the masses of nut jobs en route to scout the scene of the crime, taking their all-important selfies. They'd all be spouting their thoughts and prayers for the missing girl. Hashtags like #findthepenyfanone littered with self-centred photos of narcissists pretending to help search. It happened all the time. Some Z-list celebrity involved in a car crash and a day later, a thousand people turn up, blocking traffic for miles just to gawp at the skid marks on the tarmac. Pathetic, but such was the social media life these days, someone would rather take a selfie for likes than help a victim. Mark would never find himself falling into that trap. Selfies were so last season. Now it was all about the subscribers on his YouTube and TikTok accounts.

Mark didn't have much time before the most important vlog of his career so far. The launch of his online clothing drop was imminent and today would be the first chance his followers would get to see it. A teaser to the main event. The sun was about to rise at the top, the deep orange glow threatening to explode from its hiding place at any moment.

It was going to be the perfect shot. Nothing tells the followers of his fitness channel he's a go-getter more than being at the top of a mountain before dawn. He actually despised getting up at 4.30 each morning, but for the sake of his online persona, it was absolutely necessary. If it's good for Dwayne Johnson, then it's good for Mark Winters. And what better place to document it than the place it all started; Pen-y-fan mountain. He just hoped the events over the weekend wouldn't cause an issue and take the wind out of his sail.

Deciding to record a vlog of his weight loss journey was the best thing that ever happened to Mark. That first video of his three hundred pound frame hiking the mountain earned him thousands of followers in a matter of days. He had gone viral, earning a spot on the local six o'clock news that only increased his popularity some more. A career change followed, leaving behind the boring world of I.T. to become what he had only dreamed of being; an online influencer. The weight loss continued, fuelled by increasing subscriptions, YouTube sponsors and clever product placements. Fitness trainer qualifications were considered, then dismissed, deciding the online world didn't need to see a C.V. to be inspired, just a tanned, muscled Adonis with pearly white teeth who had at one point been fat himself. Today he wore his rather fetching two-tone lime green tracksuit, complete with MWF logos under his jacket. A prototype likely to earn ten thousand likes and two hundred comments in the first hour on how to get their hands on one. He licked his lips at the prospect. As good as it was to make money from the social media companies, they could pull it from under his feet at any moment. For serious cash flow, his online shop was vital. It was time to start the ball rolling. It was going to be a great day.

Mark scanned the summit. A handful of early risers here and there, but nothing to get into a tizzy over. An older couple dressed in full hiking gear stood near the stone signage. If they didn't move soon, he'd ask them to. There was also a younger, middle-aged guy in a high viz vest with scruffy hair. He was taking off a heavy-looking rucksack, and as he dropped it to the floor, the crack of his arse peeked over his waistband. Mark creased his nose in disgust. No way could he let him in shot. With a bit of careful camera work, he could make it look like he was totally alone. Today he was using his phone to record a live stream but would upload a follow up with his Nikon afterwards. It was an expensive bit of kit, perfect for the quality visuals the clothing range deserved. Laying his jacket in a quiet spot, Mark could still see his breath as he exhaled, the morning air at the summit yet to warm up. Perfect. The illusion of hard graft made all the better with some heavy breathing adding to the effect.

Mark straightened out his tracksuit top, the high quality cotton fabric sliding between his fingers. He ran them over the expert stitching of the MWF logo. Time to make his millions. Opening his YouTube channel, he started a live video and turned on the charm with his expert camera presence and posh vowel pronouncing voice.

'Hey guys, good morning and welcome to a special live episode of Winters' fitness.' He held the phone high, the camera set to selfie mode as he circled to show off the impressive surroundings. 'We are live from where it all started, the ever amazing summit of Pen-y-fan mountain. It's 6 am and I'm here for a special announcement.'

The elderly couple stood close by, confused expressions on their faces. Not subscribers to Mark's channel, it seemed. At one point, the woman opened her mouth to answer as Mark spoke to the camera, clearly not understanding what was going on. He turned to get the stone cairn in shot, the National Trust sign illuminated as the rising sun bounced from it.

Fighting the nausea and foul stench, Eddie removed the rucksack and dropped it to the ground with a heavy thud. It was easier this time around, the smells and visions fading since the last visit he made. He pulled his jeans up and checked over the other visitors at the top. It was a good idea to get there early, even if it was a struggle after the drinks he had put away last night, but it would be heaving in an hour or two and he wouldn't get through the job unchallenged. It would be difficult enough even if he was alone, such was the size of the task in front of him.

The older couple may cause a problem. No doubt they'd have a few choice words for him, so hopefully they'd buy his cover story he worked for the Trust. Catching the early morning Brecon bus and getting off at the base was a good idea, though, just in case. The young fella in the vomit coloured tracksuit talking to himself wouldn't cause an issue. He'd keep his distance. Eddie reached in to his rucksack and removed a yellow fibreglass handled sledge hammer matching his hi-viz vest, a crow-bar and a three-quarter size railroad pick. He had thought about bringing a full-sized one for extra leverage, but as he was catching the bus to the base of the mountain, he'd likely earn some queried looks. Climbing the rising stones to the centre, he threw down the crow-bar and pick. Without warning, he picked the sledge high above his head and, with a long, wide arc, pulled it down onto the back of the plaque. With just two more efforts, the face stone came loose. Eddie expected it to put up a bigger fight considering the amount of hands touching it each day, but the cement holding it in place was years old and weather-beaten.

'I hope that's official work and not vandalism, young man,' the old man said, his small chuckle attempting to keep the conversation light. He looked down at the limited tools at Eddie's feet, unconvinced.

'Aye, the plaque is being renewed this afternoon. Visitors will be without it for today, I'm afraid.' He turned back, lifting the heavy plaque away to reveal a series of vertically set stones heavily plastered with aged cement. It was going to take some time to get through them, time he didn't have. He picked up the crow-bar, setting the point into the cement course ready for the first strike, when a tap on his shoulder stopped him. It was the young guy in the tracksuit.

'What the hell do you think you're doing, mate? You've interrupted my live stream.' The perma-tanned cretin had his hands on his hips, his dyed blond hair wafting over his sweat band. He held a stern frown on his face, doing his best to look serious. 'I'll have to start it again now.'

*A right diva, this one. So much for not causing trouble.* 'Sorry Sir, but we're in the process of changing the stone. Your love dream or whatever you called it will have to wait.' Eddie said.

'Well, you'll have to wait until I've finished my vlog pal. Put the stone back in place so I can restart it. I'll be about fifteen minutes, then you can do what you want with it.'

Eddie tried one last time. It was easier than using force. 'Sorry Sir, it has to come out now, so if you can stand back over there I can get on with it. Cheers.'

The lad spoke sharply. 'Listen here mate, you're a public servant and I pay my council tax, so you work for me. Put the stone back or I'll video this nonsense and send it to your complaints department.'

Eddie stood upright. His position on the stones had him a good foot taller than the lad. Much to Eddie's frustration, the lad didn't cower. Instead, his chest puffed out like loaded bagpipes as he lifted his chin in a show of power. Eddie wouldn't have been shocked if a plume of peacock feathers shot from his arse.

'First off, I'm not your mate. Second, I work for the National Trust, not the council, and third, if you don't sling your hook, I'm going to snatch your phone and launch it back down to The Storey Arms. Now piss off before I ruin your tracksuit.'

The lad pulled his phone in front of him, camera at the ready. Before he could press record, a hand snatched it away as another slapped across his cheek. The boy went down, sleeping before he hit the gravel floor. He landed side on with a thump, rolling onto his back where he stayed face up, eyes closed. The lime green colour of cotton up one side of his pristine tracksuit stained darker as it sponged the ground moisture up. Eddie shook his head. It was barely a slap, but sure enough, the lad laid spread out, snoring away contently. Looking across to the older couple, they were fifty feet away now, rushing back down the mountain as they looked over their shoulders, panicked expressions on their faces. Eddie had to get moving before the lad woke up.

*Nice one Eddie. Now you'll have to take the long route down.*

Working with purpose, he smashing away at the weak points of the cement, prising the jagged stones out one by one and dropping them to the side. He continued digging, not sure what he would find, but a feeling began to muster in his stomach. The lower he got, the easier they came, centuries of tightly packed clay and moss no match for the crow-bar and pick. The empty, sick feeling grew with each stone he pulled away. Eventually, he reached a flat slab that took everything he had to pull away as it sucked at the wet clay around it. A deep hollow lay beneath. His stomach knotted and his chest clamped tight. Eddie pulled his phone and switched on the torch. He was right. The hollow was around four feet deep and littered with cloth parcels.

*A cist. Too small for a grave. What was it for?*

He couldn't imagine the Trust knew they were there. The parcels would have been archived. But his gut feeling had been right. The women in the video had made a deposit here, although he couldn't imagine how. An offering of some sort. But to who? And to what purpose? Eddie didn't take the time to open any of the items. Dropping to his knees, he scooped up the contents of the hollow into his rucksack. He had to get his head down deep into the crypt to reach the bottom parcels. Some were evidently older than others, looking extremely fragile, the cloth enveloping the contents barely holding together. Sweat dropped from his forehead from the strenuous effort. Running out of time to make a getaway, he propped as many stones as he could back in to position, and lifted the plaque back to the front. The new arrangement looked like a dog's dinner next to the original, but it didn't matter. He had what he came for. Right on cue, the young lad murmured and raised a hand to announce his return to the living world. Eddie pushed him over onto his side, placing a bottle of water into his hand as the lad muttered something indecipherable.

Lifting the rucksack onto his back, Eddie staggered off over the brow to the East, the direction the girl had been taken. He'd have to trek over to Tal-y-bont and catch the bus from there, avoiding the last of the search parties if they were still ongoing. He looked back one final time. He had made a hell of a mess of the cairn. The young lad sat upright now, facing away, scratching his head, his back covered in brown and dark green stains. Eddie continued on, the curdling feeling staying with him. *Something in the bag, no doubt.*

The old couple would likely alert the police, but no-one had seen which direction he'd left. By the time they'd have given their statements, and the police had checked the registrations at the car park, he'd be long gone.

## Chapter 18

The thick smell of ash and char hit the nostrils a long time before they could see any damage. The morning sun had long risen over the mountains but was yet to do its duty of warming the valley. On approach, the winding B-roads hid the farm from view and the sudden and stinging pungency assaulting her nose came as a shock from so far out. Price regretted wearing her best trouser suit this morning. No dry cleaners in the country would get this smell out first time. Turning towards the farm, the aftermath looked apocalyptic. Red Fire Service appliances littered the grey dead scenery. Spent fire fighters stood zombified, all life and enthusiasm sucked from them over the course of the night, spraying the last of the smouldering embers close to the access lane. It was a miracle they saved the farmhouse, the expertise of the Mid and West Fire Service setting up a control line between it and the flames proving invaluable. Coupled with the wide lane separating the house from the fields and a dead wind, luck had played its part. In all directions from the valley, sunrise hinted at a fine day, yet the lazy grey smoke continuing to rise from the recently extinguished hillsides gave the spooky look of a foggy winter's morning.

A group of firefighters met them as they pulled into the farmhouse turn off. One stood in a fresh looking uniform, holding a polystyrene cup, barking orders to the rest that, by the look of them, had clearly worked through the night to save the farm. He wore a pristine white helmet suggesting it lived in the boot of his car and only came out for special occasions like this one. A stark contrast to the others, who looked completely and utterly spent, faces black with smog that would take a nail brush and plenty of elbow grease to scrub off. Spotting the approaching car, the officer pointed to a free spot amongst the numerous appliances to park up. Hibbard negotiated the tight turn for the only available space in the yard as the fire officer waited for them to approach and introduce themselves. Hibbard shook his hand first.

'I'm DCI Hibbard, South Wales Major Crime, this is DC Price.'

Price offered her hand to the man. His grip was soft and welcoming.

'I'm Station Manager Vince Tandy. Thanks for coming. Pretty good timing, actually. My crew just finished at the source point. You'll be able to get up there soon. I'll get my crew manager to take you over.'

Hibbard looked towards the fields. The view was barren wasteland, straight out of a Hollywood blockbuster. 'The farmer did all this?' he asked.

'Pulled a petrol tank across the fields with the tap open, dumping the fuel. Then lit himself up in his slaughter barn. With the weeks of dry weather, the entire valley was up in minutes.' Tandy pointed a thumb back over his shoulder. 'These poor bastards have worked through the night with just a handful of helicopter drops to assist them.'

'I'm sure they've done a great job,' Hibbard said, unaware of the condescension in his voice. Tandy looked to Price, who fought with all her might to keep straight faced.

Tandy continued. 'The farmer's wife is with the neighbours.' He handed Price a slip of paper with the address. 'Some of your guys are with her now.'

'Station Manager Tandy?' Price said. 'Do you know why they've called us in? Major Crime I mean?'

Tandy let out a deep sigh, his eyes looking to the ground for a reasonable response.

'We don't see many incidents like this in Mid and West, Detective. My guys don't normally get to see anything sinister. RTCs, as bad as they are, always have an innocence about them. Do you know what I mean?'

Price nodded. Even the drunk or drugged drivers that kill behind the wheel don't plan for it.

'We've had the odd suicide in the past, too. But I know this one has hit them for six. The pain the guy must have been in, and for the length of time before he died, too. It's heartbreaking. His body is untouched, but we've no idea how he got to where he was or what he was doing. It's standard to call in CID on an arson case. They were here for some time, but then we showed them the note and they said they had to call you guys in. I'm not sure why.'

Hibbard and Price shared a confused look. Tandy caught it. 'It's easier if Darren just shows you.' He cupped a hand around his mouth as he called for his crew manager.

'Apologies, but I need to get back to the station to write up the report. I'll leave you in Darren's hands. Good luck Detectives.'

Price frowned as she watched Tandy get into his jeep. His last comment, wishing them luck, for some reason, made her uneasy.

'Do you have wellies with you, Detectives?' Crew Manager Darren Lewis said, a tired frown on his face. 'Best you get them on to cross the fields. The ash sticks to everything.'

They returned moments later with their trousers tucked into their new footwear and followed Darren across the road to the field opposite. He led the way, ambling through the devastated, scorched fields. On one occasion, they had to stop and change direction due to a patch of smoldering ash deciding to reignite. Darren radioed in for his crew to follow up with their beaters. Groans sounded from the other end of the radio. They wouldn't be going anywhere yet. The man looked spent, feet and arms dragging like he was ready to sleep for an eternity. The adrenaline must have long worn away by now, but the firefighter continued to show his professionalism. Last thing he needed was two Detectives to babysit. Or maybe that was a good thing. Maybe whatever they were about to find, he was looking forward to dumping in their lap and running for the hills.

The remains of the slaughter barn loomed ahead. A ruin of charred, soaked wood and discoloured corrugated metal sheets sat entombed in steel frames Price guessed as livestock pens. A burned-out tank, the side bright blue from the fire damage, sat with an enormous hole ripped into its belly. It was attached to a forked tractor, the cab of which seemed miraculously untouched from the flames. The steelwork still held its bright green paintwork in an otherwise solemn surrounding. Two firefighters were still busy dousing some of the debris from a portable bowser. They looked across at the new visitors. Darren stopped ahead and turned back, a concerned frown on his face.

'We found the note in the tractor cab when we searched for survivors. Took it with us in case it went up. It's back at the farmhouse. I'll get it for you when we're done here. We'll have to keep a wide berth of the barn for now. There's still a lot of heat from the metal work inside. It's acting like a giant radiator.'

They continued on, arcing around the barn before Darren stopped once more, hands sagging at his sides. His head dropped a moment, then he looked over his shoulder to the two officers. 'Brace yourselves. It's quite a sight.'

Price's face fell as they caught him up. Something pulled at her gut and squeezed, forcing a burning sensation to rise at the back of her throat. She gulped and swallowed profusely. It was her body's reaction to the change in the smell, the aromas of charred wood and grass overpowered by the horrid and unmistakable stench of burnt hair and flesh. It held so thick in the air she could almost taste it. She looked across to Hibbard, who wore his own mask of horror, then back to the lone oak tree at the centre of the field. It stood completely untouched, the colours of lush, green foliage and healthy brown bark emanating from an otherwise black and grey, miserable landscape.

As if holding the huge oak upright, like a sickening network of roots, a tangled mass of dead pigs lay around it, their bodies scarred in varying degrees of black and red burns. It was difficult to make a count, but Price guessed there must have been at least forty. They had sought the last point of safety, squeezing the life out of each other as they pressed in around the thick trunk of the oak. The pigs closest to the middle had escaped the wrath of the flames, only to be crushed by the following hogs desperate to escape the fire. Cruelly constricted of their last breaths, they stood squeezed upright like prone wax figures as the pigs closest to the flames crushed inwards. Bile rose in her throat as Price remembered a photograph she once saw in school of Holocaust victims, attempting to reach the ventilation grills in the gas chambers. They had formed a human pyramid as the strongest prisoners climbed over the weakest in last ditch attempts to find a breath. She recalled being sat at her desk, closing her eyes and imagining the screams and the panic they must have felt. The circle of carcasses around the tree displayed a sickening array of barbecued shades. Whites and greys of spent charcoals. Deep maroons and browns of seared, well-done flesh. Pinks of uneven, uncooked meat. She fought hard not to vomit.

And then she saw him. The mass around the tree had taken her eye from what knelt before it. Price regained her composure, blinking her eyesight clear to reveal the corpse of who she assumed was the farmer, Richard Evans. The body knelt towards the tree, twenty yards out, black and unrecognizable, all clothing, hair and skin burnt away. Muscle, tissue and organs shrunken to lumps of charcoal. Scraps of melted fat hanging from bone. She turned to Hibbard, his face a piece of cold marble. His head slowly shook from side to side as he attempted to make sense of what he saw. The three stood in silence until Price broke it.

'We were told he set himself on fire in the barn?' She asked, eyes locked on the body.

'He did. Drenched himself in petrol. You see the trail behind him? He dragged himself there.'

Both detectives turned to the firefighter. He nodded his agreement what he just said was ridiculous. 'Yeah, crazy right?'

'That's got to be over a hundred metres away. How is that possible?' she asked.

'Fully ignited, death averages between thirty and sixty seconds. Add an accelerant and it dramatically reduces from the intense burst of heat and asphyxiation. His even colouring suggests he went up as a fireball. He should have been dead in seconds. I don't know how, but he dragged himself there. You can tell from the claw marks in the soot. I've asked every single one of the lads. None of them have seen or heard anything like this. Some of them are in a right state. The Station Manager is contacting our counselling department. I've got a feeling some of the team are going to need it.'

Price was the first to step closer, as near as she dared. She arced around the body, keeping the mass of pigs in her peripheral. From this distance, the closest to the tree still looked alive, as if trapped and waiting patiently to be freed. Crouching down, ignoring the black soot that had likely transferred from her boots to the butt of her trousers, she inspected the body. Kneeling in a praying position, his hands stuck out unnaturally in what Price recognised from her basic forensic training as the strange phenomena 'boxer's pose.' There was science behind it, the extreme heat causing victims to assume the position from muscle shrinkage. She leaned over to look at the face, all skin and lips burned away to reveal a sadistic grin. Empty eye sockets. Burst from the intensity of the flames, probably back at the barn. Standing again, she looked back towards it. Darren was right. The marks did look like he dragged himself there. How the hell did he manage it? And why?

As the other two joined her, Price walked to the pigs. Those pinned to the tree still had their body hair. Seeing them upright but very much dead gave her the creeps. Eyes wide open, their last fearful emotion still etched into them. She held her eyes on one in particular as she walked around the tree, an enormous pink and black boar. A powerful looking beast, strong enough to make it to the centre of the circle, hugging the tree to fight off every other trying to take its position from the intense heat. Not powerful enough, however, to withstand the crushing forces subjected on it by the rest of the frightened and desperate pigs. His eyes held on hers as she circled the oak, refusing to let her leave him. Another memory came to her, of her grandfather, who she adored for so many years until his own passing when she was fifteen. He kept a painting of Jesus Christ, hands together in prayer, behind his office desk that followed her wherever she stood in the room. It freaked her out no end. Her grandfather often joked he would pass it down to her when his time came. To her relief, a friend of his received it in his will instead.

Price looked up at the tree with puzzlement. Not a burn mark in sight. The leaves were fresh, healthy and vibrant, more fitting to a lush meadow than a desolate wasteland. As she walked around the back, something caught her eye. In the trunk of the gigantic oak, a piece of the bark had been cut away, revealing the lighter flesh beneath. Carved into it was a symbol. A symbol she had seen before. Recently.

It was a Triquetra.

She turned to Darren. 'I think you'd better show us the note.'

## Chapter 19

Sitting on the paisley couch, Margaret Evans held hands with her neighbour and best friend Reena Williams. Receiving her frantic call last night, Reena and her husband Alf had raced the two miles of country road in their Landrover Defender to the farm. It had been such a frightening experience for them, Reena screaming directions at her husband as he negotiated the twists and turns of the track roads. Alf did his best not to leave their home after dark these days. Even though the weather was going through a recent dry spell, an unusual occurrence for typical Welsh summers, the roads held year round surface water from the mountain streams, and potholes and divots appearing deep enough to at some point, harboured miniature landmines. Alf had been an agitated mess all the way there, mumbling to himself as he concentrated on the road, his wife keeping a running commentary at his side on when to brake, when to turn, when to change gear and when to put his foot down. The last half mile had been an eerie experience. Driving into no-man's-land as the blue and white lights flashed sporadically beneath the devastating blazed landscape above.

A Fire Service Jeep received them at the farm turn off, where a spooked Margaret was waiting with an officer. She had broken down at this point, falling into Reena's arms just in time to save her from hitting the tarmac road. They had stayed for some time, begging and crying with questions the officer couldn't answer, watching in horror as appliance after appliance filled with firefighters arrived and passed them by. Eventually, with the lack of information and the night drawing on, Reena had suggested retiring back to their own farm, to the relief of the accompanying officer. Margaret had reluctantly agreed, spent the remainder of the night, and at the request of the Fire Station Manager, stayed put.

It was Alf who broke the tension, tenderly carrying in a silver platter so wide he struggled to get through the doorway of the small sitting room. It held a large teapot with matching cups and saucers stacked to one side that rattled away as he nervously set it down. It would normally be Reena hosting the guests with the refreshments, but she was busy propping up the recently made widow beside her. He laid it down on the coffee table, almost losing a cup as he did, then backed out of the room before anyone had a chance to ask him to stay. Price's eyes flashed to the two plates, one loaded with Welsh cakes, the other fresh scones, beautifully flanked by bowls of cream and jam. Skipping breakfast, her stomach ached for one, yet she begged it not to make a peep. Now wasn't the time for indulgence, even if strangely offered them during such a difficult time.

To her embarrassment, an 'oof' noise escaped from Hibbard as he shuffled closer on his seat to pick up a plate. He filled it with the two biggest scones on show, before going to work with a spoon on the jam and cream. Everyone sat in silence as he expertly loaded the first of the cakes into his mouth. Price gave him her best death stare that went ignored.

*Looks like I'll be doing the talking.* 'Thank you again for letting us speak with you, Mrs. Evans.' Price said. 'I know it's been a long night for you. We just have a few more questions the other officers didn't touch on this morning. Is that OK?' she lowered her head, an attempt to make eye contact with the grieving woman. She responded with a small, almost unrecognisable nod as her eyes remained fixed on her lap. The only noise came from Hibbard's lips smacking together.

'Mrs. Evans, do you have any idea why your husband would do what he did?'

'She has no idea,' Reena answered for her, quick as a flash. She sat tall in her seat, a far cry from her friend. 'The other police officers already asked her. You don't even know if it was Richard. It could have been anyone. There's always some idiot starting grass fires around here. Ask the firefighters they'll tell you. And you don't know... you don't know if it's Richard who's still out there. You... you don't know,' her voice trailed off unconvincingly.

Margaret patted Reena's hand. 'It's ok, Reen. Let her be.' She turned to Price, her body sagging even more as she exhaled. 'We've been married thirty years this year. A lot of happy memories. Two beautiful daughters. They're on their way up from Cardiff now. Kate's twenty-eight. She's given us two wonderful grandchildren, Evie and Lucas. And our son-in-law we couldn't ask for better. He's an architect. Doing very well for themselves. Then there's Carys. She's twenty-six and a trainee solicitor. Such ambitious children. I don't know where it came from, what with Richard and I being such home birds.' She trailed off with a weary smile as her eyes glazed over.

Price scuttled forward in her chair. 'Mrs. Evans?'

'Thirty years.' Margaret said, shaking her head. 'Thirty years and he kept it from me.'

Price looked to Hibbard, who stopped mid-chew, a rim of cream around his lips. She looked back to Margaret. 'Kept what from you Mrs. Evans?'

'The sale of the farm. Thirty years and he couldn't tell me he'd had enough of it. He doesn't..., I mean, he didn't know that I knew he planned on selling it. One of the estate agents from Brecon phoned on Monday as he was tending to the cattle. Told me they were willing to consider charging a flat fee instead of a percentage if we agreed that day. I didn't have a clue what he was talking about. The lad soon flustered when I demanded he explain himself.'

'Mrs. Evans, I'm a bit lost.' Price said, looking at Reena. Reena only shrugged her shoulders. 'You've told us you saw your husband drive his fuel tank past your kitchen window and across the road to your wheat fields. The investigation officers have confirmed it as the accelerant. I'm sorry to say, it appears your husband deliberately started the fire. So the question is, why would your husband set fire to the farm if he planned on selling it?'

'I… I don't know.' Margaret replied. Reena let go of her hand and filled a cup with tea from the pot. She gave it over to Margaret, who took it with both hands. The cup rattled in its saucer and after a couple of seconds of trying to settle it, she gave up and put it back on the table. 'After the agent called, I checked our computer but I couldn't access Richard's profile. He must have changed all his passwords from when I set it up for him. He's quite good at it now, much better than me. He spends hours in the study on it in the evenings. I think… I think he talks to people on there. Not like when I talk to the girls on that WhatsApp thing, though. I don't hear voices, but I think he messages people on there.'

'Do you have visitors to the farm? Anyone you don't know?'

'We get visitors several times a week. Some picking up produce, some delivering. People back and fore regularly. There aren't many pig farms around here anymore. It's mostly just cattle and sheep. Richard butchers the swine himself. They're still popular with the local restaurants. We have them at numerous stages of development, so we get pickups all year round. It helps keep us afloat. Sometimes he gets phone calls in the middle of the night. People come to the farm and he takes them to the slaughter barn.'

'What for Mrs. Evans? Does he explain what they do at the barn? Did you hear any of the calls? See any of the people who come?'

# THE ESCORT TO THE GRAVE

'He sleeps in his study a lot. Has a fold away in there. I don't hear the calls. He told me he trains farmhands on butchery and delivering piglets. I don't get involved in any of it.'

Price looked to Hibbard again. He caught the look and jumped in. 'Mrs. Williams, could we have a moment with Mrs. Evans alone, please?'

'Reena is my closest friend. She stays.' Margaret said, feeding her own arm through hers.

He put down his empty plate and licked his fingers, before pulling a clear ziplock bag from his coat pocket, the suicide note inside. 'Mrs. Evans, I'm sure you've been told your husband left a note in his tractor cab.' He fingered the bag in his hand, keeping the writing towards him. Everyone looked to it. 'We'd appreciate it if you'd be able to identify the handwriting, and hoping you might shed some light on what it means.'

Margaret said nothing. A tear fell down her cheek as she held out her hand. Hibbard lifted from his chair as he reached the note across the coffee table. She took it with both hands, drawing a deep breath as she read it. More tears flowed that she wiped away with her hand.

'Is it your husband's handwriting?'

A small nod.

'Do the words mean anything to you, Mrs. Evans?' Hibbard asked.

No answer. Just a shake of the head.

'How about the symbol?'

Another shake of the head.

'Mrs. Evans, did you ever hear your husband discuss any children with anyone?'

'No. What are you saying?'

'The note mentions children, Mrs. Evans. We don't think he's talking about your own. Did he have any visitors to the farm recently? Maybe someone you didn't know? Did he make trips away from the farm for any length of time?'

'Only to pick up feed or hay.' She set down her cup forcefully, frustration clearly showing. 'I'm sorry, what are you getting at here?'

Hibbard decided to show his hand. 'Mrs. Evans, on Saturday morning, a woman abducted a young girl from the top of Pen-y-fan mountain. She's still missing. The symbol your husband has drawn was also found at the scene of the abduction.'

'What are you saying? What the hell would it have to do with Richard? He's just a farmer. A good man. An honest man.'

'An honest man who keeps secrets from his wife, Mrs. Evans. Receiving secret phone calls and visitors in the dead of night. Locking himself away for hours on end in his study, communicating with people online.'

Margaret and Reena pulled faces that could curdle the cream. The tension was building, like an inflating balloon close to its breaking point. All Price could do was sit and watch, wait for the inevitable explosion, and see if any information fell out when it burst.

'I'm sorry this is all a shock to you Mrs. Evans', Hibbard continued. 'But your husband burned the farm while busy completing sales to finance the rest of his life. We've found vast sums of cash in his study. I'm assuming not being allowed in there, you knew nothing about it? Why would he keep it from you? And what changed? What happened to make him compromise all that?'

Margaret stood up. 'Maybe he was setting *me* up for the money. And our girls. Maybe someone else started the fire. Maybe... maybe it's someone else in that field.'

*Poor woman,* Price thought. *Defending him to the end.*

'You said the estate agent phoned, attempting to get you to commit to them to sell Mrs. Evans. That means your husband had only received valuations for the property. It wasn't even on the market. The agents would need to come to the farm, photograph it, make full assessments. It's a graveyard down there now. Why would he burn it knowing full well the farm would never sell afterwards? Unless he was trying to hide something? Cover something up?'

'Get out.' Margaret spat. Reena stood next to her friend. Joined in defiance. 'My husband was a good man.'

The two detectives rose from their seats in silence. Hibbard held out his hand. After a moment, Margaret handed over the ziplock bag. 'I'm sorry for your loss,' he said.

They showed themselves out as the muffled wails of despair continued to bleach out through the stone walls. Price felt sorry for the woman, losing the man she had loved for so many years in such terrible circumstances. That wasn't the reason for her pity, though. It was the apparent betrayal, the disloyalty, the breach of trust her husband had shown in his conniving behaviour, and her defensiveness to protect him until the very end. It was a sure-fire sign of mental and emotional abuse.

Her eyes flicked sideways to Hibbard as he negotiated the farm lane to the main road in silence. As much as she hated to admit it, she was impressed. His ability to turn the screw, as barbaric as it may have seemed, got the desired result. They needed to know if she was hiding anything. 'That was heavy,' she said.

'You have to learn to check your emotions at the door and deal with them later. It's never nice, but it has to be done. Easiest way to find out if she knew anything. Hit them when they're at their lowest, before they have time to think. The truth will out.'

'But she doesn't know anything, right?'

'She's got no clue.' Hibbard said. 'Still believes he was a good man.'

'Do you think it's connected to the Morrison girl?'

'I've no idea. But we've got two mobile phones and his computer. And I'll bet my left nut there's something on that hard drive to give us some answers.'

## Chapter 20

Price stared up at the statue outside Merthyr Tydfil Central Library. The immortalised depiction of some industrialist and entrepreneur long since passed towered over her, gazing out in silent contemplation. Henry Seymour Berry, the plaque read. A celebrated inhabitant of a town steeped in history. Today he adorned a fetching hat of an orange and white traffic cone as he kept watch over the Castle Inn across the road. Merthyr Tydfil was a famous participant in the Industrial Revolution and fondly protected by many in the town, proud to say they lived in such an important area. Then there were the people who got drunk and found hilarity in dressing up a statue of 'some rich, dead geezer' with traffic management accessories. Price caught herself tutting, then silently chastised herself for having no idea who the man was either.

Climbing the steps to the revolving door, she pushed through, popping out into a small hallway the other side. The door continued to rotate behind her as she took in her surroundings. Considering her relatively decent education and the fact she'd lived in the town all of her twenty-six years, Price couldn't recall ever having set foot in the building before. There was a musky smell in the air, probably from old books. The predominant material through the building appeared to be various kinds of dark stained wood. It was everywhere. Decorative panels and mouldings covered every internal partition wall. A carpenter's wet dream. True to library etiquette, the lack of common background noise gave it a noticeable, eerie atmosphere. No conversations or ringing phones, no fingers tapping on keyboards, just silence. Such was the fast-paced twenty-first century she considered it a strange moment when absolute quiet ensued. It gave her the creeps.

A wooden partition stood straight ahead, frosted coloured glass panels inset blocking what lay beyond. To the left of the partition, a red sign with white lettering read 'Entrance', another reading 'Exit' to the right. Price made her way through to the area opening to the main library floor. Packed shelving units adorned the back and side walls, signs high above directing perusers to the relevant subjects. Free standing shelves ran diagonally across the well-worn carpet. Save for the thousands of authors, the room sat empty.

'Can I help you?' a voice said from behind her.

The break of silence caught Price off guard, who surprised herself by letting out an audible shriek. She snapped around, momentarily confused as she failed to find the culprit.

'Down here, my lovely,' a gentle voice said. 'Can I help you with anything?'

Price peeked over the stack of novels sat on the counter. Sitting atop a foldaway stool, a ragged copy of *Stephen King's Misery* opened in hand, was a little old lady that appeared she had been around as long as the building itself. The stereotypical librarian, she even had the half-moon glasses and blue rinse hair. Price doubted she could even lift herself off the stool and had, in fact, been stuck there all morning.

'Any good?' Price nodded to the book in the woman's hands.

The woman sniffed and crinkled her nose, trying to work out where the camp-fire was. Then she looked to the book cover as if forgetting what she was reading. 'One of his better ones. His new stuff is a load of shite. Give me the older stuff any day. Read this one a few times. She doesn't break his legs in the book, see. She cuts his foot off and cauterises the wound with a propane torch. Should have done that in the film, instead of arsing about with a sledgehammer.'

She broke the stereotype, this one. If Price expected a squeaky clean grandmother who pronounced every syllable perfectly, she got the tattooed truckdriver version.

'I'm looking for a friend of mine. Name's Eddie Venter. He asked me to meet him here.'

The woman dropped the book to her lap and considered it for a moment. 'Mmm, what does he look like?'

'White, about five foot ten. Dark hair. Average build.'

The woman cackled. 'That's a good one. You must have the wrong person. Average build? The scruffy bugger has turned into a right pudding lately. Needs a haircut too. Just not looking after himself. What have we got if we haven't got our health? Am I right, missy?' She didn't wait for an answer. 'He's upstairs with Joyce. She's the librarian. They've set up a room for you.' She pointed back the way Price had come. She laughed again. 'Average build. Stairs are next to the revolving doors.'

Price frowned, properly confused now. 'You don't work here?'

'Do I sound like I work here, love?'

'Umm no I suppose you don't.' Price replied. 'Thanks.'

The woman kept going. 'Such a lovely boy, Eddie. Been to hell and back, you know. Don't you go breaking his heart now, not unless you want to end up like Paul Sheldon here.' She held up her copy, a grin spreading across her deep wrinkled face. 'The book version.'

'Uh OK' Price said. 'I'll keep that in mind.' She made for the stairs, unhooking the barrier rope at the bottom step and replacing it behind her as she went. *A right sweetheart, that one.*

'Nice girl. Smells a bit though,' the woman said, settling back into her novel.

# THE ESCORT TO THE GRAVE

Price climbed the winding staircase to the first floor. She came to a corridor of wooden doors with frosted glass panels, only one of which was open at the far end. She decided to try it first. As she walked towards it, a door with gold embossed lettering reading *Research* sprang open. A tall lady, elegantly dressed in a dark business skirt suit with a white shirt and an impressive beehive hairstyle, stood guard. She looked to be in her late fifties and also wore half-moon glasses. Price couldn't help but admire her style, very chic. She reverted back to stereotyping. This must be Joyce.

'Can I help you, young lady?' the woman said with a flat monotone bore-you-to-death voice. She eyed Price from head to toe and back again. Her brow furrowed as she looked up and down the corridor to find the source of the stink. Something smelled like a burnt roast dinner.

'I'm DC Lauren Price,' she said, holding up her warrant card.

At this, the woman's eyes widened and her lips parted to reveal a perfect set of pearly whites. She caught under Price's arm. 'At last', she hissed, pulling her through the door. 'I've been like a jack-in-the-box waiting for you to turn up.' She slammed the door behind them, the frosted glass shaking violently as it met the framework. Eddie stood propped over a large table littered with opened leather-bound books and parchments. A second table against the wall displayed a collection of unwrapped squares of cloth holding numerous coins, small pots, and what looked like primitive tools. Pinned up maps and white boards lined the walls. A trolley sat in the corner with more books and rolled up scrolls. Price could smell the age of the materials, unaware of the other overpowering scent.

Eddie creased his nose and wafted a hand in front of his face. 'You been to a barbecue?'

'Hilarious. I can't get the smell off me.' She raised the crook of her elbow as she sniffed. 'I've showered twice at the station and had to throw out my best suit. That stink from the pigs was horrific. I'll never forget it. I don't think I'll eat a bacon sarnie for a while.' She glanced back to Joyce sheepishly, forgetting momentarily she was there.

'Joyce knows everything, Price.' Eddie said. 'I do all my research here. If there's written archives of anything, Joyce can find it. And it always stays within these four walls. Right Joyce?'

Price turned to her again. Joyce stood tall on her heels, folding her arms across her puffed out chest, face stern and purposeful as she looked down her glasses. A moment of triumph. 'Of course Eddie. Librarians always keep their word. It's the police you have to watch out for.'

Price smirked. Joyce responded with a matching one. Then she melted into an excited teenager again, clapping her hands together. 'I'll make us some tea. Give you pair a chance to catch up on your eventful mornings. I need to check on Betty, anyway. Make sure she hasn't killed anyone.'

'I got a warning.' Price replied. 'Something about a blowtorch.'

Joyce rolled her eyes. 'I bet she's pulled a horror novel off the shelf again. I've told her how aggressive she gets reading Koontz or King. You can't reason with her.' She pulled the door closed as she left, the glass rattling again.

'So the wife didn't know anything?' Eddie asked.

'She was clueless,' Price replied. 'His computer and phones are being handed to digital forensics. Shouldn't be long before they find something if it's there.'

'Did you bring a copy of the note?'

'I'm risking a lot taking a photo of it. Hibbard would crucify me if he thought I was feeding you information.' Pulling her phone, she swiped to her gallery, giving it over to Eddie. He stared at the phone for quite some time, appearing to read it more than once. 'Swipe left.' she said. His face grimaced as he scanned them, attempting to make sense of it. The last one was of the markings in the tree. His eyes glinted when he saw it.

'What do you make of it?' he asked, handing the phone back over.

She read it aloud. 'Eternal torture awaits us all. Payment for the pain and suffering of the children. The wages of sin is Death, and so it receives us.'

At the bottom of the note, the farmer had drawn, rather crudely, the same symbol she had found carved into the tree. The Triquetra.

Eddie rubbed at his cheek. His nails scratched through the stubble like coarse sandpaper. 'The wages of sin is Death.'

'Romans six, twenty-three,' Price said, effortlessly. 'For the wages of sin is death, but the gift of God is eternal life in Christ Jesus our Lord.'

Eddie sat back in his chair, a smirk rising at one side of his face. 'Well, that rolled off the tongue easily enough. You've got the whole bible locked away in there. I didn't have you down as the churchgoing type.'

'In a former life,' Price replied. She marched on. 'CID called us in because of the note. They'd been briefed to if any suspicious activity east of Pen-y-fan involving possible missing children or odd symbols were identified. They figured it may relate to Ellie Morrison's disappearance.'

'What do you think?' Eddie asked.

'I'm not seeing it.'

'There is the symbol?'

'I agree, it's one hell of a coincidence. The same as the one on the tree, and the same one the dead woman gave to Mrs. Morrison. But could both incidents really be connected? Some kidnapping scheme gone wrong? I don't know. And why the hell would the farmer be involved? I can't help but think it's just that, a coincidence.'

'Have you seen the symbol before?'

'I've looked it up. It's used by several religions. The Celts used it a lot in their myths and stories, but it's a common emblem. Walk into any new age hippy shop selling holistic therapy and alternative medicines and you'll see it plastered everywhere.'

'You can't find stuff like this in no shop.' Eddie said, thumbing in the direction of the side table. Price wandered over, picking up a heavy gold coin from a cloth looking frail enough to turn to dust at any moment. She looked to the other items, picking up one of many small pots that again, had the symbol carved into the ceramic lid.

'It's an urn.' Eddie said, rising to stand next to her. 'There's a bunch of them, some older than others. Sarah Morrison reported one of the women holding a pot in her hands when her daughter got kidnapped, right? And the coins, just like the one they gave her.'

Price looked confused. 'Where did you get this stuff, Eddie?'

He didn't respond, but cast his eyes away to hide the smirk creeping onto his face.

Price lifted a hand to her forehead. 'Jesus Christ, you're the one that couple reported on the mountain this morning. Destroying the Trust plaque and beating up some kid. They think it was some nutter after a souvenir.'

'I didn't beat anyone up. He started getting mouthy, and I gave him a backhander. The lad got in the way.'

'You can't just go around beating people up, Eddie. I *am* a police officer, you know. I should arrest... what is all this stuff?'

'I found all this in a cist deep under the plaque at the top. After I saw the video of the two women, I couldn't help but think the cairn meant something, so I looked it up. They're ancient burial spots, where worshippers would leave gifts along with the remains of loved ones, as close to the heavens as possible, ensuring a safe passage to the afterlife.'

'You don't believe in all that stuff, do you?' Price asked.

'They're offerings.' He pushed a large delicate looking book towards her, pages open ready. It was nothing like she had felt before, more material than paper, bound in a cover made from heavy looking, dark brown leather. The open pages displayed an intricate drawing, an etching full of black and grey detail. It was as beautiful as it was barbaric. Price ran a finger around the gold-coloured edge as she took in the scene. Three cloaked figures kneeling at a mountain top. Ahead of them stood another figure, its face hidden by the shadows of its own cloaked hood, looking back at them. All across the ground were dozens of naked bodies, twisted in death, the faces aghast with pain and suffering. Naked, winged demons filled the sky as they landed to collect the dead. Some were hoisting them from the ground. Beneath the etching was a description. She squinted as if doing so would change the words to English. Eddie put her out of her misery.

'The Escorts to the grave pay homage to Arawn.'

'You speak Welsh?'

'No, Joyce does. Anything look familiar?' Eddie asked.

Price looked back to the etching again. 'The cloaks. Are you telling me we've got some nutcases running around re-enacting pictures from some old book?'

Eddie nodded. 'Some sort of cult. I think they took the girl from the mountain to be sacrificed, and somehow involved the farmer.'

'You don't know she's dead, Eddie.'

'Well, if she's not already, I think we're running out of time to find her alive.'

He let the words hang as she rubbed at her forehead. 'Who's Arawn?' she asked.

'The Celtic god of the dead, revenge and terror.'

They shared a quiet moment, one of those uncomfortable, not knowing what to say next, kind of silences. A realisation dawned on him.

'This is your first one, isn't it?' he said. 'Missing child case?'

She said nothing. Her eyes told him everything.

'Have they searched the farmer's house?' he asked.

'Found stacks of cash in shoe boxes. The wife doesn't know where it came from. What else are you expecting them to find?'

'Maybe nothing. Hopefully something.' Eddie said, offering at least a touch of optimism.

Biting her lip to stop the confession from falling out of her mouth, Price looked to the floor. Her knees wobbled, and she pulled the seat out from the table, dropping into it heavily. Eddie was clearly putting everything into finding the girl, and she was playing him. The guilt churned in her belly. She leaned forward, resting her elbows on the table and propping her head with her hands.

'I need to find her alive, Eddie. You know that, don't you? I'll do whatever it takes. You understand that, right?'

'Yeah,' he replied. 'Yeah, I do.'

'What's your story Eddie?' she asked. 'Why are you and Enfield so close?'

Eddie eyed her cautiously. He sat in his chair and leaned back in thought, his tongue pushing around in his cheek as though searching for leftover food.

'It's a long one and you haven't got time. But buy me a pint tonight and maybe my lips get loose. In the meantime, I'll keep looking for answers here while you see if they've found anything more from the farm.'

# Chapter 21

Iefan Morris collected the tray of coffees at the counter. The forward facing cup read Ivan in black marker. Not surprising, more often than not, it either read Ivan or Evan. He couldn't remember it ever being spelt correctly in the last year he had been coming here. They probably couldn't be bothered or were too busy to try. It didn't really matter, though. What did matter was the contents were correct. He was a standard cappuccino, nothing difficult about that, but the others got more complicated. Freddy took a Caramel Macchiato, Penny a Honey Almond milk Flat White, and George a Pistachio Latte. The team got awful grumpy if they got them mixed up, taking it out on him like it was his fault. It's not like he could just take the lids off the coffees and work out the individual ingredients from their scents alone, like some caffeine wizard. Ridiculous, just like the price; nearly twelve quid he had to stump up every four working days for. He didn't care it was his task to pick them up daily, such is life as the only team member living close to a fancy coffee shop, but the prices were as sickening as the almond milk Penny insisted on.

At one point a few months ago, he had tried to drop out of the round, citing make believe doctor's advice on cutting out the caffeine, but it didn't stop the rest of the team treating him like a leper with the flu. He tried to get them to change the coffee shop. 'Buy local' he would say, 'help the independent traders', but again, they dismissed the idea as sacrilege. It was premium brand all the way, including the premium prices. The drive to the station north on the A470 was a good twenty minutes that always took the edge off the heat of the coffees, another thing that blew his mind in their insistence, and every time he walked through the office doors they would launch themselves at him for their fill before it got cold.

Today was no different. Penny met him at the entrance like the caffeine junkie she was, excitement and desperation on her face for her morning hit as she took the cardboard tray of drinks away from him, giving him a chance to take off his summer rain jacket.

'Got a good one coming in for you today, Iefan,' she said, as she inspected the tick-boxes on the side of each cup. 'Farmer's hard drive being recovered. Guy committed suicide and burned out his farm.'

'Sounds awesome,' Iefan replied as he rolled his eyes. 'Sheep rustling online these days?' Penny smirked and made off to George's desk, dropping a cup down onto the empty space. She passed another to Freddy, who took his without looking up from his monitor, instead lifting it skyward in a thank you gesture.

'What are you working on, Penny?' Iefan asked.

'Drugs bust in Cardiff, all class-A stuff. A network of runners taken into custody. Making a start on a bunch of phones and tablets this morning. George wants a full timeline of text messages by the weekend to see where it's coming in from. Probably Bristol or down from Manchester, but we'll know soon enough.'

It was no surprise she got all the best stuff coming in. As the lead engineer in the Digital Forensics Department at Merthyr Police station, Penny always got the important projects from George, the team leader. She sometimes delegated to Iefan, the junior engineer on the team, and he relished the opportunity to get his teeth stuck into a proper case where actual crimes were committed and where he wouldn't die of utter boredom searching files for tax fraud evidence.

# THE ESCORT TO THE GRAVE

There were moments when he wondered if he'd made the right choice, joining the police force. Some of the guys he graduated with were making triple figures working for private firms. The big corporations like Amazon paid handsomely for analysts who could track hackers and restrict access to their sensitive information. Some areas in the public sector still paid well too. Ever since hackers infiltrated the NHS systems in 2015, the Government had learned their lesson and threw billions of taxpayer's money into creating and recruiting divisions of engineers, proactively making life so much harder for the thousands of computer criminals attempting to bring down services every day.

Yet for Iefan, it wasn't about the money. At twenty-four, he was certainly doing well for himself. There weren't many people his age earning close to forty grand. And it would only go up the more experience he gained. He was earning the equivalent of an experienced Sergeant and within two years would be on par with an Inspector. No, for Iefan, it was all about the thrill of the chase. His father had been an old school copper, working the beat over the neighbouring valley of Aberdare. He was a big hulk of a man that struck fear into many a criminal until he retired ten years ago. Unfortunately, Iefan had taken after his mother's side, and failed to take on the physical attributes his father was feared and respected for. Growing up, his father's obvious disappointment in his career choice in computing hurt Iefan. It wasn't until he began pursuing digital forensics at university his father had showed any interest. Even in his last years before retirement, there was a growing need for computer experts to work within the force. He could see the importance of the department, and even went as far as to tell Iefan he was proud of him when he graduated and started working for South Wales Police. 'Following in his footsteps,' he had said. It had brought them so much closer.

He had made significant progress with Penny's last case involving a phishing scam, turning out to be a spotty teenager in the Rhondda stealing credit card details from pensioners with cleverly disguised emails and text messages. But it still wasn't meaty enough for his liking. And now, now he was being given some farmer's computer to pull what, exactly? If he burned out the farm, it was likely for evidence of his favourite. Insurance fraud. Boring.

From behind the toilet door, a flush sounded, then out popped George Jones, vigorously shaking his hands. His mouth puckered and eyes lit up when he spotted Iefan, cleverly deducing his coffee had arrived. He scurried over with an expectant look on his face. Picking up his coffee, he took a greedy gulp, knowing with the travel time it would be at his desired temperature. An 'ahh' noise bellowed out from the portly man. 'No blooming paper towels in there again. I'm going to leave a note for the cleaner this time.' That was George's style, passive aggressive. He wouldn't dare complain to someone in person. It was emails and texts and notes all the way. Never one to raise his voice or swear, he was quite simply a nice man. With a white ring of hair stretching from ear to ear that long ago allowed the crown of his head to poke through, and his big round frameless spectacles, he looked as harmless as he was. Behind the jolly exterior, however, lay an intricate and organised mind respected throughout the force. He also had a knack of delegation that always seemed to work.

'Has Penny told you what you've got coming in this morning?' he said as he pushed his glasses back up his nose. The coffee was still hot enough to steam them up.

'Yeah, some farmer's hard drive.' He couldn't hide the lack of enthusiasm. 'Maybe I'll find an elaborate potato smuggling racket.'

George chuckled. 'Now, now, Iefan. Lowest form of wit and all that.' He leaned in, looking left and right to exaggerate the imaginary secret he was guilty of exposing to absolutely no-one. 'Did she tell you who wants the data?'

Iefan raised a brow. George was clearly enjoying himself. He repeated the movement, looking left, then right, then lifted a hand to the side of his mouth as he whispered, 'Major Crime. DCI Hibbard suspects potential involvement in that girl going missing off the top of Pen-y-fan mountain. The MP's daughter.'

'YES!' Iefan shouted, loud enough to wake the dead, a fist pumping the air. He momentarily forgot the cup in his hand and juggled to keep it upright. *Something for me to get my teeth into at last.* He turned and ran for his desk. The others smiled as they watched him go. His mind wandered as he booted up his workstation. He pictured the Chief Constable in her full dress uniform, presenting him with an award for finding the vital information in their search for the missing girl. She held a plaque in front of Iefan as cameras flashed and raptures of applause from detectives and reporters alike filled the press conference. His proud parents wiping away their tears of joy.

The officers delivering the equipment had barely got a foot through the door before Iefan raced over and prised it off them. George felt the need to apologise on his behalf, stressing his eagerness to do a decent job as the reason for his rudeness. Jumping straight to it, Iefan worked with an enthusiasm he hadn't felt for a while. It was time to prove to George and the gang what he was made of. It didn't take long for him to get results. The man was a farmer, not a programmer. Nothing appeared encrypted. Pulling the hard drive and bypassing the operating system, everything became readable. Either the man didn't expect it ever to be taken, or didn't know how to protect the data in the first place. Iefan suspected a bit of both. The last of his cappuccino long forgotten, he pulled up the first of the folders. Inside were a volume of files, images and videos, all labelled in alphabetical order. The first read Abigail.jpg, the second, Abigail.mp4. Iefan swallowed hard as he scrolled down the list. His heart drummed a beat as his fingers trembled above the keys. Every letter of the alphabet had several names against them, some girl's names, some boys, all with corresponding photo and video files. Iefan closed his eyes, hoping it wasn't what he suspected. He clicked on the first file. An image filled the screen. A lump rose and caught in his throat, clogging his airways. He gulped the sensation down, the heat instead rising to his forehead and temples. His breath spasmed short and fast, then a ringing sound filled his head as his chest constricted. The room swirled around the screen, the light colours of the walls and ceiling and desks darkening to highlight the appalling image in front of him. With a monumental effort, dragging the last of the air from his shriveled up lungs, he called out, his voice squeaking pathetically.

'George! Penny!'

Penny was the first to his station, grabbing hold of his hand and swivelling him away from the screen. She made herself big in his eyeline, forcing his focus onto her. 'Iefan, listen to me. Focus on your breathing now, please. Slow it down, that's right.' She grabbed the armrests, pulling the chair as she inched backwards, away from his desk. 'That's it, good, keep breathing. In, out, that's it.' Freddy came into view with a bottle of water. Penny took it and listed the bottle to Iefan's mouth. She held her other hand under his chin, expecting him to lose half of it.

'Can't. Can't breathe.'

'You're ok. Keep drinking, that's it. You've had a shock, that's all.' She looked over his shoulder, back to his desk. George sat in Iefan's place at his terminal, head in his hands. He lifted and looked to Penny. His lips squeezed together as his head shook back and fore.

Iefan kept his eyes on Penny. He swallowed hard once more. 'Is it what I think it is?'

# THE ESCORT TO THE GRAVE

'I'm afraid so.' George said. 'We'd better get DCI Hibbard down here pronto.'

## Chapter 22

From the hilltop layby, Eddie could see the entrance to the Morrison estate at the bottom of the twisting country lane, sandwiched between rows of oaks standing guard at the roadside. The house sat on picturesque grounds worthy of an elegant wedding brochure. Large electric gates led to a circular gravel courtyard, an intricate stone fountain detailed with hand carved cherubs at its centre, doubling as a turning point for any vehicles entering and leaving the grounds. A double garage and outbuildings, built to match the yellow sandstone of the main house, littered the far side, all held in by the ten foot high walls running out of view behind the house. A marked police car currently sat guard at the front gates to warn off any over enthusiastic reporters. Following yesterday's press conference, it surprised him a pack of broadcasting vehicles wasn't clogging up the country lane leading to the estate, rather than the lone van sat opposite the entrance. Then again, David Morrison had granted the BBC access to the family home earlier that morning. Eddie had watched the broadcast this afternoon. A follow up warts and all exclusive interview, celeb reporter Heidi Ellenburg sat across from Morrison, who had not only subjected his wife to the charade this time, but his eldest daughter too. He paraded them in front of the cameras, faces blotched and raw from the endless emotional drama. At one point, Ellenburg attempted to engage both women, only to receive a passive nod or shake of the head in return. For the most part, they sat holding hands with their heads lowered, as David answered all the pre-approved questions with equally practiced answers, then proceeded to demolish the reputation of the Major Crimes Unit of South Wales Police. Ellenburg played her part, not once challenging Morrison on his opinions. She could have countered with how they had used every resource available to them. How they had worked around the clock to find her. How they took on the investigation from another borough force. Yet she played along with the Morrison narrative. It was interesting viewing, he had to admit, expertly navigated by reporter and politician alike. They kept individual names from blame during the damning interview, knowing full well it held additional credibility to do so. The icing on the cake was Morrison's slating accusation the department had used 'alternative methods' and had 'dabbled with the occult' to search for his daughter. Considering Eddie couldn't get reprimanded the way the scapegoat in the Major Crime team would be, it surprised him Morrison hadn't smeared his name with the opportunity.

He sat and waited, a cold cheese and onion pasty his only company. During the interview, Morrison had 'accidentally' let slip he would visit the station for updates later that afternoon, 'to make sure progress is being made in the search for my daughter'. It was likely the missing broadcast vans were now camped in the station car-park to get a prime shot of the MP walking in, rather than a poor one of his blacked-out Jaguar leaving the family grounds. He certainly knew how to pull the strings of the media puppets. And it was perfect for Eddie, too. All he had to do was wait.

As the front door to the house opened, David's car, parked outside the double garage, came to life and pulled around the fountain to rest at the house entrance. The driver stepped from the car, rounded to the passenger side, and opened the rear door. Morrison left the house, followed by an older man with a briefcase and a young woman with a shoulder bag Eddie assumed was his legal team. The older man sat up front with the driver as Morrison and the young woman got in the back of the car, the driver closing the door behind them. As the entrance gates crept open, a photographer leapt from the van across the road and began snapping. The driver pulled forward next to the police car, allowing the gates to close back behind him. Car windows lowered briefly, then raised, as the Jag made off up the hill towards the layby, followed closely by the media van. Stepping out of the car, Eddie rounded to the rear where a spare tyre and wheel brace lay on the gravel floor of the layby. Underneath, a scissor jack was in position. Taking one knee, he waited until the roar of the three litre V6 approached the brow before winding the jack. The Jag flew past in a blur, the occupants clearly in too much of a rush to rescue the hapless and needy driver. Such a shame.

Lowering the jack, Eddie weighed up his options. He loaded everything back into the boot and climbed back into the driver's seat. Daylight was yet to fall behind the valley. He checked his watch. The patrol outside the gates would likely clock off at seven, still an hour away, but would likely get replaced by a night shift guard. Jumping the wall deeper into the woods was a strong possibility, but if they spotted him before getting to Mrs. Morrison, then he'd blow any chance he had of speaking with her.

Deciding to try the easier, more diplomatic approach, Eddie dug out his phone. He wasn't a fan of social media; it being loaded with tossers and narcissists, but it was amazing the details he had found out about targets, and even more so his clients, from what they were willingly giving up on Facebook, Twitter and Instagram. It was something his journalist wife had shared with him back in the early days. Gwen would always friend request people she barely knew, hoping to harbour information on a big story, and pathetically, nine times out of ten, she would get a positive response. She would gain valuable intel on targets in minutes. After that, it was a simple decision for Eddie to sign up to every platform he could.

# THE ESCORT TO THE GRAVE

He opened Facebook, running a search for Sarah Morrison. A list of them appeared, but none with profile photos matching the one he was after. Her settings were most likely set to private. She was a politician's wife, and he wouldn't be the only one trying to get hold of her over the past couple of days. He tried Twitter next, giving up after a few minutes. It was Instagram where he hit the jackpot, finding her profile straight away. He sent a follow request and waited, hoping she would take the bait. Yes, her daughter was missing, but if she was anything like he thought she would be, the phone would be by her side, constantly on, ready and waiting to ping for news. He also banked on David Morrison telling her who he was. While she may share her husband's views on people like him, he hoped it would intrigue her enough to at least hear him out.

Ten minutes passed with no response. He tried a message. *My name is Eddie Venter. I am trying to find your daughter and need to speak to you urgently. I am currently in my car at the layby overlooking your home. I need five minutes of your time.*

Eddie propped the phone on the steering wheel and waited. No response. A trek in the woods looked inevitable.

He fired the car up, ready to find a quiet spot away from the main road. As he was about to pull from the layby, the patrol car moved off from its post at the front gates, up the hill toward his direction. No point in moving now. They'd be with him before he could turn around. The car disappeared momentarily, then came back into view as it crested over the hill. Two stern faces with accusing eyes leered at Eddie, then slowed and turned into the layby. They pulled next to him and lowered the driver's side window, continuing their ever so menacing, intimidating stares.

Eddie lowered his in return. 'Sorry guys, I'm not working tonight, but if you come back tomorrow, it's twenty quid a blowie.'

The officers didn't see the funny side. 'Mrs. Morrison has instructed us to escort you onto the premises. Follow us, please.' The driver raised his window before U-turning back towards the house. Eddie did as told. As they approached, the gates opened. Pulling the patrol car to one side, allowing Eddie to pass, the officers watched closely, same stern faces questioning his every move. Eddie parked in front of the left garage roller doors and walked the short distance to the house. The front door opened before he got there, a shy little woman with hair pulled back in a ponytail watching him approach. She only seemed to look at his feet, save for an occasional stolen glance upwards, and her hands took turns to pick at each other. As he reached her, she stood to one side, allowing him to pass. 'Please go through to the sitting room. Mrs. Morrison will be through shortly.' It came out rehearsed, like she had said it a thousand times. Eddie felt like he should know where the sitting room was. 'Can I offer you a beverage, Sir?'

'Ah, no thank you.... '

'Ana. I'm the housekeeper.' She bowed as she backed out of the room as though greeting some sort of dignitary. He couldn't help think a certain man of the house had instructed her to do so. *The Pompous twat.*

Eddie remained standing as he waited. A collection of photographs at the fireplace drew his attention. Matching solid silver frames filled the huge marble mantel. Faces of two pretty young girls smiled back in a variety of poses. Some held photos of Sarah posing with them. At the centre of the mantle, a large black-rimmed frame sat out of place, all four members of the Morrison family in full pose. The adults stood at the back, children seated at the front. Awkward hands on shoulders and forced smiles told him the frame didn't live with the others, a showpiece David placed there for the cameras Sarah had forgotten to remove since. The political ambition of the man was almost as impressive as his lack of empathy for his own family.

Towards the back of the deep mantel, Eddie spotted a frame of a lone figure. An older woman, bearing the same button nose and doe eyes as Sarah, grey bobbed hair and crow's feet around the eyes, the only difference. He picked up the frame, taking care not to nudge the others over. *Her mother.*

'Beautiful, isn't she?' a voice spoke behind him.

Eddie turned to meet Sarah Morrison. Her eyes were raw with emotion. Dark shadows spread out beneath them. Her face hung slack with fatigue and wore her red hair pulled back in a loose ponytail. Dressed in grey jogging bottoms and a T-shirt three sizes too big, she looked exactly what she was, a woman desperate for her daughter back. Under normal circumstances, Eddie doubted anyone other than her daughters and the housekeeper would see her like this, including her husband.

'Your mother?' Eddie asked.

Sarah walked over, taking the frame from Eddie. She ran a trembling finger over the image. 'She left us over seven years ago and I miss her just as much as I did the first day,' she said. 'I don't know how many times I've heard people say to give it time. But it's just a cliché, isn't it? Something people say because they don't know what else to.' She placed the frame back in its rightful place. She stared at the black frame, her eyes turning cold. 'Do you know what I mean, Mr. Venter?'

He knew exactly what she meant. Time wasn't a great healer at all. Time didn't do shit, except prolong the pain and misery until your own time runs out.

'I do.'

She turned to look deep into Eddie's eyes. She held his gaze for a long moment. 'Yes. Yes, I think you do, don't you?' She turned to the settee, offering him a seat. 'Did Ana offer you a drink?'

'She did, thank you.'

'But you turned her down.' Walking to the drinks cabinet, she turned over two crystal tumblers from the tray and poured two fingers from a decanter into each. She gave one over to Eddie. He took a sniff.

'It's one of David's fancy bourbons. I'm not one for the stuff myself, but, well, it takes the edge off lately.'

They shared a silence. Not an uncomfortable one. It seemed almost necessary. Sarah sat down first. She grasped the glass with two delicate hands as she sipped at the drink. It was an effort not to spill the contents. She lowered the glass to her lap, where it was safe to take one hand off. She gestured to the couch next to her.

Eddie did as instructed and perched leaning side on, into the back of the settee to get a view of her. Her reactions would tell him the truth, not her words. Sarah continued to sit facing forward, nursing the glass in her lap. He suspected the decanter had been refilled more than once in the past week.

'Thank you for agreeing to see me, Mrs. Morrison. I'm sure you've had enough of visitors the last few days. There's just a few things I'd like to ask you and I'll be on my way. I'm sure your husband has told you who I am?'

Sarah took another sip of the bourbon, her eyes held firmly on the glass, then slowly nodded.

'And what has he told you Mrs. Morrison?'

'That you're some private investigator friend of the Detective Superintendent in charge of finding my daughter. That he's wasted all this time searching for her by employing a ghost hunter, and you all think she's dead. My Ellie, my beautiful baby.'

A lone tear fell down her cheek. She didn't bother catching it.

'Do you want me to be honest, Mrs. Morrison?'

'It's Sarah. And yes, I want you to be honest. I'm tired of all the lies being told around me right now.'

'If she's still alive, we're running out of time to get her back.'

# THE ESCORT TO THE GRAVE

Sarah nodded as she took his words in. A narrow smile rose at the corners of her mouth. She became more animated, her body turning towards him, her posture strengthening. Behind the tears filling them, her eyes looked stronger, more purposeful.

'You are wrong Mr. Venter.'

Eddie stared back for some time, searching. She held his gaze until he could take no more. He looked to his glass, unable to find the right words. The swirling amber liquid invited him to take it. He obliged, knocking it back in one burning swallow.

'Do you love your husband, Mrs. Morrison?'

Sarah's mouth opened, but nothing came out. The pause told the truth. Eddie looked to her. 'As bad as it sounds,' he said, 'when I first heard David Morrison's daughter got kidnapped, I couldn't help but think he was involved. That he had something to do with her disappearance, some sort of point scoring exercise with the public en route to his meteoric rise to the leadership. Then, miraculously, she'd get found unharmed. He pushes a family man persona I find hard to digest.' He let out a resigning sigh. Sarah kept quiet. 'But I don't think even your husband would do something like this.'

Sarah nodded. 'Believe it or not, we were in love once.' She took a sip of her drink. 'And he was a good father, too. He lived to provide us with his undivided attention. Now I share him with a tart of a PA and an entourage of advisors. The worst part? I'm very much a part of the persona. I play along, the perfect wife. It's not a terrible deal. I love my children with every ounce I have. Everything I do is for them. So if I need to play a role and keep them happy and free from harm, then I will.' Another tear fell down her cheek. 'Is that wrong?'

'No, Mrs. Morrison. It isn't.'

'Are you ready to tell me why you think my daughter is dead, Mr. Venter?'

Eddie looked back at the empty glass, wishing it full again. He was all in now. No turning back. In almost seven years, he hadn't shared his *entire* story with anyone, not Peter, not Jane, not even Wendy, his therapist. There had been plenty of rumours, of course, and he'd made no effort to confirm or deny any of it. It was how he'd kept himself fed and watered over the last few years. Yet something felt different now. Something he didn't understand, like when he passed out at the mountain top, stopping him from following her daughter's kidnapper as she carried her away. There was a reason for it, a transition occurring he couldn't figure out, and he couldn't help feeling he was being drip fed the answers. Now this feeling had brought him here. To speak and to share with a woman he'd never met before. A willingness to explain it all when he'd refused on so many other occasions. Something deep down in the pit of his stomach told him it was the right thing to do. He couldn't say why, but she needed to know. She had a right to.

He blew out a huge breath, composing himself. 'Almost seven years ago, I lost my wife when the car she was a passenger in lost control and nosedived into a tree. You may remember it. It wasn't far from here. The car broke through corner barriers and plunged down the valley. I was a police officer at the time and first on the scene. I'll never forget the look on her face as she died, like she was begging for help. But she was dead. I kissed her goodbye then concentrated on saving the driver.' He gestured to the decanter. 'May I?'

Sarah looked to her own and downed the last of it. She gave Eddie her glass. 'Please.'

Eddie filled the two glasses with another couple of fingers. He passed Sarah's back. 'As it turned out, my wife was still alive. I failed to register a pulse, but it was there. The paramedics told me. They battled for an hour in the wreckage to save her. They wouldn't admit it at first, but the truth is, if I had tried when I got there, they might have had a chance. I have had to live with that ever since.' He eased himself back into his seat next to her, his eyes on his glass as he turned it between his fingers. His chest heaved with effort.

Sarah's hand fell onto his, settling him. She spoke with a soft tone now. 'But you saved the driver?'

'I did. She never fully recovered, but she's alive. Her name is Jane Enfield. Detective Superintendent, Peter Enfield's wife.'

Sarah frowned. 'Mr. Venter?'

'Please, call me Eddie.'

'What does this have to do with my daughter?'

He took a small sip of the bourbon. 'You may think I'm crazy, but the night my wife died, everything changed for me. I was working miles from the scene, completely oblivious to it all, but something caught hold of me and wouldn't let go, taking control of me, telling me she was in trouble. I don't know how, and have no recollection doing it, but I ended up driving straight there. Something sent me to that very spot, willing me on, wanting me to find the wreckage first. Wanting me to find her body, to see the look on her face as she died. It's a curse, Mrs. Morrison. Toying with me. Mocking me. Punishing me. And ever since, it has continued to do so. Like it's keeping me on a leash, letting me off long enough into thinking I'm free of it, and then when it wants me, it yanks me back with force, showing me it's still in charge. When it decides to, it tortures me, messes with me, taps into my mind until I think I'm going crazy. It takes over my senses and my perception of reality. Instead of spring flowers, baking bread or fresh cut grass, it gives me the scent of decay, rot and filth. Instead of stunning landscapes, ocean waves or a setting sun, I see torture, pain and suffering. And in the place of beautiful music or children's laughter, I am tormented by screams of agony and loss. It consumes me, beats me down into wanting to die, desperate to end my misery. And then, when I'm at my lowest and I don't think I can take anymore, it feeds me something that keeps me going. The scraps of information, enough to think I might one day make the difference, to get there in time, to save one of them.'

'What do you mean, it?'

'My curse, Mrs. Morrison. It's death, ridiculing me. It calls to me, telling me it has taken another, where to find them, but refusing to let me save them. It only feeds me after it takes them, when it's too late to make a difference. I don't know why it chose me, but ever since the night of the crash, death taunts me.'

'And it showed you my Ellie was dead?' Sarah asked, alarm in her voice.

'I attended the scene Monday morning, but I could still see it. I saw her body carried from the mountain,' Eddie replied, all aware he wasn't directly answering the question.

Sarah's hands hid her face as the tears came full flow, her body trembling. She leaned forward into a crouch, making her body small, deflecting the pain. His own hands shook as he reached into his back pocket, pulling and unfolding a white piece of A4 paper, a photocopy of the symbol he had seen many times in the last couple of days.

'It's never been wrong, Mrs. Morrison. Each time it has shown me a death, it was how they came to pass. But something was different this time. It refused to let me follow her. I blacked out on the mountain. It must mean something. I have to find out why. What can you tell me about this symbol?'

Sarah raised her head. She took the paper, the tears stopping momentarily as she inspected it. She wiped her face with her sleeve. 'It was on the coin the woman gave me before she collapsed. Before the other woman took Ellie.'

'Have you ever seen it anywhere else, other than the coin?' Eddie asked.

She smiled then. 'Yes, yes, I have. It's why I know she's still alive. It was on a gift my mother had delivered to Ellie when she was born.'

'I found more items at the top of the mountain with the symbol on Mrs. Morrison, in a cist. Grave goods: tools, urns, coins, all with this symbol. It's called a Triquetra. I've been looking it up. Everything in the religion seems to revolve around it, and around the number three.' His finger traced the three points of the symbol in turn. 'The movement of life, Past - Present - Future.'

Then he pointed to them again. 'Life - Death - Rebirth'. Sarah looked at him, bemused concentration etched deep into her face. Eddie continued. 'Body - Mind - Spirit. It means many things.'

And then he said, 'The triple deities. The Morrigan.'

Sarah's face turned to puzzlement. 'The what?'

'The Morrigan. She is the Celtic goddess of fate. The foretelling of doom.'

He moved closer, expecting to lose her any moment now. 'Throughout the ages, the Morrigan was described as a trio of sisters. Representatives of each of the three Celtic nations: Ireland, Scotland and Wales. Three every time.'

Sarah sat in silence, wide eyes dashing in their sockets.

'You said the old woman who died had a Scottish accent, Mrs. Morrison?'

'Yes, she did.'

'And the other woman, the one who took Ellie. Was she Scottish too?'

'I... I don't think so, no. She didn't say much. She may have been Irish.'

'Three representatives, Mrs. Morrison.'

She looked at Eddie again. 'But that's only two?'

'Your daughter is Welsh. If these women are part of an ancient Celtic religion, then she completes the trio.'

'Then she is not dead, Mr. Venter.' Sarah said with a newfound enthusiasm. A smile broke on her face.

Eddie rubbed the pain from his forehead. 'At some points in history, the Celts worshipped the Morrigan as deities. At other times, sacrificial representatives. The Morrigan was the goddess of fate. They believed if the Morrigan took the fall, it saved the fate of the masses.'

She placed her glass down and rose from her seat. 'The story you shared, of your wife. You haven't told many people before, have you, Mr. Venter?'

'No, I haven't told anyone the whole story. It's not something most people would take seriously.'

'But you shared it with me, because you knew I would believe it. Come with me, please.' Sarah rose from her seat, placing her glass down on the table. She offered her hand to Eddie. He took the invitation, placing his own glass down before rising and allowing her to lead him to the staircase. They climbed to the first floor, down the landing to a closed door. 'This is our spare bedroom, where my mother would sleep when she stayed with us. It's mostly the same as when she was still alive. Only Ellie spends time in here now. She sits and plays with her toys and chats away as if my mother is in the room with her.'

'How long ago did she pass?'

'Ellie never got to meet her. She died before she was born. She would have doted on her just like she did with my eldest.' Sarah pushed open the door, revealing a perfectly kept room: a large double bed, crisply made, and a dresser table overlooking the rear garden. Sarah walked to a series of built-in wardrobes. She opened the doors to reveal assorted stacks of bedding and towels. She stretched to the top shelf, up onto her tippy toes, taking three pulls to gain purchase on what she was after. She turned and set on the bed one of the piles, opening it to reveal it protected a shallow, ornate box. It was a rich, dark wood, engraved with hand carved details only a master woodworker could produce. Intertwined details of stems and leaves of ivy ran around the perimeter of the lid made with gold inlays. And central to the lid, prominently declaring ownership of the box, was another gold inlaid symbol. A Tree of Life, and at its trunk, a Triquetra.

Eddie walked to the box. He held out a finger as he traced the symbol across the smooth, detailed lid.

'You are the first person I have ever shown this box to, Mr. Venter. You shared your most intimate secret with me, and now I share you mine. You want to know why I didn't tell the police I had seen the symbol before? Because this is the gift my mother gave to Ellie, along with this note.' She held it out to Eddie.

*My darling Elinor. I am sorry I never got to meet you, but it was my time to go. You will grow up to do the most wondrous things. Your sisters will show you the way, and she will deliver your key when you are ready. ~Nana~*

Eddie's mouth fell open, his head swimming in confusion. Wondrous things. Your sisters will show you the way. A throbbing pain pulsed at his temple, splitting his mind in two. The tension continued to build, like a coiled spring ready to pop. He thought back to his own message, the one from his dreams. The woman sat next to him in the hospital corridor.

*You will do wondrous things together, Mr. Venter. When the girl is ready, you will find each other, and you will do the most wondrous things.*

'Mr. Venter, for some reason I can't explain, my mother, who never got to meet her second born granddaughter, had this delivered to me after she had left us. Ellie hadn't even been conceived by the time of her death. This box, along with her note, saying when Ellie is ready, its contents will be presented to her. It is why I know my daughter is still alive, because *my* mother never lied to me.'

'So the coin the woman gave you…'

'Was an assurance, Mr. Venter. That my baby will return to me unharmed.'

Eddie looked back to the box, shaking his head. 'What is it? What's inside?'

'I have no idea. It's locked and without a key.' She pointed to the note. 'At first, I was desperate to open it. I'm not known for my patience. It was from my mother, after all, the woman I adored most in the world. After she died and I found out I was pregnant, I felt a deep guilt she would never know she had another granddaughter. It was a lonely time for me, and then this came with her message. Somehow, she had known all along I would have another baby. Another girl I would name Elinor. I can see her now, with a big smile on her face, writing the note and sealing the box. She had set up the delivery and will one day do the same with the key. Of course, I thought about revealing it to the police, in case there could be a clue as to her whereabouts inside. But while I worry a stranger has taken my daughter, I can't help but think it's all connected. You see, the woman, before she took my daughter, she spoke to me, and I couldn't believe I was hearing those same words. But I've had time to think it over, and I know it is to do with my mother, somehow. I take comfort in knowing she is watching over her, and will deliver her back to me, safe and sound.'

Around the corner, at the top of the second floor staircase leading to her bedroom, fifteen-year-old Jenny sat hugging her knees with one arm, the other wrapped around Border Collie Bandit. He buried his head into her lap and gave a quiet whimper, sensing her sadness. She wanted to run to her mother, hug her, tell her everything would be ok. That she believed her. They would find Ellie alive and in good health. She had been taken for ransom money, or as leverage to bribe, to get one over her father, the ever popular, deceiving MP. They would get in touch and give Ellie back and she would say they treated her well, and she spent her days watching cartoons and eating McDonalds

# THE ESCORT TO THE GRAVE

followed by ice cream and slept in a bedroom looking just like her own.

But she couldn't. She had heard everything the man had to say downstairs, and just like her mother, she had believed his story too.

Including the part when he thought her sister was dead.

## Chapter 23

Strolling down the High street, Eddie welcomed the cool evening air. It was a fair trek from his flat at the north-east end of the town to the centre, but taking advantage of the late summer evening and the downhill slope, he'd decided on the leisurely approach. It gave him a chance to think. The visit to Sarah Morrison had been necessary, as well as productive, for both of them. The woman had pleasantly surprised him, his preconceptions misjudged. She was, he had found, to be a mother first, lonely woman second, MP's wife third. Expectations of a high maintenance, ambitious woman driving her husband's rise in politics were the polar opposite of what confronted him. He felt guilty to the point an apology was necessary. He liked her, he'd decided.

Strolling down the top end of the town centre, the aromas of various takeaway restaurants stirring to life filled the air. 'For Sale' and 'To Let' boards outnumbered occupied shops, the tell-tale signs of local businesses inability to compete with online shopping and the gigantic retail parks pummelling them into closure. Eddie recalled his younger years in the nineties, when bustling pubs dominated the top end of town, competing for business, putting on live music four or five days a week. The nightlife in the town was electric, customers travelling from miles out to sample it, every other door protected by a couple of bouncers in their distinct dickie bow attire, or restaurants awaiting their tables to be filled from the hungry and drunk alike. Nowadays, save for the odd barbers and tattoo studio, the steel of roller shutter doors, plywood covered windows and fading overhead shop signs told the predominant theme of sadness and days gone by.

Further down the high street, the buildings presented a busier picture. The old Town Hall Eddie only ever remembered as the Chambers night club, now fully renovated as an Arts centre. The Castle Inn sat opposite the public library he had left only hours ago. It was a second home to every dosser living around the town centre, the underpriced cider and overcooked egg and chips all too inviting. A steady stream of drinkers kept the staff busy from the 8am opening to midnight last orders. Further on, a group of suited office workers sat outside Vardie's, a high end cocktail bar with trendy mood lighting and a drinks menu to match, the birth child of a local entrepreneur who saw the need for something different in the town. It was a diamond in the rough. Unlikely to have succeeded in what otherwise looked a dying town centre, it had become extremely popular in the couple of years it had been open. It showed others it was possible.

Eddie continued through the pedestrian area of the High street. More derelict shop fronts fenced him in from both sides. He stopped at the window of a jeweller displaying their wares behind the toughened glass. Hundreds of cheap earrings and necklaces shone back above their price tags. In a portioned off area, various gold and silver items, two toned with details of the distinct rose colour associated with them, sat littered around a central sign reading Clogau Gold. Charms of love spoons and daffodils and forget-me-nots. Welsh dragon rings and rugby ball cufflinks. Several pieces held the theme of the Tree of Life, popular in Celtic folklore, the trunks of the trees in silver, the leaves in the orange gold giving them the name. The price tags for these items warranted the premium spot they commanded in the shop window. Beneath the green and gold Clogau sign, sat a lone necklace, the large pendant the centrepiece for the display. It was completely rose gold colour, the fine intricate details bouncing off the under shelf lighting illuminating it. The three pointed symbol wound around itself in an eternal pattern. The Triquetra.

Eddie spotted the back of Price at the bar as he walked through the door of the Royal Crown Inn. She turned as he approached, two pints of cider in hand, a smile spreading across her face. She nodded to an empty table and Eddie followed. It was far enough from the stage they wouldn't have to shout at each other over the noise of the next up-and-coming band the pub had booked and was busy setting up their equipment on. Price sat with her back to the wall, giving herself a view of the room. Eddie sat to her left and took a sip of his pint. The pub was busy, but not to the point of annoyance. Laughter and loud discussions competed with rock ballads on the jukebox. A group of thirty something women shared two ice buckets holding a bottle of Prosecco each. One of them, with wild blonde hair and huge jangly earrings, brayed like a donkey as she laughed at her own joke. Price winced at the sound. In a previous life, it would have annoyed Eddie too, but in the last few years, something about the pub atmosphere and the drinks they served seemed to hold a calming influence over him. The stale smell of beer, the bustling noises of banter. He did his best thinking in the pub. When his mind became muggy from the alcohol, when his motor skills became suspect, a contradicting clarity came to his thought processes.

'I've been to see Sarah Morrison.' Eddie said.

Price's eyes flicked across to him. 'At her house?' she asked. 'Was her husband there?'

'I waited for him to leave. He mentioned he'd be attending the station during his heartbreaking interview on the BBC.'

'Jesus Eddie. If he finds out who you are and what you're up to, he'll play hell with us.'

'Didn't you watch his interview? He already knows who I am. And so did Sarah.'

A look of realisation hit her. 'That's what he meant by the Detective Superintendent wasting time on alternative methods? He was talking about you?'

'Hibbard knew Enfield had asked me to look at it. My guess is he's in Morrison's pocket, feeding him information.'

'Other coppers have seen you, Eddie. There were bobbies at the bottom of the mountain too.'

'Unlikely. A man as high profiled as David Morrison isn't going to mess around with police constables. They're on a need to know basis and never kept in the loop. No, David Morrison has a detective on his payroll. And the only people who knew were Hibbard, and you.' He looked at Price with a wry smirk.

She dropped her head to look at her drink. 'Look, Eddie…'

'Don't sweat it, Price. I know Hibbard instructed you to get pally with me. You didn't think I'd actually believe you wanted to partner up with an alcoholic PI, did you?'

Price's shoulders relaxed, as though a weight she had been propping up had finally shifted. 'He wanted me to keep tabs on you. He may call you and your methods rotten, but still wants to know what progress you're making.'

Eddie laughed into his near empty pint glass. 'Hibbard thinks I've already drunk away my last brain cells. He thinks I'm just a thick liability.'

Price shook her head. 'I don't think so. He has some level of respect for you and what you do. He wouldn't have me to spy on you otherwise.'

A wine glass knocked over on the women's table. A collective 'woah' sounded as they each slid backwards on their chairs to avoid the spill. The blonde donkey brayed again.

'Did you give him the items I found?' Eddie asked.

'Yes, and he's not stupid either. He knows it was you who found them.'

'So why isn't he pulling me in? To find out how I knew they were there?'

'I convinced him you've still got a lot of information we need. He's willing to hold off for now. But he'll definitely want to drag you in at some point.'

'You can tell him everything. I'm not bothered. All that matters is the people who did this get found. I'd rather you told them everything I know if it means they find who killed her.'

'You don't know she's dead, Eddie.' Price said before downing the last of her pint. Her empty pint glass returned to the table with force. 'I'd prefer you acted that way until we find a body.'

'I can't do that. But out of courtesy, I'll mind you are. Ready for another?'

'Yeah, why not?' She drained the last of her drink, stopping Eddie as he rose with the glasses. 'But I can't go mad. Hibbard's calling a briefing at eight tomorrow morning. As I was leaving the station, Digital Forensics called him down to their department. I'm guessing they've found something tasty on the farmer's computer.'

Eddie's eyes creased. 'If the two incidents turn out to be related, he'll definitely want to pull me in over the contents of the cist.'

'Not yet. I told him about our meeting at the library. The stuff you're finding. He's set up a team in the incident room looking some of it over.'

Eddie thought back to the symbol again, on the coins, the urns, the tools. What did they mean, really? How did it all fit? 'Let's get another drink in. I promise you'll make your briefing in the morning.'

Price watched him go, pleased it was out in the open. She didn't enjoy playing him, or more like attempting to. He'd surprised her by announcing he'd known all along. She liked that. She had underestimated him, and so had

Hibbard. It was almost like they forgot he used to be a police officer himself.

Returning with two full glasses, he placed them down, then left again, coming back this time with two vodka chasers.

'What part of 8am briefing did you not understand, Eddie?'

Eddie sat and smirked, then downed his in one. He looked to her expectantly. She responded, knocking back the drink, her eyes shutting tight as she pushed the glass away on the table. She sucked through her teeth at the aftertaste. 'Hibbard told me you used to be in the force?'

'Seems a lifetime ago.' Eddie replied.

'What happened to you?' She sipped at her pint, avoiding eye contact momentarily. Eddie noticed.

'Don't tell me Hibbard hasn't told you.' He said. 'I bet he's given you a full breakdown of how my life fell apart.'

'I thought you might want to tell me the actual story, instead of me relying on those apple women.' She took another sip of her pint.

'I've got a shrink I pay extortionate amounts of money for that pleasure.'

A spray of cider burst from Price's mouth. A couple of the noisy women looked over disapprovingly. Eddie chuckled.

'You see a shrink? I can't imagine you spilling the beans lying on a couch, Eddie. That's a belter.' She wiped a tear from her eye as she calmed back down.

Eddie smiled as he took a drink. He liked her. Even though she'd tried to play him, she had done it with good intentions. And she'd come clean without confrontation. He would let her in, albeit it at arm's length.

'It was part of the deal when I had my suspended sentence. I had to go through twenty sittings with a shrink. Turns out she's pretty good at what she does. Now I just keep going to play hell with her.'

'What were you arrested for?'

'Drunk and disorderly. Criminal damage. ABH.'

'Quite a collection.' Price said.

'My life was down the toilet. After my wife died, I got pissed and assaulted the arresting officers. Hurt one badly. Peter almost ruined his own reputation backing me up, but he couldn't protect me. I hit a copper after all. I got a suspended sentence instead of jail time, though.'

'What was she like?'

'She was everything.' Eddie replied. 'My everything.'

'And she passed away?'

'Peter was my DCI back then. He used to keep his distance from the team. Never socialised with us. Kept everything pure business. So it became a bit weird when my wife came home from one of her classes one day and says she's made a new friend. Turned out to be Jane Enfield, Peter's wife. They became inseparable. For months, they would pick each other up and go to the gym, do lunch, go shopping. It was all so strange for me and Peter, but since then we've become friends ourselves.'

'What did she do?'

'She was a freelance journalist. I used to tease her it was just a posh way of saying she was a private investigator, but twice as seedy. Maybe that's why I started doing this after I got sacked, I suppose.'

'Bet that was odd. A journalist and a copper living together?'

'We had a deal, a pact of sorts. We never discussed her work. Or mine. Kept everything separate. She always joked the day she needed the police for help would be the day she gave up being a journalist. She never asked for my help at all, ever. Probably why we got on so well. She had her own study she'd lock herself away in while she worked. It's all still there too, just as she left it. I haven't been able to stay there since the accident.'

'Stay where?' Price asked.

## THE ESCORT TO THE GRAVE

'Our house. I haven't been able to since the night she died. Too many memories I'll never get to experience again. So I try to block them out instead, with this mostly,' he pointed to his glass. 'So I live in Sam's flat above the shop instead, and he and his family live in my house. It works a treat. Bet you think I'm crazy now, right?'

'I don't think you're crazy. You're grieving. But blocking out the memories with drink can't last forever, you know.'

'That's what I'm hoping.'

They shared a quiet moment. Eventually Price continued.

'Didn't your family rally round you? Or the in-laws?'

'Never knew my old man and my mother passed in my twenties. As for Gwen's? Her father couldn't stand me when she was alive and certainly didn't hide the fact when she was dead. Her mother tried for a while, hiding her calls to me from her husband, but it soon fizzled out. Not that I gave a crap. The house was Gwen's, paid for by her parents. It left a sour taste in her dad's mouth when he found out she'd left it to me. He even threatened to take me to court to win it back.'

'Sorry Eddie.'

'Yeah, me too.'

'They were together the night she died? Your wife and Enfield's?'

'I was just about to come off duty. Then something told me she was in trouble, like some crappy spidey-sense. Everything went blank after that. I don't know how or why I got there, but I ended up travelling in the opposite direction and straight to the scene. I got to Jane in time, but Gwen died. I went off the rails then, and I've been a first class screw up ever since.'

The band started their sound checks, the lead guitarist strumming away, altering the amps as the lead singer stood out in front, directing him. The drummer banged out a warm up on his set, the sound of the bass drum overwhelming. Eddie and Price shared a look. They finished their drinks, then headed for the door.

The temperature had dropped since the sun went down and Price put on her denim jacket, pulling her hair out from the collar. They strolled up the deserted high street as the music faded.

'So what's with the bible bashing?' Eddie asked. 'You spend your Sundays singing Kumbaya and spreading his good name?'

Price smiled as she dug her hands deep into her pockets. 'Like I said, in a previous life, it was something like that. I grew up a good little girl to devout Catholic parents. They were pretty strict with it, so naturally, I rebelled in my teenage years. Ended up moving away to Uni and came back an atheist.'

Eddie smirked. 'Bet they took it well.'

'Like a kick in the nuts with Doc Martens on.'

'But they're ok with it now?'

'My mother tries to see past it.'

'And your Dad?'

'Our relationship was never really the same afterwards. I may as well have told him I was the devil himself. He'd rarely talk to me, and if he did, it would be to chastise with some of his favourite passages. Or to tell me how much I'd hurt him. It got pretty ridiculous. Funny how some people can talk of repentance of sin, but then be guilty of pride and be unable to forgive. We ended up having a major bust up. I stormed out, and we never spoke again. I joined the force, and he ended up dying of a brain haemorrhage.'

'That sucks,' Eddie said.

'Eddie, why are you so certain the girl is dead?'

The change of subject threw him. He thought of the locked wooden chest hiding in Sarah Morrison's wardrobe, her explanation for it, and her mother's note. *You will grow up to do the most wondrous things. Your sisters will show you the way.* He thought of the mysterious woman from his dream, those icy blue eyes piercing his soul. It was no coincidence. It couldn't be. *When the girl is ready, you will find each other, and you will do the most wondrous things.*

'I'm not sure of anything anymore,' he said.

# Chapter 24

**Thursday**

A full team of construction workers jack hammered away at Price's skull, splitting it into a thousand pieces of mind thumping aches. Sipping at her coffee, she did her best to keep them at bay, but they were insistent in their pursuit. *Damn you Eddie Venter, you drink too much.* She couldn't remember the exact time she got home, not long after 10pm, but she still managed to fall asleep in full make-up and the clothes she wore out. At least she'd got her denim jacket off. She had found it screwed up in a ball just inside the front door. Drinking on a school night, not a good idea. Attempts to mask the stale smell of alcohol with excessive amounts of mouthwash and perfume had only given her the scent of someone trying to hide a hangover. It was unlikely to fool anyone. Her belly groaned a sick hollow feeling. A dripping toasted bacon sandwich with lashings of brown sauce came to mind, but her stomach told her it couldn't manage it for another couple of hours. She'd stick to the coffee for now. Swallowing every thirty seconds didn't help, her mouth hyper-salivating to the point she was dribbling like she'd been tranquilised.

It startled her to see the incident room so full, looking like the entire Major Crime team were in attendance, as well as many of the on duty uniforms getting their positions early for the briefing. Or was she late? All the seats around the large conference style table were full, their occupants crammed together in more chairs than the table would allow for. Few standing spaces remained, the cork and white boards loaded with photos and maps of ongoing cases lining the walls hidden from view. Hibbard raised an eyebrow as she crept in, watching as she tiptoed away to find a spot amongst the late arrivals with a sheepish hunch.

He scanned the faces in the room as everyone quietened down. There had been murmurs amongst the team something big was coming. They looked to him expectantly, hungry for progress. Sat at the front were the foursome making up the digital forensics team, heads hung in a subdued, tired and dejected manner. They all sat in silence. The youngest member, a handsome lad named Iefan, sat with his eyes glued to his lap, picking at something on the back of his hand. His face was grey, drained of all colour, and of the four he looked most ready to run from the building and never look back. The team leader, George Jones, sat closest to Hibbard in front of an open laptop. Price couldn't help feel he forced the smile at his face, hiding some news Hibbard was about to reveal. This really didn't look good.

'Alright everyone, I appreciate you all making it on such short notice, but George and his team have bust their arses all night on this one, and they've hit on something big.' Hibbard walked behind George, resting his hand on his shoulder. George's face turned a plum tomato colour. 'You're all aware approximately four o'clock on Tuesday afternoon, a farmer by the name of Richard Evans lit up his pig barn with himself inside it. Made a right mess. Mid and West Fire Service worked all night putting it out.'

DC Leighton Hadley's hand shot to the ceiling. 'We heard they had a *crackling* time, sir.' A collective groan filled the room. Someone from behind pushed him in jest.

'Shut your face, Hadley,' Hibbard spat through his bared teeth. 'Now's not the time.' His hardened stare was enough to melt the constable into his chair. Hibbard's eyes switched to movement at the entrance and several heads turned with him. Detective Superintendent Enfield leaned against the closed door, his hands crossed in front of his chest, a drawn and withered look of sorrow on his face. No-one had heard him come in. He stared toward the front with a blank expression.

'Sorry Sir.' Hadley said, turning back and dropping his head in shame. Enfield didn't respond. The room fell silent again.

'Due to the suicide note and evidence found at the scene, it initially appeared there were links to the kidnapping of six-year-old Elinor Morrison from Pen-y-fan mountain on Saturday morning.' He held up a smiling photo of her. 'Some of you have been working on the link between the two in hope of finding the girl.' He glanced at Price, who met his gaze. 'That's why you're all in here. George's team has pulled the data from the farmer's computer and mobile phones. They're still working on the information, but haven't found anything linked to the girl yet, and we still don't know the identity of the dead woman from the mountain.'

Heads turned to each other with disappointing whispers. They had been hoping for better news.

'Settle down. We still can't rule out the links either way. Unfortunately, they've stumbled on something even more sinister. George?'

George let out a heavy breath before rising from his seat with a thin-lipped smile failing to reach his eyes. 'Um, thank you DCI Hibbard,' he said, his voice thick with uncertainty. He coughed to clear it. Lifting himself out of his chair, he pulled the back of it away from him, an attempt to gain more room in the restricted space, instead tangling his legs underneath. He stumbled momentarily before righting himself. Penny, sitting next to him, held out her hands, ready to catch him. 'Sorry about that,' he said to no-one in particular. He cast a nervous glance to Detective Superintendent Enfield at the door. Enfield's eyes were at his feet now, head lowered as he rubbed at the back of his neck. George held an open hand across the table toward Iefan. Iefan's gaze stuck firm to his lap. 'Uh, our junior engineer, Iefan here, was yesterday tasked with pulling the information from the farmer's hard drive. He made light work of most of it with remarkable speed. Fantastic work. Really well done. Making huge strides in his devel...'

Hibbard stepped in. 'George?'

'Ah yes, sorry. The evidence he found... well... came as a bit of a surprise. The sort of thing we normally find encrypted, really. Maybe as a farmer, he didn't quite have the expertise to hide the information.'

He sat back at the laptop in front of him. He picked up a remote, turning on a large flatscreen television behind Hibbard, who stepped to one side to allow everyone a view. The screen filled with a view of George's laptop, the mouse cursor running over it wildly. He clicked here and there before opening a folder, revealing a series of names in alphabetical order. The names were big enough Price could read them from the back of the room. For every name, there were two files. She felt sick again, but this time it wasn't the alcohol.

George swallowed hard and clicked on the first file. Abigail.jpg. It pulled up an image, filling the screen and scorched itself deep into Price's mind. Flames rose in her throat she somehow kept down. A collective gasp filled the room, then silence.

The close up of a young girl's face, no older than ten or eleven, her dilated black eyes staring out to the audience in the room. Her pale skin riddled with mottled blue patches, the process of pallor mortis well underway. Her mouth open, holding a shocked expression caused from the loss of muscle tension in death. She was so young, so innocent, so undeserving.

George blew his cheeks out as he closed down the photo back to the file list, then moved the cursor over the next file. Abigail.mp4. Rubbing his forehead with the back of his hand, a bead of sweat trickled down his cheek that he caught before it reached his jaw. 'Every name has two files, an image and a video. Brace yourselves.' He clicked on the second file. A video popped onto the screen George unnecessarily maximised. The same child, same face in death. George clicked play. The camera slowly pulled away, revealing the body lying naked and prone on a stainless steel table. Underneath it, black plastic lay curled inwards as though someone had freshly cut it away from the body. The camera started a slow 360 degrees around the table. Artificial white light shone from above, illuminating the undeveloped body in a cold blue hue and casting a wicked darkness all around it. As the camera panned, Price could see purple blotches where the skin met the plastic, the surefire sign of the blood pooling from gravity and lack of circulation. Her eyes squinted as she recognised details. She inched closer for a better look, not realising until she hit the person sitting at the table in front of her. A sniffling sound came from somewhere in the room and several heads dropped, having seen enough, desperate for someone to end the video.

The camera panned around the other side of the body, the shadows of the background lifting to reveal an open plastic curtain, beyond which was the expanse of a wooden barn. Inside the curtained area, galvanised meat hooks hung from low beams. A second stainless steel table beneath them held a variety of butcher's saws and knives and a green rubber apron. The camera continued on its sickening course, revealing more details of empty stainless steel pens. The video ended after twenty seconds. George closed it down back to the file list.

Hibbard took the lead again, giving a desperate George his leave. He blew out with relief as he settled into the back of his chair, pulling a handkerchief from his trouser pocket to mop more perspiration from his face. Despite the nature of the videos, Hibbard spoke with a calm and assuring tone, probably down to the fact he had already had time to come to terms with the contents. Nevertheless, Price had to respect his professionalism. 'All files came from the same mobile phone uploaded to his computer. A search of his farmhouse revealed he kept a secret phone, receiving incoming messages and calls from one other phone only. The network operators have identified them as pay-as-you-go, so we can't trace. Text messages to this phone, along with the plastic wrappings seen in the video, indicate the victims arrive at the farm deceased. His wife has stated a number of vans come to and from the farm for produce, that she knows some, but not others. There are over fifty names on the image list, all appearing to be fourteen years or under. It appears this guy may have been the end of the line of a possible trafficking ring. Officers have found stacks of cash amounting to almost four hundred thousand pounds at the farmhouse. I'll be nominating a few of you to a specialist team to try and identify these children, teaming up with the Public Protection Unit. George's team is still sifting data to find out how the farmer got involved in the first place. In the meantime, we've made a request UK and European wide for any information regarding possible crime syndicates involving the kidnapping of children. There's too many on this list for them to just get picked up locally.'

From his seat at the table, DC Gareth Jones lifted a weak hand in the air. Hibbard nodded to him. 'What has he done with the bodies? Are there any signs of them?'

All eyes were back on Hibbard. Price knew what was coming, just as half the room did, but was glad it got asked all the same. No-one wanted to hear it, but they needed to. Hibbard's eyes closed and Price saw a moment of faltering, a vulnerability, the machismo he so loved to display evaporating.

'All the photos and videos show different children, but the same content. Some date back over two years. No evidence of what he does to them. However, his wife described him as a master butcher. Equipment found in the barn suggested the same. The tables and equipment you see in the videos, all used for slaughter. There's a mincer in there, and a band-saw. Forensics are trying to pull hair and blood from them to determine if human flesh has been through them, but they're badly burned from the fire and they're not confident they can lift anything.'

Another wavering hand lifted, this time from DC Hadley. 'Why would he mince human flesh?'

Looking to the door, Hibbard saw Detective Superintendent Enfield was no longer there. He hadn't seen him leave. His eyes went back to the Detective Constable.

'You saw the video. So they'd be easier to digest,' Hibbard said, rubbing his head again. 'The man was a pig farmer.'

## Chapter 25

Leaving the car at one of many turn-ins surrounding the Tal-y-bont Reservoir, Eddie hiked the remaining couple of miles, taking the scenic, off-road route in towards the Aber village. The sky was a miserable slab of concrete threatening a downpour at any moment. He played the part of hiker well, his grey cargo trousers, matching boots and black rain jacket giving anyone who spotted him the impression he explored the rolling hills of the welsh countryside for fun. There was a time that wasn't far from the truth. During his teenage years and into his early twenties, days spent boxing and running, Eddie had been a solid piece of gristle, weighing just over half what he currently carried. Nowadays, his muscle hid beneath a thick layer of fatty neglect.

A trek in the hills was a common thing back then, especially after he had met Gwen, who enticed him into exercise in the great outdoors as often as she could. He welcomed it in his fitter days, but now he couldn't think of anything worse. A muggy head from last night's drinking didn't help. Progress was slow, his decision to avoid the access lanes and hence any patrolling officers proving time consuming. The steep fields, rock walls and wire fences separating them made for difficult obstacles to negotiate with a hangover. At one point he rolled an ankle that had him cursing at the bemused sheep, watching him from a distance as they chewed their cud. The early morning air held an unusual humidity that soaked Eddie's shirt through with sweat, his rain jacket sucking to his body like cling film over a cooked joint of meat. Just as he expected, his head throbbed before he could see the devastation. Yet something was different, a milder, gentle drum at his right temple that eased when he applied pressure with his fingers. Not like the other occasions. Since that first time, shortly after the crash, they had always been intense, mind splitting aches producing tidal waves of sensations. And then two days ago, at the mountain, before he had seen the old woman lying dead, and the girl carried away, it had been so extreme it had erupted into a loss of consciousness, like he was being refused to follow.

Now it was different, easier to handle. Like an invitation. A transition was happening, but why?

The acrid smell of burnt grass poured over the crest of the hill above him. He was close. His hands began to tremble, and he looked for somewhere to put them, tucking them into his shoulder straps of his rucksack as he climbed, his tired legs screaming for rest as they drove up and up. Reaching the top, he dropped his hands to bear crawl the last few yards on all fours, turning to sit and ease the pain of the lactic build up in his sore muscles. Looking to the valley below, he surveyed the damage. Everything was shades of black and grey, accentuated by the morbid slate sky above. Pulling a pair of binoculars from his rucksack, he concentrated on the farmhouse in the distance, a sad monument that just days ago would have sat proud in a splendid landscape. He zoomed in, making out a couple of white vehicles on the forecourt, belonging most likely, to a couple of Police Community Support Officers left on site to patrol the grounds and keep unwanted guests away. Unwanted guests like Eddie. Although Enfield had requested he attend at the mountain, Morrison's interview and attack on the Major Crime Team had put paid to his attendance being required at the farm. It was better this way. After Price's confession regarding DCI Hibbard's scheming last night, flying under the radar and working alone was the right way to go.

# THE ESCORT TO THE GRAVE

Descending the hill toward the ruined fields, Eddie kept close to the waist-high stone wall leading there, hiding the bulk of his body from view of any eagle-eyed patrol at the farmhouse. The crisp, char-grilled aroma filling his nose made way for another, a foul, pungent odour he'd expected and dreaded in equal measure. Although the smell was distinct and obvious as to its identity, it was far more bearable than before. Scaling the wall, he dropped to the other side, taking in the wasteland ahead. The giant oak sat untouched at the centre of the main field, its limbs rich and plentiful, like the mirage of a desert oasis teasing him to join it. Behind the tree, Eddie could make out where the slaughter barn once stood, the unwanted debris now scattered clear, the equipment inside already forensically examined, bagged and tagged, sitting in an evidence warehouse somewhere miles from here. Some of the steel pen frames still stood defiantly, warped and heat damaged, but refusing to give up. He walked along the perimeter of the field, keeping one hand running along the top of the cobbled wall. A high speed whirring noise began to ring in his ears, a steady sound intermittently broken up by an even higher-pitched scream. He recognised it as the sound of a working band-saw, getting louder and louder as he closed in on the scrapheap. He stopped short of the debris. Leaning against the wall for support, he closed his eyes, waiting for the vision.

The intact slaughter barn stood ahead of him, cloaked in late night darkness. Artificial light peeked out through the gaps in the wooden planked walls. The huge doors pulled closed. He opened his eyes and walked to it, the healthy, untouched grass crunching beneath his feet. The whine of the band-saw continued from within. Pulling at one entrance door, it gave reluctantly, and he crept in. Oblivious to the usual farming smells of muck and shit and straw, he moved forward, as the dominant stench of death filled his nose instead. He paused a moment, again unable to understand why it was different this time, more bearable and tolerant. Making his way to the back, he stopped as the farmer, dressed in a green hard plastic apron and blue vinyl gloves, stood over a steel table, whistling as he sawed and cut and hacked. Streaks of blood and tissue covered his gown and hands and face. The farmer skipped between band-saw and mincer, feeding palm sized portions into the hopper, collecting the finely chopped meat at a bucket the other side. The excruciating scream of bone and cartilage as it caught on the blades was nauseating. Eddie squeezed his eyes tight, and silence fell, if only for a short moment.

The unmistakable sound of raging fire. Crackling of flame on wood. The creak of warping timber. The squeal of super-heating metal.

He stood in the barn as the fire blazed around him. Flames and smoke rose up the walls, engulfing everything in their path. The straw lined floor sizzled and cracked and wisped into the air. He felt the heat licking at his body, but it refused to burn him. His lungs filled with all-consuming smoke, yet it didn't overpower. A path of straw sizzled out ahead, leading the way. An invitation to follow.

He slipped through the doors and out into the field. It was daytime now, but not today, the blazing sun holding court in a clear blue sky, slowly being ruined by the cloud of billowing smoke as the fields burned to cinders below. A blanket of destruction worked its way through the long dry grass, transforming it into a bleak and desolate landscape like an evil cast spell. Eddie walked towards the tree, the flames parting as he neared before rejoining to continue their onslaught as he safely passed. His fingers massaged at his neck to take the bitter charcoal taste from his throat. Twenty metres out, he stopped again. The raging monster continued to work in all directions, consuming anything and everything it could without prejudice. It hungrily reached for the giant oak at the fields centre, the pigs grouping beneath, panicked and desperate to escape it. They squealed and screamed for mercy as the flames and the unsympathetic heat worked closer and closer. Above them, amongst the foliage of the tree, the mocking caws of crows fought against the deafening sound of the fire, as they sat a noisy audience to the carnage below. The pigs continued to fight for position, the bigger, more powerful hogs smashing and trampling over the weakest in last critical attempts to find salvation. They hugged the trunk as the flames closed in, finding a moment of relief that couldn't last. The immense heat forced the weaker pigs inward as their skin blistered and hair scorched, their last acts of desperation overpowering the strength of the swine at the centre. They squeezed them in, choking the life from them with final, ear-splitting squeals of surrender. And then the flames around the tree died with them. The only sound left was the contemptuous jeering of the birds.

Eddie watched the horror, unable to interfere, yet unable to turn away, as a realisation manifested. The shape they formed in their last throws of life resembled the mound at the mountain top. The concentric shape winding up toward the middle. The smaller, outer stones lying horizontal, propping up the larger, central, vertical ones.

At the crashing sounds from the barn, he looked back. The roof collapsed inwards as its supports gave way; the flames roaring from within at the sudden rush of oxygen. Black smoke billowed high into the sky. And then more movement, deliberate, as one of the gigantic wooden doors creaked open and the screaming, burning mass that was once Richard Evans crawled out. Eddie winced as the scorched figure scraped along the ground, blackened fingers digging in to pull the rest of him along. The last of the flames snuffed and died on his back. Scraps of clothing, skin and flesh fell away as he hauled across the ground, leaving behind a vomit inducing slug trail of bodily fluids and remnants. The man wailed in agony, dragging his way to the tree, begging forgiveness, his suffering and torture unbearable to hear. Only when he reached the spared grassy edge did he fall back on his haunches, hands held aloft to the skies as he begged to the heavens, allowing Eddie to see the remains of his face. All hair singed and skin melted away, smouldering white wisps of smoke snaking into the air from his snuffed out body. Cheek and jaw and neck muscles cooked into solid joints of meat. Eyes long since burst and liquidised from their sockets. A hideous, grotesque sight.

Then she stepped from behind the massive trunk, dressed in her long black cloak, the woman haunting Eddie's dreams. Noticing her visitor, she cast Eddie a smile and welcoming nod, stealing the breath from his lungs. The hoarse cawing of the crows ceased, and the mortifying, charred remains of Richard Evans slumped forward with accepting misery. Rounding the pile of corpses under the tree, she flicked her hair behind her in a confident display of power as her two wolfhounds followed obediently. She stopped in front of the farmer, her face a snarl of hostility as she stood over him. Her dogs pulled up beside her, their ghost white coats a chilling contrast to their grim backdrop. They growled hungrily at the pathetic figure collapsed in front of them. The woman crouched lower, gripping the last of the man's crumbling jaw in her fingers. She stared deep into his empty eye sockets with menace, her face twisting with venomous hate. The farmer whimpered and cowered, fearful of what came next. And then the woman spoke.

'Nothing you can do will make up for your sins, Mr. Evans. Your torture is merely beginning.'

## Chapter 26

Retrieving the car, Eddie took the scenic route back to his flat. Taking in the breathtaking views around the Tal-y-bont and Pontsticill reservoirs on the way afforded him time to reflect. He had done well to dodge the weather on his trek back from the farm, but now the grey sky had refused to hold off any longer, sending a soft drizzle down into the valley as a friendly reminder summer was ending. Images of the mysterious woman clogged his mind like a blocked artery, refusing him little chance to concentrate on anything else. So many times he had seen her in his dreams, of that night at the hospital in the ICU corridor. The dream was always the same, their interactions never altering. Her arrival as he waits alone for news on Jane, sitting next to him, dressed head to toe in black. Her alluring pale face, hungry blue eyes and seductive red lips. Her long silky hair. Her lecture on grief, the damning speech about his wife's injustice.

And her message about finding the girl.

His dreams had been a mixture of fantasy and reality for so long he had learned to live with them by now, never really knowing what the woman or her messages had meant. Now he had seen her when he was awake, albeit during one of his visions, in another place, in another time. Something *was* changing, transitioning. But what exactly? And why now?

Cresting the hill, the first houses of Pontsticill village came into view as his mobile phone rang. He pulled over at the roadside to answer.

'Afternoon. How's the head today?'

'Like someone's taken a sledgehammer to it,' Price replied. 'I didn't need the hangover with the morning I've had, believe me.'

Eddie jumped in. 'Me first. I've been to the Aber valley. The farmer's connected to Morrison's daughter.'

'Why? How do you know?' Price asked. 'What did you find convincing you of that?'

He could open up, tell her everything. Lay all his cards on the table and hope she'd be able to see past the craziness and accept not everything is explainable as matter of fact and set in stone. She'd admitted she'd heard plenty of rumours about him at the station. Here, he at least had an opportunity to show his hand. Tell her what he'd seen and give her the opportunity to make her own mind up. But it was his burden to bear, not hers. And once she knew, heard it from the horse's mouth, then she could be just another of the growing crowd who didn't believe, and judge him as a crazy madman like the others. Yet, for some reason, her impression of him did matter, but now wasn't the time.

'Just a hunch,' he said.

'Well, I really hope you're wrong,' she replied.

'Go on.'

'I don't know how much I should elaborate yet,' Price said, letting out a heavy sigh. 'But we've found the reason he torched the place.'

'He was disposing of bodies,' Eddie said. 'Using his butchery equipment.'

There was a long pause. 'How... how could you know?'

'Look Price,' Eddie said. 'You've shown a lot of faith in me. Most people would rather walk barefoot over broken glass than get mixed up in my life. Reputations are at risk when I'm involved. Just look at Peter. Do you need that shit on your plate?'

'I need to find the girl, Eddie,' she replied. 'I don't care what it takes.'

'Then tell me everything you found on the farmer,' he said. 'And the next time we meet up, I'll tell you everything about what happens. When I see them.'

After the call ended, he sat at the driver's wheel for some time. The rain had intensified, drumming a soothing rhythm on the windscreen. Deciding to make a pit stop before heading back to the flat, he drove the short distance to the Enfield's home. As suspected, Peter's car wasn't in the drive. Making his way to the front door, Eddie rang the bell and waited patiently for an answer, sitting on the supporting wall of the porch canopy to hide from the downpour. A young tabby cat leapt next to him from the other side of the wall, shook the rain from its coat, then nudged its head under his hand for a nuzzle. His hand vibrated from the content purring the feline made, as its long tail looped around his wrist as he stroked it. A full two minutes passed, but from experience, he knew it didn't warrant a second ring. Eventually, a shadow fell behind the frosted glass, the sound of a latch turning, then the door slowly eased open as Jane wheeled backwards out of the way.

'She's a stray, been coming here for weeks now. Peter started feeding her and now she's here every day. Won't sleep in the house though, and we haven't a clue where she goes at night, but every day she comes back. You coming in? Peter's still in work.'

Eddie followed her through, as did the cat. He inched behind her as she expertly negotiated the hallway. The cat wasn't so patient, darting past the two of them to investigate the smells emanating from the kitchen. 'I've come to see you, not your hunk of love.' He reached down and planted a smacker on her cheek. 'And for a bit of whatever smells so good out there.'

They made their way through to the kitchen, Jane leading the way. It was a large room, specially adapted with extra width between the lowered marble countertops and the central island, creating enough space for a wheelchair's turning circle. Pull down cupboards hid clever and elaborate shelving perfect for disabled users. Some pulled out to reveal modern appliances. The huge sink had leg room underneath. A large pot of stew bubbled away on the cooker, steam rising into the overhead extractor. Jane wheeled towards it, pulling a wooden spoon from the side and giving it a stir.

Eddie sat and marveled at the woman's resilience. 'I'd offer to help, but I don't want to,' he said.

Jane smiled. 'It's lamb stew, won't be ready for another hour, though. Will you stay for some? I'll put the kettle on.'

Her tenacity was remarkable. Stuck forever in a chair, yet she held a determination that would humiliate anyone complaining about their own bad luck, including him. It was why he enjoyed coming here. She may have been a constant reminder of what he had lost, but she kept him in check. Showed him whatever crap you're hit with, there's always a way to overcome it, even if it takes a lot of hard work. When he came here, spent time in her company, she showed him life was worth living. It was the opposite of how he was when alone with his demons and a full bottle, contemplating ending it all.

It was a coin toss which side would win.

'Has Peter told you why I was here at the start of the week? The case he asked me to look at?'

'The Morrison girl. Terrible thing. I can only imagine how frightened she must be,' Jane replied. 'They don't live far from here, you know, just the other side of the village. Don't know them myself, though.'

'How's Peter been with it all? Since it happened?'

Jane stopped mid pour. She put down the kettle and gripped the tyres of her chair. Pulling one side and pushing the other, the chair made a tight 180. 'You're worried about him?'

'Yes. If this doesn't work out, they'll want someone to blame.'

# THE ESCORT TO THE GRAVE

'Worry about yourself for a moment, Eddie.' Jane said. 'That's your problem. You worry about solving other people's issues and neglect your own.'

'Isn't that what I do for a living? Solve other people's problems?'

'Yes, of course, but if you don't take time to sort your own out, how do you expect to help anyone else?'

He'd heard something similar many times from his psychiatrist, but it was the type of advice he never paid much attention to. It never made sense and so he found it easier just to ignore it.

As if reading his mind, Jane asked, 'Are you still meeting with Wendy?'

'Yeah, I still go. Don't get much out of it, though.'

'She's good at what she does, Ed. She helped me so much those first few months, you know.' Her hand went to her leg, smoothing out the canvas fabric of her trousers. 'After the crash.'

Silence fell over the kitchen, save for the gentle bubbling of the stew. Jane continued to stare at her lap for a long moment. Eddie watched as a sad look enveloped her, her head lowering as the corners of her mouth drew downwards. Then her hands went to the chair again as she turned back to finish the tea, and he noticed, to wipe a tear from her eye.

In the past, they had talked about Gwen a lot. They would sit together in the lounge with a stiff drink, Jane's favourite jazz music playing she had tried and failed to get Gwen into, and talked for hours about the woman they both grieved for. Eddie would sit wearing an etched smile as she relayed memories of embarrassing stories involving herself and her friend. Then he would repay the favour, telling Jane tales of dates they went on, and how she would pretend she was a fabulous cook yet somehow manage to burn water, and how she would purposely wind him up when she'd watch Christmas films in the middle of spring.

He couldn't recall ever seeing Jane like this, though. Each time they would talk of her, it would be Eddie breaking down and seeking comfort. She always held a strength in her grief, and now he saw it was for him she did so, refusing to show her vulnerability when he had so easily shown his. It had been nearly seven years now, and still it hurt deep, but Jane's ability to rebuild her life after everything she had been through always impressed him. Now, he realised, she simply hid it away instead.

He listened as she tried to mask her sniffling sounds, the spoon pinging off the sides of the mugs as she vigorously stirred the tea.

'I miss her too.' Eddie said.

The noise stopped suddenly. Her head lowered again as she turned back to Eddie. She offered him his mug. 'It was the worst day of my life, and it all happened so fast. Laughing and joking one minute, then... do you think you'll ever move on, Ed? Ever heal enough to forget, even for a minute? Would you feel guilty if you did?'

He shook his head. 'I can't, and even if I could, I'm not sure I'd want to.'

'I'll never forgive myself for taking her from you.'

Eddie wanted to hold her and tell her it wasn't her fault. That it was a freak accident no-one could have prevented. Torrents of harsh rain had pummeled the valleys for weeks, the country road surfaces slick with rain, mudslides washing down onto the narrow lanes cut into the mountain landscapes. There had been yellow weather warnings in place for days, and somehow they had pulled off the road down into the steep valley below. The car exploded through mounds of earth and brush as it blasted toward the valley floor. Luck momentarily on their side, the steep drop turned to a levelled bank, slowing the car as it dragged the woodland debris beneath its wheels, but not enough. Their fate arrived in the form of the tree, the massive trunk inviting the car into it, taking the oncoming force with ease.

# THE ESCORT TO THE GRAVE

The steel shell of the car was no match, crumpling like a piece of aluminium tin foil on impact.

'Do you ever think about it? The crash?' Eddie asked.

'All the time. I see Gwen staring back at me in the car. In my dreams, she's still alive. Begging me to help her, but I just sit there.' She wiped another tear from her cheek. 'I wish I'd never met her, Ed. If I hadn't, she'd still be alive now, and you wouldn't be alone. Instead, she saved me. I can't help think she knew what she was doing, leaning across and turning the wheel the way she did.'

She was right, of course. The accident investigators concluded the car had attempted to change direction in the last second, the back end lurching out to the left to avoid a head on impact. The passenger side had taken the brunt of it, crumpling in on itself as the car spun around to face back up the valley the way it came. And then Eddie had somehow arrived and found the devastation.

'You know, I've never understood what you were doing there, Jane? On that road.'

'We were on our way back from lunch. I was taking her home.' Jane replied.

'But I don't understand why you took that route home?'

Jane was quiet, eyes searching for the right words. 'We were supposed to be going to the gym that day. You know why Peter doesn't like us discussing this when he's about, don't you?' she didn't wait for an answer. 'Because our marriage was in trouble. That's why Gwen and I went to the pub instead. I talked, and she listened.' Jane's eyes turned glassy. Pulling a tissue from the box on the counter, she dabbed it under them. 'We drove for some time after we left the restaurant. I'd never met anyone who could offer advise like Gwen, but more importantly, anyone who could listen the way she did.'

'Why haven't you told me this before, Jane?'

'I thought you'd hate me for it. Blame me for the crash. I was a mess, Eddie. Peter and I had been arguing for weeks.

I thought my marriage was going to be over and I shouldn't have been driving that day. Gwen tried to get me to pull over and let her drive the rest of the way, but I wouldn't listen. I was too selfish and wrapped up in my own problems to see I was putting her in danger. I hate myself for what I've done.'

Eddie held Jane's hand. 'I don't blame you, Jane.' He gave his best reassuring smile, hoping he sold it. She took it and gave one in return.

'Why were you and Peter arguing?'

'Work, of course. We never saw each other. Not much has changed in that regard. I wish he'd retire and finally put his feet up.'

Eddie smiled. 'He's a busy man, that's for sure. Maybe he'll consider it once they find the Morrison girl and figure out what's gone on at the farm. I'll try to convince him too if you like?'

'What farm?' Jane asked.

'Uh, I'll let Peter fill you in,' Eddie said. 'Now, how long is that stew going to be? I'm starving.'

## Chapter 27

Picking up the decanter to his eye line, David Morrison's face screwed up at the dregs of bourbon remaining in the fine crystal vessel. If he'd put away more in the last few days than normal, he'd forgive himself for doing so, what with his youngest daughter being kidnapped. He hadn't of course, with all the interviews and press conferences and calls coming in from London, he needed to keep a level head and box clever, as he'd never been in the public eye more than he did right now. That only left one other possible culprit. And the number of missing crystal tumblers from the set tray told him what he needed to know. He sighed loudly. He may not have been the best father in the world this last couple of years. Eldest daughter Jennifer barely grunts a response at him these days, but in his own way, he loved the three women he shared his life with. The first couple of days following the kidnapping, he had been naïve enough to think they took Elinor for ransom, and waited to be contacted by some mystery disguised voice on the phone telling him how much money to stuff in a suitcase and where to leave it. He'd watched far too many Hollywood blockbusters. It was his personal assistant Victoria who first suggested political influence on the motive, but for the life of him, he couldn't think who would do such a thing. He mixed with all sorts of people in his line of work, the straight shooters, to the crooks in fancy suits, but no-one jumped out at him as a prime suspect. Maybe a business owner looking for a bargaining chip on a major deal, or a campaigner he'd fallen foul of needing to teach him a valuable lesson. He'd pondered this for some time, concluding he had to agree with the police it was highly unlikely. It had been five days now, and he had to believe if any of these scenarios were correct, then some-one, somewhere, would have been in touch already. It made sense then the third scenario, the one he had feared so much, was the likely reason.

Elinor's kidnapping was random, taken to be used for whatever purpose, and tossed away afterwards. Sarah didn't believe it, though. Something the woman said on the mountain, that they had chosen her. But then again, Sarah was a mess, and not thinking straight when she made that statement, anyway. It was her fault they'd taken Elinor in the first place, and now she clung to the hope they wouldn't hurt her.

David replaced the decanter and walked through to the kitchen. The grey gloss cabinets and white marble worktops were a stark contrast to the high ceilings lined with oak beams running through the rest of the house. Ana, the housekeeper, was busy loading the dishwasher. He held out a hand, stopping her from shutting the door, peering in at the used dishes. She stood back in silence, giving him space, all too aware of what he was searching for. He opened the top drainer, pulling a face at the three used tumblers stacked ready for a wash cycle. He turned to Ana, raising an eyebrow. 'Mrs. Morrison?'

As usual, Ana's face remained neutral, her shoulders rising to meet her ears. 'She likes to call for a fresh glass rather than a top up.'

David turned back, pushing the drainer closed. 'Well, at least we know how much she's drinking then.' Behind him, Ana shook her head, her lips pressing together. Leaving the dishwasher door open, he made his way to the staircase. Ana rolled her eyes as he left.

Climbing to the first floor landing, he passed the bathroom to his left and master bedroom to the right. The door was wide open, revealing a bed made with the precision a 1960s hospital matron would be proud of. Ana was an excellent housekeeper, and worth every penny he paid her. Continuing down the corridor, he reached the spare room to his left, unused since Sarah's mother had died. To the right was Elinor's room, the door covered with multi-coloured stick on butterflies and bumblebees. Pushing open the door led to an onslaught of pink every six-year-old girl would be envious of. Everything imaginable the colour of candy floss. Custom painted walls with cherry blossom trees flowering in springtime, with pink birds and even a pink owl sat on its branches. Rugs, furniture, pillows and bedspread, all varying shades of his daughter's favourite colour. A transparent net canopy draped the head of the bed, mimicking the sleeping quarters so many princesses enjoyed in her favourite Disney films watched a million times over. He sighed and rubbed at his forehead as he saw his wife Sarah, lying on the bed facing away, her legs tucked to her chest in the foetal position. One of his missing crystal tumblers sat empty on the bedside table next to her. Below the window overlooking the courtyard, a dressing table held an open music box, the ballerina figure long finished spinning to its tinkling tune. A large oval mirror stood behind it reflecting Sarah's unconscious face, a light snore keeping in time with each breath she exhaled. David eased the door closed again, creeping away not to rouse her. He couldn't handle the twenty questions he would have from her on any news if she woke.

At the end of the landing, he rounded the corner to climb the stairs to the second floor, to be met by a single white door. A thumping sound came from behind it David guessed at some sort of self-loathing music. His first knock on the door went unanswered. The second turned to a bang of the fist. The door pulled inwards with force as his eldest daughter Jennifer answered, wearing a set of giant headphones and a screwed-up face like she smelled something she didn't approve of. Considering he could hear the heavy metal tune through the door, he only imagined what it must have been doing to her eardrums. She creased her brow as she looked him up and down, a greeting he'd seen many times from her since she hit puberty. Turning away, she headed back to her double bed, snapping shut her laptop and pushing it to one side. She lay in its place, pulling in a threadbare soft plush black and grey donkey to her face he recognised as Elinor's favourite, the toy he'd seen his youngest carry everywhere around the house. Although Jennifer took after him in the looks department, her hair so much darker than Sarah and Elinor's, she'd never looked more like her mother than she did now, even down to the way they both lay on the bed. The girl looked completely cried out, her cheeks and eyes chapped raw, her face drawn to the point she looked like she'd lost considerable weight in the space of just a few days. At the foot of the bed, Bandit lay with his head on his paws, eyes glancing up at him, then darting away. David tried to recall ever seeing the dog in here. He always slept in Elinor's room, or stood guard outside her door whenever she was in school or at a friend's house, waiting for her to come back. Was he just missing his best friend and consoling her big sister? Or was he not expecting her back?

David walked around the bed, back into Jennifer's eyeline. He pointed a finger at his own ear, and she took the hint. She raised her head, pulling the earphones down around her neck. The screaming din wailing from them hurt David's ears, giving him brief concern she was damaging her own. Picking up her phone, Jennifer pressed a button, and the sound stopped. Her head hit the pillow once more.

'Is *that* what they call music these days?' David said, a poor attempt at an ice breaker. Without invite, he plopped down on the edge of the bed, forcing Jennifer to pull her legs further up to her chest. She gave a silent scowl David failed to register. He looked back down to the dog. 'I didn't know Bandit sleeps in here. I always thought of him as Elinor's dog.'

'There's a lot you don't know,' Jennifer mumbled. 'You've got to be around here to notice stuff.'

'Touche,' David said. 'Work has really taken over the last few years. I haven't been much of a dad lately, have I?'

Jennifer didn't answer. She pulled up to a seated position against the headboard, tucking her legs in with her arms. An uncomfortable silence held in the air. Bandit broke it with a pitiful whine.

David looked at his lap. 'Your mother's sleeping in Elinor's bed. How long has she been there?'

'Since Sunday, pretty much. She comes out for another drink and goes back in. She's a wreck. She blames herself.'

'Your mother's not to blame.' David replied.

'I know *she* isn't.' Jennifer snapped, as she dropped her forehead to her knees.

David's head flicked toward her. 'That's not fair, Jennifer.'

Her head came back up as she met his gaze, eyes blazing. 'Isn't it? You used to come on those walks with us. The five of us all spending time together, as a family. Now you'd rather spend it with your slut of a PA. If you were there, that woman wouldn't have taken her.'

Hearing enough, David stood from the bed, startling Bandit, who moved to the corner. He jabbed a finger toward his daughter. 'If I remember correctly, you weren't there either. Too busy sitting on your phone in the car. Any excuse to be on Facebook or chat to those arsehole friends of yours. All wasters. Ever thought if you were up there they wouldn't have taken her? Maybe you should take some of the blame. Ever thought of that?'

'A million fucking times' Jennifer screamed, her eyes welling up. 'And I know Mam thinks it too. Every time I try to talk to her, she turns away. I know she blames me. And now Ellie's dead. And she'll never forgive me for it.'

David's eyes creased into deep lines. 'What are you talking about? Why would you think Elinor's dead? Have people been saying that? Have you been talking to someone?'

Jennifer lowered back down on her side into the foetal position, closing her eyes tight. David grabbed her by the upper arm, pulling it into an awkward position, forcing her to look at him. She winced as Bandit barked a warning. David ignored him. 'Tell me, Jennifer,' he said, shaking her arm. 'Tell me right now. Why do you think Elinor's dead?'

She tried her best to pull away. 'Get fucking off me.'

'Tell me, you little bitch,' he hissed as he twisted her arm.

Jennifer's face contorted in pain. 'Because... the man who came here told Mam she was. That's why.'

David relaxed his grip. He let go of her arm, allowing her body to drop back to the bed. She hissed through her teeth as she checked the tender spot. 'I hate you. I wish it was you who was fucking dead.'

David ignored the insult. He leaned over her. 'Who's been here? What man?'

From behind him, a quiet voice sounded. 'Keep your hands off her.'

David turned to the door. Sarah stood wearily, like a stiff breeze would send her back down the stairs head first. Her bloodshot eyes the result of a gallon of liquor and an equal amount of tears.

'Who's been here? Who have you let in this house without my permission?'

'Eddie Venter,' Sarah replied.

He stood inches from her now, chest pounding, teeth clenched. She looked up at him defiantly, pulling her shoulders back and puffing out her chest to match his. His fury took over. With a short, swift backhand, he slapped her cheek, sending her sprawling to the thick carpet. Jennifer raced to her side, throwing an arm around her to block any more blows. Feeling a little braver, Bandit ran to position himself between the women and their attacker, barking furiously in attempt to ward him off.

'Get the fuck out!' Jennifer shouted.

'You let that nutcase into my house? When?'

Sarah looked up. 'After you'd paraded us in front of the world like some sick puppet show. Your daughter's been kidnapped and you're still lording it up with all your kiss arse flunkies. He came here and drank your bourbon and sat in our living room and told me she's gone. And all the while, you're playing games with those gutter journalists and turning it into a big publicity stunt. You're disgusting.'

David stamped out of the room, slamming the door behind him. A collective sobbing noise came from behind it. He took out his mobile phone as he walked back down to the first floor.

It answered on the third ring. David kept his voice low, knowing Ana could be anywhere right now. 'Eddie Venter has been in my house, drinking with my wife and filling her head with all sorts of rubbish. I want him gone. You hear me? Gone. Either he goes or you do. Make it happen.'

## Chapter 28

DCI Hibbard sat alone in his office, the adrenaline of the morning briefing and the subsequent hours in delegation of tasks finally wearing off and taking its toll. He had worked furiously overseeing the setting up of the investigating teams to get them hitting the ground running. Now came the lull of the first day closing, exhaustion setting in fast. Sitting side on in his chair, he kneaded the knot in his back that begged to be put in a horizontal position.

Through the office window, the teams of officers continued to work away, tapping at keyboards, phones to ears, searching the reams of paperwork and maps and photos lining the walls of the incident room. It was late afternoon, yet they continued to work with enthusiasm and purpose. With the office door closed, the voices were nothing more than a steady muffled hum of worker bees climbing over each other to find their own share of the nectar and combine it with the others to turn it to honey.

Hibbard let out a yawn, deflating back into the chair with it. This was pretty much his life now, living from incident room to incident room. A continuous stream of investigations as case after case melded into each other without respite, so much so, you couldn't tell where one ended and the next began. All work and no play, and for what? He was the Senior Investigation Officer for this case, but here he was, carrying out all the hard work while Enfield sat in the big seat. Then again, he couldn't possibly see how this case would end well. It was for the best he wasn't in charge. Not yet anyway.

*Careful what you wish for, John.*

He still got to play occasionally, of course. It's not like he was turning into some old man. He was smart, good looking, and although his hair was more grey than black these days, his waist was still the same size as his twenties. Most importantly, he could still get his fair share, even if it was just with the one woman these days. That was his choice, though. She was absolutely dynamite in the bedroom, and equally captivating out of it. She was funny, intelligent and, dare he say it, enjoyable company. He couldn't get enough of it, to the point he failed to imagine another woman holding a candle to her. It was a strange sensation, one he hadn't felt before, even when he was married. A fluttering in his belly when she walked into a room or when he saw her name on his mobile phone when she called. He struggled to keep things professional and not giggle like a schoolboy when he smelled her perfume or heard her voice. Since they'd begun their relationship, he could genuinely say he hadn't looked at another woman the same way.

*Could it be the L word he keeps hearing about? No, it couldn't be. Don't be ridiculous.*

Even his feelings towards ex-wife Bella had been different. Their marriage had seemed to be built more on familiarity than love, at least from his perspective, anyway. Eventually, his ever-increasing workload and inability to switch off from the job had seen them drift apart. She had begged him to try and save their marriage with a weekend away in the Cotswolds alongside a promise to reduce his working hours. It was a last-minute decision to stay and help with a sexual assault case that did it. Obsessed, she had called him. On his recommendation, her best friend had joined her on the trip, not for it to go to waste, and no doubt encouraged her to keep her suitcases in the car on her return.

He often wondered if he should have listened back then. Life would have been so much easier with less stress. But where would he be now? Still in uniform, most likely. Patrolling the streets and holding neighbourhood watch clinics with the PCSOs. Fuck that. He was only forty-seven and still had real ambitions to accomplish before he hung up his boots with a fat pension and even fatter lump sum payout.

He should have been happy to be involved in such a high-profile case as this. All going well it would serve a reminder to ACC Bentley he was overdue for promotion to lead the department, and the fact the case involved David Morrison should have been a blessing, such was his political prowess in influencing decisions amongst the senior management of South Wales Police. They were more politician than police officer themselves. He had imagined finding the girl with ease, returning her to the MP as the hero of the hour with a slap on the back and a promotion in waiting. But it hadn't worked out that way. She had been missing for too long now, almost a week. Confidence amongst the team on finding her alive was diminishing, and with the findings at the farm mushrooming beyond anything he had dealt with before, he couldn't help but second guess himself, to think it was one case simply too big for him.

And now Morrison was getting crazy with his demands.

The door to the incident room crept open, and a defeated looking Detective Superintendent Enfield walked in, his face ashen, shoulders slumped. Hibbard watched through the office window at the man he'd looked up to for so many of his early years. The ever cool character he'd tried his best to model himself on as a junior officer, now giving off nothing more than of a man mentally done. He certainly didn't envy him anymore, especially now, dealing with this case. The vultures were circling, waiting to pick the bones. Enfield wandered aimlessly to the white boards and to the enormous map of the Brecon Beacons valleys stuck there, littered with red pins and marker pen circles. The busy noises and bustling energy that moments ago charged the room fizzled out like a spent sparkler doused in water. Heads dropped, eyes averted, hearty discussions turned to whispers.

He didn't help himself, mind you. Leaving the briefing early this morning had set the tongues wagging, and no doubt every officer in the building wondered how long it would be before the old man broke or got kicked to the curb as the scapegoat. Spotting Hibbard in his office, Enfield wandered over. He knocked as he entered, a small token of respect to the lower rank officer. Hibbard reached behind him, flicking the kettle lever on to boil.

'You read my mind,' Enfield said as he closed the door behind him. He sat across from Hibbard, positioning himself to see back into the incident room.

'You look like I feel, Sir,' Hibbard said, dropping two tea bags into mugs and filling them with water.

'You must feel like crap then, John,' Enfield said, a sad smile barely breaking through. 'Because I know I look like shit.' He looked out of the window, the room having returned to its energetic ways. 'They've worked hard on this, and so have you. But it's all going to blow up soon. The media are all over us.'

*You. The media are all over you.*

'I'm sorry, Sir. We haven't even been able to identify the dead woman, never mind the living one who took Morrison's daughter,' Hibbard said. He poured in some milk and pushed a mug toward Enfield. 'The worst part is we weren't even supposed to be involved in this in the first place. But that's politics for you, I suppose.'

Enfield looked across the table to his understudy. He took the mug in two hands on his lap. 'You've done your best on this, John. You've put everything you've got into it. Whatever the outcome, I know you'll do well off the back of it when everything blows over.'

'And what about you, Sir?'

'I'm more or less done. It's just a matter of time.'

The two men sat in silence. A full minute passed as they both nursed their drinks. Hibbard straightened in his chair. He couldn't take it any longer.

'Why did you do it, Sir? Why involve Venter in such a high-profile case as this? The guy is a first class fuck up. One way or another, the press was always going to get wind of it. He's made a mockery of this whole thing. You must have seen it coming? Why didn't you listen?'

Enfield stared into his cup. 'I've given my life to this job, John. We've solved countless cases and put hundreds behind bars. And do you know what they'll remember at the end of it all? This. How I led the unit that failed to save the MP's daughter. And do you know what? I deserve it.'

He put down his cup, then walked to the door. Palm resting on the handle, he turned back to Hibbard.

'I'm finished whether they find the girl dead or alive. Last thing I'll be doing before I go is putting your name forward to replace me. I just hope my recommendation will still be worthy of consideration. You're a great leader, John, and a good friend.'

He walked out of the office, closing the door behind him. He stopped momentarily outside, giving a last look to the team in the incident room, nodding away with a blank, lost in thought, reminiscing expression.

As he walked from the incident room, hands buried deep in his pockets, he failed to see the wide grin making its way across DCI Hibbard's face.

## Chapter 29

St. Michael's Inn prides itself as the oldest pub in Wales, with tales of folklore dating back to the Norman invasions. Sitting at the heart of the Abergavenny valley, the pub courtyard overlooks the Skirrid mountain to the east, where the now ruined chapel of its namesake once sat, and the Black mountains to the west. Legends are told legal proceedings and even public hangings took place on site in its former occupation as a courthouse, and now, thousands of visitors come from far and wide each year to take in the macabre stories on offer. Other tales involve the Welsh uprisings of Owain Glyndwr holding rallying points in the cobbled courtyards outside. Built in the 17th century, a good two hundred years after Glyndwr's reign, there was a pretty big hole in that particular claim. A large percentage of the annual takings rely on the myths and vague historical anecdotes surrounding the pub, and the landlord, Stuart Richards, offers no apology in marketing it as the oldest, but also the most haunted in Britain as well. The limited rooms on offer were consistently booked up seven days a week through the months of October and November, sold along with the ever popular Halloween ghost hunter packages. The tourists lapped it up. Grown men and women revelled in searching the grounds in the freezing cold and at dead of night, scaring each other with horror stories like school kids, getting so spooked there was to be no sleep in them. Stuart never understood it himself, but they paid handsomely for the experience, so who was he to argue? And so the pub decor told the fables in all their glory. The cold flagstone floors and immense fireplaces sold the haunting atmosphere. Wood-panelled walls held portraits of the supposed spirits roaming the corridors late at night. A favourite with the visitors was the aged rope noose hanging from 'the execution beam,' from when the building operated as a Court of Law and the unfortunate souls put to death. They weren't to know it was a B and Q purchase Stuart made when he took over the pub license. He played the role of custodian well, reciting the history of the pub and the surrounding areas like a museum curator, but it was his wife Christine who really sold the experience, leading those weekly midnight tours of the nearby graveyard dressed like a seventeenth century maid. Between them, they shamelessly played on the pub's history, and in doing so made a pretty decent profit when so many others had been forced to close their doors in recent years. After all, they were keeping a local pub alive and gave something the villagers could continue to enjoy. So what was a little white lie, or a bunch, if it meant being able to keep the door open, the fire burning, and the bar pumps full? Another of their 'centuries-old traditions' was the 'demon tankard,' a steel cup they filled every night with ale, leaving it out on the doorstep to appease the Devil himself. Locals and tourists loved it, especially when they were told on retrieval of the cup, it was miraculously empty. Drank by the evil one himself, and not thrown into the bushes as any skeptic would have you think.

    Stuart lowered the tanker down to the flagstone doorstep, tipping the top two inches of the cheapest beer he served onto the cold floor as he did, and pushed it close to the corner so anyone leaving the premises wouldn't kick it over. He made a sign of the cross, starting with a touch to the forehead like any good catholic would. All part of the act, of course. Truth was, the only time he ever went to church these days was for a funeral. He checked back over his shoulder, peeking through the glass of the foyer door. Christine was serving at the bar, two people waiting. Perfect time for a sneaky ciggy. The nights were drawing in now, cooling far more than they did a couple of weeks ago. He stood alone, looking back to the pub, the quiet broken only by the sounds of the wind whipping up around him. The warm yellow hue of the pub sign glowed in an otherwise black landscape. Taking a seat at one of the picnic benches out front, he dragged in a pull of his cigarette, the red ember glowing brighter as he sucked in. Each one was to be savoured these days. Christine ragged his arse about it big time ever since Eric, one of their most loyal regulars, died last year from the big C. Otherwise, life was good for Stuart at the moment. He was relatively healthy for a fifty-five-year-old with a wonderful wife, even if she nagged from time to time, and a steady business that was never a dull moment. He couldn't ask for more.

Taking a last pull on the cigarette, he stubbed it out on the side of the pine table, flicking the butt away and exhaling a cloud of white smoke that swirled and danced in the breeze before taking off into the sky above him. Rising from the seat, something caught his eye. In the gloom of the lane leading to the pub, there was movement from the shadows, getting brighter, coming towards him. A shuffling sound, a dragging noise of gravel underfoot. Stuart narrowed his eyes to focus, attempting to identify the oncoming figure, flashes of white and red highlighted by the moonlight. The noise continued, and finally, as the figure came into view, fully illuminated by the car park lighting, he saw a lone girl. A child, ambling sporadically forwards ready to collapse any moment, her bare feet and knees dirty and scraped with sores. She shivered profusely, her hands wrapped around her body, a blank look of deep shock moulded onto her pretty little face. Her once white lace dress was torn, blackened and scorched and smoldering in places, and for a moment, Stuart thought it was her long red hair that set fire to them. He ran to the foyer door, opening it enough for the sound to get in. The busy noise of pub life came out to greet him, but he shouted over it.

'Christine!' he screamed, before turning back to face the child coming towards him.

His wife came straight away, the fear and panic in his voice alarming enough for her to drop whatever she had been doing. 'What the hell are you shouting for? I nearly dropped a full pint...' Her mouth fell open as she took in the young girl. She stole a glance to her husband, who returned the look. 'Stu, go get the fleece blanket behind the bar, bottom shelf,' she whispered, doing her best not to startle the girl into fleeing. 'And call the police.' He did as requested, darting in through the door and out of sight. Lowering herself to the girl's eyeline, Christine inched closer. 'Hi there,' she said, a soft tone to her voice. 'Are you ok? Are you hurt?'

The girl's eyes stayed rooted downwards, her long red hair falling over her face, hiding the majority of it. Every so often, her head twitched off to her left shoulder. She gripped something in one hand, a gold metallic object, clamping her thin fingers so tight around it they looked ready to break. Her arms trembled uncontrollably, setting off the rest of her body into fits of unnerving quakes. Stopping a few feet in front of Christine, her skinny and bloodied bare legs looked ready to buckle at any moment. The landlady resisted the urge to grab her and pull her in straight away. 'You're safe now, little bird,' she said. 'No one can hurt you now.' She reached for her hands to see what she was holding, but the little girl snatched back defensively. The bustle of noise returned, with Stuart racing out through the door, blanket under arm, phone to his ear. He slowed his approach as he met his wife, who took the blanket and opened it out. Creeping forward, she held it out as though attempting to save a spooked wild animal, holding her breath as she eased it around the girl's shoulders. She knelt in front of her, lowering her head again to try and catch the girl's eye.

'Umm, she's about six or seven,' Stuart said into his phone. 'No, she's alone. I think she'll need an ambulance, too. Send someone straight away. Yeah that's it, The St. Michael's Inn.'

'You ok, honey?' Christine said as she tucked the blanket around the front of the girl. She looked to her feet, covered in dirt and bruises and dried blood. 'Where have you been?' The girl didn't respond, just continued to stare vacant, low and away.

'I'm not sure,' Stuart said to the operator. 'Just a sec.' He looked down to the girl. 'What's your name, little one?'

Christine looked to her husband. 'Don't you recognise her?' She rose from her knees to a crouch position, pulling the girl in close to her and rubbing her hand up and down her arm for warmth. 'She's the little girl the police have been looking for all week, the politician's daughter.' She thought a moment, then recalled the information she was searching for. She looked deep into the girl's eyes, hoping it would light something behind them. The blank expression remained. 'Her name is Elinor. Elinor Morrison.'

# Chapter 30

Eddie held his head in his hands as he sat in the quiet corridor. The faint tones of life support monitors through the double doors to the ward his only company. Squeezing his eyes tight, he saw Gwen's face, blank of expression and soaked with blood. Her eyes, lifeless and fogged over, the spark behind them extinguished forever. Her mouth lay slack, hanging open in a silent cry for help. Lips dried out and cold as the early signs of deterioration set in.

But then, something different, movement from her jaw and chin as they worked to form the words. Her lips and tongue became animated as they shaped the syllables, slow and deliberate, a whisper, all she could manage with her last breath. 'Listen to her, Eddie. She will help you find the truth.'

The woman in the black cloak approached and sat next to him, her heels clacking across the cold hospital floor. The pang of guilt came as he took in her beauty, transforming his grief and pain into a rising tide of anger.

But then, something different.

'Who are you?' he spat in demand of an answer.

Undeterred by the outburst, the woman grinned, pulling loose strands of jet black hair behind her ear. 'You already know the answer, Mr. Venter, but you still won't accept it. Even after all I have shown you already.' Eddie turned his body to hers, and as before, she grabbed his face with those sharp painted nails. 'The girl will show you. She will help you find the truth,' she hissed through gritted teeth, the words dripping with venom as they fell from her tongue.

'What truth? What will she show me?' Eddie begged with desperation. She turned his head away, her lips coming an inch from his ear. The hairs on his neck stood to attention as a shiver snaked its way up his spine.

'The truth about the crash, Mr. Venter. Why your wife is dead.'

The photo frame dropping from his hands to the floor woke him. It took a moment to come to his senses, deducing he was back to reality, alone in his dark and dingy flat. The television played some black and white movie, illuminating the vodka bottle and the foil wrapper of Fluoxetine on the coffee table. They only ever came out for special occasions, when his depression sank so low no amount of alcohol could let him forget. Since his first visit to the crime scene at the mountain earlier in the week, Gwen had taken up more and more of his conscious thoughts, that only escalated following his investigation at the farm. Every time he closed his eyes, he saw her. Those beautiful almond eyes once full of love and passion, he would stare into and attempt to read for hours on end, now only remembered clouded and empty, stolen by death. Plagued with that lasting image for so long, he was losing grasp of how they had looked before. The photo could only do so much. Was this what people meant when they said time heals a broken heart? Or was it the case of time helps you forget? If that was the truth of it, fuck that. He couldn't, *wouldn't,* allow it. With his memory of his wife fading, he knew who was at fault. The other woman invading his thoughts, his visions and his dreams. She was taking over his mind, picking at the last threads of his sanity. Last night it had been unbearable, to the point he'd made another failed visit to the Blue Pool, and returned to the flat drunk and muddied and desperate for peace. Four of the powerful tablets and a mouthful of vodka had, at least, been enough to knock him out for a short while, but it proved brief respite. He had dreamed of them again, both his wife and the other woman, and this time, it was different.

They had both spoken to him.

Picking up the photo, he laid it back on his lap. Gwen's face stared up at him as he kissed at her cheek. They were so happy back then, young and carefree and living for the moment. Now look at him, full of confusion and anger and desperation. He ran a finger down her face, but it was the other voice echoing in his head.

*The girl will show you. She will help you find the truth.*

Eying the box of Fluoxetine, he contemplated pressing out the last four tablets from the foil wrapper. Picking up the remote, he switched off the TV, allowing the room to drown in darkness. The pain living between his eyes momentarily lifted as he pinched his fingers at the bridge of his nose. The relief was short-lived, as it returned when he pulled them away. He took a swig of the first bottle that came to hand from the table. The burn of the vodka warmed his throat and settled his aching stomach.

A violent buzzing sound startled him, his mobile phone coming to life as it vibrated on the coffee table. Pushing a carton aside, he picked it up, the clock on the screen reading a quarter after two. A text message alerted on the screen.

*They've found her. She's alive.*

The vodka threatened to resurface as he read it again. The girl was alive. Her mother was right. And he was wrong.

Eddie hit the green button and waited. The phone rang twice before she answered.

'Hey Eddie,' was all Price offered.

'Where did they find her?'

'At some pub, over Abergavenny. The landlord called it in. She's in shock, but she's not hurt. A few scratches and bruises, and some signs of dehydration but otherwise, she's ok. The doctors say there's no sign of physical abuse, thank God, but she's being kept in for a couple of days. I'm here

# THE ESCORT TO THE GRAVE

with Hibbard and thought you'd want to know straight away.'

'Where has she been, Price?'

'We don't know. She's not talking, hasn't said a word since they found her. Not even to her parents. From what the landlord has told us, we think she's somehow escaped from wherever she was held and wandered down from the Black Mountains.'

The Black Mountains. Was it a coincidence? Or something more? During his countless hours at the library, Joyce had stuck many books under his nose surrounding the myths and legends of Wales, including the Black Mountains. One tale in particular had stood out of the Skirrid Fawr, an individual elevation within the range known locally as the 'Holy Mountain.' The legend told of the dramatic landslide at its north end caused by an earthquake, or possibly a lightning strike at the moment of Jesus Christ's crucifixion. A load of crap, of course, but there were details that piqued his interest, in particular, the chapel built there by the Roman Catholics as a monument to the significant event. St. Michael's Chapel it had been called. The building no longer stood at the site, having long been reduced to a handful of stones marking the outline of the foundations. It was the fable surrounding the chapel's demise interesting him the most, supposedly burned down and demolished hundreds of years ago by local villagers, following accounts of sacrificial ceremonies carried out by the resident Catholic priests.

'Are there teams out combing the mountains?' Eddie asked.

'There's a team out searching local to the pub, but they'll be expanding through the mountains at first light.'

'Tell them to check at the Skirrid Fawr summit, at the ruins of St. Michael's Chapel.'

'Why there Eddie?' Price asked. There was a tone of frustration in her voice. 'What do you know of it?'

'Something from my research at the library. It's probably nothing. It's just a ruin. But they should check there, just in case.'

'Why didn't you mention it before?'

'There's hundreds of stories of places around Wales like that.'

'I'll pass the information on,' Price said. 'Look, I need to go now, but can I offer some advice?' She didn't wait for an answer. 'Keep your head down for a bit. The press will be all over this in the morning, and you can imagine what Morrison is like already.'

'I need to speak to her, Price.'

'Who? The girl? Did you hear what I just said?' she spat. 'Keep away, for everyone's sake. Why do you think the Morrisons would let you anywhere near her, anyway? Didn't you tell Sarah Morrison you thought she was dead? For Christ's sake, Eddie, think about it. Morrison will want someone's scalp for this. It'll probably be Enfield's. If you were anything of a friend to him, stay away from the girl and hope it blows over.'

'I'm sorry Price,' Eddie said. 'For everything.'

Price's voice softened again. 'I almost believed it, you know. When you said she was dead. I almost believed *you*.'

'I'm sorry,' was all Eddie could offer again.

'I'd better get back,' Price said. 'I'll pass on your message about the chapel. Did you say it was St. Michael's?'

'Yeah, on the Skirrid Fawr.'

'That was the name of the pub she turned up at. The St. Michael's Inn. Probably named after the place. Look after yourself Eddie.'

'You too Price.'

The call ended, pitching the room back to darkness. Eddie's head hit the back of the settee, the cold leather soothing at his neck. He should have felt relief. The girl was alive and unhurt. Traumatised, by all accounts, but physically unharmed. It could have ended so much worse. He rubbed furiously at his face with the palm of his hand, an attempt to wake himself up enough to function. His head hurt from the million thoughts running through it.

Something wasn't right. Since Enfield pulled him onto the case to find her, he had somehow misunderstood the clues. His curse, for so long reliable in its consistency, appeared to be transforming into something he couldn't interpret. It gave him an overwhelming feeling this wasn't the end. Not by a long shot. It would continue to get worse, continue to goad him, continue to use him.

Pulling up his phonebook, Eddie hit the green button again. It rang for an age, and he was about to give up, when a tired, solemn voice answered.

'You've heard?' Peter said.

'I don't know what to say, Pete,' Eddie replied. 'I don't know what to make of it all.'

'There's nothing to make anything of, Eddie. You were wrong. We were wrong.'

'What happens now?' Eddie asked.

'You know the score, Eddie. We didn't find her, and we sure as hell haven't caught the offenders. Morrison has started raising hell already. As bad as it sounds, we're lucky the team has fallen on something bigger, so the whole department won't get dragged through the mud. But as far as this goes, the Chief Constable will need a scapegoat...'

'... and you're it,' Eddie finished.

'I had to make the call and wake ACC Bentley earlier. He's consulting with the Chief and will call me in tomorrow morning. They'll likely demand I take my retirement.'

'I'm sorry Pete. I don't know how this happened.'

'It's my fault, Ed. You told me not to involve you, but I didn't listen. I'm just thankful the girl's alive. All this talk about losing jobs and slinging mud, and we've forgotten the important part. She's safe. She's back with her family. I wouldn't change a thing if it meant a different outcome.'

'Is Jane OK?'

'I haven't told her yet. She's asleep in the house. I'll wait till the morning. I doubt I'll get any myself. My phone's been red hot since they found her. I'm in the annex writing my intention letter.'

'Pete. I'm sorry.'

'Me too Ed, me too. But hey, we've all got to retire sometime, right?'

Ending the call, Eddie picked up the vodka and blister pack, popping the last four tablets out and downing them in one swallow. There was nothing he could do now, except try to sleep through until sunrise and wake with a clear head, and begin working out what it all meant.

Closing his eyes, he recalled the first time he realised what was happening to him. The head doctors had told him he had experienced 'bereavement hallucinations' during the crash, a phenomenon where a loved one has phantom perceptions of a partner dying. They usually existed as a dull pain, or even hearing the deceased call for help, but they couldn't explain how he had managed to find the scene of the accident. The doctors made a collective opinion it was indeed unexplainable, but would categorically be a one-off experience. They were wrong. For weeks, terrible visions, smells, and sounds haunted him, but not from the crash. Sights that made him want to dig his eyes out in protest. Desperate cries and screams and wails of terror and pain and torture, but not of people he knew and loved. Strangers filled his head with the most unimaginable horrors. Positive he was losing his mind, he turned to alcohol to keep it at bay, but they persisted. Until the realisation of what it all meant, he lashed out, the mix of alcohol and frustration and grief taken out on others. It started with him losing his job, just a month after the crash, getting drunk and assaulting the arresting officers. Smashing the windscreen of their squad car as they turned up didn't help, and in a fit of rage as they attempted to restrain him, he had punched out, breaking one of the officer's jaw. The man received a lengthy layoff and a healthy payout for his troubles. Eddie saw a couple of hundred hours of community service, an order to attend a psychological assessment followed by subsequent meetings, and a middle finger from the constabulary.

The drinking continued, as did the grieving. At first, he believed the doctor's explanations of his 'hallucinations', accepting his mind as broken and needing repair. But then, they had led him to his first body, that man in his garage. The penny dropped, and he realised what was happening to him. A curse, some sick, twisted gift plaguing him ever since. He had started investigating shortly afterwards, a weak attempt to find purpose, but no matter how hard he tried, however many times it happened, he could never find the living. He only ever found the dead. Some gift.

As the tablets and alcohol took effect, and he drifted back into a deep sleep, the mystery woman's words sounded again.

The girl will show you. She will help you find the truth.

The girl was safe. Once she willingly gave up information on her whereabouts, they may even find the kidnappers, and find out why they took her. If they didn't, it would get chalked up they panicked, bottled it, let the girl go to avoid getting caught. She was young enough to forget. She could recover, bury the experience in the back of her mind and continue on with her life. But something, deep down, told him things would never be the same for her again.

Or for him.

# Chapter 31

## Monday

Sarah Morrison pulled the pink unicorn patterned curtains to one side, giving her a better view out to the courtyard. At the gates, the uniform police officer on guard duty was leaning in towards the passenger side window of the saloon car pulled up to them. Stepping back, he made a waving gesture towards the house, where a second officer pressed a remote to open the gates. The car moved on, parking up to the side of the garage, next to the family Range Rover. Two women stepped from the vehicle Sarah couldn't help think looked like some sort of comedy duo. The first one she recognised from her initial interview following the kidnapping, and she had also turned up at the hospital after they found Ellie. She was a pretty little thing, dressed in a smart trouser and suit jacket combo, her dark hair slicked back into a formal bun that looked very professional. Her companion, a stark contrast she hadn't met before, looked middle-aged, a robust woman that appeared at least six feet, wearing a tartan skirt suit three sizes too small. Every second step she pulled on the bottom of the skirt hem as her heels struggled to find purchase on the gravel surface. The younger one caught under her arm like a makeshift crutch, helping her across the courtyard and out of sight, the porch roof hiding them as they made their way to the entrance.

The doorbell buzzed as Sarah turned to the bed, a worried frown etched on her face. Perfectly still above the freshly made covers, staring to the ceiling with an unreadable expression, youngest daughter Ellie lay in her favourite butterfly pyjamas. Her left hand wrapped tight around the shaft of the large ornate key they had found her with. Futile attempts had been made to take the item from her since her reappearance, each occasion resulting in the child breaking into a full meltdown. She had drawn blood scratching the police officer who tried late Thursday night, and screamed the house down yesterday when Sarah had tried when stripping her off for a bath. It was the only sound to have come from the girl in the last forty-eight hours, a sound that sent Sarah sprawling across the bathroom floor in fear and despair. As well as evidence in her kidnapping, the key had become her new comfort blanket, and Detective Superintendent Enfield had permitted it could stay with her if it meant she remained calm and didn't hurt herself. Because of the political clout of her father and the current hold he had over the department, further riling the family by confiscating the key with force would undoubtedly result in even more bad press for them, and so Enfield had cowered.

Sitting at the edge of the bed, she eyed what she could see of the key, the intricate detailed symbol on the head staring back at her. During her interview at the hospital, she had told the police she had no idea what it could be for. She didn't know why. Any sensible person would have confessed straight away in hope it would reveal the truth. But something made her hold back, a maternal feeling, like she was protecting her daughter under the watchful eye of her very own mother. The truth was, she didn't really know, not yet anyway. Memories came back of that night the box was delivered to her doorstep, her mother's note to her unborn granddaughter. Had she made the right decision not telling anyone yet, her husband included? Yes. The box was for Ellie, and she should open it without prying eyes from strangers. But it may hold a clue as to her whereabouts this past week. The conflicting thoughts constantly scratched at her, a niggling dull throb refusing to go away.

Taking Ellie's free hand, Sarah leaned over her in attempt to make eye contact. Ellie continued to stare through her. There was a quick rap at the door. Waiting for an answer before opening, Ana stood at the threshold, keeping a respectful distance, aware of Sarah's need to rebuild the mother-daughter bond.

'The police officers are here, Mrs. Morrison. Have you decided where you will welcome them?'

Sarah kept her eyes on her daughter. 'Ellie honey, some nice people would like to speak to you to see how you're doing. Come on downstairs for a minute, ok? Ana will make you a nice glass of milk and we'll go speak to the nice ladies.' She nodded to Ana, 'we'll come down to the living room.'

Ana made off, leaving the door open. Sarah gently pulled at Ellie's hand, using her other to move her legs sideways off the bed. The little girl responded as she lifted into a seated position, allowing her mother to cover her bruised feet with her fluffy slippers. Leading her out of the room, Sarah looked back to the end of the landing to see eldest daughter Jenny, sat crouched in a ball at the foot of the second floor staircase, eyes pained from the tears long dried there. On seeing them exit the bedroom, Bandit rose from his curled position at Jenny's feet, taking off up the stairs with his tail between his legs, letting out a solemn whimper as he went. Jenny watched them head for the stairs to the ground floor, her mother leading the way as Ellie shuffled behind, head hanging low and eyes down at her feet.

Entering the living room, the two women stood to greet them, the short one introducing herself again as DC Lauren Price. She had a kind smile, a caring one Sarah warmed to. Ellie paid no attention, her eyes rooted to the floor ahead. The tall woman with frizzy brown hair and loud clothing spoke with a well-to-do voice clearly put on, as she introduced herself as June Whitman, the assigned family liaison officer. Sitting back in her armchair, she tugged

# THE ESCORT TO THE GRAVE

pointlessly at her skirt, attempting to cover her knees with nowhere near enough fabric. An A4 notepad spared her blushes as she prepared to take notes.

'Is your husband joining us, Mrs. Morrison?' Price asked.

'He's gone back to work. It's a busy time.' Sarah replied, sighing as the words came out.

'Hello Elinor,' Price said as she leaned lower to catch her eye. 'My name is Lauren. Those are beautiful pyjamas you have on there. Are butterflies your favourite?' She gave her a chance to respond, but her eyes continued to pick out a spot on the floor.

Sarah walked Ellie over to the larger settee, gently lowering her down to the seat and tucking the red hair hiding her face behind her ears, revealing her pale, blank face. Leaning in front of her, she spoke softly, her voice wavering with emotion. 'Ellie baby, the nice lady just wants to know who took you from the mountain. If you can help her, then they might stop her from doing it again. Can you do that?'

Ellie's face gave nothing. Sarah's head lowered in defeat. She turned and sat next to her, the tiredness and sorrow etched into deep lines on her face. Each woman took turns trying to get through. They made jokes, told stories, asked hard questions about the last week, all desperate attempts to invoke a reaction. Price showed Ellie a photo of the women, hoping for something. Anything would do, a smirk, a sneer, a look. The only movement that came from her was to tighten her grip on the key when Price asked what it was for. At least she could tell she was listening. She tried once more.

'Elinor, after you turned up at the pub and those nice people called us, some of our officers searched the mountains to find out where you had been. To try to find who took you from Pen-y-fan. They came across something interesting on the Skirrid Fawr mountain, close to where you showed up. Does the name ring a bell, Elinor? How about St. Michael's chapel? Do you know it?'

A flick of the eyes. Not much, but enough.

'Elinor? Is that where the woman took you? What did they do with you there?'

Sarah interrupted. 'What did they find, detective?'

'Candles, Mrs. Morrison. Hundreds and hundreds of them. The site is a ruin, only a handful of stones and rubble, but someone had been there recently. It looks like they were carrying out a service of some kind.'

'What... what kind of service?' Sarah stammered.

'We don't know.' Price turned back to Ellie, dropping to her eye line once more. 'Elinor? Is that why you had a lovely lace dress on when the nice people found you? Have you been to the place with all the candles? What did you do there, Elinor?'

Ellie's eyes stayed on the floor, face neutral of expression. Price had lost her again. She turned back to Sarah. 'Forensics tested everything collected from there over the weekend, but nothing has come up. No prints, no clues. We still haven't been able to identify the woman who took her, or the woman who passed away at Pen-y-fan, but we won't give up Mrs. Morrison. I promise.'

All three women stood at that, calling time on the meeting. June recommended a brilliant child psychologist, leaving her details for Sarah to muse over, and Price left her own business card as Ana showed them to the door.

For what felt like ten minutes, Sarah sat beside Ellie, the ticking of the mantel clock putting her in a daze matching her daughters. She had hoped with patience Ellie would break first, but it was a stand-off she couldn't win. And so, she decided, it was time. With Jenny hiding upstairs and David back working in London, Sarah needed to reconnect with her youngest daughter. Rising from the settee, Sarah looked back to her daughter, at the skinny, empty shell of what only a week ago was a bubbly, energetic bottle of pop.

What had happened since then? Was she committing the mother of all sins by not sharing this with the police straight away? She could always tell them afterwards if the box revealed anything sinister, and they would understand when they saw her mother's note. Almost seven years had passed Sarah had kept the box a secret, and when her daughter had been returned, that moment when she had hugged her and pulled her in tight and thanked the lord for keeping her safe, that moment when she saw the key, the moment of realisation, she knew deep in her heart she had never been at risk. Her mother, the wonderful woman she adored and missed every day, who never got to meet her second granddaughter, had looked after her this last week, keeping her from harm.

Oblivious to her mother's movements, Ellie continued to stare at the rug as Sarah took to the stairs. She moved fast, taking the flight two treads at a time. At the bottom of the landing, Jenny's head raised from her knees at the oncoming rush of noise, a confused look at her mother's urgency. Sarah darted into the spare room, coming out moments later, straining under the weight of a package wrapped in a flowery patterned duvet cover. She leaned back to counterbalance the obviously heavy parcel. Puffing with effort, she headed back down the stairs to the living room, followed at a distance by a curious Jenny in tow. Pausing at the bottom tread, Jenny sat gawping as her mother dropped the package down on the coffee table in front of Ellie with a softened thud. Purposely working her way around to the back of the table, she unfolded each flap of material in hope it struck a reaction from her daughter. As the last corner dropped to reveal the box, Ellie's head turned across and up, the deep red, black and gold colours of the beautiful lid sparking her to life. Looking to the stairs, Sarah's face lit up. Jenny stood at the bottom now, her neck craning in attempt to get a better view, all the while keeping a nervous distance in case of an outburst.

When Sarah looked back, Ellie's fingers were already tracing the lid, caressing the well-polished inlay details. A tear fell down Sarah's cheek as she watched her daughter run a line around that familiar symbol at the centre. Her fingers moved to the lock, equally intricate and imposing, her tiny forefinger feeling out the shape of the hole. Pulling the note from her pocket, Sarah read it to herself in silence, something she had done a thousand times before, then offered it out to her daughter with a shaky hand. Ellie took it, a smile threatening to break out as she read it. Her thumb rubbed across the top of the paper as her cheeks filled with colour. Mirroring the young girl, Sarah broke into her own smile as she looked back at Jenny. It was contagious, Jenny following suit as she eased into the living room.

'I don't know how, but your Nana left this for you, baby,' Sarah said, her eyes full to the brim. She came around the table to kneel next to her. 'She knew everything about you before we even did.' Reaching out for Ellie's cheek, she stroked it gently. 'I love you so much, baby. I'm sorry I let that woman take you.' Pulling her into a hug, her one arm fell out in gesture to her eldest. Dropping to her knees the other side of Ellie, Jenny began sobbing as she joined the embrace. Ellie's arms stayed down at her side, allowing the hug to happen, never really joining in, her eyes stuck firmly on the box. Eventually, the reunion broke, both Sarah and Jenny wiping their faces as they leaned away. Ellie's eyes went to the key as she held it in two hands, then reached out to insert it into the lock. It fit perfectly, the long shank disappearing until only the head was visible. Jenny jumped at the loud click from the case as Ellie turned the key, and Sarah sucked in an audible breath. Fighting the almost seven-year curiosity, she allowed Ellie to take the lead, as the little girl stood to lift the lid up and over the back. All three peered in at the red, plump velvet cushions keeping the contents in place. A stale, musky scent filled the air, smelling of age. Staring back at them, tucked in position, its deep brown leather border carved and stamped with hundreds of tiny interlaced leaf shapes, was a large book. It was around A3 in size, the thick robust binding protecting the spine, giving it an air of strength and importance. Little wonder the case was so heavy. Sarah dipped her fingers into the sides, the velvet cushions sinking to allow purchase. She lifted the book from the case, revealing a selection of deep red and black chalks and charcoals hidden beneath. Jenny pulled the box away, giving her mother room to lower the heavy book in its spot. The book was untitled, the front cover or spine un-named, just loop after loop of delicately carved leather vines and leaves, all working toward the tree at the centre that matched it's protective case, and the symbol at the heart of it. A Triquetra. Ellie's eyes widened as she touched at the symbol, then moved to the right side to pull at the front cover. As the heavy leather creaked open, Ellie's face lit up with excitement, eyebrows raised and teeth sneaking through the wide, thin smile.

Sarah and Jenny shared a look of confusion.

# Chapter 32

Eddie had spent the majority of the long weekend trawling through endless books and manuscripts at the library. Joyce dipped in and out when she could, fetching documents from the archive room in between manning the main desk downstairs. She had really come through this last week, pulling in favours from her contacts at the National Museum of Wales, who worked overtime to find as much information from their extensive archives on the subjects she gave them as possible. Dangling the carrot they were assisting a criminal investigation and able to channel their inner Robert Langdon, had excited the scholars to no end. Joyce even found a university professor working in Carmarthen able to translate the earliest of the Brythonic language scriptures they had found that the Welsh language had grown from.

Through the ages, the symbol had been heavily worshipped, the Silures tribes of South East Wales decorating weapons to fight off the Romans, through to modern day artwork being popularly recognisable as 'Celtic knots.' Steeped in history and surprisingly not confined to the Celtic nations, many regions through Europe and Asia, from Germany to Japan, adopted the symbol in some form or another. What he found, however, was wherever it was used, a common theme appeared adopted. It symbolised the celebration of life-death-rebirth or, alternatively, body-mind-spirit. Yet as deep as his research sent him into histories around the world, it was the Celts drawing his attention the most, not just because of its familiarity, but also because of its coincidences to his recent experiences.

# THE ESCORT TO THE GRAVE

He kept referencing back to the Morrigan, or 'the three Morrigna,' where several mythical stories through the ages of Irish folklore labelled them as a trio of sisters responsible for escorting the souls of dead soldiers to the next place. Other fables told the Morrigan as the goddess of fate, foretelling of death. The more he delved into the myths through the centuries, the more confusing and contradictory it appeared. Irish tales remoulded, crossing the sea into Scottish Gaelic, in turn transforming and travelling south to become Welsh legends. He trawled the archives, pulling manuscripts telling ancient tales of Irish Banshees, Scottish Bean-nighes and Welsh Cyhyraeths. He pictured families sitting around the winter fire as the elders told ghost stories of Psychopomps and deities, passing down the fables to the younger generations who cast their own spin on them to scare the wits from their own children and grandchildren years later. Some documents he had to pass over, written in ancient Scottish and Irish Gaelic dialect he would have to get additional help trying to translate.

One interpretation caught his eye in particular, an ancient-looking document of scrolled parchment in early Welsh. Joyce had done her best to write it down in English for him to understand, the translation not making sense in parts due to the sentence structures of the Celtic language. The story of the Morrigan retold as the three sisters representing the Celtic lands. They spoke of life, death and rebirth, visiting those ready to depart to the Otherworld. The Celtic nations of Ireland, Scotland and Wales. There were other smaller areas documented, Cornwall, Brittany, and the Isle of Man also teeming with their own branches of Celtic history. Yet it was this one manuscript calling out to him. It spoke of a sister watching over each nation, roaming the lands in search of souls to harvest and send on to the next place. Extracts told of their duties as the Escorts to the grave, their work in choosing and preparing the journey to the afterlife.

*And the Morrigan walked the lands, harvesting the souls for the Otherworld. And Arawn called to each sister, 'souls of the damned belong to me, and will not be pardoned. And so I call you to escort them through purgatory, where they must lay at my feet in death.'*

More extracts stood out. *'And the sister lay at the sacred place. And Arawn called to her, my child, your time to rest has come. Take my hand and I will lead you to eternity, for another must take your place.'*

Many times, his eyes stung as the words on the pages blurred into one big mess, but he plowed on. At some point Joyce found him slumped in his chair, snoring away, and sent him on his way with a peck on the cheek and orders to get some rest. Eddie didn't put up a fight on account he had planned to visit Gwen.

Driving the short journey back to his flat, he dumped his car in the rear lane behind the Miner's and after purchasing a bottle of Jim Beam, he walked the short distance to Pant cemetery. Gwen wouldn't approve of the drinking, but then, she wouldn't exactly be over the moon with his wallowing in self-pity either. Trundling his way up the steep path to her resting place, he cracked the top from the bottle and pulled a first swig. He took in the mix of well-maintained and regularly visited plots, with their blooming bunches of multi-coloured summer flowers, to the cold, desolate graves of the occupants long forgotten. Some still adorned the single plastic roses in their tin flower vases the council had long ago added, the faded sun damaged petals adding to the misery of the untended plots. Here and there, red and white hazard tape surrounded headstones considered at risk of collapse from the years of harsh weather on a mountainside graveyard.

Arriving at Gwen's plot, Eddie slumped on the hard grass in front of the headstone. Sunlight peeked through the cloud laden sky, illuminating the black marble face of the stone, the shadows filling the deep carved, gold painted

# THE ESCORT TO THE GRAVE

letters giving them an additional three dimensional appearance.

Gwenno Catherine Venter
Born 19th July 1982
Died 6<sup>th</sup> September 2012
'Till we meet again.'

Eddie turned and lay back, swallowing a harsh glug before allowing his head to drop and rest at the foot of the headstone. He checked his watch. Half four. Plenty of time before he got kicked out. Closing his eyes, he floated away to his favourite moments.

The occasions. The Christmas market in Manchester, where they ate Brockwurst and drank mulled wine and laughed so hard at Eddie's Bambi impressions on the ice rink. The trip to Rome where Gwen dragged him around every tourist attraction the city offered, and after three exhausting days of following her like a lost puppy, he had gone down on one knee to ask her to share her life with him.

The little things. The alternating cinema picks, hers romance, his sci-fi, and the hours of ribbing they would give each other following so many terrible choices. The cute purring sound she made as she slept, that only seemed to happen lying on her right side as she faced him, and how he would watch her until she woke before telling a little white lie she hadn't made a sound. Her tone deaf singing in the shower. The love hearts she doodled on slips of paper and sneaked into his packed lunch. Small pieces of memories that always cut the most, yet always brought the biggest smiles.

The sound of shouting woke him. He lifted his head from the gravestone in time to see a whining, yellow, Labrador dog belting past him up the path, dragging its empty lead behind where it's human should be. Thirty seconds later, a middle-aged blonde woman followed, huffing desperately as she went. She stopped at Eddie's level, bending over with hands on knees, wrinkling her nose at him as she struggled to suck in some air. 'Cujo!' she shouted, before waddling off up the path a little further.

Eddie checked his watch. Five forty-five. Stumbling to his feet he picked up the half full bottle, taking another pull as two men dressed in orange walked up the path towards him, council workers clearing the cemetery ready to lock up, shaking their heads and rolling their eyes and nudging elbows at the familiar sight.

'We're locking up soon, Eddie,' one of them said. 'Make your way out please fella.'

He lumbered down the hill towards the exit, his feet dragging as he went. Walking past the flat bed council van, he threw the empty bottle into the open top bin at the entrance overflowing with dead flowers, fresh cuttings and plastic wrappers. Walking through the main gates, he was oblivious to the figure through the blur of headstones, sitting at one of many tribute benches littered around the cemetery, watching him as he left. She sat with one arm draped over the back of the bench, her two wolfhounds taking turns to receive strokes under their muzzles from their master. From the tree above, a lone crow landed on the armrest of the bench next to her, quizzically tilting its head at the woman with the long hair matching its own silky black coat. She held out a hand. The bird accepted the invite, hopping to her pointed finger with grace.

Through the entrance, Eddie turned back toward the village, ready to hit the nearest pub and find more solace at the bottom of a glass. The hatred he felt for his own self-pity had countless times taken him to the thought of suicide, and yet his weakness had won over on each occasion, forcing him to continue on his path of self-destruction. Maybe this was the purgatory he had read about earlier at the library. It was him laying at Arawn's feet, begging to be taken to Annwn, the Celtic otherworld. It was Arawn toying with him, prolonging his pain, enjoying the torture he inflicted. Stuck between not dying and not really living, perhaps the very definition of purgatory.

Similar to many working class towns in the South Wales valleys, Merthyr Tydfil and its surrounding villages were an alcoholic's dream. Every other street had a public house competing for business. Most took the attitude of 'if I don't serve them, someone else will.' Reaching the doorway to the Black Lion, Eddie shambled in, already looking a mess, knowing he would look a lot worse when he left. A man who once held such a sharp mind, an intelligence and intuition his peers looked up to, a detective the talk of the force for all the best reasons, now an empty shell of distaste few spoke of. He was the rosette winning restaurant that ten years ago flourished, that found a rat in the kitchen and now sat empty with boarded-up windows. The high school sports star destined for top flight football that snapped a knee and now taught junior school students. He was a million what-could-have-beens ending up in the gutter as nothing more than a first class fuck-up.

But when he drank, filling his belly with warmth and swirling his mind with the intoxication, none of that mattered. It was the moment that counted, everything else shut out and ignored. He even tried to forget Gwen in those moments, but she was stuck there, haunting his sleep and daydreams alike. And so was the other woman.

Demanding he learn the truth.

# Chapter 33

## Tuesday

Hands trembling, Malcolm Glover completed the online boat hire and powered down his laptop. Letting out a sigh that could wake a sleeping dog, he looked to the wall plaque taking pride of place above his office desk, the black interlaced symbol etched into a gold plate on its mahogany mount. He had been told they had used a different symbol back in the day, before the Grove Druids separated and rebranded with this other Celtic symbol as its emblem, the Triquetra.

Wiping a tear with the back of his hand, he rose from his chair, uncertain his legs could support him through the morning. Both career and personal life had been good to Malcolm Glover in his fifty-nine years, although he would never admit it was anything but hard work. As the son of a lifelong miner, he had followed his father's advice, keeping firmly away from the pits. He had been lucky, his parents having backed his plans to do so much better in the long term, rather than pressure him into finding work as early as possible. His friends had all taken the literal plunge down the mineshafts to start earning, taking home their sixty-two pounds a week and acting like weekend millionaires. From day one Malcolm had seen through the short-sightedness of it all, and so, with his father's blessing and support, studied finance at university. This turned out to be a wise decision, meeting and courting his wife Elaine while picking up the all-important qualifications that saw him earn three hundred

# THE ESCORT TO THE GRAVE

pounds a week as his friends fought at the picket lines. It was the start of a life of well-timed moves.

The 1980s were a difficult time for many people. High interest rates, taxes and inflation pinched most families through the valleys. Malcolm and his family were an exception. Stock investments, as well as savvy property and land purchases, including large portions of three separate industrial estates when the manufacturing industry was decimated, had completely exploded as the economy recovered in the latter stages of the 80s. Selling off most of his portfolio before the '91 recession, he had amassed a personal fortune to see him through the rest of his life and then some. Not bad for a man just hitting thirty, but he refused to slow down, printing money overnight as he invested in upcoming pharmaceutical and computing companies to earn him eight figures at the turn of the millennium and his fortieth birthday. After months of nagging, Elaine eventually got through, and they moved to their idyllic mansion in Brecon with their daughter to wind things back and enjoy the spoils. Personal fortune allowed the side product of boredom and laziness to creep in, the business ventures he was still involved in more like hobbies than money-making schemes. Golf and shooting filled his days with like-minded people, the rich and hardworking alike, becoming secretary, then president of both clubs keeping him almost as busy as the early days of business building and enterprise.

It was 2010 he was introduced and welcomed into the Grove Druids, elite membership earned by a select few, his fiftieth birthday marking his induction as a Bard. It was by far the best day of his life, the celebration unlike anything he had witnessed before. From then on, nothing else came close. Business became even more of a bore, as did home life. Shamelessly, he spent more and more time with the other members, arranging functions and the all-important monthly ritual ceremonies, learning the history of The

Grove as it split from the ancient Druidism in the 13th century, and then from other branches in the 14th, becoming an even more secret organisation in its transformation. It wasn't an easy educational process, considering the Grove Druids refrained from recording events on paper. Google would bring up a blank. Patience and teachings from his fellow Grovers, tales passed down through the generations of members became his way of learning as he worked through the ranking system a year at a time. As a lifelong control freak, it pulled him from his comfort zone, turning out to be a breath of fresh air he was experiencing for the first time in his adult life.

Throwing plenty of money at it, something many other members couldn't spare as much of, Malcolm took charge of renovating the hilltop temple with a much needed new roof and complete internal refurbishment. His efforts didn't go unnoticed as he quickly rose to the rank of Ovate, and eventually Druid. The generosity continued. Throughout the temple, the amazing amount of flagstones making up the flooring were lifted, reconditioned and reset, another of his endeavours. He treated the road leading into the grounds to a much needed resurfacing. Next month, he'd booked his carpenters in to start on each of the twenty arched oak doors in the building, rejuvenating them to their former glory at eight-hundred quid a pop.

Through well thought out calculations, he was on course to become Arch-druid of the South, Mid and West Wales Grove by his sixtieth birthday. The current Arch-druid, although a fine, respected man with strong connections, didn't have the money to influence as he did. There wasn't a single person he had met through his working life who didn't enjoy the little under the counter brown envelopes. Voting time would be no different. His fellow members, no matter the profession, would welcome those packed envelopes. Doctors, Judges, Police Officers: all more than willing to take the cash to sway their votes. Money talked even in the Grove Druids. It was a dream until last night, he was patiently waiting and planning to realise.

Until his visitor at the temple.

As project manager and financial secretary, Malcolm had been running through the books in the temple chamber. It was late afternoon; the sun descending behind the hills, allowing the late summer air to cool. Not that it mattered. Contrary to the old stone exterior, the temple was full of mod cons now, mostly thanks to Malcolm. The well maintained air conditioning system kept the ambient temperature at a comfortable eighteen degrees all year long.

A knock at the chamber door had startled Malcolm into dropping his pen. He was sure he had locked the entrance doors. Only a select few members held keys, but nevertheless, the accounts weren't for prying eyes, only for his as temple secretary, and the sitting Arch-druid, and he returned them to the hidden chamber safe to lock away before answering.

Sitting back at the large oak table, he called out with an air of regency. 'You may enter.'

The door pushed open, causing Malcolm to frown. A young woman stood at the doorway. Her long black hair hung straight over her shoulders, but through it he could see the gold triquetra symbol on her chest. She was breathtakingly beautiful, mid-thirties at a guess, and her hands pressing at her waist hinted a figure to die for beneath her long dark cloak. She stood leering at the doorway, her pale blue eyes fixed firmly on Malcolm's. Words stuck in his throat, his mouth attempting to free them like a fish gulping for air. The woman spoke first.

'Hello Mr. Glover,' she said. 'I wish to speak with you regarding particular dealings at the Grove.'

Malcolm sat back in his chair, his puzzling expression adding lines into an already creased face. Tugging at an earlobe, he tried to make sense of it all. 'How did you get in here?' he asked. 'I locked the main hall doors.'

'I used my key, Mr. Glover.'

Malcolm's voice became louder, sterner. 'You're not a member here. Who gave you a key? Are you a member's wife?'

Very few women were members across the whole of the Grove Druid religion. There were certainly none in the South, Mid and West Wales temples. Giving a key to an outsider was a major offence carrying grave consequences.

'Who are you?'

The woman leaned against the doorframe, raising a hand to inspect her nails. 'I am Mara,' she said nonchalantly. 'And I hold a key for *all* Grove Druid temples, Mr. Glover.'

*Holy shit.* Through the teachings, Malcolm had heard of holders of such keys. Grand druids roaming through the countries. Travellers carrying with them the secrets needing passing on. His confidence wilted as his tongue swelled in his mouth. The woman approached and rounded the table. Rising from his chair, Malcolm stumbled as he kicked it onto its back.

'H-h-how do I know you're Grove?' he said, looking backwards for means to escape around the table. The fallen chair blocked his path.

She held out her hands, turning them palm up. Running diagonally on each hand from forefinger to wrist were long healed scars. Malcolm looked to his own, the tell tale initiation marks matching hers.

'I'm here to share important news, Mr. Glover. Will you receive what I offer?' Reaching into her cloak, she pulled from it a familiar ceremonial dagger. The silver blade curved backwards, the gold handle twisting ropes of Celtic patterns and knots. With a wry smirk, the woman ran the blade across her left palm, opening the age old wounds once more. Malcolm winced as drops of blood fell to the stone floor of the silent chamber with a tap-tap-tap. Raising an eyebrow, she waited expectantly. Taking a moment to draw and hold his breath, he held out a shaky left hand. She drew

# THE ESCORT TO THE GRAVE

the blade across as Malcolm sucked back in through clenched teeth. The blade cut deep, too deep for his liking, blood pooling in his cupped hand threatening the white cuff of his shirt. Dropping the blade to the table, the woman grabbed his bloodied hand into hers, forcing them together, their warm, slippery fluids mixing as one.

She pulled him closer, his face inches from hers. He had always been faithful to Elaine through their marriage, but smelling the sweetness on her breath, he found himself desperate to kiss her. Her piercing blue eyes bore into him. He saw a finality in them, an icy sharp look sending fear and panic coursing through his body. His legs buckled, his spine folding in on itself as his body begged for support. Before he could go down, the woman locked her lips with his, her plump wet kiss sending a surge of adrenaline through his veins. Somehow, Malcolm's legs found the purchase they needed, pushing him back upright as her tongue massaged his. A wave of ecstasy washed over him, his mind flying through clouds of intense euphoria.

And then everything changed. Bliss turned to misery as his mind switched to unimaginable horror. All around him, fire rose from the ground, licking at his body, threatening to scorch his limbs. The heat singed at his fingers as he tucked his arms in, a desperate attempt to make himself smaller. Through the flames, faces peered back, pained and tortured and crying. Faces he had seen before but couldn't quite place. Faces of boys and girls, young children, begging for mercy. They called to him by name, agonised shrieks, pleading for him to help. And then he saw a girl he recognised from just three weeks ago, the one they had used in their last ceremony. Her desperate eyes bore into his, and unable to take anymore, he turned away. Realisation took over him, each face now recognisable as previous sacrifices. Their expressions shifted, no longer wincing, now wrathful, hungry smiles etched in place. The flames rose higher, engulfing the children from view, inching ever closer to him. Squeezing his body tight, he screamed desperately for escape, the hair from his arms and head burning away as his skin turned a wax texture, before erupting into huge yellow watery blisters. A last cry for mercy as his eyes dried out and his lids scorched like tissue paper. Drawing in a final breath of searing heat, his lungs shrivelled to nothing.

The flames disappeared. His knees hit the cold flagstone floor of the darkening chamber as the tears streamed down his face, a soft whimper escaping him belonging more to a small child having lost its mother. He leaned forward on all fours, searching for air, gulping greedily. Rolling into a seated position, he looked for the woman, but she was gone. Sticky, drying blood covered his hands and face where he had spread it in his terror, the open wound slowing its release as it clotted. His chest heaved as he took in the mess, fingers finding his face, checking for damage. It all felt so real. He closed his eyes and the girl's face returned, the one he saw in the flames. She spoke to him now, eyes full and woeful, pleading for him to cease the pain, stop the torture and make amends. Douse the flames. Flood them out. The woman had shown him what he had done. The pain and suffering they had caused. Those poor children. He had a chance to make amends, and there was only one way he could. Douse the flames.

A sleepless night ensued, worry over what dreams would come. He spent his morning in his office, hiding from his wife and her twenty questions, but now it was time to get moving. Lumbering into the kitchen, he found Elaine pulling her apple crumble from the oven. She always cooked it early on, both of them preferring it cold after their evening meal. She paused as he lumbered in, his bloodshot eyes and grey face giving him away. Pulling her into a tired hug against his trembling body, he held it a little too long, and her hands went to his shoulders as she pushed him back into view.

'What is it Mal? What's going on?'

# THE ESCORT TO THE GRAVE

'Just some work stuff, that's all,' he replied. 'You know I love you, don't you?'

Elaine's eyebrows dropped to an even deeper frown. 'Mal, you're scaring me.'

He let out an unconvincing chuckle as the embrace finished. 'Me saying I love you scares you? Charming.'

'Are you sure it's just work stuff?'

Malcolm's long pause told her no. He reached for his car keys from the rail hook. They jangled in time with his shaking hands. She walked towards him again, her hand meeting his forehead.

'Are you coming down with something?'

'Maybe,' he replied, trying to end the interrogation. 'I'll pick up some tablets from the pharmacy on my way home.'

'Where are you off to?' Elaine asked.

'I've got some stuff to take care of for the club. I'll be home later.' He kissed her then, not the usual peck he gave on his way out, but a lingering kiss full of love and emotion. He held her gaze for a long moment, and then walked away, shoulders slumped from the tremendous weight holding them down. Pausing at the door, he turned back, managing a shallow smile to his loyal wife, then turned and left.

Following a purchase at the local builder's merchants, Malcolm made his way to Llangorse Lake, just a fifteen minute drive from their Breconshire home. He pulled his Aston Martin into the boat hire car park and killed the engine. A stiff breeze was up this morning, the lake waters looking cold as they rolled sideways, making the canoe club members work harder as they progressed from one side to the other. Malcolm counted a couple of other row boats already on the water, one close enough for him to make out a family enjoying the last few days of the summer holidays before school started back.

Walking to the boat hut, a teenager with spiky blue hair sat chewing a pink piece of bubblegum that looked big enough to choke on. Kind enough to pull her attention from her phone a moment, she checked his reservation, eyeing him up and down as she passed over a life jacket and health and safety leaflet. To be fair, he warranted the look, considering his blue dress shirt and cream corduroy trousers were more suited to a bottomless brunch on a super yacht than a rowboat on a Welsh lake. The girl blew an impressive pink bubble that popped over her lips she dragged back into her mouth with her tongue. Pointing to a rack of oars off to the side of the hut, she said, 'Boat six. Keep an eye on the clock, saves me getting the tannoy out.' She gave an exaggerated smile that disappeared as soon as she looked back to her phone.

Selecting two oars, Malcolm set them into boat six ready, before returning to the car. He opened the boot, pulling out a builder's bag of stone chippings, and heaved them up onto his shoulder. He dropped it into the boat, returning for the carrier bag accompanying them and threw his keys into the boot before closing it. His eyes filled now, blurring his vision as the sun continued to warm his face. He heard laughter ring out from the water as two kayakers splashed at each other. It was due to be another beautiful day. Pushing out into the water, Malcolm took some time to figure out his rhythm. He made a clumsy three hundred and sixty degree circle that reddened his cheeks, causing him to look around with embarrassment. No-one seemed to pay notice, the kayakers heading for the far side and the nearest boat two hundred yards away. He crept his way to the centre of the lake, dragging the oars in the water to slow the boat to a stop. Confident it was the seven metre depth he had researched on his laptop last night, he opening the carrier bag, pulling from it a length of blue rope. He tied one end around the bag of chippings, using his penknife to cut a tail four metres long from the surplus, and knotted it around his ankles. His whole body trembled now, as the small boat began listing as he stood. He swiped away the snotty fluid from under his nose as the faces came back to him, egging him on. With care not to flip the boat, he stood tall and looked out across the lake. The family in the row boat caught his eye, their matching luminous life jackets standing out against the murky waters and woodland backdrop. The young boy at the front looked back at him, a broad smile on his face, clearly enjoying himself. He gave Malcolm a little wave, calming him enough to return the gesture.

He really was making amends. So many children were unable to enjoy these summer boating trips because of him, because of the Grove. Before the woman came to him, they had been necessary offerings, nothing more than living gifts to the druid lord. He had played his part, robbing them of the happy moments this young lad was experiencing now.

Catching hold of the rope tied around the chippings, Malcolm hoisted the bag over the boat with a splash, the rope cutting into his legs from the weight as it tried to follow. He gave one last look to the boy, but he had turned away, back to his family. Relaxing his muscles, he followed the chippings into the water, the shock of the cold tensing his body into full spasm. The faces came again, happy now, smiling thankfully as he sank into the depths. They spoke to him, all together as one, calling in unison.

'Douse the flames.'

The chippings raced to the bottom, disturbing a plume of silt that enveloped Malcolm as he followed it to the depths. He thought of Elaine, the pain she would feel in what he was doing, and what he had already done. Then he thought of the children, the fear and pain they had felt in what he and his fellow Grovers put them through.

Now he was the sacrifice, to her and to them. Making amends, dousing the flames. As the searing pain in his lungs burned, and his body begged for air, his mind went to the woman who came to him. Mara. She would be happy with him now. He was making up for his sins. *He* was the offering, easing *their* pain. Then he heard her voice, her final instruction, a last task before she would take him.

*Give him the code.*

His hand dug into his pocket, pulling the knife once more. Bending his knees, he pushed with the last of his strength as he rocketed toward the underside of the boat, stopping suddenly from the opposing weight of the chippings. His calculations had been perfect, his hands just managing to touch at the slimy wood. He dug the knife in, pulling and dragging it with all his might to leave the impressions in the soaked timber. Heat raged through his chest, firing him on to finish. Then it was done, and as he blew out the last of the air in his lungs and sank back to the lake floor, the knife dropped from his limp hand to find its new home amongst the silt.

And then, appearing in the muggy water ahead, the woman smiled a wicked grin, as his brain took over the involuntary muscles and called for the lungs to be filled. He fought with a last thrash of his body, until his airways opened, allowing the murky water and black filth to flood them instantly. As the green and grey of the waters fell away, and everything turned dark, the woman spoke once more.

'Nothing you do can make up for your sins,' she said. 'Your torture is merely beginning.'

## Chapter 34

DCI Hibbard collared DC Price at her desk, pointing a finger at her, then in direction of the door. Confused, she followed out to the corridor just as Hibbard disappeared through the double doors leading to the rear station staircase. She picked up to a light jog to catch up as Hibbard waited for her on the other side with his arms crossed, then continued down the stairs as she came through.

'George's team has made more progress on the farmer. Best we find out what before we announce to the team.'

They descended to the ground floor and through a winding corridor to the back of the building, to a door marked Digital Forensics Laboratory. Hibbard knocked once and walked in without waiting for a response. It wasn't the type of laboratory Price had ever been in before. No white coats and test tubes, no incubators or Bunsen burners. It looked more like a hi-tech graveyard, where redundant computers went to be torn apart and tossed to the scrapheap. Disassembled motherboards and hard drives littered the high shelving lining the walls, the counters below home to tool chests and technician's maintenance equipment. Important looking servers with tangles of wires winked furiously from the corner. At the centre of the 'lab', a series of desks held elaborate and expensive looking computer setups that made her own PC look like a Fisher Price.

The four making up the forensics team crowded around a single monitor operated by the seated Iefan Morris.

'Ah, DCI Hibbard,' George said, as he clapped his hands together. 'Thanks for coming down. Iefan here has been making tremendous strides with your man, the farmer.'

'He's not my man, George,' Hibbard replied in a flat tone. Price did well to hide her grimace.

'Uh yes, sorry, sorry,' George said, shaking his jowls in apology. 'Please come over to Iefan's station. He's found some very interesting information.' George scurried back around towards his own team. Hibbard and Price followed, rounding the table to the seated technician. As they approached, the other technicians stood back to allow them a better view.

'Iefan, if you will?' George said.

Iefan cleared his throat as he looked around to Price. She caught his look, giving him a radiant smile, turning his face a lovely shade of cherry. Hibbard raised an eyebrow at the boy. Penny and Fred looked to each other and lowered their heads with a snigger. George scratched his head, clearly missing something.

'Uh, ok,' Iefan said, turning back to his screens. 'I've been looking into the farmer's search histories online. He wasn't particularly secretive. It's almost like he never thought of erasing anything before... well, before doing what he did.' Iefan clicked onto the farmer's bookmarked pages, pulling up a website, talking all things new in the farming community. Within the website was a tab labelled 'chat rooms'. He clicked the link, the homepage disappearing and loading up a new community chatroom page. The top left corner read the farmer's user ID, frustratedfarmer1. Iefan clicked his mouse and scrolled down. Hundreds of titles ran up the page too fast to read. 'There's hundreds of threads on here I've had to scan going back five years. Luckily, the website highlights the user interactions in red, so it's saved me hours of work.' He kept scrolling down, stopping every so often to check the thread dates.

# THE ESCORT TO THE GRAVE

Eventually he arrived at a post dating back almost three years, pausing before he opened it. 'There were other posts the user was interacting with before this one,' Iefan said, 'but this is the first and only one of significant interest.'

Price moved in for a closer look, leaning down next to him. Iefan squirmed in his seat. From the back, Penny and Fred shared another look and smiled.

The forum title read *Butcher with own facilities required - cash in hand waiting.* The post submitted by user *Hog-Roast-Delights-UK.*

'Jesus,' Hibbard said. 'Not exactly discreet.'

George responded first. 'Apparently, it's a common thing in the community. Lots of people rear animals, but not so many can slaughter and butcher, so they turn to local farmers who can. Catering companies regularly turn to them too, and many farmers welcome cash in hand so they don't have to declare it, apparently.'

Iefan clicked on the thread title. The page opened up, revealing a lengthy conversation between the poster and the farmer. A couple of other users had posted their interest, but they went ignored. From Richard Evans's desperate sounding responses, they had hooked the right man. The conversation held little clues, Evans simply listing off his facilities, equipment and contact details, but little else in the form of evidence.

'How do we know this is our man?' Hibbard asked.

Iefan opened his mouth to answer when Price's face fell even closer next to his and the screen, completely invading his personal space. His eyes flicked across, then back to the screen, and he swallowed audibly.

'They don't discuss what the product is,' Price said.

Iefan turned to her, eyebrows raised and mouth open in awe. He broke into a wide smile, showing off the dimples in his rosy cheeks. Price looked back to him, her own smile rising at the corners of her mouth, before looking back over her shoulder to Hibbard.

She pointed at the screen. 'See here. Evans asks about what they need butchered and how much, and they avoid an answer, instead asking about his facilities.'

Hibbard turned to George. 'Have you been able to trace the poster?'

'We contacted the website creators this morning for an IP address. They could have kicked up a fuss about confidentiality, but were actually very accommodating. They're currently checking their servers and getting back to us this afternoon. Then it's a case of getting the location from the service providers.'

'Brilliant work,' Hibbard replied. 'How long will it take?'

'Probably a day or two at most,' George said.

Price turned to Iefan, nodding. 'Well done Iefan,' she said.

His hand rubbed at the back of his neck. 'Uh thanks...'

'Lauren,' she said. 'My name's Lauren.'

Hibbard's phone ringing broke up the party. 'George, as soon as you get the location, I want to know. Keep up the good work.' He clicked his fingers at Price and gestured to the door, walking off in its direction. 'DCI Hibbard,' he said as he lifted the phone to his ear.

Price rolled her eyes. 'See you around Iefan.'

She followed Hibbard out as the love-sick pup watched her go, slumping back into his seat, finally exhaling the breath he'd been holding. Penny walked back over and stuck a finger under his chin to push his mouth closed. Iefan swatted her away as Fred pinched his cheek. 'Smitten kitten,' he said with a chuckle.

Hibbard and Price made their way back up to the first floor, met by the caller, a Detective Constable named Williams. She gave chase as they made their way back to the Incident Room. 'Interpol's been in touch, Sir,' Williams said, handing over printouts as they settled back in the IR, 'Following our requests for leads into potential child

# THE ESCORT TO THE GRAVE

smuggling rackets. A Major Valenov has left details for you to call him back. He's given us lists of missing children in Latvia he believes have been victims of an elaborate criminal kidnapping ring. There's photos of some of the children too. The team just started trying to match them to the files on the farmer's computer.'

'OK, good work,' Hibbard said as he flicked through the lists.

'The last list should interest you, Sir,' Williams said.

Hibbard cocked an eyebrow as he pulled the last sheet to the front. A list of names, Eastern European men's names, printed in either black or red.

'What am I looking at here?'

Williams's eyes flashed to Price and back to Hibbard. 'That's a list of names from the Kovalenko crime family in Belarus. They've found every name in red on the list dead in the last two weeks, including the heads of the family. The names in black, Major Valenov believes to have fled into Western Europe, in hiding most likely. They haven't been able to locate them, but he believes this group are responsible for trafficking children throughout the Scandinavian countries and into France, Germany and the UK, and he has a theory a rival gang has decided to take out the entire family network. The thing is, every one of the gang deaths appears to be suicide, but Major Valenov is convinced they're staged. He's sending over files as we speak.'

'Sir?' another officer called from her station. Hibbard and Price made their way around the table to her. 'First files coming through from Interpol, sir.' She clicked on a folder, opening a series of files. The first one read *Ivan Azarenka*, noted as a high level soldier in the family. Opening the file led to a detailed police report of the crime scene.

Hibbard pointed to a sub page on the screen. 'Photos. Open it.' The officer followed her orders. The first photo filled the screen, a mugshot of Azarenka. She clicked on the next one, same face, this time the eyes void of life, face grey and mottled with thin blue and purple veins. A steel background gave away the morgue slab where they took the photo.

'Next,' Hibbard demanded. Photos of the body filled the screen, as found in his Minsk home garage, hanging by the neck. The man's head twisted off at an unnatural angle from the dislocation. Stripped to the waist, he wore pale blue denim jeans, soaked through from the blood running down his chest, along with the body fluids he'd let go in his last throws of death. Beneath his bare feet, lying in the blood pooled and coagulated there, was a large Bowie knife. Small chunks of flesh, finger-tip size pieces littered the pool, cut out from the man's own torso. The deep wounds cut out a shape, the deep red, almost black, dried blood and flesh forming a symbol striking a shocking contrast against the man's pale skin.

Price and Hibbard looked to each other, then back to the screen.

'My god,' Hibbard whispered, as he took in the shape he'd seen so often this last week. 'What the hell have we gotten ourselves into?'

## Chapter 35

### Wednesday

'Where are we going, Eddie? I thought we were going to walk my handsome prince Mossy?' Wendy Bickerton-Smith asked, looking at the little ball of noise yapping from the back seat of Eddie's Ford Focus. 'And you promised to take us for lunch.'

'Aye, I'll take you for a slap up meal in a bit.' Eddie said.

Spotting his smirk, Wendy rolled her eyes. 'Bloody Cefn cafe again, I suppose. Better book myself in for a tetanus shot later.'

Eddie drove through the twisting road leading to the Morrison home, the trees lining either side blocking the sunlight, giving the single width lane a rather ghostly, unwelcoming appeal. Cresting the hill back into the open, he pulled into the layby he had used before, overlooking the house. Mossy paced back and fore on the back seat, whimpering as he lifted his front paws to peer out the windows either side.

'What's wrong Mossy baby?' Wendy asked as she shifted to get a better look at him. Opening the driver door, Eddie stepped out and closed it behind him. There was no sign of a patrol car at the property gates, and no press trucks, likely due to David Morrison giving the reporters everything they needed with his interviews following his daughter's return. Parked by the garage, the family Range Rover sat next to David Morrison's black Jag. There would be no chance of getting to speak to her with him at home. Not that Sarah Morrison would likely let him, anyway.

Mossy continued to pace and whine from the back seat, clearly agitated, Wendy reaching back desperately trying to grab a hold of him to pull him to the front seat. Eddie went to the rear door, opening it enough to grab the dog under one arm. His paws pushed at Eddie's chest, a pathetic growl developing from his throat.

Wendy climbed out, making her way around to them. 'Mossy, what's got into you?' she said.

'Got his lead?' Eddie asked, taking it from her and clipping it onto his collar. Dropping the dog to the gravel, Mossy began pulling away with desperate attempts to head in the opposite direction.

'Something's wrong with him, Eddie. He doesn't like it here. Eddie?'

Looking back to the house, Eddie could see the figure at the first-floor window, watching them, her little hand raised to wave at him. He gave a wave back and even though he couldn't quite see from this distance, he just knew Ellie Morrison was smiling. Another figure approached from behind her, pulling the curtain to one side. Sarah Morrison spotted Eddie, looked back down to her daughter, then to his surprise, gave her own little wave.

'Fuck sake Mossy!' Wendy shouted, forgetting any notion of elegance and class her double barrel name had suggested, as the dog made off up the road, lead in tow. 'Eddie, help,' she pleaded as she scurried away awkwardly in pursuit, her red heels giving way every other step on the loose gravel.

It took them three quarters of an hour and a mile up the road before Mossy would return to them. They had crossed two fields, at one point climbing over a wire fence that saw Wendy fall in a pile of horse manure. The words spat from her mouth as she attempted to clean it from her legs with her chiffon scarf had Eddie doubled over laughing. The dog refused to go back the way they had come, Eddie having to collect the car as Wendy waited on the side of the road like some drunken hitchhiker. Far from amused, she practically threw the dog and her filthy heels onto the back seat before dropping in next to Eddie. The enclosed space in the warm weather intensified the pungent scent of shit clinging to her. Eddie wound down the driver side window. Wendy glared a hole right through him, her hair sticking out like she'd been dragged through a hedge backwards.

'Right, enough of the bullshit,' she said. 'What was that all about?'

'The house belongs to the Morrison family. I saw the girl in the window when Mossy made off.'

'And to what purpose did you feel the need to bring myself and Mossy along?'

'I needed to find out if Sarah Morrison would let me speak with her daughter.' He started laughing. 'You and Mossy were a bonus.'

'Bastard,' Wendy said with a smirk.

His brow furrowed as he turned to her, a stern look in his eye. 'Look, we've spoken a million times about what happens to me when I'm on a case, when I find a body.'

'Eddie, it's your subco…' Eddie held up a hand, cutting her off.

'Ever see the videos of dogs refusing to leave a gravestone, or move from the scene of an accident their owner was involved in? I don't believe it's because they miss their owner. I think it's because they can really see them, smell them, hear them calling. It's because they know they're still with them.'

Wendy's eyebrow tilted its favourite shape, the one she made when Eddie sat across from her in her therapy room.

'When the girl went missing, the family dog refused to climb the mountain. The search team's dogs refused to go up too. It got me thinking. When the farmer died, his dog was nowhere to be seen, and now Mossy wouldn't go near the Morrison house either. It's all linked. The dogs can sense what's happening.'

Wendy blew out a heavy sigh. 'And what exactly is happening, Eddie?'

'I... I don't know yet.'

'Eddie, you're crazy,' she said.

'Well, I wouldn't need to pay you a small fortune if I wasn't, would I?'

Wendy puffed out a huge breath. 'Take me home, Eddie. I need a long soak in the bath and a large glass of wine.'

---

Eddie dropped Wendy off at her front door just as the phone rang. Wrestling it from his pocket, he hoped it would be Sarah Morrison. The illuminated name staring back surprised him. It must have been three years since they spoke last.

'Elaine? You ok?'

'Hey Eddie. It's, uh, been a long time.'

'What's going on Elaine? Is it Mal?'

The call fell silent a moment, then a sniffling sound. 'He's dead,' Elaine said.

'What happened?'

'Will you come here Eddie, to the house?'

'I'll be there in an hour.'

The drive to Brecon was just long enough to make a couple of phone calls en route. Just like his own home, the Glover's house brought back nothing but bad memories. The last visit hadn't gone particularly well, a full slanging match concluding with Eddie grabbing Malcolm by the throat, telling him under no circumstances would he ever see him again. Pulling up to the gated driveway, the house had changed little since the first time he'd been there, when he had turned up full of good intentions to win over Gwen's parents. He was a good man back then, charming and respectful, with a decent career, but above all, madly in love with their daughter. Following that introduction, he'd realised even if Gwen had brought Prince William into the family home, it wouldn't have been enough for Malcolm Glover. The evening didn't go well. Trouble brewed the moment he turned his nose up at the bottle of wine Eddie handed over to Elaine.

Pressing the intercom button, he waited for a response. Instead, the gates opened, allowing him to drive through and park up next to a brand new white Porsche Cayenne he guessed as Elaine's. Malcolm would undoubtedly own some ridiculous looking fluorescent Lambo, or some two seater Shelby that takes him ten minutes to get in and out of. That was Malcolm Glover, practicality always playing a distant second to an opportunity to flaunt money.

Opening the front door, he hardly recognised the shell of the woman he'd once known as his mother-in-law. Raw, spent eyes, unkempt hair, and bedraggled, creased clothes looking like she'd slept in them. A far cry from the Elaine Glover that played the part as a millionaire's wife so well. She melted with relief as she allowed Eddie to take her into a hug before pulling him into the house. They held onto each other for a long time through a mixture of freshly shared grief and long awaited reunion. Eddie waited for her to pull away first, her hand taking his and leading him into the sitting room where they both shared a stiff cloth covered settee. He had hoped they would move past the room, into the kitchen or the large conservatory overlooking the garden, but he resisted the urge to pull back on her hand as she led the way. It took a moment for him to look up at the walls. Frame upon frame of the Glover's family album adorned them, like a shrine to the lost. Official school photos, beach holidays, equestrian comps on her pony, Bella. One thing he could say about Elaine and Malcolm, they loved Gwen with everything they had.

Grief is a strange emotion, personalised in every way. Eddie kept just one photograph of Gwen, the happiest of pictures that broke his heart every time he held it in his hands and swallowed more liquor. He had others, of course, albums filled with special moments. Photos dressed up on nights out eating good food, mud soaked and carefree watching bands perform at Glastonbury, faces painted at the stadium watching Wales play rugby. Now they sat gathering dust in the house they once shared that he couldn't bear to set foot in and yet couldn't bear to sell either. A strange emotion indeed, grief. Here, the Glovers held a celebration of their daughter's life. Their grief appearing at the opposite end of the spectrum to his, choosing to reminisce with pictures, hold her close at the front of their minds and see her every day as the baby, the toddler, the schoolgirl, the woman. Was that the secret to relieving the pain? Was he trying to push her away, lock her out of his head and instead trap her there to burrow around in his mind?

Elaine saw the shamed, stolen glances he made around the room as he sat with his shoulders hunched and head lowered, rubbing at the back of his neck. As she took the display in for herself, a smile rose that couldn't quite reach her eyes.

'Don't you keep photos of Gwen, Eddie?'

'Just the one. The rest are in the house.'

'Still haven't been back there, I take it? Why are you holding on to it?'

Eddie shrugged his shoulders. 'Closure,' was all he could think to say.

Elaine cocked an eyebrow. 'You're keeping the house empty for closure? That doesn't make much sense, Eddie.'

'So I *don't* have to deal with the closure.' He dared a brief glance to the wall ahead of him. 'I don't want to move on. I just want her.'

'You think me having all these photos of Gwen means I've moved on? Listen to me Eddie.' She took his hand in hers, tapping the back of his with her free hand. 'You somehow feel guilty one day you'll learn to live again and enjoy it. Have a sense of purpose. Maybe even fall in love again. But here's the thing, Eddie. No matter how your life ends up and who you share it with, Gwen will always be a part of it, and she'd be devastated if she knew what this was doing to you.'

Eddie nodded. 'You've just lost your husband and you're giving me advice about my wife I lost nearly seven years ago. You're a selfless woman, you know that?'

It was Elaine's turn to hunch her shoulders. A deep frown took over her face as she looked down at her trembling hands. 'Will you help me, Eddie?'

He gripped her hand tight. 'Of course I will, Elaine.' Eddie already knew the course of events leading up to Malcolm's death. He'd phoned one of his contacts in Dyfed Powys Police to get the information en route, who'd read off the interview notes from the boat hire worker and the young family present on the lake.

'He took his life, and I've no idea why,' she said, shaking her head. 'Life has been so good the last couple of years. He's been happy, content even. Last week we planned a month long cruise around the Caribbean. And then yesterday morning, everything was different.'

'How so?' Eddie asked.

'He was stressed, like I haven't seen before. No, I tell a lie, only once before.' She pulled a hand away to wipe a tear. 'When Gwen died.'

'Any idea why?'

'He said it was work stuff. But I know it wasn't the truth. He never got stressed like that over work. Then he said he was going out all day to sort something for the club. But he was at the temple the night before and didn't come in till late.'

Eddie snapped to attention, his neck jarring as he turned to her. 'The temple?'

'Some gentlemen's club. He never told me much, and I never liked to ask, because he'd get all defensive, you know? So I just left him to it. Took up a lot of his time, though. Far more than the golf and the shooting clubs ever did. He'd be out most evenings.'

'What are we talking about here, Elaine?' Eddie asked.

'Druids.' Elaine said. 'Grove Druids, they're called. He's been a member the best part of ten years now, I'd say. I remember the first time he told me they were swearing him in. Said it was the best day of his life. He had such a smile on his face. Then when he saw I was a little offended, he played it down as just a club for him and his mates to get pissed at, which was pretty much the truth. He'd get in some right states when they had their monthly meetings there.'

'Druids,' Eddie repeated, his eyes dancing back and fore. 'What do you know about them?'

'Like I said, not much,' Elaine replied. 'He was very secretive about it all. They're all high-powered types, the members. Pillars of society. A select few. He was very proud to be part of it. And with him winding down the businesses and relaxing a bit, I thought it would keep him busy. I assume they're a bit like the Freemasons. Secret handshakes and all that you know?'

'Did he mention any of the other members by name?'

Elaine thought about it. 'No. Never. He'd bring home his ceremonial robes from time to time for me to handwash. Beautiful material, such amazing colours. But other than that and his inauguration plaque in his office, you won't find anything to do with them here.'

'Where's the temple?' Eddie asked.

'Somewhere up towards Talgarth. He never said exactly.'

# THE ESCORT TO THE GRAVE

'Weren't you ever suspicious, Elaine? Some secret society Malcolm spends so much time with?'

'I know what you're getting at, Eddie, but let me tell you something. A woman can tell when a man is in love with her.'

'I... I didn't mean...'

Elaine held up a hand. 'Gwen could tell you adored her, and I could tell the same about Malcolm. Women just know these things. I just thought the club was a harmless way for him to spend his time. He seemed happy until yesterday.'

'I'm going to go to the lake to see if I can figure this all out. I need to try and locate that temple, too. See if this club has anything to do with this. Can I see Mal's office?'

They both stood. 'Of course,' Elaine said. 'Go on through and I'll make us a cuppa. Do you remember where it is?' She stayed put as Eddie walked through the kitchen towards the back end of the house, stopping at the tall oak door to the office. His hand lost grip on the knob as he opened it, the door swinging back violently on its hinges. Eddie barely registered the noise as he focused in on the plaque mounted proudly above Malcolm's office desk, alarm registering on his gob-smacked face. A gold etched plate with dark wood surround, the Grove Druid Emblem sitting smack in its centre.

The three pointed symbol staring at him, again.

## Chapter 36

Pulling into the boat hire car park, Eddie killed the engine and took in the scenery, dropping an elbow onto his open window. The evening was cooler now, but still pleasant. Smoking barbecue smells filled his nose from the camping field further over, the aroma of cooking meat sending his stomach into a frenzy. A group of twenty-somethings prepped their kayaks at the water's edge below him. They chatted as they pulled them up the banking towards a car hitching a trailer at the back, completely unaware or carefree of the events that happened here just yesterday. Driving into the grounds, he'd expected to sense it. But as he drove down the gravel path toward the lakeside, the bomb-dropping migraines never materialised, no mind spinning nausea, no deluge of vomit inducing aroma saturating his sinuses. Only a mild warning of a fuzzy head and empty stomach called to him, demanding he get some alcohol into his bloodstream at the earliest opportunity.

Is this really where Malcolm died? He really should have sensed it by now. Events at the mountain and farm had been different, and now this was continuing the trend.

Leaving the window down, he climbed out and made his way to the hire shack. A young girl with spiky blue hair leaned on her elbows, chewing noisily as she eyed him up and down. As he approached, she pointed a finger up to the sign above her head. Large chalk lettering reading 'Last hire 6pm. Last call in to dock 6.45pm.'

'I'm after some information.' Eddie said.

'About yesterday,' the girl said.

# THE ESCORT TO THE GRAVE

'Were you working?' Eddie asked.

The girl blew a large pink bubble that popped over her lips. She smiled as she pulled it back into her mouth with her tongue. 'Might have been.'

Eddie pulled a ten-pound note from his pocket and held it up between his fingers.

The girl chuckled. 'Might have got you somewhere in the nineties, old timer, but I can't buy twenty Bensons with that these days. Try again.'

Eddie grumbled as he dug back in, pulling another tenner out.

The girl swiped them away. 'What you wanna know?'

'The guy who killed himself, you remember him?'

'Yup,' she said as she blew another bubble.

'Don't elaborate too much now,' Eddie said.

She rolled her eyes. 'Yes, I remember the wacko who tied himself an anchor and threw himself over,' she said.

That was the thing these days. So many of his and older generations viewed and labelled youngsters as 'snowflakes' now. A collection of over-sensitised protesters of anything and everything. But where Eddie's generation had grown up relying on crappy documentaries and low budget 80s horror flicks for blood and gore, today's kids could find anything they wanted just logging onto YouTube. If anything, they had become completely desensitised. Some mid-life crisis committing suicide was a walk in the park for kids nowadays. She was probably just gutted she didn't get a video of it.

Eddie looked out at the lake. 'Where'd it happen?'

'Well, the guy drowned, so out there, obvs.'

Eddie smiled as he turned back to her. 'Point to the spot.'

'Smack bang in the centre,' she said. 'Deepest part is seven metres.'

'Did you speak to him? How did he seem to you?'

'You mean did he seem like someone about to off himself? Not really, no.'

'I need a boat.' Eddie said.

'Then you'll have to come back at eleven tomorrow morning. Last hire was six o'clock.'

'Fifty quid for twenty minutes,' Eddie said.

The girl threw him a life jacket. 'Boat four. Oars at the side rack.'

'Which boat did he use?'

'Boat six. It's the one dragged out onto the bank. Police told us not to use it until they give the OK.'

'Has to be that boat.'

The girl raised an eyebrow. A smirk raised on the corner of her mouth.

Blowing out a resigned sigh, he pulled another twenty quid from his pocket. This was getting pricey.

It took almost twenty minutes for him to get the boat back in the water, the loose gravel shoreline giving way under foot as he dragged it backwards, gaining himself waterlogged boots and knee soaked jeans for his troubles. He nearly went overboard as he got in, the vessel rocking violently as he desperately tried to balance himself out. A sniggering sound came from the hire shack and if it wasn't for the fact he'd likely fall in head first if he tried, he would have turned around to tell the girl to shut her face.

Eventually, he steadied himself enough to row out to the centre of the lake. The easy summer sounds were relaxing. The creak of the oars against the brass of their oarlocks as they pulled through the water soothed the pain in his head, as his brain continued to call for more alcohol in his body. He hadn't drunk since last night, and it was beginning to show. A sheen of sweat glistened on his brow as he eased the oars back one last time, allowing them to drag in the water and slow the boat to a stop. Eddie watched as the ripples died behind the boat, settling to remove any evidence they had ever been, just as his visions had done over the years. Before the events at the mountain, the ripples had been animated and obvious, easy to identify and interpret. Over time, they dissipated, until there was no evidence left even to him a crime had taken place. Now, however, the ripples began as nothing more than a shimmer across the surface, a blink and you miss, type of deal. He didn't know how to feel about that. For so long he had wished himself dead from his curse, and now it appeared to be easing, he found himself unsure, maybe even afraid, it was disappearing completely and leaving him for good.

There were a couple of boats still out on the far side, anglers reeling in and packing away their equipment to make their way back to the jetty, but otherwise, the lake was empty. Under normal circumstances, if this was the spot Malcolm had died just a day ago, he would have known about it by now. It should be a struggle to stay on the boat. Instead, he sat there, somewhat baffled by the lack of response his body made. Closing his eyes, he lowered himself back off the seat to lie with his back resting against the bow. He lay there a moment as the boat resettled, the lapping of the water against the hull and the rocking motion singing him a gentle lullaby. The sounds faded, and his grip released from the boat's edge as the first of the visions surfaced.

It was not Malcolm's death that came to him.

It was a young girl's face, a frightened adolescent, her eyes wide and brimming and begging for help. She muffled a plea for mercy through her gag, but not to him. Eddie stood frozen to her side, unable to move, unable to help, damned to bear witness. Her wrists and ankles strained against the leather straps holding her to the vertical wooden crucifix. She jostled to be free, her sweaty body wriggling in desperation. All around her, hundreds of candle flames flickered, casting their shadows to dance against the cold flagstone floor and the painted stone walls behind. The first figure approached, cloaked in purple and white ceremonial robes, a gold curved dagger in his hand. He wore a mask adapted from the skull of a stag that hid the top half of his face, an impressive set of antlers branching out from the temples. His mouth pursed as he and the rest of the masked figures chanted words from a language Eddie couldn't understand. They all wore identical robes, but their own masks appeared individual and personal to each of them. All adorned smaller, more juvenile versions of the leader's antlers, their skulls all differing in shape and species, doctored in design. Some had teeth, some pointed fangs.

Eddie frantically scanned the crowd, moving from face to face. They continued to chant at the young girl strapped to the crucifix. Then his eye caught on a mask in particular, with small stubby teeth allowing him to identify the jawline and smirk of his now deceased father-in-law.

*Malcolm, what the hell have you done?*

The leader stopped in front of the girl. Eddie's eyes went to the man's mouth as he spoke to her. Again, there was the feeling of familiarity about him he couldn't quite place. Eddie screamed for him to stop as he touched at the girl's cheek, but it was no use. Ignoring her obvious and overwhelming fear, rejecting any notion of pity, he rested the cold tip of the dagger on her chest plate and forced it in. The girl let out a pathetic whine behind her gag, her eyes draining the last of the life from her. A sick gurgle found its way out before her head dropped toward her chest. Pulling the blade away, the masked figure lifted it high as the group cheered, hands held aloft as they fist pumped the air.

The girl disappeared, and now a boy no more than ten years old was in her place, the same look of fear in his eyes as the masked figure approached again. The group chanted. The boy pleaded. The dagger plunged into his chest. Eddie screamed for mercy, and this time felt his body release, his legs buckling as he fell back towards the cold flagstone floor. He closed his eyes, waiting to hit the ground, but it never came.

He was underwater, stood on the lake bed. Above him, he could make out the underside of a boat, rocking and thrashing a deep echo through the depths. The disturbing splash of a weight dropping into the water as it raced toward the floor in front of him, followed by a second splash from the surface above. As it hit the floor, the weight threw up a bloom of silt, temporarily clouding his vision. Eventually the filth resettled to the floor, and a figure he recognized as Malcolm came into view, his legs tied to the weight. He floated a moment, already looking so peaceful waiting for death. Suddenly, he pushed off the lake bed toward the boat. Eddie expected a scramble for the surface, desperate and regretful as he clambered for air. Yet he appeared to accept his fate, taking his knife to scratch a final message into the underside of the boat.

Satisfied with the message, Malcolm blew out the remainder of the air in his lungs as he sank back to the depths. He made one last thrash of his body, and as he did, a face came into view from the dank, murky waters.

The woman winked at Eddie in acknowledgement, then turned back to Malcolm. As his body relaxed from the water filling his lungs and throat, she spoke.

'Nothing you do can make up for your sins,' she said. 'Your torture is only beginning.'

All he saw was blue and white sky. His hands gripped the sides of something rough, wooden. His body rocked back and fore matching the sounds of water lapping around his head. He was back in the boat. Laying there a moment, he watched the clouds drift from one side to the other, trying to match the tempo of his racing heart to the sound of the water. He tried to make sense of what he had just seen. He expected to see Malcolm's death, but the others? The children?

*Those kids. My god, those poor kids.*

Pulling himself up into a seating position, he rubbed at the burning sensation behind his eyes. A tinny voice called out that for a moment he thought was still in his head.

'Boat six, time's up, boat six, return to jetty.'

He looked back to see the girl with the blue hair walking away to the hire shack, megaphone in hand. Taking his time rowing back to shore, the children's faces continued to haunt him. He had little doubt who they were. It was time to phone Price, and if she was willing to show him some photos from the farmer's computer, he may even be able to identify them.

His visions were continuing to change. Now he had seen what Malcolm had been part of, the reason behind him taking his life. But for what purpose? He still couldn't save them.

A line of moored boats and pedalos sat in the shallow waters tied off at the jetty edge. Eddie rowed past them all to the shoreline and dragged the boat out as far as he could onto the gravel banking. It was no simple task, the weight of the boat resisting and digging into the gravel as he pulled. Using all his weight, he pushed on one side of the boat to reveal the bottom, using an oar to prop it in position. It took a few efforts to get right; the oar slipping out of position on the loose gravel and soggy hull. Lying down on his back, he used the torch from his phone to illuminate the muggy underside of the rowboat. Fresh scratch marks had been dug into the soaked wood he struggled to make out from his position. Switching the phone to the camera, he took a snap of it instead.

There was a series of numbers, five in total.

7, 38, 19, 28, 21.

He had no idea what they meant, but would be sure to ask Elaine when he phoned her. Removing the oar, the boat dropped back down to a safe position. He took the oars and life jacket back to the shack. The girl was behind the counter locking a money box ready to take with her.

'Thanks for your help,' Eddie said.

## THE ESCORT TO THE GRAVE

'Find what you were looking for?' the girl asked as she began winding the shack awning.

'Maybe,' was all he offered back.

'Did you know him?'

'He was my father-in-law,' Eddie said.

'Woah, that sucks,' the girl said. 'Sorry to hear that.'

'I'm not,' Eddie said as he walked away. 'I'd kill him again if I had the chance.'

## Chapter 37

Price's answer phone took his call. Keeping it short and sweet, he was sure she'd phone back on hearing his cryptic message. 'I know how the children ended up at the farm.' The trouble would start when she asked how he'd found out.

He needed her on his side now more than ever, and although she might not see it right now, she needed him. His misread over the girl had made her feel and possibly look a fool to her superiors, and she was unlikely to trust him or his methods anytime soon. Back in the car, he tapped out a message to Sarah Morrison, asking if she would be willing to meet with him again, this time with Ellie present. It could go either way. She had waved back at him at the bedroom window, a decent sign he'd be welcome. Avoiding her husband was probably the best course of action at the moment, although he'd love nothing more than to gauge the man's reactions to some of his probing questions at some point. Not that he'd be confident of him giving much away. The guy was a politician, after all.

The sickly, hollow churn continued to curdle his stomach. His mouth had a dry texture like it had been filled with sawdust, and he constantly found himself trying to moisten it with saliva. The cool breeze holding the sweat at bay on the lake had disappeared, and now sweat soaked through the majority of his shirt, turning it a navy shade of blue. He wondered how severe drug addicts coped, going cold turkey, locking themselves away for days on end and vomiting the linings of their stomachs up in bouts of sheer agony. No way he'd be able to do it himself. The dependancy on alcohol wasn't something he could put a date to, even though he started drinking daily after the accident. At first, he had disguised the alcohol as pain relief, a way to dull the senses and blot out the world. Medicine for his warped and troubled mind. Eventually, he had figured out and came to terms with his new found curse, and yet continued to drink, anyway. Before long, the dependancy crept up on him, backed him into a corner until all he could do was accept what he had become. It had been his friend for so long now, a loyal companion, welcoming him every day and never judging him. The bottle never looked down its nose at him.

Driving back down the A470 toward Merthyr Tydfil, his phone pinged with a notification of a message. Result. Sarah would see him providing he got there before her husband returned home at 9.30pm. He checked his watch. 7.15pm, just enough time to call in and update Peter. It deserved more than a phone call.

Back at their Pontsticill home, Jane answered the door and gave a sympathetic thin-lipped smile.

'Hey Jane, how's he doing?'

'Not too good, to be honest,' she said. 'Spent most of his time shut away in his annex. Go round the driveway. He's in there now.'

'You ok?'

'Been better Ed. You?'

'I think we're all feeling a bit shit, to be honest.'

'Yeah, I bet. But she's alive. That's the main thing. Go on round.'

He announced his arrival at the annex with a quick rap at the front door and waited. There was a time Peter would have told him to just walk in, but the way things were at the moment, it would be better to tread carefully. As much as Peter would blame himself, Eddie knew a large portion of it was his fault. True enough, on answering and seeing Eddie at the bottom of the ramp, Peter gave a silent and solemn nod of the head to follow before turning and walking back to his office. He was back in his chair with a drink in hand before Eddie reached the office door, turned toward the view over the reservoir as the last of the sunlight dipped behind the mountains. A half empty decanter of whisky sat at the centre of the table. Although desperate for one, a drink wasn't offered, and so he wasn't about to help himself.

'I've always loved this view,' Peter said. 'It's what sold it to me when we moved here all those years ago. I was just a Sergeant then, a good officer, a good person.'

'You still are Pete. Don't give up on me yet.'

Peter scoffed as he swallowed his drink. 'You're going to offer me advice on not giving up? Really? Next you'll be telling me I'm drinking too much.'

Eddie ignored the insult. 'I'm on my way to the Morrison estate. Sarah Morrison has agreed to meet with me again, with her daughter there. I'm determined to find out what happened to her, to find out the truth.'

'The truth is she's alive,' Peter said, still failing to make eye contact. 'Leave it go. Accept you were wrong and move on. I certainly have.'

'I misread the signs, Pete, but I wasn't wrong. Something's happening to me I can't explain right now. All this started with Gwen, and now it's changing because of this girl. I need to find out the connection. And the Morrison girl holds the key.'

Peter's gaze dropped to his lap. 'She's not the answer to anything. Your faith in your abilities was misplaced. It's not your fault. You've been grieving all this time, and it's been your way of dealing with it. A coping mechanism And I took advantage of it, of you. I'm sorry.'

'You sound like my shrink,' Eddie replied.

# THE ESCORT TO THE GRAVE

'I've been a poor friend,' Peter said. 'Allowing you to keep going on this path of self-destruction. I should have helped you a long time ago. I've let you down.'

'Get a grip of yourself Pete. This isn't all about you.'

'Fuck you Eddie.'

'Fuck you right back, Pete.'

Peter let out a defeated belly laugh that seemed to go on forever. His head rocked back in his chair and he had to hold his hands over his stomach from the ache of the much needed humour. Eventually, he settled back down and finally turned to make eye contact with his dear friend. They shared smiles in silence before Eddie broke it.

'Gwen's father killed himself yesterday.'

The grin evaporated from Peter's face, his mouth falling open like a broken trap door. 'Jesus Christ. How?'

'Tied a weight around his ankles and threw himself in Llangorse Lake.'

Peter shook his head as he blew out his cheeks. 'I'm sorry to hear that, Ed.'

'I'm not,' Eddie said. 'You never knew the guy. Hated me from day one. Always said I wasn't good enough for Gwen and blamed me for everything he could. The guy was a wanker.'

'Well, I'm still sorry. Any idea why he did it?'

'It's why I'm here. Because I think he was involved in the deaths of the children found on the farmer's computer.'

Peter nearly fell from his chair. He blinked furiously, as though he were seeing stars. His lips moved, trying to form words that just wouldn't come out. 'What? How?'

Eddie brought Peter up to speed, deciding to leave out the details of his little stakeout of the Morrison farm in the morning, instead starting his explanation at his mother-in-law's phone call. Peter listened intently, occasionally looking back to the window as Eddie went through it all. When Eddie got to the part of seeing the children being sacrificed, when he was in fact on a boat in the middle of

Llangorse Lake, Peter refilled his glass and added another two fingers to a second, sliding it across the desk to Eddie.

'What actual evidence have you got of his involvement? This cult you're talking about? Where are they?'

Eddie eyed the amber liquid as it resettled in the glass. The pain in his stomach begged for him to drink it. He ignored the call, but was unsure how much longer he had the strength to do so. 'Elaine doesn't know, and neither do I. She thinks they have some lodge or temple or whatever they call it up towards Talgarth. I'm going to see if my contacts in Dyfed Powys know anything about it. I'm guessing it'll bounce back a no hit, but it's worth a try.'

'I can't help you, Eddie. With my resignation in, I'm not in charge of the investigation anymore.'

'I'm not asking you to, Pete. I'm here telling you this out of friendship and loyalty. You've done your best with this, something you weren't supposed to be involved with in the first place, and they've thrown you under the bus for it. Well, I'm going to find out the truth, and bury every last one involved.'

Leaving Peter in the annex, he walked back around to the front of the house just as the streetlights switched on, the orange glow barely holding off the blanket of night dropping over the valley. It was a sleepy village, Pontsticill. Picturesque by day, turning remarkably eerie by night. A scattering of country estates and farms overlooked the string of well-lit cul-de-sac estates branching off from the main road, where the majority of the village population resided. Peter and Jane's house stood toward the north end, with the Morrison estate just a few minutes' drive southwest, back toward Merthyr town.

# THE ESCORT TO THE GRAVE

There were no sentries at the gate this time around. The press had moved on to their next big story following Ellie being found alive, and while those responsible were still at large, there was always a meatier meal to be had. Eddie could imagine the Chief Constable herself phoning David Morrison to tell him they were pulling the guards from his property. No doubt he would have made his feelings known. After all, there's only one thing worse than a politician always in the news, one that's never in it. David Morrison was not for back benching.

After a brief wait, the gates opened and again, Eddie parked beside Sarah's Range Rover outside the double garage. The front door opened before he got to it and this time, instead of Ana the housemaid, it was Sarah herself. She looked out towards the gates and the dark road beyond, beckoning Eddie to hurry along and join her inside like some lover she was desperate to keep secret. She pushed Eddie in behind her, giving one last look out over the lit courtyard in case someone watched from the shadows. Eddie waited for her in the living room. She strode in, looking more alive, more animated than the last time he'd been here, understandably so. She wore her hair down over her shoulders and her make-up-free face had a healthy, determined look to it, even if it pinched together as she looked out the window. There was a yellow tinge to her one cheek, a healing bruise not present the last time he was here. As big a prick as David Morrison was, he hadn't sized him up as a wife beater. Emotional and mental abuse maybe, but not physical.

She had surprised him with her agreement to let him come here again, especially with everything he had told her the last time. Eddie admired the strength she displayed, even if she was clearly nervous of her husband's impending return. Eddie's judge of character rarely let him down. It was one of the things that made him a talented investigator, but it had done just that with his initial impression of Sarah Morrison. He had expected some stuck up socialite and instead got a down-to-earth mother who doted on her children. It was a mistake he felt guilty for jumping to conclusions over. Just like his opinion of her daughter's disappearance.

'Thanks for letting me come,' Eddie said. 'I'm a little surprised you did.'

A broad smile warmed Sarah's face. 'I told you she was still alive.'

Eddie's eyes dropped to his hands as he tried to hide the tremors overtaking them. 'Yes, you did, and I owe you an apology.'

'No, you don't,' Sarah said, her eyes sparkling with purpose. 'I've had time to think this past week. All that matters to me is my Ellie is safe. And while we still don't know who took her or what happened, all I know is I'll never let anyone take her from me again. I'm going to spend the rest of my life helping her get back to the way she was. And you're the first step.'

'What do you mean, Mrs. Morrison?' Eddie asked.

'Mr. Venter…'

'It's Eddie.'

She forced a smile, but this time, her eyes held concern. She took his hands in her own, then slowly nodded toward him. 'I think she's right. You're a good man, and you do need her help.'

Eddie shook his head in confusion, his eyes narrowing to form a silent question.

'My daughter was found five days ago in complete shock. Wouldn't speak. Refused to even look at me. She just stared off into space. I couldn't even tell if she was listening to me when I told her I loved her. She just sat there in a daze, holding the key they found her with. The psychologist who assessed her called it traumatic mutism.'

'Her key?' Eddie asked, his eyes widening with excitement.

Sarah chuckled at his response. 'I held off for a couple of days to see what would happen, but when there was no change, I decided it was time to see if almost seven years of waiting was about to end.'

'And did it? Was it for the box?'

'It was. When I showed it to her and she opened it, she became my daughter again, if only for a short time.'

'Why? What happened?'

'She came alive again when she saw the box, all excited, like a long-lost friend had arrived. She opened it with the key and my mother's gift was there, and even though I was confused, I thought everything would be fine again. But it wasn't. The one thing keeping me from going crazy when that woman took her was the belief my mother would watch over her. Of course, I couldn't know for sure, and all I wanted to do was to find the woman responsible and strangle the last breath from her. Then Ellie was delivered back to me with the key opening my mother's gift from before she was born. What do you make of that, Eddie?'

Eddie shook his head again. It was exhausting trying to make sense of it.

'She took the gift to her room and drifted back into her own little world. For the next three days, all she would do was sit at her table with it. Wouldn't talk to me, wouldn't look at anything but the gift. And then I saw what she has been doing with it and I was horrified. Stuff no six-year-old girl should be capable of producing. It made me wonder what happened to her before they found her. What she had been exposed to. What she had seen. My emotions have been all over the place. One minute I think she's going to be fine, the next she's back in her own little bubble.' She rubbed Eddie's hand with her thumb. 'Until this morning.'

Eddie's eyes narrowed again. He had no idea where this was going.

Sarah caught the look. 'She saw you at her window, Eddie. And she came back again.'

'What do you mean?' Eddie asked.

'I was in her room with her this morning. It may sound strange, but it's as much mesmerising as it is worrying, watching her with it. She just sits there at her desk, her little hand and elbow moving so fast, and I swear she's not really looking at what she's doing. She was making another one, but then she stopped, and she stood from her chair and looked out her window. And before I could move, she started waving to someone, to you. And she melted into my daughter again. Told me she loved me. We both cried for so long. Then my eldest Jenny came in and we all cried some more. And when things settled down, and I built up the nerve to ask her some questions, she just told me to bring you here. That she needed you to help her, and she could help you too. Do you have any idea what she means? Why she is asking for you, Eddie?'

Eddie shook his head in silence, struggling to find an answer. He was about to ask about the box, but Sarah got in first.

'Are you ready to see her?' Sarah asked, pulling him by the hand before he could reply. They made their way up the stairs, passing the guest bedroom he had been in last week. Stopping at what was obviously a young girl's bedroom, Sarah knocked and waited, an unusual thing for a mother to do with a daughter so young. Eddie looked to the end of the landing, where another staircase led to the second floor. Peeking around the corner were Jenny and Border Collie Bandit. Eddie held up a hand, and both heads disappeared.

Sarah knocked again, but didn't wait this time. She opened the door tentatively and peered in around the door, before opening it fully to present their guest.

'Honey, Mr. Venter is here to see you.'

# THE ESCORT TO THE GRAVE

Eddie stood at the doorway as Sarah walked in. At the writing desk, beneath the large bay window, Ellie Morrison sat with her back to them, her long silky red hair hiding most of the chair she sat on. From the doorway, Eddie could see her preoccupied with something, her head lowered toward the desk and right arm working furiously. He inched closer as Sarah put a hand on her daughter's shoulder. There was no response from the girl as she continued to work away on whatever she had in front of her. Eddie looked to her bed, eyeing the heavy box Sarah had shown him during his last visit. The lid was closed, but the locking mechanism lay flipped open, the head of a key sticking from it. The key they found her with, adorned with the three pointed symbol he was sick of seeing this last couple of weeks. The thought of it all made his head swirl. He edged closer to the bed, finding himself reaching out to it, feeling the intricate design beneath his finger-tips yet again. Sarah looked to him, and when he saw her, she gestured for him to join them at the desk. Eddie obliged, quietly sliding over as to not disturb the girl. On approach, the girl's elbow stopped moving, and he could see she was holding a piece of charcoal in her hand she now placed onto the large piece of yellowed paper in front of her. Eddie got as close as he dared, trying not to spook her. He peered over her shoulder to the drawing, as she continued to rub at the markings she had made with her fingertips of her left hand, blending the harsh charcoal lines into soft detail. A mix of emotions flooded him, now he understood what Sarah was getting at. Amazement came first at the quality of the black and grey drawing, work no six-year-old he knew was capable of creating. He was no art expert, but he suspected even the most seasoned of critics would be in awe of this young girl's capabilities, and equally shocked at the content.

Following the rise of social media, painters and sculptors continued to push the boundaries of what was acceptable to be considered 'art'. Shock value and political statements became as important as the quality of the work itself. But every artist had an agenda. A reason to paint. A reason to choose a subject. And for some reason he couldn't imagine, here was a six-year-old girl, drawing the most shocking images of death.

Eddie kept silent as he took in the grotesque picture. It looked more belonging to a copy of Dante's Inferno, such was the horror of the subject. Ellie used her left forefinger, gently blending the details of the man's gown, expertly creating the tones of shadow and highlights to give the impressions of folds in the cloth. An icy shiver pierced between Eddie's shoulder blades as he recognised the robes the figure wore. Beside it was a firepit, and although the medium was charcoal, expertly drawn details and fine outlines showed the hot coals spewing from it. A branding iron lay heating in the pit, with another in both his hands of that familiar symbol as he pushed it into the chest of a screaming, topless man kneeling before him. A line of figures knelt behind, calmly awaiting their turn. Beside the robed man stood another, wearing a matching gown, the top half of his face hidden behind his giant mask. A mask made up of a skull and antlers he recognised from his vision at the lake earlier. The figure pulled back the hair of the most recently branded figure as he ran a knife across his throat. Arterial blood sprayed out onto the flagstone floor ahead, where other bodies crawled away, freshly opened up and bleeding dry. Eddie recognised not just the men in the robes, but the room from his vision as well. It *had* to be the temple.

*But why did Ellie know them?*

In the bottom left corner, she had written a date. 29th August 2019. Tomorrow's date. Crouching to her eye line, he peered around to her side, now able to see what Sarah had meant about her daughter not quite being 'with it'. She was staring at the paper, or rather he noticed, through the paper, paying little or no attention to the macabre creation in front of her. Her finger made small circles to blend the charcoal, as if the action created her trance-like state. Then, as if realising she was in company for the first time, her finger stopped rubbing at the sketch as she looked to Eddie. Her eyes focused as a beaming grin broke across her pretty little face. Pouncing from the chair, she wrapped her arms as far around Eddie's back as she could get them, her face burying into his soft belly. She squeezed and nuzzled into him like he was a relative she hadn't seen in months, rather than some stranger she'd never seen before. She held him long enough for him to look to Sarah, who crossed her arms with a bemused look on her face. Her eyes moved up to Eddie, and he saw some relief there. As confusing and worrying as her daughter's behaviour was, she had responded to him. She was Ellie. Her daughter again.

Ellie broke from the embrace and took his hand, leading him over to her bed she climbed up into, resting her back against her pillows, and sliding her legs under the covers. Reaching for her favourite donkey plush toy, she cwtched it into her cheek as Eddie sat at her feet, his hand resting on the mysterious box. Sarah sat with him and they both stared at the little girl, who looked ready for someone to read her a bedtime story.

'It's nice to finally meet you,' Eddie said. 'It's been quite an adventure this last couple of weeks, hasn't it?'

'Yes it has, Mr. Eddie,' Ellie said. 'I've been on a *big* adventure.'

'Can you tell us where you went, Ellie?' Sarah asked. 'When the lady took you?'

'Oh Shannon is so lovely, Mammy. She's my sister now. We had such a nice time together. We went on a long walk over the mountains and she told me all about where she's from. Do you think we could go visit her soon Mammy? She says Ireland isn't too far and we could go on a boat and she'll come and meet us when we arrive. Oh please say yes, Mammy. We could make jam sandwiches to take with us.

You could come too, Mr. Eddie. Shannon can't wait to meet you too.'

Sarah looked to Eddie, giving a small shake of her head, then back to her daughter. 'Uh maybe honey, maybe.'

'I thought you only had one sister, Ellie?' Eddie said. 'Jenny isn't it?'

'I've got two more now,' she said. 'Isn't that exciting? Although, I only got to spend time with Shannon this time. Mara says I won't get to meet Bonnie until she's six like me. But then I'll be older too.' She frowned and dropped her head.

Sarah opened her mouth to ask a question, but nothing came out. Eddie's eyes flickered, frantically trying to piece it together. 'How old is Bonnie now, Ellie? Where is she?'

Ellie looked to the ceiling as her finger touched her lips. 'Today is Wednesday, so that makes her, um… ' She started counting with her fingers. 'Ten, no, eleven days old, I think.'

'And where is she, Ellie?' Eddie asked.

'She's in Scotland, of course, where she was born. I really can't wait to meet her. I told Shannon and Mara I've always wanted another sister to play with, because Jenny's getting older now and doesn't like to play dolls with me anymore. And now I get to be the big sister. It's so exciting.'

'Ellie, who's Mara?' Sarah asked.

'She's my mama. She's so pretty, and she has the most amazing pet dogs. Apart from Bandit.'

Eddie scratched at his forehead. *The dogs.*

Sarah's face had taken on a sour look. 'I'm your mama, Ellie.'

'No, you're my mammy, silly. Mara is my mama.'

Eddie jumped back in. 'Did they hurt you Ellie?'

She laughed at that. 'Don't be silly, they're my family. We had fun.'

'Where did they take you?'

'To one of Mara's favourite places.'

'Do you know where it is? What it's called?'

'Michael's Chapel,' Ellie said. She gave a wide yawn. 'I'm really tired now, Mr. Eddie.'

'St. Michael's Chapel?' Eddie asked.

'Yes,' she said with surprise. 'Have you been there, Mr. Eddie?'

He recalled his last conversation with Price, asking her to pass on his theory about the site. Looking to Sarah, he said, 'It's a ruin on the Skirrid Fawr mountain. Close to where they found her.'

'The policewoman who came here on Monday asked about it. She said the search team found candles there, like someone had recently carried out some sort of ceremony.'

'What policewoman?' Eddie asked.

'Uh, a detective constable,' Sarah replied. 'Young, pretty woman. Black hair in a tight bun. Can't remember her name. I've got her card in the kitchen.'

'Price?' Eddie asked.

'That's her,' Sarah said. 'DC Lauren Price.'

'What does ruin mean, Mr. Eddie?' Ellie asked.

Eddie turned back to her. 'It means piles of stones.'

'Oh no, Mr. Eddie. It wasn't a pile of stones. It was a big chapel. That's like a church, but not as big. Mara loves it there. We played lots of games and we lit candles and she told me all about her, and Shannon and Bonnie and Agnes.'

'Who's Agnes honey?' Sarah asked.

'Agnes is the lady we left on the mountain Mammy,' Ellie said in a casual tone. 'She's gone now. She was a sister for so long.'

'Do you know her last name, Ellie?' Eddie asked.

'Clark. Agnes Clark. Such a nice lady. I wish I could have got to know her more. But that's not how it works.'

'Tell me more about the sisters,' Eddie said.

Ellie smiled at him. 'I'm really sleepy now, Mr. Eddie. But I'll tell you more tomorrow.' She reached for the lid of the box, flipping it open to reveal the leather book and two more yellow sheets of paper rolled up into scrolls. Across each of them, a red wax seal stamped with the triquetra symbol kept them from reopening. She pulled them from the box, giving them to Eddie. 'These are for you, Mr. Eddie. Will you come back tomorrow and see me again? I'm sure you'd like to know more? And I'll have two more of these for you, too.'

'Yes please Ellie, if you and your Mam will have me.' He looked to Sarah, who smiled back her response. They both rose from the bed as Sarah picked up the box and tucked it under. Ellie grabbed her donkey and snuggled under the covers. Sarah gave her a kiss and told her she'd be back to read her a story after she'd seen Eddie out.

'It's ok Mammy, I'm very tired.'

Eddie walked to the door, stopping as Ellie called out. 'Mr. Eddie?' she said. 'Mara told me about you and Gwenno, too.'

His eyes widened like dinner plates. 'About me? About...Gwen? How? Who is she, Ellie? Who's Mara?'

Ellie smiled again as she looked to her donkey, rubbing noses with it like some eskimo greeting. 'You know who she is, Mr. Eddie, and tomorrow you'll find out some more. Goodnight.' She blew a kiss before dropping her head to her pillow.

Sarah turned out the light, leaving the bedroom door ajar as they made their way back down to the ground floor in silence. Passing the darkened living room, they walked straight toward the front door. Stopping at the porch, their eyes met, the gaze holding as they stood in silence. Her yellowed cheek glowed in the soft overhead light, and as he looked at it, Sarah's hand came to her face. 'Want to talk about it?' Eddie asked.

'Maybe tomorrow,' she said. 'If you decide to come back.'

# THE ESCORT TO THE GRAVE

'I'd love to,' Eddie replied as he opened the front door and stepped out. 'If that's ok with you, and Ellie.'

'David will probably be out all day. I think it's best if we don't tell him you've visited her for now. I'll let you know what time is good for Ellie. She's got a real soft spot for you, Eddie, and I'm starting to see why. Goodnight.'

Eddie smiled as she closed the door. Walking back to his car, he climbed into the driver's seat, failing to notice the recently disturbed gravel marks leading into the closed garage to its side. His fingers caressed over the scrolled paper in his hands, its yellowed colouring and thick, cloth-like texture showing its age. He drove out from the property, waiting beyond the gates just long enough for them to close behind him, deciding it best to look at Ellie's drawings at home.

The last thing Sarah needed was her husband finding out he'd been there.

# Chapter 38

Sarah turned the light out in the porch and watched Eddie's battered Ford disappear from view. She couldn't quite understand why or how he was linked to her daughter, but she was pleased it was there, that link. Her daughter was responding to him and while she felt a rather large pang of jealousy, it was nothing to the overwhelming relief someone had got through. Some maternal instinct, a feeling deep down in the pit of her stomach, told her everything would be ok. Ellie would help him with his own demons, and in turn, he would help her become her little girl once more. It was a trade she could accept, however strange it might appear.

Everything they had talked about upstairs had blown her mind, but she was confident together, the three of them would figure it all out. Make that four of them. This last fortnight, her full attention had been on her youngest daughter, and she could forgive Jenny for thinking she was being left out. She was still just a fifteen-year-old girl, even if she tried to act so much older these days. No doubt she had her own questions she wanted answered, considering she had witnessed Ellie's reaction to her nana's gift, as well as the disturbing drawings she had created with it. And since Ellie's return, her sister had kept her distance, almost as much as Bandit did, as if scared to get too close. But she deserved to know, to be included, to be loved by her mother and sister, and become their perfect little girl-group once more.

Now was as good a time as any. She would speak to her straight away. Turning from the front door, she made her way back to the staircase. The distinct sound of ice rattling in glass stopped her climb. She inched into the darkened living room, spotting the haunting moonlit silhouette sat at the sofa.

'How long have you been home?' she asked.

'Long enough to see what you've been up to,' David said as he swallowed the last of his glass. Picking up the decanter, light glinted off the crystal as he filled it some more. 'So tell me, what did I say to confuse you so much about that man coming anywhere near this house and this family again? What did I say I would do if you let that piece of shit in here again, huh?' Rising from his seat, he stalked toward her, the contorting menace on his face dipping in and out of the shadows as he approached. 'You've disobeyed me again. You let that bottom dweller in to spout more of his bullshit and fill not just your head with it, but my daughters, too. My fucking daughters!' His hand clamped around Sarah's throat as he pushed forward and pinned her against the wall. Her head smashed into the photo frame behind it, cracking the glass. 'You ungrateful bitch. Everything I've given you over the years and this is how you repay me. You had nothing. You were nothing. Just a ten-a-penny tart, slutting herself around college looking for a free ride. Nothing more than a glorified prostitute. Fucking disgusting.'

Sarah's hands found his wrist but had little effect, his forearm still holding the powerful twisting muscle he'd built there from his younger years. 'You... you're... hurting me,' Sarah wheezed as she kicked out, her eyes rolling back.

David released the pressure just in time, a well-rehearsed move perfected over the years. Sarah slid down the wall, taking the photo frame with her that smashed as it hit the floor to her side. Her legs shot out from underneath as she slumped there, rubbing at the pain in her throat. 'I want my daughter back. He can help her,' she gasped. 'You? You don't give a shit about anyone but yourself. You call me disgusting? I'm only disgusting because I fell for you. You're a power hungry psychopath. Well, you can rise to power without us. We're done. Me and the girls won't be here anymore for you to fool everyone as some family man. You're nothing more than a fake.'

Lowering himself into a crouch, David grabbed a handful of her hair and pulled her head to one side. Her eyes brimmed with tears.

'Eddie Venter is a dead man,' he said. His eyes fired back at her like he meant every word. 'And if you think you're going to ruin my career by splitting this family up, then you'll be fucking joining him. From now on, you'll do what I say, or so help me, I'll use all my power to ruin what little reputation you've got left. Remember who let their daughter get taken from the top of a mountain? That wasn't me. It was you. And I'll make sure the world knows just what a crappy mother you really are. You forget what I do for a living, Sarah. Manipulating the press is part of my job. And now I suggest you do yours, playing the happy wife and the sorry mother. Anything else and I'll bury you with Venter.'

As if to seal the deal, he pushed her head back, knocking it against the wall behind her, rattling her senses. It made a loud thud, and she slumped even further to the floor, doing her best not to show her pain. Her shoulders trembled as the tears flowed.

David rose to his feet in victory. 'Clean this shit up. If I find out Ana's done it, she's fired.' He walked off toward his study, pulling his mobile phone from his pocket before slamming the door behind him.

At the top of the stairs, Ellie and Jenny held hands, staring down at the crumpled heap sobbing below. They moved as one until they were with her, the three of them joining in their union of grief. They wrapped themselves up in a tangle of limbs as Sarah and Jenny cried together.

# THE ESCORT TO THE GRAVE

Ellie's eyes were on her father's study door as she stroked her mother's hair. Then she spoke. 'It will all be better soon, mammy. It will all be better soon.'

# Chapter 39

Driving away from the Morrison estate, Eddie called his contact over at Dyfed Powys Police, the same who'd given him the details on his father-in-law's suicide. 'Hey Jimmy, it's Venter. I'm after some information.'

'Again, Eddie? You're going to get me fired.'

'All for the greater good, Jimmy, you know that. And it's not me that's going to get you fired. It's the fact you can't pick a horse from a three-legged donkey, and need people like me to keep palming you those purple notes with the queen's head on to fund the habit.'

Jimmy let out a deep sigh. 'What do you want, Eddie?'

'I'm looking for some sort of building up around the Talgarth area. Some sort of chapel or lodge, like the Freemasons use, you know the type.'

Silence on the other end. 'Jimmy?'

'Why would you be looking for a place like that, Eddie?'

'It's linked to the suicide at Llangorse Lake we spoke about this morning. Do you know any places?'

'No, can't say I do. I'll ask around the station. There's a few on shift from up that way. Maybe they know of a place.'

'Cheers Jim. Ring me later with an update.'

'If you don't hear from me, then it's a dead end. I'm a busy man Eddie.'

'Please!' Eddie replied. 'Busiest you'll get is ordering your takeaway.'

A few minutes later, after pulling up outside the shop, Eddie's phone rang again, Price's name filling the screen.

'Just got your message,' she said with an air of frustration. 'Care to elaborate?'

'I think I know how the corpses ended up at the farm,' he said.

'I'll play along,' Price replied.

'My father-in-law killed himself yesterday. I think he was part of the cult we've been making theories about.'

'You made those theories, Eddie.'

'Stick with me, Price. I think this cult has these kids delivered from somewhere and they sacrifice them for whatever disgusting, perverted reasons they have. Then they get taken to the farm to be disposed of. They could be kids slipping through the net, forgotten by the system, children few people would care to even ask about.'

'Kids from Eastern Europe,' she replied.

'Price? What do you know?'

'You're right about the kids being trafficked. Interpol sent photos to us yesterday of missing children. We've matched some of them to the videos on the farmer's computer. The farmer made up the names on the files, but our guys are working through the list and it looks like they all came in from Eastern Europe, specifically Latvia. They've also sent us lists of dead or missing members of a well-known crime family in Belarus. It looks like they've trafficked these poor kids all over Europe.'

'This is why, Price. These kids are being smuggled all across the continent with promises of a new life, only to be slaughtered.'

'Not anymore. It looks like someone's beating us to it and killing this family off one by one, unless they're moving in on the business and taking it over.'

Eddie thought for a moment. His eyes averted to the scrolls on the passenger seat. 'Price, I've got to go. I've got something I need to look into. Are you around tomorrow for a catch up?'

'Eddie, how do you know your father-in-law has anything to do with this?'

'I saw him do it. When I went to the spot he killed himself at, I saw what he and his friends did to those kids. And there were others. Lots of them.'

'Jesus Eddie, another leap of faith?'

'Trust me Price.'

'Didn't get me very far last time.'

'I suppose that's why you didn't tell me what the search team found at the chapel ruins on the Skirrid?'

'I said you should keep your head down, Eddie. I'm trying to do the same. How did you find out, anyway?'

'Sarah Morrison told me when I went to see her and Ellie.'

'You don't listen to anyone, do you? Did they let you in?'

'Meet me tomorrow morning and I'll tell you all about it.'

---

Switching on the table lamp, the living room lit up in a sad, jaundiced glow as Eddie fell into the settee, swallowing him up. The room reeked of stale booze, and it set his hands trembling and mind to the bottle in the kitchen cupboard. Looking to the photo above the fake fireplace, Gwen begged him to leave it there. Letting out a heavy sigh, he lifted himself to a seated position as he made space on the coffee table.

*Keep your mind clear, and on the girl, Eddie.*

Placing the first of the scrolls in front of him, he cracked the hardened wax stamp holding it, the flakes sprinkling to the table and carpet beneath as he spread it out. The used tumblers littering the table came to use, one positioned in each corner to stop the picture rolling shut again. Eddie's mouth dropped open at the content. Again, the drawing was appalling and breathtaking in equal measure. The girl had drawn the farmer, deep inside the barn, kneeling and holding a lighter aloft as the flames melted away the last of the skin covering his body. The drawing had amazing detail, down to the grains in the wooden planked walls and singed hay littering the floor to wisp into the air. A date written in the same charcoal as the picture was in the bottom left corner. 20th August 2019, the day the farmer killed himself.

Removing the whisky glasses, the scroll rolled in on itself. Eddie removed it from the table and replaced it with the second. It was a picture of Gwen's father throwing himself off the boat. Again, it was intricately and expertly drawn, the likeness uncanny, and a picture no normal six-year-old girl should be capable of imagining, never mind creating. Malcolm's face grimaced with effort as he heaved the bag overboard to drag himself under. The bottom left corner read another date. 27th August 2019. Yesterday. Eddie let out a puff of air, trying to make sense of it all. Something unexplainable was happening here, and not just to him. Then, in the background of the picture, he noticed something. A blurred smudge, shaped just like a person. Amongst the pine trees behind Malcolm, at the far end of the lake, a lone black figure stood watching. It was difficult to make out, but the shape was definitely human, looking out from the treeline to the spectacle on the water.

Reopening the first drawing of the farmer in the barn, it surprised him he'd missed it before. He had to hold the drawing up so the light from the table lamp caught it just right. Lurking in the depths of the barn, amongst the background shadows, the outline of a figure stood watching. Again, he couldn't make out any details, but he knew. He knew it was her, the woman from his dreams, the woman plaguing him over and over. He had seen her in his visions when he had gone there, mocking the farmer as he begged for forgiveness. And now she plagued Ellie too, warping her mind as she drew the grotesque scenes. The question was there, but he felt he already knew the answer. He had seen Ellie creating one of them back at her home, dated for tomorrow. He had little doubt these were drawn prior to the dates on the drawings. He would confirm it with Ellie tomorrow, but he was confident in what he was seeing. She was predicting people's deaths.

## Chapter 40

### Thursday

DCI Hibbard sat behind the wheel of his Audi in the Holiday Inn car park at Coryton Interchange, wishing he was thirty minutes north, hiding under his bed. He'd been up all night, and taking a quick look in his overhead mirror, he realised he very much looked that way, too. His normal healthy tan now had a sickly tinge. He could definitely feel a cold coming on. His head was muggy like he nursed a hangover and his bloodshot eyes itched like they held dried out contacts. He'd never suffered with hay-fever before and wondered if it was even possible for this time of year.

Coryton Interchange is the main link between the A470 and the M4 motorway that runs from West Wales all the way to London. It was the last place he needed to be right now. He was still leading the investigation into the Belarusian trafficking racket, until he guessed, word caught of the scale of it all. Then it would get pulled from under his feet and given to a higher-ranking officer to take all the plaudits when he'd done all the donkey work himself. He'd been close to telling David to go fuck himself this morning. He should have. The fact was, he didn't have a chance to. He'd answered the call only to hear that annoying little bitch PA of his tell him to be here, alone, at 7 a.m. sharp. She'd hung up before he could say anything. No doubt Morrison was sitting next to her when she called, the self-righteous prick.

The black Jaguar pulled into the car park and eased into a space over the far side, away from prying eyes in the hotel lobby. Hibbard leapt from his seat, slamming his door behind him as he cursed the length of the walk to the car. It was an obvious attempt to show dominance. The tinted windows hid the occupants from view. He tried the rear door handle, finding it locked, and huffed until the front window lowered enough for him to see the top half of the driver's face.

'Up front,' the driver said.

Hibbard huffed again as he traipsed around the bonnet of the car to the front passenger door like a pouting teenager. He got in, looking back behind him to see the PA sat behind the driver. Her eyes stayed glued to the laptop in front of her. He wrenched his neck around a touch more to Morrison sat directly behind him. He turned back around, facing front, and said nothing. A long silence ensued.

Eventually, Morrison broke it. 'Go for a smoke,' he said.

For a moment, Hibbard thought he was talking to him, but then the laptop snapped closed, and the PA and the driver got out.

Morrison waited until the door shut, leaving just the two of them. 'I thought I told you to get rid of that imbecile, Eddie Venter.'

'This isn't the Bronx, David. I can't just shoot someone in the street. And I've had more pressing priorities lately than taking out some piss head flirting with your missus.' He regretted the comment as soon as he said it.

'Your department's ineptitude in finding my daughter threatened to derail my progression,' Morrison said. 'If they had found my daughter dead, I'd get thrown into the backbenches and left to rot. Seen as a liability. It would have taken me years to get back into this position, if at all. You were damn lucky they found her alive, John. All of you. Because now that piece of ass standing outside has turned this into the public's wet dream. They can't get enough of the story.'

'Then what's the problem?' Hibbard asked.

'I've already told you. Eddie Venter is the fucking problem. He's filling my wife's head full of all kinds of nonsense, my daughters too. He's threatening to pull the curtain down on everything I have built. They're all acting crazy. The stuff Elinor's been doing, my god. And it's all because of him. I've been up all night working out how to get him out of the picture, and there's only one way. Now get rid of him, John. This is your last warning.'

Hibbard's head sank in defeat. He sighed, then let out a whisper. 'I'll figure it out.'

'Get it done today,' Morrison replied. 'If you ever want to be somebody in this shit-show you call a police force, then Venter goes today. If I find out he's still breathing when I return tonight, then I'll make sure you're manning the doors of Asda before the week is out. Now get the fuck out of my car.'

Hibbard stepped back into the rising sunlight hurting his already straining eyes. Without a word, Morrison's driver and PA dropped into the car and took off back toward the busy main road.

# Chapter 41

DC Price pulled into the retail park, surprised to see a fresh-looking Eddie perched against the bonnet of his car, two takeaway cups in hand. He looked different from the last time she had seen him, pleasantly so. As bad as it sounded, he didn't look as unkempt as usual. His hair and face had found a razor since they last met, and the polo shirt and jeans he wore actually looked clean and freshly ironed. Most of all, his face looked somewhat healthy. No bags. No drawn features. He actually looked good, for Eddie Venter standards. As she walked over, he held out a cup, which she took with a smile.

'Alright?' Eddie asked, taking a sip of his own drink.

'I'm ok,' Price replied. 'Look Eddie…'

'Don't sweat it, Price. I let you down. I'm hoping it hasn't done you too much damage?'

She sipped her coffee, letting out a content purr. 'Hibbard's a hypocrite. He tried to give me grief about getting too close and falling for your nonsense, even though it was his idea in the first place. Even tried telling me I'm lucky to still be on the investigation.'

'He'll do a lot for self-preservation,' Eddie said.

They both mulled over that last statement.

'So, are you coming with me to the Morrison estate?'

'How have you managed to pull that?'

'Boris Johnson's love child isn't there. Sarah text me to say he left for London early this morning.'

'First-name terms and text messages. Sounds like you're getting close?' She smirked as she took another sip from her coffee.

# THE ESCORT TO THE GRAVE

Eddie smiled back at her, his eyes sparkling with enthusiasm. 'Come with me and meet Ellie again. There's something you need to see, and I promise she's a lot different than when you would have seen her last,' he said.

'Now?' Price asked.

'After you've run a check on any missing persons by the name of Agnes Clark.'

'And who might that be?' Price asked.

'That's your dead woman from the top of Pen-y-fan mountain.'

Price phoned the details in to the investigation team, then listened intently as Eddie relayed everything that happened at the lake with his father-in-law. Once up to speed, she followed him to the Morrison house.

Ana answered the door and showed them through to the living room, where she promptly disappeared. They sat in silence for a good minute until feet bounding down the stairs had both their heads turning. Rising from his seat, Eddie's gut took the brunt of the force from the enthusiastic child rushing in for a hug. Ellie caught around him and squeezed hard, burying her head into him as Sarah and Jenny giggled from the bottom of the stairs. Price stood off to one side gawping, marvelling at the girl's transformation.

'She's missed you, Eddie,' Sarah said. 'Hasn't stopped talking about you since you left yesterday.'

'Well, I've missed her too,' he replied, looking down to the girl like an uncle would a favourite niece. He ruffled her hair so it covered her face. She laughed and squeezed again. Price pursed her confusion. She was no expert, but the trauma Ellie showed just a couple of days ago indicated it would likely take months, even years to improve from. Yet here she was, bouncing in like an excited puppy.

'And who've we got here?' Eddie asked, looking over to the two at the bottom of the stairs. 'You must be Jenny. It's nice to finally meet you.'

Jenny walked over and joined the embrace. 'Thank you,' she said. 'You brought her back to us.'

'I haven't done anything,' Eddie said. 'I just think this young lady here is ready to share with us. Right, Ellie?'

Ellie nodded her response and took his hand in hers. She reached out for Price to take her other and led them to the stairs. They passed Sarah, who gave a weary and tired smile Eddie spotted. He took Sarah's hand in his. 'Ellie, why don't you and Jenny take Lauren to your room, and me and your mam will follow you up? Lauren would love to see what you've been up to?' He nodded to Price, who spotted the worrying look on Sarah's face. The red marks lighting up her neck looked raw and fresh.

'Come on Ellie, I'm excited to see your room.' She gave a gentle pull and Ellie giggled again as the three of them darted up the stairs and along the landing. Reaching the bedroom, Ellie ran and dived on the bed like any normal six-year-old would. The firm mattress bounced her back up, and she squealed some more as she reached for her plush donkey for a cuddle. Jenny lowered herself into the miniature armchair at the corner of the room, her eyes firmly on Price, waiting for her reaction.

Price looked around the bedroom as she wandered forwards, toward the table beneath the bay window. 'Such a beautiful room Ellie,' she said. 'Pink is my favourite colour, too. I don't get to wear it much at work, though.'

'It's ok,' Ellie said. 'I like red and black more now. Just like our robes.'

Price looked to Jenny. Hey eyes deceived the thin-lipped smile she wore. She was clearly concerned about Ellie's behaviour, even if her younger sister seemed so happy.

'Robes, Ellie?'

'Mine are red ones, like my sisters. I'll get them at the party. I can't wait. They're beautiful. Mara's are black and really suit her. She's so pretty. Prettiest woman ever.'

Price looked at Jenny again, who responded with a slow shake of the head.

Sat on the table was the box Eddie had told her about. He wasn't joking about the beauty of it. She imagined a woodworker spending endless hours creating the intricate inlaid lid, polishing it up with immense pride as he turned it into the piece of art sat before her now. Turning back to Ellie, she pointed a finger at the box, a request to look inside. Ellie nodded her approval. Lifting the lid revealed even more beauty, a stunning leather book surrounded by plump velvet cushions. At its centre, those symbols again. She resisted the urge to pluck it out from its spot, instead running a finger across the intricate details adorning it.

Eddie and Sarah came in moments later, joining her at the table and looking over her shoulder. 'Amazing isn't it?' Eddie said. He turned to the little girl on the bed. 'Mam says you've got some more drawings for me, Ellie?'

'Yep. Can you bring it over, please? I'm sure I'll be a lot stronger next week when I'm seven, but right now I can't lift the box when the book is in there.'

Eddie did as asked, lifting the book out and positioning it in front of Ellie, who shifted her legs to cross them under her. Creaking open the book, she found the first of her drawings, and turned it to show him with pride. Price gasped her surprise. Turning to Eddie, she saw the shock on his face too, his eyes wide in alarm and mouth hanging open. Her eyes moved to Sarah, then Jenny, and she realised by their faces they'd already seen the work. The quality of the picture matched that of the book and the box, the shadows and light shaded perfectly in the charcoal media. A blended swirl of moonlight peeked through the tree canopies, illuminating the figures on the grass bank below. Littered among the broken glass, a man's body laid sprawled out on the floor, his face and eyes blank in death. Standing over him, hands dripping with bloodied cuts and wearing the very same clothes he wore now, was Eddie. He was looking to his side, speaking to the third person in the drawing, a cloaked, hooded figure, it's features shadowed and hidden from the moonlit view. Written in the bottom corner of the drawing was another date. Today's.

'Do you like it, Mr. Eddie? It's my favourite one,' Ellie said.

'Um, it's really good Ellie,' Eddie said. 'When did you draw it?'

'Last night,' she replied. 'And it got me so excited.' She pointed to the dark figure in the picture. 'You're going to see her again. Tonight.'

Price waited for Eddie to ask, but the question never came. Clearly, he already knew who she spoke of. 'Who is it, Ellie?' Price asked with a touch of impatience. 'Who's in the picture?'

'Mara, of course,' Ellie replied. 'Mama.' Price looked to Sarah, who grimaced as she rubbed at the back of her neck.

'Ellie?' Eddie said, as he sat on the bed. 'Tell me about the pictures. Do they come to you when you're sleeping?'

'No, Mr. Eddie. They don't come to us. We find them,' she said.

'Do you know what they are, Ellie? What you're drawing?'

'Of course, people doing their sooey-sides.'

He tapped her hand. 'Ellie, you're drawing these pictures before they happen, aren't you? You're seeing what these people are planning to do before they do it, right? How are you doing that, Ellie?'

She smiled at this. 'That's not what I'm doing, Mr. Eddie.'

'Then what is it, Ellie? Help me understand. What am I missing? What exactly are you doing?'

Taking the drawing from his hands, she ran a finger over the darkened figure stood next to him. 'Mara will explain it all, Mr. Eddie, if you let her.'

'Who's the man on the floor, Ellie? Do you know him?'

# THE ESCORT TO THE GRAVE

'He's one of the bad men who take the children. There's not many left now.'

Eddie and Price shared a look. 'What children, Ellie?'

'The children that end up at the farm.'

'And the drawing of the man in the boat?' Eddie asked. 'He was something to do with them too, wasn't he? And the men in your last picture, with the masks?'

Ellie smiled again, this time to her donkey. 'You're starting to get it now, Mr. Eddie. Aren't you?'

'Can you tell me more about the sisters?' he asked.

'No. Mara will explain that too, when you're ready.'

'Ready for what, Ellie?' he asked. 'What am I going to be ready for?'

'For the answers, Mr. Eddie.'

'What answers?'

'About Gwen, of course. Why she had to leave you. I wish I got to meet her, Mr. Eddie. She sounds like such a wonderful person.'

Eddie's hands went to his temples as he shook his head back and fore. 'What the hell is happening?' he whispered. The room fell silent for a moment. After collecting his thoughts, Eddie spoke again.

'Ellie? Is Mara the woman who keeps coming to me? In my dreams?'

'Yes, Mr. Eddie. She told me about when she visits you, but you try your best not to listen. Maybe you will now, now you know she's for real.' She reached under her bed, pulling from under another rolled up scroll, wax stamped and sealed, handing it to Eddie. 'Can you keep a promise, Mr. Eddie?'

'I'm the best promise keeper ever,' he replied.

'I drew that one last night too,' she said, pointing to the scroll in his hands. 'But you need to promise not to look at it until after…'

'After what, Ellie?'

'Until after this one,' she said, pointing back to the one in her book. 'After this one happens.'

Eddie jumped as his phone rang, sending Ellie into a fit of laughter. It caught on, the mood in the room suddenly lifting and there were giggles all-round. He pulled the phone from his jeans pocket and rose to the window as he answered. 'Hey Jimmy. You got something for me?'

'How do you do it, Eddie?'

'Do what?'

'What is it? Séances? Tarot cards? Ouija Boards is it? You're like some sort of mystical wizard.'

'One minute, Jimmy,' Eddie said. He gave Price a look to follow, then to Sarah. 'Just need to take this call. Hope you don't mind.'

On the first floor landing, Eddie switched to speakerphone. 'What is it, Jimmy? What have you got?'

'We got a call in the early hours from some housewife missing her husband. She was worried sick, saying he was acting all weird and stuff, panicking he was going to do something stupid, you know? The Duty Sergeant fobbed her off, told her he was probably out with some mates, getting pissed. Told her we'd send a couple of cars out looking, stuff like that.'

'Keep going,' Eddie said.

'Then we got another one. Same thing. Guys wife having a meltdown. Said he was going to his temple, but she could tell something was wrong.'

Eddie frowned as he looked to Price. 'Did she know where it was? The temple?'

'No,' Jimmy said. 'But the third one did. Sarge sent a patrol car to the location. The attending officers won't be sleeping well for a while.'

Eddie asked, but he already knew the answer. 'What did they find?'

'A bloodbath. Bodies everywhere. Some sort of mass pact. Looked more like an abattoir than a chapel.'

# THE ESCORT TO THE GRAVE

'What's the location, Jimmy?'

'Sorry Eddie, no chance. CID are all over it. They see you turning up, they'll be asking who told you. Or think you're involved somehow.'

'I can keep my mouth shut, Jimmy. It's all linked to something a lot bigger, reaching overseas.'

'They've already made the connection. They'll be calling your mates in Major Crime to get up there any minute.'

The phone went dead. They shared a look, then headed back into the bedroom. From her bed, Ellie gave a beaming smile as she rubbed noses with her donkey again.

'You see Ee-aw,' she said. 'The baddies always lose in the end.'

# Chapter 42

They were barely out of the door before Price's phone exploded to life. Her answers were short and sharp, and she refrained from asking any questions herself. When she ended the call, she turned to Eddie. 'Everyone's been called in. Dyfed Powys Police have requested our presence as soon as possible on a major incident at a property in the Talgarth area. We're waiting on DCI Hibbard to come in, then we'll be heading up there.' She let out a big breath as she rubbed at her face.

'You're going to find a lot of dead bodies, Price, a complete mess. Just like Ellie's drawing. Will you believe it then?'

'If that's what we find, then that drawing will be evidence. And a lot of people will wonder where it came from and how it ended up with you. You'll be considered a suspect, Eddie.'

'But you don't think that.'

'What makes you so sure?'

'Because you haven't arrested me,' he said with a smile. 'And why would I show you the drawing if I was the one who did it? Now answer my question. Will you believe what she's doing when you see the bodies?'

'Who's to say she didn't draw it afterwards, someone else feeding her the information?'

'Whatever for?'

'I… I don't know,' she said, turning away to open her car door.

'It's ok Price. For a long time, I didn't want to believe what was happening to me, either. Just keep one thing in mind. You saw the drawing. The guy slitting the throats wore the weird mask with the antlers. If you don't find it there, my guess is he's still out there somewhere.'

Arriving back at his flat, Eddie found Stretch, the landlord of the Miners, sweeping out front. Without looking up from his broom, he spoke just three words, enough to turn Eddie's face sour.

'You've been summonsed.'

'Thanks for the good news,' Eddie replied. 'How much?'

'Five,' Stretch replied.

Five hundred quid. A hefty price for what must be hefty information. But Eddie knew the score. He owed his early years to the club, and it relied on charitable donations now more than ever. That meant he should expect to double it and now a grand would come out of his pocket. The information had better be worth it. He'd originally planned on taking a few hours to look over the research Joyce emailed over from the library while he waited for an update from Price, but it would have to wait now. Instead, he went straight to his bedroom and removed the back panel from the wardrobe, revealing a stack of cash in used twenty-pound notes. Counting out the thousand, he slipped it into an envelope and pocketed it. His eyes moved to the bottom drawer of the bedside table, where he kept his favourite switchblade. In his mind there was little doubt Ellie's drawing from earlier, where he stood very much alive over the very dead body, was absolute. He wondered if he even had a choice how the next few hours would play out. She had seen how this evening would end, and whether he took the knife or not wouldn't have any bearing on the outcome. Or would it? She had shown him the eventuality, so wouldn't his decisions over the next few hours change everything, anyway? If he jumped on a plane this afternoon, then it would all get avoided, but the fact he hadn't done so, and didn't intend to either, only added weight to the argument his free will meant nothing in the grand scheme of it all.

The Slaughterhouse gym had seen some tremendous fighters over the years. Steeped in rich history, it had seen many British and European champions starting their careers in the modest gymnasium. They had, a number of years back, even boasted a World champion in featherweight Martin Collins, but the success of Mixed Martial Arts becoming a mainstream sport had seen youngsters deflecting in their droves, and recent years saw the club scraping by on meagre membership. It made him wonder how Don managed to keep the club doors open at all, but then again, the club was all he lived for.

Eddie loved coming here. The thud of the heavy bags taking hits. The click of skipping ropes as they skimmed the floor and the whirring as they sliced through the air. The slapping of sparring pads getting worked. Shouts and screams from the coaches as they walked the room giving brutal opinions on loose hooks and weak uppercuts. The familiar smells of stale sweat and deep heat. He loved it all. Today, however, was a different story. He'd been called here for a reason, and he couldn't help but think it had something to do with the hundred grand Bentley sitting outside, currently being guarded by some knuckle dragging individual in a tracksuit who stared him down all the way through the car park.

Inside, aged promotion posters from fights gone by lined the brickwork like wallpaper, stuck every which way with no sign of order. Famous faces mixed with local heroes. Ali, Frazer, Foreman. Winstone, Owen, Thomas. All silently casting their expert eye over the amateurs in front of them. Respectfully keeping close to the perimeter, Eddie made his way around the gym to the far end, avoiding the throng of sweaty, grunting bodies as he went. A few paused long enough to give him a welcoming nod, and Vic, who even back in his teenage years Eddie had thought was the smallest and oldest man alive, and who was right now putting a promising hulk of a heavyweight through his paces in the ring on the pads, stopped and waved, narrowly avoiding a short right from his trainee for his troubles.

Eddie waved back, but kept moving toward the back office, rapping on the door and interrupting the mumbled conversation behind it. A response within came in the form of 'Yeah?'

If Vic was the oldest man Eddie knew, Don James, the owner of the Slaughterhouse, must have been a close second. He also happened to be the toughest bloke he'd ever met, a man that hit like a mule and moved like a ninja. Many people over the years had made the mistake of dismissing him as some flat capped, five-foot-eight, leather skinned pensioner, only to regain consciousness minutes later looking up at the clouds, wondering how they got there, what day of the week it was, and why they were missing most of their teeth.

'Eddie Venter,' Don said, looking him up and down from behind his worn office desk. 'What did I tell you all those years ago about keeping yourself in shape? I suppose it's my fault. I didn't explain that shape wasn't supposed to be a jacket potato.'

'Nice to see you too, Don,' Eddie replied as he shut the door behind him. 'Thought you'd be dead by now, considering there's cathedrals littered around the country younger than you.' His eyes moved to the third person in the room, sat with his enormous back to him. The man stayed facing forwards and Eddie moved off to the side until he recognised him.

'You know who this is?' Don asked.

'I do,' Eddie replied with a single nod. 'But never had the pleasure.'

Frank Noonan remained in his straining seat, steepling his shovel hands as he looked Eddie over. His large eyes creased together and his lips pursed as he frowned surprise, before turning back to Don with a nod of his own. Not quite what he was expecting, it seemed. His expensive business suit oozed class, but easily cancelled out by the masses of gold he wore over his neck, hands and wrists. He ran his fingers through his chalky hair hanging just short of his massive shoulders, then eased his fingers through his walrus moustache, shaping it as he sized up the man before him.

'I've been hearing your name a lot in the last twenty-four hours, lad,' he said with a thick accent sat somewhere between West Walian and Irish. 'Fortunately for you, I recognised the name and where I'd heard it before.' He stopped a moment, clearly waiting for a response. Silence ensued, Eddie not rising to the bait. From experience, he knew it was wise to keep conversations one way traffic with men holding a certain type of power. Interrupting the head of the biggest crime family in Wales would not go down well. He would answer when asked a question, nothing more.

Frank recognised it, the unspoken etiquette, the respect. A smirk lifted his moustache up one side. 'Don and I have done a lot of business over the years. He's shaped many of my fighters into bareknuckle champions. I've earned nothing short of a small fortune off the sweat this man has put into them, and the money I've put back into this club could never make up for his hard work and loyalty. He has my utmost respect, something few people earn from me.'

Eddie stole a glance at Don, who stared back in silence. The warning in his eyes told Eddie to keep his mouth shut and listen, something he intended on doing anyway.

'Respect and loyalty are also the reason I know your name, Mr. Venter. You see, this man sitting with us has yours, and you have his. Am I right?'

'You are,' Eddie said.

# THE ESCORT TO THE GRAVE

'I know your name because Don has spoken of you many times before, Mr. Venter, of your talent in the ring in your junior years. And he's used your example in teaching other talented boxers. Mainly to show them how easy it is to fuck things up, of course.'

Eddie raised an eyebrow at Don. Don's face remained unapologetic.

'Nothing happens in my community without me finding out about it, Mr. Venter. I've built a solid reputation on it. Maybe I'm getting lazy in my old age, but unfortunately one of my competitors has managed to hide a line of business from me I would never have allowed to continue if I had found out sooner. A line of business I was preparing to go to war over to stop. I was ready to take those inbred Donahue's lives, Mr. Venter. Every bastard one of them for what they have done. Plans were in motion. Now, you might wonder why I would tell you all this? Well, as it turns out, I didn't need to plan for anything. Instead, I've received information someone has been doing my bidding for me. Wiped them out completely. Last night, every male member worth carrying that stinking name travelled to some place in the Beacons and failed to return home. I have word my great rival, Gerry Donahue, two of his three sons and four nephews, are no more. Baited into attending some business and slaughtered like pigs. I have done some digging this morning, and my little birds have found that Dyfed Powys police are currently in attendance at an incident in the Beacons fitting the description. They are yet to be formally identified, but it appears Donahue, his family members and soldiers are a part of that incident. I have a police contact there who can't blow his cover by identifying them himself, but has kindly told me what those dirty bastards have been up to.'

Eddie didn't doubt it. Men like Frank Noonan paid handsomely for inside information from a variety of sources all over the country. There was little to be surprised about someone within the force coughing up details for cash. They'd get regular little envelopes off Frank for a variety of information. But the last thing they needed was to have their superiors questioning how they knew so much about crime families from miles away if they hadn't been directly involved in investigating them. Whoever Frank's contact was, they'd keep quiet, play dumb, and wait for someone else to identify the bodies.

Frank stood from the chair that creaked in relief. He was a mountain of a man who towered over Eddie. He straightened his silk tie before shooting his cuffs. 'Which brings me to you, Mr. Venter. This morning I received an unexpected call from none other than Gerry Donahue's distraught wife, begging me for help. To put decades of rivalry aside and help her eldest son Ronan seek retribution. Early this morning, Ronan received a tip off, informing him of what has transpired, his entire brotherhood killed, and the man responsible for their demise. And out of respect for my friend here, along with the wonderful thought the sneaky little fuck Ronan Donahue could follow his sorry excuse for a father into the ground, after she gave up the name I dropped everything to reach out to Don, and to yourself of course.'

Ellie's drawing of the kneeling men, branded and throats opened up. It had to be them, the line of men awaiting their fate in the temple.

'Who made the call to the son?' Eddie finally asked.

'They don't know. Only that the call came in informing him that you, Mr. Venter, were responsible for decimating their family. Now, the fact you haven't asked me what those filthy vermin have been doing leads me to believe you're not quite the innocent party in all this. Is that a fair assumption?'

'I have nothing to do with their deaths,' Eddie replied.

# THE ESCORT TO THE GRAVE

Frank twisted his moustache as he pondered this. He stared deep into Eddie's eyes, searching. 'Yet you still haven't asked, Mr. Venter.'

'About the children?' Eddie asked. 'That these Donahues have been trafficking children in from Europe and selling them off to some sick cult?'

A broad smile stretched across Frank's face. 'So you are involved. Excellent work Mr. Venter.' He slapped a giant mitt on Eddie's shoulder that threatened to dislocate. 'Although I'm told it was not the Donahues who trafficked them into the UK. They merely purchased them to sell on again.'

'And I'm guessing they were the ones disposing of them afterwards as well,' Eddie said.

'Sickening business,' Frank replied, holding his hand out to Eddie. 'But I'm not surprised. They always were a nasty bunch. I spared his wife the details of their enterprise. I didn't feel the need to rub her nose in it anymore than necessary. She has, after all, lost her husband and children, even if they were filthy scum.'

'Thank you, Mr. Noonan,' Eddie said, taking his hand.

'I've left a healthy donation for the club with Don here. Feel free to do the same, Mr. Venter. You do, after all, owe your life to him. I wouldn't have bothered reaching out if you meant nothing to him. But then again, you've done more for me in the last twenty-four hours than you could possibly know. So maybe I'm here to thank you.'

'I had nothing to do with their deaths, Mr. Noonan,' Eddie repeated.

'So you say. Keep your eyes open. You wouldn't be the first man Ronan Donahue has done in. He'll be coming for you. And he won't be offering fisty-cuffs to settle it.'

Could Ellie's other drawing, of him standing over a prone body, be him? Could it be this Donahue?

'He'll be gone by tonight,' he replied.

'I can see why you like him,' Frank chuckled, as he shook Don's hand and headed for the door. 'Best of luck to you.'

The door closed and Don dropped back into his seat like he'd been holding his breath the entire time. 'What the fuck, Eddie? I've always known you didn't mind a spot of bother, but you don't want to get tangled up with this lot. They don't settle with fists.'

Eddie reached into his back pocket, pulling the cash and dropping it to the desk. 'Guy in the ring with Vic moves well, good footwork.'

'Got potential,' Don said. 'Needs work on his head movement.'

'See you around Don.'

## Chapter 43

The journey from Merthyr to the temple, in the sleepy village of Talgarth, took all of forty-five minutes. The Major Crime team of eight handpicked to attend by Hibbard travelled up the A470 in an unmarked Mercedes people-carrier, and for the most part was a jovial affair like they were off on some team building exercise. They joked and ribbed each other and took bets on what they were about to find. All they had been told was Dyfed Powys CID had called them in again, similar to the incident at the farm, after deducing a potential link to their own investigations.

Hibbard sat in the front passenger seat, and although he'd no doubt received his own brief of what to expect, offered no clues to the rest of them, clearly enjoying some of the ridiculous theories fabricated behind him. Price struggled to share in the light mood, her mind somersaulting with visions of bodies Ellie had drawn. She kept her gaze out at her back seat window to avoid drawing attention, watching the rolling hills zip by in a blur. Being pulled in two directions was beginning to show, and she struggled with the notion the events of the last couple of weeks may be down to such unexplainable means. She didn't believe in that sort of stuff. How could a six-year-old girl really be predicting such awful events? Was this part of some elaborate scheme to fool her into believing she was? Eddie believed it, but surely his faith was misplaced. Through all his troubles, she knew he was a good man, and she *really* wanted to believe him, and Ellie too, but for so long she had worked on facts rather than faith, and no matter how hard she tried, her mind continuously searched for reasoning rather than accept there was none. There was still no proof, as it stood, the girl drew anything before it happened. All rationale continued to point to someone telling her what to draw. A witness to the murders.

Yet for some reason, she *did* believe Eddie was there at the house yesterday when she had drawn this piece. And she now had to accept with great reluctance if she could believe that, then her way of thinking should change if they found what they suspected at the temple. She hoped the girl was wrong, and it was all a big mistake. That she wasn't being asked, yet again, to have faith. If he could see her now, her father would laugh his ass off, then reel off one of his favourite passages; *Faith doesn't make things easy, it makes them possible. Luke, one - thirty seven.*

'Earth to Price? Come in, Price?'

She came to, eyes moving to each of the faces staring back at her, Hibbard included.

'Welcome back,' DC Hadley said. 'Thought we'd lost you for a minute. I asked, what do you think we're going to find?'

She shrugged her shoulders and huffed. 'So far up in the sticks? Got to be a sighting of Bigfoot.'

The rest of the team chuckled and turned back around. Hibbard continued to stare. She caught his look but couldn't hold it, averting her eyes to her phone vibrating in hand. A text message.

*Bodies are crime family of gang leader Gerry Donahue from West Wales, responsible for receiving trafficked children to deliver to Druid cult. Family and soldiers lured to temple under guise of business deal and taken out. Call made to Donahue's wife and son from suspect in early hours.*

How the hell was Eddie getting the information? She tapped out a quick response.

*Ten minutes away, will report findings later.*

# THE ESCORT TO THE GRAVE

Two minutes out, Hibbard turned to give his brief. The mood turned serious as they listened to the limited information he had. Many bodies in one building. Some identified, some not. Forensics were already on scene and authorised to make a start. It was pretty much all he had. Price winced at the thought she possibly knew more.

The entrance to the temple grounds sat at the end of a row of semi-detached houses. High pillars flanked the gates, with a circular stone wall surrounding the grounds, opening onto a path wide enough for single file traffic to drive up to the building at the top of the hill. Although the grounds looked similar to a church setting, the building itself was anything but. It was a large, simple two-storey structure, cube shaped with a tall peaked roof. No extravagant stained glass windows or stone carvings in sight. The front of the building had no windows at all, and interviews with the neighbours below had revealed they all mistook it for a Masonic lodge of some sort. They had seen people congregate at the building many times, decent looking people, quietly going about their business. During their late evening events there, the members showed the utmost respect to the residents, coming and going quietly to avoid stepping on anyone's toes. They would even see members litter picking and weeding around the area, doing their bit for the community. The members would chat with the neighbours, hold charity fundraisers on the grounds, handing over cheques and donations to the village councillors and town mayor, and although seen as secretive and mysterious, never considered a threat among the local community.

The gates to the temple grounds had been taped off hours ago, but a gaggle of onlookers continued to hang around, and now held their phones aloft as the black Mercedes van pulled up, like they were expecting an A-list celebrity to get out. A uniformed officer guarding the entrance untied the tape from one side to allow them to pass, then reattached it as they continued up the path. Disembarking from the van, they made their way to the large white tent set up across the building entrance. A member of the forensics team received them, suiting them up in disposables bracing them ready to enter the building. Hibbard hung back with the CID Detective Inspector, a short, bald man he seemed to have met before, gathering the information on who they had identified so far.

Price joined the rest of the team as they followed two forensic investigators in. Stopping at the entrance, she looked at the lone, blue circular plaque adorning the large wooden door. Written in gold letters around the circumference were the words *The Ancient Order of the Grove Druids*. Sat at its centre, also in gold, was the Triquetra symbol. Price crossed the threshold, meeting up with the rest of the team at the temple foyer. A faint smell permeated the air, and she couldn't tell if it was the fousty-mould scent common to every old, damp chapel, or the decomposition process already underway. One of the forensic investigators offered an open tub of Vicks Vapor Rub around the group and each of them dipped a finger in to rub under their noses, before covering them over with their masks. That answered that, then.

Led through the internal doors to the main hall, they all stood fixed on the crime scene. A large team of forensics worked away like a colony of busy ants, climbing over each other to piece it all together. Price spotted a stressed looking Deborah King, Hibbard's flirting Forensic Co-ordinator, pointing and shouting instructions to her team. A photographer stood at her side, showing her a shot she had just taken, and as their bodies parted, Price took stock of the massacre behind them.

Still kneeling upright on the cold stone floor, in arced rows facing the main altar, were the mass of bodies positioned as if taking part in some sickening prayer service. They knelt with their hands interlaced in their laps and chins tucked to their chests, and she wondered how they had not fallen onto their sides in their last moments. A slug trail of blood ran from each body, leading from a communal point at the altar to each of their final resting places.

Walking down the centre of the formation, her paper overshoes rustling on the flagstone surface, Price looked left then right, dipping her head to try and identify any of the men. Cause of death was obvious, all appearing to bear the same injuries, wide and deep gashes from one side of the neck to the other, long run dry. All were topless and had identical raw brand marks to their exposed, paling chests. Beside the front altar, two wrought irons sat in a cooling fire-pit, each capped with *that* triangular symbol. She looked back at the bodies. Although pulled down to their waists, some men appeared to be dressed in identical, once white robes, now heavily stained from the sticky mess of blood they were drenched with. Older men of retirement age, members, Price guessed, belonging to this temple.

Others wore casual wear, tracksuits or jeans, scruffy younger men in their twenties and thirties, save for one or two looking older, all victims of equal fate. Price moved back down the makeshift aisle, doing her best to dodge the tacky trails of blood, taking a quick count of over thirty bodies as she passed them. All faces gave away their last moment of terror, mouths hanging slack and eyes popping from their sockets, and she imagined the immense panic and pain they must have felt as the knife ran through their necks. The smell was stronger here, penetrating through her surgical mask and the menthol ointment under her nose. As she tiptoed around the throng of bodies, she looked to the walls. Large portraits bordered with ornate golden frames lined them in chronological order, paintings of previous members sitting proudly in their ceremonial robes. Some held titles ahead of their names, dating back hundreds of years, but she had no idea who any of them were. Earl,

Lord, Sir. Important looking men of times gone by, all apparently sharing the honoured title of Arch-druid, as the name plaques at the base of the frames suggested. Each plaque held a date, the last reading 2000 - 2010.

Walking back to the altar, she stopped again. Gallons of dried blood and tissue stained the grey flagstone floor. There was little to argue about what happened here. Each man had received their brand at the firepit, had their throat opened at the altar, then somehow dragged themselves back to their final kneeling place to bleed out. *Exactly like Ellie's drawing.* Price tried to imagine the men crawling back across the stone floor as the warm fluid emptied from them. *How in God's name had they managed such a thing?*

Above the fire-pit, a gold plaque with large lettering read *Arch-druid Incumbent,* beneath an empty space similar in size to the portraits around the room. Small holes were visible where fixings had been pulled from the wall.

'Missing frame,' Hibbard said as he appeared next to her.

Price jolted away, caught off guard. 'Jesus Christ!'

'You can call me Sir,' Hibbard replied with a smirk.

'Haven't been able to locate it,' Deborah King said as she also magically appeared next to him. 'Good to see you again, DCI Hibbard,' she said. 'It's been a while.'

Price rolled her eyes. If they thought they were fooling anyone, they needed their heads examined.

'Do you have a time of death?' Price asked.

'Twelve to fourteen hours,' Deborah replied.

'That's all? They smell like they've been dead a lot longer?'

'Yes, they are a bit whiffy, aren't they?' Deborah chuckled. 'But from the age of some of them, they might have been decomposing for years!' She threw her head back in laughter. Hibbard joined her as she rested her hand on his chest. Once they calmed down, she reiterated. 'Twelve to fourteen hours, Detective.'

# THE ESCORT TO THE GRAVE

*From midnight onwards.*

Ellie's drawing was all Price could see. The mystery man running his blade across his victim's throats, the sinister skull mask with the antlers. She turned to Hibbard. 'Did CID find any masks?'

'How did you know?' Hibbard asked, his eyes narrowing again. It was fast becoming his go-to-look towards her.

'Theories are like arseholes,' she said, shrugging her shoulders. 'Everyone's got one.'

'That's opinions,' Hibbard replied, raising an eyebrow. 'And yes, they found a bunch out back, weird looking things, animal skulls with horns.'

'Antlers,' Price and Deborah said together.

The three of them stood in silence. Hibbard stared Price down, working his face into a deep frown, searching.

With a sideways glance, Deborah cleared her throat and pointed to a door in the corner. 'Um, they're through there.'

Without taking his eyes from his Detective Constable, Hibbard spoke. 'Deb, give us a minute.'

Deborah lowered her head as she backed away. She stomped off in the direction of two forensic investigators stood chatting at the main doors.

'Mind telling me how you know that?' Hibbard asked when out of earshot.

'They're all similar, aren't they? The masks?'

'Let's go find out,' Hibbard replied, taking off toward the door. They walked through to a large locker room where two more forensic investigators were busy photographing more evidence. A number of lockers laid open, casual clothes, shoes and wallets strewn all over the floor. On the back wall, facing the lockers, hung a large display of masks. There were over twenty in total, no two identical, but all similar in material and appearance. They stared back at the two officers with their hollowed eye sockets and sinister grins, the skulls of what looked like deer, some more mature than others, with varying amounts of tines or points to their antlers. Price scanned each one, counting furiously. There was one empty mount above the rest of them she guessed belonged to the mask from Ellie's drawing. She had counted the points on it, sixteen for the Monarch, king of the stags.

The Arch-druid's mask wasn't there.

'Spill,' Hibbard said.

Price pulled in a deep breath, then let it out in one big blast through her nostrils. 'It's the Morrison girl, Elinor. Don't ask me how, but uh, she predicted this would happen.'

'She told you about this place? The bodies? The masks?'

'No, she drew it. I saw it this morning, when we went to see her.'

'We?' Hibbard asked, an eyebrow raising high up his creasing forehead.

Price looked to her feet and sighed. 'I went there with Eddie Venter this morning, Sir. It was unbelievable. She drew it all, the mess out there.'

'A drawing? She did yesterday? And all this stuff?' Hibbard said, looking to the masks, shaking his head. 'I suppose she told you about all this stuff, too?'

She stayed quiet long enough for him to turn back to her. 'Price? The masks?' He walked right up to her, fully invading her personal space, his body mere inches from hers. Puffing out his chest, he forced her to look up at him.

'How did you know about them?'

She closed her eyes, wishing the simple action would teleport her away, then gave another sigh. 'There was one in the picture. Eddie told me about the others. A man who killed himself at Llangorse Lake two days ago was his father-in-law. When Eddie went to the scene, he had a vision of what the guy had been doing. He was a part of all this. This cult, or whatever it is. Eddie's convinced they're responsible for the children at the farm. It's all linked, Sir. Look.'

# THE ESCORT TO THE GRAVE

She gave her phone to Hibbard, Eddie's text message about the crime family members on the screen, the same ones now dead next door.

'They're the ones in plain clothes CID haven't been able to identify out there. They were responsible for delivering the children here, to these sickos.'

Silence fell in the room as he took it in. The clicking of the forensic investigators' cameras had ceased. They were both too busy staring at the detectives.

Hibbard scowled as he read, his eyes flicking back and fore. 'You're right, Price. It is all linked. Linked through Eddie Venter. How could you be so blind? I'll be calling in and seeking his immediate arrest. It's obvious he's complicit in all this. Why didn't you say anything earlier?'

'With respect, you're wrong, Sir. Eddie Venter is the reason we've been able to link any of this at all. He's an ally.'

'And you're a liability if you believe any of his crap,' Hibbard snapped, loud enough to startle her. 'Now I'd suggest you decide where your loyalties lie, and quickly.'

'That's not fair,' Price spat back. 'It was your idea for me to work with him in the first place.'

'And relay information back to your own team,' he replied as he handed the phone back. 'Not withhold it. And certainly not to leak anything you find back in his direction.'

She looked to the phone and her reply to Eddie. *Will report findings later.* As much as she'd like to argue, Hibbard had a point. But she had seen the drawing with her own eyes. With the time frame on the corpses at twelve to fourteen hours, the drawing could only have been made afterwards if Eddie was involved. But he couldn't be. She trusted him. Whatever was happening, the visions he claimed to see, the information he found, she couldn't help but think it may really be something unexplainable.

'Come here,' Hibbard said, grabbing under her one arm and pulling her to a corner. 'Eddie Venter is a manipulative piece of shit, always has been, and it's my fault you've fallen for it. But you've found out some vital information linking Eddie Venter to this. Now it's time to bring him in and lean on him to tell us the truth. You've done well. You've a bright future in this department, a shoo-in to climb the ladder. If we get convictions on this, I'll be putting your name forward for Detective Sergeant. So, like I said, remember where your loyalties lie. Find out where he is, and quietly. I'm going to brief the team we're moving out soon. I want to know where we can find him before I call it in.'

Price watched him strut back through to the main hall, then turned to the forensic investigators, who promptly looked away to downplay their eavesdropping. Her head felt like it was going to explode as she looked up at the masks sneering back at her. Deciding she needed some space, she wandered through the next door and into the secretarial chamber, a large room furnished with a grand oak writing desk and chair. More portraits lined the walls, accompanied by displays on sideboards of what appeared to be ceremonial daggers and axes in glass cases. Some had what looked like bone handles, beautifully carved into different shapes. Others were even more ornate, encrusted with gold and gemstones of every colour and size. High behind the desk was another picture, a huge framed painting of a dark figure sat atop a pearly white horse. His face hid in the shadows of his hooded black cloak, yet his glowing red eyes lit enough to make out the sinister grin of a fleshless human skull. A grand set of antlers protruded high from his head. Price counted their tines. Sixteen for the Monarch, the same as the figure in Ellie's picture. At the feet of the horse stood two wolfhounds, their fur matching its own white coat. The tips of their ears glowed red, the same as their master's eyes. The group posed at the summit of a mountain

Price recognised, the telltale valleys of the Brecon Beacons in the distance giving it away. The dogs growled at a group of slaves as they worked to set a mound of stones at the peak. She recognised it as the cairn at the top of Pen-y-fan.

The late afternoon sun streamed in through the solitary arched window of the chamber, illuminating the dust motes suspended in the stale air. Rounding the desk, she leaned back against it as she looked to the shimmering gold plaque beneath the painting. It was a name Eddie had shown her at the library, although the depiction of the character was much different this time.

*Arawn - Grove Druid Lord of the Otherworld.*

She thought of the man in Ellie's drawing, holding back his victim's hair to reveal his throat. Troubling her, was the expressions on the kneeling men's faces, placid looks of acceptance. The monstrous mask the man wore was undeniably an homage to this Druid God, proving it clear it was some sort of sick ritual they had stumbled on. Closing her eyes, she worked her head from ear to shoulder, ear to shoulder, an attempt to loosen the stiffness creeping into her neck. Leaning on the table edge, her latex covered fingers furrowed under the lip of the desk, then stopped as they felt something abnormal there. Price kept her eyes closed as she blocked out the rustling sound of approaching paper covered footsteps entering the room, concentrating on what she had found. Her left middle finger took purchase and pushed in what felt like a button. A loud thud came from the painting facing her as she opened her eyes once more and turned to meet the new arrival.

'What was that?' Deborah King asked as she stood with a puzzled expression. She inched closer as Price turned back to the painting, the right-hand side now protruding an inch away from the wall. She slipped her fingers into the gap and pulled, the enormous portrait pivoting on the hidden hinges at its left side, to reveal a heavy duty steel wall safe. A large silver combination dial sat in the middle, inviting her to chance her luck and open it.

'No touchy. I'll call the team in to dust for prints,' King said with enthusiasm as she bounced around and called out from the doorway. Moments later, the room was filled with forensics again, working over the desk button and newly found safe. Price stood back with her arms crossed, watching them work, soon joined by Deborah again.

'Great work Detective,' she said, nudging her elbow with her own as though they were becoming best chums. They both watched as a forensics officer brushed at the frame of the painting. 'I'm no safe cracker, but I'm guessing it's going to take some time to get into it. That bad boy looks serious.' She let out a snort like she'd said something hilarious.

Price stared at the safe, busy thinking about Eddie, or more precisely, Eddie's father-in-law. Eddie told her he was apparently the secretary for this place, meaning he must have had the responsibility of balancing the books and the finances running through it. Sensitive and important information, so it would be fair to assume he would need a reliable way of storing such documents. Access to a hidden safe would be perfect.

Eddie had described Malcolm's last moments to her in detail. She remembered thinking at the time the only way he could know all that stuff was if he'd actually been a witness when he did it. If his gift was to be believed, then in a way, Eddie *was* a witness. She tried to imagine Malcolm beneath the boat, looking up to the belly of it in the glum water before his lungs raged and forced themselves open. The calmness and quiet before the panic overtook him. It was during that time he managed to reach back up to the underside of the boat to leave his last message. How could Eddie possibly know about it without having seen the event unfold himself? When he had described what his father-in-law had done in those last moments, running his blade through the wood, she couldn't quite believe it. No-one had thought to check the underside of the boat, not even the frogmen who pulled Malcolm from the bottom of the lake. But Eddie had known the marks were there. He had watched the man carve those numbers, though not when he had made them.

'I think I might know how to get into it,' Price said as she continued to stare at the safe.

King frowned back at her. 'How could you possibly know that?'

Price turned to her, grabbing her by the shoulders, eyes wide with excitement. 'Deb, you're in regular contact with the pathologists across the boroughs. Do you know of anyone working on a drowning in the last couple of days? Pulled from Llangorse Lake?'

'I do,' King said, shrugging her shoulders. 'Straight forward enough. It was Eddie Venter's father-in-law.'

Price's head flinched back. 'You know Eddie?'

'Of course,' King replied, shrugging her shoulders. 'Everyone knows Eddie. He's one hell of a boy. I've worked with him on several of his discoveries. Never fails to amaze me.' A broad smile rose on her face. 'Working with facts and evidence for so many years, I was resolute in the pursuit of deductive reasoning and the truth. Nothing ever came close to the science. Eddie Venter certainly blew that out of the water. What can I say? He made a believer out of me. Showed me there are some things even science can't explain. He phoned yesterday to see if I could find out any details on the postmortem. It was open and shut, pardon the pun. Lungs flooded, cause of death, drowning.'

Price ducked her head and looked back to the door, lowering her voice to a whisper. 'I need your help, Deb. As we speak, DCI Hibbard is making calls to arrest Eddie on suspicion of involvement in this case. He thinks he must have been in on it because of what he knows.'

'That's surprising. John is normally so open-minded,' King said with a giggle. 'In certain situations, at least. But if I know Eddie, nothing will stick.'

'What if I told you I think the guy in the mortuary fridge was the user of this safe? That he carved a series of numbers into the bottom of the boat he threw himself from before he died? Or that the police missed them completely, but Eddie found them when he went to the lake?'

'Then I'd say you're a believer of Eddie's methods too, DC Price.'

Price stared back, pondering her statement.

'So you think Eddie knows the code to the safe?'

'I think so,' Price said. 'But if Hibbard sees us open it, he'll want to know where the code came from.'

'Then we keep it from him until we know either way. Can you get the numbers?'

Price pulled her phone from her pocket. 'Let's find out.'

# Chapter 44

Ronan Donahue sat in the driver seat of his silver BMW in the depths of the alleyway overlooking the Miner's Arms. The sun had dipped behind the rows of terraced houses running on either side of the alley, ready for the darkness to swallow up the car.

The evening air still held an uncomfortable humidity that soaked his forehead, and now a trickle of sweat made its way down the small of his back. He desperately wanted the air conditioning on, to feel the cool breeze soothe his face, but he daren't run the engine and risk blowing his cover. Set back up a short hill opposite the high street, the alley was a perfect vantage point over the pub, the neighbouring shop, and more importantly, the door to the flat above it. It ran between the rear ends of two terraced streets, the gardens and garages to the properties backing onto it, and the last thing he needed was some curtain twitcher coming out to see who was messing around outside. A couple of youngsters had walked past and given him the stink eye already, no doubt wondering what an unfamiliar car was doing in their territory.

He'd had to hide the handgun he was loading the clip into at the last second, realising he needed to be more careful in case he made someone nervous enough to dial 999. The gun was now back in his jacket pocket as a back-up, but the weapon he planned to use, his trusty twelve bore sawn-off shotgun, hid away in the boot. It was a perfect length, the butt able to tuck under his arm so the barrel hid neatly away under the bottom of his jacket. The shortened barrel also made missing from close range extremely difficult, giving plenty of room for error. It surprised him how much power and noise it had added to the gun. Both times he had previously used it, his victims had bled out within a minute. Now it sat loaded, ready in the boot, waiting for its third. This time it would be different, though. A slower, more painful death. A shot to the knees would be plenty to get him talking, but if he was careful, he could prolong the bastard's agony long enough for him to get the information he needed before sending him on to the next place.

He shifted in his seat as his arse cheeks ached with numbness. He'd only sat prone for an hour or so, and already he was doubting the information on the piece of shit that killed his family. He couldn't understand why his father hadn't called on him to attend with them last night. After all, he was more involved in the Druid business than the rest of them. He set up the initial meet between his father and the Belarusians, as well as the arrangements with the Druids over in the Breconshire valley. He was even the brains behind the disposal plans, finding that farmer had been nothing short of a stroke of genius. He had masterminded and brokered the deal that earned the Donahue family a sizable fortune. But for some reason, his father saw fit to leave him out of the meet at the temple.

Was it fate he had eluded the trap? Or something his father knew? A niggling feeling played on repeat he had not so much escaped, but rather, spared. It troubled him to think for what purpose. *Don't be a twat. Dad wouldn't lead everyone into a bloodbath, knowing they wouldn't be coming out of it. They had fooled him as much as everyone else, the stupid fucking tit.*

The voice on the phone early this morning told him he had been at the temple, witness to the slaughter, somehow managing to escape. He even identified the man responsible, saying this piece of shit, Venter, some leader of a local criminal gang in Merthyr, had heard of the contract and was muscling in on the Donahue business with the Druids. Hours of frantic phone calls and visits to his father's and brother's places had confirmed they were all missing, and Malcolm, his contact at the temple, wasn't answering his calls. The only thing he could do was see it for himself, and after driving all the way there, he found it swarming with pigs and forensics, confirming his worst fears.

Ronan wasn't stupid. He knew the voice on the phone was lying. There was more to it than he let on, but he had no choice to go with it. He had no way of finding the caller other than to go through this Venter. Hobble the bastard to torture the information from him. He would give up the voice on the phone, and then he would receive an equally unwelcome visit and similar treatment afterwards. He'd show up soon, and once he'd dealt with him and the voice on the phone, he could go back to rebuilding the Donahue name for what it's always been. He was the head of the family now, and unless he acted quickly, then those dirty, stinking Noonans would move in on his turf before his father's and brother's bodies were in the ground. He still couldn't believe his old girl had begged for their help. He could have told her Frank Noonan wouldn't do fuck all for them unless they gave him everything. He'd get his come-uppance soon enough, though.

Wiping away more beads of sweat from his head, he hoped the sun going down would cool the air quickly. Below the lane there was movement, the door to the pub swinging open for two men to step out, pint glasses in hand. One offered the other a cigarette, and they stood watching the traffic pass as they smoked. Ronan clenched his teeth from the craving. He thought about risking it and lighting one up, but the job in hand got the better of him and the pack on the passenger seat stayed closed. He'd been told this guy Venter was a clever bastard, and taking him out was going to need careful and methodical planning. But that wasn't the Donahue way. They were bold in their statements. The louder, the better. Hence the shotgun in the boot.

His vengeance was coming, and he would make the loudest of statements. Don't fuck with Ronan Donahue.

And with that, the door to the flat between the pub and the shop opened.

The craving for the cigarette disappeared.

## Chapter 45

Away from the commotion surrounding the desk, Price made her way to the corner of the secretarial chamber. Eddie answered on the third ring. She left out the pleasantries.

'Hibbard's instructed me to find where you are. He wants you in for questioning as a suspect. Sorry Eddie. He finds it hard to believe you're not involved in all this.'

'He's wasting his time. He's got nothing, but if you want, tell him I'll be in the Miners.'

'I'm guessing you won't actually be there?'

'What can I say?' Eddie replied. 'Maybe I'm a changed man. But I might just turn up to see what he's got to say. Are you at the temple?'

'Yeah, and it's a mess.'

'But it's just as Ellie drew, right?'

Price's long silence was enough. 'Look Eddie, I have to be quick. You said your father-in-law was the secretary for this place, right? Well, I'm in a rear chamber office with a hidden safe…'

'The numbers,' Eddie interrupted. 'It's got to be. He's told us the code for a reason. There's something important in there, Price. Something that helps end this.'

'Do you have them? The numbers?'

'I took a picture of them on my phone. I'll send it over now.'

'Um, Eddie?' she stammered. 'If Ellie's drawing was right about the temple, then I suppose the other one will be too.'

Eddie chuckled. 'Are you starting to believe in the supernatural, Price? You'll be hanging garlic and crosses on your front door next.'

'Just be careful, funny man,' she replied. 'I'll let you know if we get in the safe.'

Forensics were busy setting up additional podium lights around the desk when Hibbard came bounding in. Making his way over to Price, he pointed a thumb toward them. 'What they got?'

'Found a safe. Dusting for prints.'

'They get in it?'

'They're calling in a locksmith,' Price said, shooting him a sideways glance.

Hibbard nodded. 'You find Venter?'

'He's in the Miner's Arms.'

Hibbard turned to her, placing a rough hand on her shoulder. 'I know you like him, Price, but you've done the right thing. Now let's go pull him in.'

'Actually Sir…'

'DCI Hibbard,' Deborah King interrupted. 'Could I have a word? I'm in need of a rather large favour, I'm afraid. And I'm hoping you could be my knight in shining armour?' She lowered her voice so only the three of them could hear. 'I promise to repay you, of course. Any way you feel appropriate.' She gave a wicked, knowing grin that had Hibbard smirking back.

'What do you need?' he replied.

'I'm in a bit of a pickle, John. Detective Constable Price here tells me she has some basic forensic training that would really pull me out of a hole, with your permission, of course. Some of my team have to move out onto another case and I'm short of some bodies, pardon the pun. I could do with DC Price hanging about for another hour or so.' She tucked her hair behind her ear and lowered her head. 'I'll drop her back personally.'

# THE ESCORT TO THE GRAVE

'We're about to make an arrest in this case, Deb. I need her with me,' Hibbard replied.

Deborah checked over her shoulder, then got close enough for him to feel her breath. She ran her fingers over the shirt button covering his chest, threatening to free it.

'Don't make me beg, DCI Hibbard. Not yet, anyway.'

Hibbard looked to Price, who tried and failed to hide the smile rising on her face. 'He's in the Miner's, you say?'

She nodded.

'I want to know what's in that as soon as you have something,' he said, pointing to the safe. He looked Deborah King up and down. 'And I'll see you later. Don't forget the kit.'

Price waited until Hibbard was out through the door. 'The kit?'

'Let's just say John likes it when we role play,' Deborah said. 'And he has a thing for forensic suits.'

Price chuckled. 'Thanks for covering for me.'

'Piece of cake,' Deborah replied. 'I get whatever I want with John. He's actually rather selfless in the bedroom, you know. All I need to do is let him think he's in control from time to time.' She clapped her hands together. 'Now, let's try to get in that safe, shall we?'

Price smirked as she checked her phone and saw the notification for a message. Opening it revealed a photo of the bottom of a boat. A scratched in set of numbers was visible in the slimy blue paint. She showed it to Deborah.

'You lot finished on the safe?' she shouted over her shoulder.

'Just lifted a lone print from the frame,' one officer called back.

'Then stand aside team!' Deborah bellowed in a deep theatrical tone, holding out an arm as if clearing a path. 'Your safe cracker awaits!'

Price gave her an amused look. She liked the kooky woman. For such a morbid job, she certainly had as much fun as possible carrying it out. Her weird personality helped, no doubt, and was probably why she and Hibbard were an item. Price couldn't imagine a normal woman putting up with him, and Deborah surprised her with her admission *she* was the one using *him* to get what she wanted. She couldn't help but admire it.

Walking toward and round the desk, the forensic officers moved aside for her to pass. Deborah followed closely, looking over Price's shoulder to get a better view of the phone as she held it in front of her. Taking hold of the dial, Price spun it a few times clockwise to reset it, then stopped on the first number, seven. She twisted it to the left. Thirty-eight. Back to the right, nineteen. Left twenty-eight, then right twenty-one. Standing back, her hands went to her hips as if expecting something to happen automatically. She looked to Deborah, who responded with a nod toward the safe handle. Taking hold of it, she pulled down hard. The heavy clunk startled them both.

Deborah let out a chortle at the successful first attempt, slapping her on the back. 'Bravo Miss Parker.' she declared.

Price looked to her and raised an eyebrow.

'Bonnie Parker?' Deborah said, holding her hands out. 'Bonnie and Clyde? The greatest female bank robber of all time? You youngsters know nothing these days!'

Heaving the safe door open, Price had to lean back to help counter the weight, following the hinged frame of the portrait at the left side. The two women almost touched heads as they peered inside the steel box. They shared a quiet moment of contemplation until the snapping sound of fresh latex gloves on skin made Price jump. Deborah reached into the dark void, pulling from the smaller shelf at the top a large book and setting it down on the desk. A forensics investigator repositioned the lights over it, as another of the team swept in with her brushes and powders, lifting another set of prints from the book cover. Deborah

## THE ESCORT TO THE GRAVE

and Price turned back to the empty safe with matching, disheartened frowns, hoping to have found more.

As the investigator carefully stored the prints away in their glass frames, Deborah offered Price the box of gloves for her to pick a fresh pair. 'Would you care to do the honours, m'lady?' she asked.

After snapping on a pair, Price opening the well-worn, delicate looking book. Inside, page after page held handwritten notes and names in columned sections, with vast sums of money alongside. It was a records book, filled with donations to the temple dating back many years. The monetary values inside were both impressive and sickening in equal measure. She flipped to the empty pages two thirds into the thick book, where the most recent of donations had been recorded, hoping to find names she was familiar with. Business titles and private donor names lined the left columns, with the donation figures to the right. There were varying amounts written in black ink, some totalling six figures. The last column held the net total dated a few days ago, 26th August 2019, at a shade over four million pounds. They had been a busy bunch, these Grove druids. Running a gloved finger down the names column, Price hoped to find something familiar. She flipped back a page, one payment jumping out at her, written in red pen.

31st July 2019, Donahue - £50,000.

Flipping another page, the name was there in red again, standing out amongst the scrawls of black ink. 30th June 2019, Donahue - £50,000.

'The red pen and minus symbols I'd guess as deductions,' Deborah said, stating the obvious. 'Purchases of some kind? But for what?'

'The Donahues are some of your corpses next door,' Price huffed as she rubbed at her eyes.

Deborah's face slackened.

'They were selling children to the wackos that owned this place, then took them away when finished with them.

Looks like each one had cost them fifty grand for the pleasure.'

Working backwards, there was an outgoing payment in red on the last day of each month, same name and amounts each time. She turned her attention to the lists of donations in black again, scanning through the names of the donors. She noticed a pattern emerging, some names and donations made on a monthly basis. *Members.* She would bet everything she owned these donor business names last night lost their directors and owners to a knife across the throat in that very hall next door. It would take a certain type of person to have access to such a club as this. A person with money. Of elite standing in the community. Someone who gets off on killing kids.

A twisted fuck.

Then she saw it.

All at once, she felt a rush of blood to the head. A dark shadow pulled down over her eyes, then lifted again. She squeezed them shut and when she reopened them, the book on the table blurred into the desk surrounding it. Bile rose in her throat and she fought to keep it down. Reaching out, her hand grabbed at Deborah's sleeve for support and she tugged at it violently.

'What's wrong Lauren? What is it?'

The next breath refused to come, and her legs lost purpose. It took everything Deborah had to keep her from hitting the floor, catching under Price's arms as she yelled for an officer to get a chair. Sitting her down, Deborah made her best attempts to calm her.

'Concentrate on your breathing, Lauren,' she said, looking into her eyes. 'You're in panic mode.'

'The book,' Price managed between breaths. Her chest heaved in and out with serious effort. Amongst the masses of scrawls in black ink, there was a name that stood out. A name she recognised.

## Chapter 46

Following her request, Eddie sent the photo of the numbers to Price's phone, then switched it to silent. He stood at his front door, the heel of his boot keeping it ajar in case of an emergency. He wasn't sure why, not when she had shown him where it would all happen. To his left, two men stood outside the pub with half-empty glasses and cigarettes in hand. One was complaining about his boss to the other. Nothing to worry about there, but for some unknown reason, his hands trembled, knowing what was to come.

If he stayed away from there, and walked in the other direction, would it still happen the way she drew, just in a different location? Or would he jeopardise the outcome by not going there at all? Thinking about it made his head hurt. Scanning the street for anything out of the ordinary, he ducked back into his doorway momentarily as a car approached from the right.

He could just say bollocks to it, walk into the Miner's and order a pint and a whisky chaser, and await his fate. Drink until this Ronan Donahue stormed in to end his misery for him. That's what he'd always wanted anyway, wasn't it, to be six feet under and pain free? He was too much of a pussy to do it himself all these years, so wouldn't Donahue be doing him a favour?

No. He had to know everything first.

Before he realised what he was doing, he was well past the pub, marching down the street with purpose toward the cemetery. Keeping his ears and eyes open for anything suspect, he made his way across the road to the locked entrance gates, pausing in the darkness to look back the way he came. Reaching high, the gate squeaked as he shimmied up and over into the depths of the graveyard. The sun had set fast, and the clear sky allowed the moonlight to reflect off the tarmac paths and lit up the marble gravestones like beacons, and so he moved with pace close to the darkness of the trees following the tall stone wall boundary. His ears pricked at the sound from behind him. The telltale giveaway as someone climbed the locked gates, entering the cemetery behind him, following him. Eddie kept moving, lower, slower, more deliberate, to avoid giving away his location, stopping from time to time to spot his pursuer moving among the shadows. And then, two hundred yards back, he saw him. The moonlit gravestone dipped into shadow by what could only be a moving body.

Now he held an even bigger advantage. He could gauge his distance, as well as the familiar surroundings. He took off, scrambling to the western wall as fast as he could. Fallen twigs snapped underfoot, giving his own position away, but he kept moving. Behind him came the thumping of feet on tarmac as his follower gave chase. Eddie rounded the last of the gravestones at the west side of the cemetery, launching himself up the ten-foot stone wall and finding each hand and foothold with a knowing ease. He had taken this route many times before in darkness, more times drunk than sober, as he left his wife's resting place to jump the wall and head to another of his favourite locations.

Landing on the other side, he blasted down the path he had created over the years in the waste high grass. The ground was hard but uneven, and although he had taken the route many times before, he had never had to at pace. Fifty yards out from the golf course fence, he growled as he rolled an ankle on a hidden rock and caught his trailing leg on the wire fence, sending a twanging sound into the air. He imagined his pursuer smiling as his prey scrambled to flee up ahead. Crossing the first of the golf course fairways, he

# THE ESCORT TO THE GRAVE

kept a steady jogging pace. Sharp needles stabbed at his ankle with each step, but he kept moving. The fence twanged again in the distance behind him as he hit the tree line between the adjacent holes of the course. The rough knee length grass swished at his legs as he ran through like a wayward golfer hacking to find his ball, slowing his progress. Eddie reached overhead, grasping for a low-hanging limb that snapped from the tree. The sound echoed through the empty course, pin-pointing his location.

He continued on across the last of the fairways, over another border fence, before bear climbing a steep hill of loose slate that seemed to take an age to conquer. He took the time to stop and look back the way he came to gauge just how close his pursuer was. Illuminated by the moonlight just three hundred yards back, the figure slowed to a walking pace, sizing up the man at the top of the hill ahead of him. They seemed to share a moment of mutual understanding as they caught a breather, before Eddie broke it, racing off and down the other side of the hill to the ruins of the Morlais Castle and beyond.

He thought of setting up an ambush at the ruins, the last remains of the stone pillars and tomb a perfect hiding spot to launch an attack. But Ellie had shown him where it would happen, and so he kept moving, until he launched himself over the last of the wire fencing and onto the steep decline of the tarmac road. His feet slapped as he sprinted down, passing the last of the houses and glow of the street lighting, down to the valley floor where it met the bridge overlooking the Taf-Fechan river. Vaulting the stone wall, he ran to the galvanised fence and worked his fingers over the coach bolts at the top, trying to find the two he had removed so many times before. The rumble of water smashing into the rocks below masked the approaching pounding of feet following him to the bottom of the darkened road. The steel bit into his flesh as he desperately tried to find the right bolts. Eventually, the first one gave, and he spun the nut away and pulled the bolt out. The second came free, and the uprights pulled apart into a V shape, enough for his body to squeeze through, just as his chaser rounded the corner. Ronan Donahue stopped momentarily, his chest heaving with effort, and their eyes met up close for the first time. Ronan growled as his hand burrowed into his jacket. Eddie declined to hang around, slipping through the gap and into the relative safety of the high grass and pitch black darkness.

The roar of the water drowned out the squelch his boots made through the ever saturated grass. Rounding the tree at the corner, Eddie came to the grass verge above the drop of the Blue Pool, now as black a void as Donahue's future. Moonlight pierced through the overhanging tree canopies, illuminating the familiar boulder he sat at so many times in search of answers, and the columns of stone cliff edge, shaped from the centuries of persistent waters pounding it. The dry summer months saw far less volume of rain water making its way down the mountains to the river, yet it was still violent enough at the falls to throw up a fine mist that soaked everything.

Thinking fast, Eddie ran to the boulder, picking up one of the empty bottles at its base then returned to hide in the shadows, his back against the tree, poised and ready to strike. He held the bottle low at his side, his right palm cupping the base, his fingers grasping around the body in a claw shape so the neck pointed outward. He wished it would transform into his switchblade, and he cursed himself for being stupid and trusting enough not to bring it.

But she had shown him how it would happen.

The drumming in his chest made him wonder if it gave him away over the din of the falling water. He took a final look to his feet, planting them to ensure he had a solid foundation for what came next, and waited.

## Chapter 47

DCI Hibbard briefed the team in the van on the way back towards Merthyr. Eddie Venter was to be considered a person of interest in the events at the temple, and it was possible the massacre there could end up linked to the findings at the Evans farm. When he finished, the team sat in silence, sharing awkward glances. They had all experienced or heard of past dealings with Eddie, DC Jones even working alongside him before he'd lost the plot. Hibbard saw the looks. None of them believed he was capable of what they'd seen at the temple. To tell the truth, neither did he. As big a prick as Venter was, he just couldn't see him as a cold-blooded killer. But he was sure he held information on who was.

Back at the station, Hibbard delegated the work. Williams and Davies returned to the incident room to relay and co-ordinate the information so every uniform and PCSO were on the lookout for Venter, and to find out more information on the temple and the Grove Druids. DC's Hadley and Jones were to follow him in another pool car to try to find him themselves. It could be dangerous bringing him in, and he had to be careful. But sending in a team of armed response into a busy pub full of drunken scum could be disastrous. He would stake him out first, get eyes on his man, and call them in afterwards.

Pulling around the corner, Hibbard found a decent spot on the hill overlooking the Miner's Arms. He'd hoped to park a little closer, at the bottom of a lane sandwiched by the rear gardens of two terraced streets, but an empty silver BMW was already there clogging up the entrance. The lane would have been ideal, nice and close to the pub and shadowed in darkness, perfect for the element of surprise. This spot would have to do, set back up the hill a little further, but still a decent vantage point. Signalling for Hadley and Jones to do the same, he positioned his car ready in case of the unlikely event Venter spotted them. He switched off the engine, and waited.

Above the corner shop sign, Eddie's flat sat in darkness. Cold calling had crossed his mind, but he quickly dismissed the notion in case he got spotted and scared him off. He also toyed with the three of them marching into the pub, surrounding him in public. Then it would go one of two ways. He'd come quietly and no-one else would interfere, or it would kick off like a wild-west saloon and they'd need a bus full of uniform to back them up. But who's to say he was even still in there? It was a complete gamble on Price's two hour old information. If he wasn't, they'd get made as soon as they walked in, Venter would get warned off, and he'd lose his only chance of catching the man himself. No, they were doing the right thing. Catch him off guard on the way out, away from prying eyes and camera phones.

He sat in silence for a long time, Hadley and Jones glancing across regularly at him from the adjacent car, not really knowing what to do. Hibbard growled at them and pointed two fingers towards his own eyes, then to the pub. 'Imbeciles,' he grunted. The interior of his car lit up from his mobile phone on the passenger seat.

'DCI Hibbard.'

It was DC Williams back at the incident room. 'Sir, George Jones from Digital Forensics has been upstairs. The service providers came through on the suspect chatting to the farmer on those forums. They've provided an address in Aberystwyth. Armed response are heading there now.'

'Great stuff. Keep me posted on any developments.'

'George left his mobile number for you, Sir. Something about arranging drinks to celebrate.'

'Jesus. Ok thanks.' Hibbard hung up, but moments later it rang again.

He looked at the name on the screen, a mix of fear and resentment overwhelming him, as he pondered leaving the answerphone pick it up. Thinking better of it, he lifted it to his ear with a grimace.

'Is it done?' David Morrison asked.

'We're bringing him in for questioning for a recent incident. I can't go into details.'

'I told you to take him out,' Morrison spat.

Hibbard reacted by moving the phone from his ear. 'And I told you this way is better. Trust me, David. He'll be away from your family and you won't be guilty of conspiracy to murder. Now if you'll excuse me, I've got some police work to do.'

'You'll regret this, John. Any thoughts you had about running the department are over. I'll make it my priority to send your career into the toilet.'

'Fuck you David,' Hibbard replied. He ended the call, throwing the phone back onto the passenger seat. He took a deep breath, pinching the bridge of his nose, before climbing out of the car. Hadley and Jones did the same, before Hibbard held up a hand for them to stop. 'Hang back a moment. I don't want to risk us getting spotted and spook him. I'm going to get closer, in case he tries to take off. If you see me moving in, get down there pronto.'

Doing his best to keep away from the street lights, he crept his way to the main street and into the depths of the small alley across from the pub, ready to pounce.

# THE ESCORT TO THE GRAVE

## Chapter 48

Holding his breath, Eddie kept his back to the tree trunk and waited, poised ready to strike. It was impossible to hear the approaching footsteps over the roar of the water below, but as Ronan crept forwards, gun held high, moonlight glinted off the barrel as it came into view next to his head. Eddie exploded into life, spinning from the tree. His left hand knocked the barrel down and away. The gun blasted off an ear-splitting shot into the muddy bank, lighting up the scene with a split second flash. Ronan snatched the gun back toward his attacker for a second attempt, straightening and exposing his body toward him. Eddie was quicker, anticipating the mistake as his right hand snapped up and forwards with tremendous power, blasting through with all his might. The neck of the bottle speared into Ronan's throat with a crunch, the blunt force crushing his windpipe and surrounding cartilage into fragments. His legs buckled, and he dropped like a bag of sand, the shotgun lost and forgotten as he lay on his back in the soggy grass, desperately clinging to life. A wet, bloodied gurgle was all he could manage as his eyes pleaded for help. Eddie glared down at the dying man, his hand dripping from the deep gash in his palm. Such was the force he had driven the bottle into the man's neck, it had exploded and cut deep into his flesh. All life drained from Ronan's eyes as they fogged over, then from the rest of his face as it fell slack and still.

Blowing out his cheeks, Eddie rubbed at his eyes with his thumb and forefinger, before crouching down to take Ronan's limp hand in his, and closed his eyes.

When he reopened them, he was in the back seat of a car. Ronan Donahue sat ahead as passenger, another man of similar age he hadn't seen before, driving. They laughed and joked as they travelled the lonely roads, oblivious to the man in the back seat with them. It was dead of night, and they passed through the sleepy residential area, in and out of orange splashes of street light. Easing through the gated entrance, they continued up into the darkened grounds of a building he guessed was the Grove temple. The mood fell serious as Ronan turned to his driver.

'This is going to be a goldmine for us, Conor lad. This is the first of many, so we can't fuck this up. These guys are dripping with cash, and they've demanded a monthly delivery. My old man says we give it six months, before we start hitting them with the excuses, lack of availability and logistical problems getting them into the UK. Sorry lads, the risk goes up, the price goes up, shit like that. We'll be charging whatever prices we like and making a bloody fortune. You ready?'

The men exited the vehicle to the boot. Two figures dressed in white robes appeared in the doorway to the temple, waiting.

The boot slammed shut behind him, and as they walked around to the front of the car toward the building entrance, Eddie could see through the windscreen a third, smaller figure, hooded head hanging low and hands tied behind its back. The men walked either side, lifting under its armpits as its tied feet dragged behind, across the gravel to the entrance. They all disappeared inside for a couple of minutes until a smiling Donahue and his accomplice reappeared holding a thick envelope and returned to the car. His nicotine stained grin was too much for Eddie to take. He squeezed his eyes shut again.

He was back at the Blue pool, Ronan lying dead beneath him. Steadying his breathing, he rose back to his feet, a harsh sneer on his face. 'Everything you deserve,' he whispered.

'Indeed it is,' a voice replied behind him. Eddie shot around, seeing the woman from his visions sat at his favourite spot at the boulder, a wry, satisfying smirk on her face. Sat on their haunches either side of her were her two hounds, their pristine fine white coats gleaming like marble statues in the moonlight. Save for their red tipped ears and hungry looking eyes, he'd have a job believing they were alive at all. The woman raised a black heel and tutted at the patch of wet, muddied clay at the toe. 'Damn it Ellie,' she said, looking up at Eddie and rolling her eyes. 'Why not a place with no mud? She knows I like my expensive shoes. My fault, I suppose. There's just so much of it in Wales.'

Eddie took a step forward, opening his mouth to speak, not knowing quite what to say. The dogs rose to all fours, a low growl developing that resonated over the rumbling water below and deep into his bones. 'Nokapt,' the woman said sternly, and they obediently withdrew behind the boulder. 'My apologies Mr. Venter. They don't know you yet, but they are good boys. Very protective over their mama. They will get used to you.'

Eddie looked to the dogs, then back to the woman, his head shaking and mouth open all the time.

'You have questions you want answering, yes?' she said, removing the heel to wipe it down. 'But first I ask one of you. Do you now understand what Ellie is really drawing, Mr. Venter?'

## Chapter 49

With one arm tucked under Price's elbow, Deborah King led her to the passenger seat of her grey Mercedes like she was helping an elderly relative to the hospital. Slamming the door shut, she raced back around to the driver's side as she shouted out to the forensic officer standing at the temple entrance.

'Mike, can you wrap everything up and organise to get the bodies to the morgue? I'll meet you there.'

'Where are you going?' her number two replied with a puzzled look.

'Something urgent has come up. I'll explain later.' She ducked into the car and roared off, gravel and dust rising from the back wheels as she raced down the winding road and out of the temple grounds.

'I feel sick,' Price grumbled.

Deborah dug into the centre console, pulling a black and white sweet between her fingers. 'Suck a humbug,' she said. 'Great for travel sickness.'

'Not that kind of sick,' Price replied, pushing the sweet away and pulling out her mobile phone. 'Just get us back to Merthyr as soon as you can.' Scrolling through, she found the number and hit the call button. The phone rang forever until Eddie's voice answered.

'You know what to do,' it said.

'Eddie, call me straight back. We got in the safe. We… we know who the Arch-druid is. We know who killed them all.' Ending the call, she scrolled through her phonebook again.

'What do we do?' King asked. 'Are you going to call it in?'

'Not yet,' Price replied. 'Not until we know exactly where he is.' She tapped on the phone again, lifting it to her ear. 'Damn it! No answer from Hibbard either. Why is no-one answering their bloody phone?'

She tried the incident room next, unsure if anyone would still be there. DC Williams answered. 'Williams where's DCI Hibbard? I can't get him on his mobile.'

'He's out looking for Eddie Venter with Jones and Hadley. We're just wrapping up here for the night.'

'Is DS Enfield there?'

'No, he's gone home too. Why what's up?'

'If Hibbard comes back before you leave, get him to call me urgently.' She was about to end the call when Williams stopped her.

'Oh, Price wait…' he said. 'We got a hit on the name you called in this morning. An Agnes Clark from Stranraer, Scotland, failed to attend Sunday service two weeks in a row. Her vicar checked in on her and reported her missing. No sign of her at the house. Looks promising she's our girl from the mountain.'

'OK thanks. Keep me posted if you hear anymore.'

King tested the car to its limits, racing through the winding country road back toward the town. The lack of roadside lighting made the journey dicey at times, the twisting tarmac disappearing from view in the car headlights on a number of occasions, causing her to slam on the brakes and correct her course. High overhead, the moon peeked through the metallic clouds, guiding them home. Price rubbed at her forehead as she looked to her phone again.

'Something's wrong,' she said. 'Eddie would have called back by now. And Hibbard always answers his phone.'

Deborah risked a glance across as she took another corner at speed. 'You don't think John has picked him up already?'

## Chapter 50

Her cold steel eyes glistened as she sat, waiting. A sly, sure grin spread wide on her thinned red lips. She leaned back onto her hands on the boulder and crossed one leg over the other. Eddie stared straight back until her hand came back to her thigh. Moving a hand over her nylon covered limb, her skirt hitched up an inch or two more. Eddie's eyes fell down to the long toned pins as Mara chuckled to herself.

'What's funny?' Eddie asked.

'Men. You can't help it,' she replied. 'So easy to manipulate.' She nodded toward the body behind him. 'Just like Mr. Donahue there. You agree Mr. Venter?'

Eddie ignored the question. 'Who the hell are you?'

'You know the answer,' she said, leaning back on her hands again. 'But you choose not to accept it. You choose not to say it.'

Eddie rubbed at his face in frustration. 'I need to hear it.'

Mara smiled again. 'Very well, Mr. Venter. I have always been so amazed by people demanding such labels. Since the beginning, people have tried to make sense of it. Everything must have a name, and wherever I am in the world, I have a different one. Some are nice names, some are downright awful. Eastern European ones are always my favourite. Marena, Morana, Mora. In Latvia, they call me Mara. It's probably my favourite, so when people ask, I use Mara.'

'And what do they call you here? In Wales?' Eddie asked.

'You already know this, Mr. Venter. Why play games?' From her pocket, she pulled a cigarette packet. She offered one to Eddie. He declined with a shake of his head, and she removed one to place between her lips. From her other pocket, she pulled a gold zippo lighter that she flicked to life. The flame reflected in her hungry eyes, giving her an air of power. Eddie looked to the lighter. There was something familiar about it. Mara spotted his confused frown and tossed it to him. Eddie flipped the lighter over in his hand.

The inscription read: *To the best dad in the world. Happy Birthday love Kate and Carys xxx*

'You can keep it if you like it,' Mara said.

Eddie tossed it straight back as a shiver tickled between his shoulder blades.

Mara grinned as she re-pocketed it. 'Here, they call me Arawn, amongst other names. Imaginative, but not one of my favourites. Ellie prefers Mara too.'

A wave of nausea threatened to knock Eddie over as the picture in the library filled his head. The figure at the mountain top. The three cloaked figures. So many dead bodies. Beneath was a description.

*The Escorts to the grave pay homage to Arawn.*

Arawn, the king of the otherworld. The Celtic god of death, war, revenge and terror.

'You understand now, yes?' Mara said.

Eddie looked to his muddied feet as if they could offer more information, his eyes working back and fore to make sense of it all. 'You're trying to tell me... you're some sort of god of death?' he said.

'Oh Please,' she said, waving a dismissive hand as she blew out a plume of smoke. 'Gods, Deities, always with the religion. Everywhere I go, you people must make names for me. And you must make sense of it, always. When will the human race finally realise they are nothing special, Mr. Venter? Deluded, yes, but special? No.'

# THE ESCORT TO THE GRAVE

'You're trying to tell me death is a person? Someone who controls who is alive and who is dead? That's ridiculous.'

'No more ridiculous than someone who sees people alive who are already dead, Mr. Venter,' Mara said with a wide smile. She patted the rock. 'Come, sit with me.' Eddie took the offer, keeping a close eye on the dogs as he propped himself next to her. One of them gave another low rumble in its throat that stopped when Mara looked to it. Eddie considered himself an animal lover, but it answered why the search dogs refused to go up the mountain that day. They had sensed it, these two waiting for them at the top, and he couldn't blame them for not wanting any part of it. These evil looking hounds had a way of striking the fear of god into you.

Pulling a handkerchief from her cloak, she handed it over, Eddie using it to stem the flow of blood from the gash in his palm. His feet kicked away the bottles littering the boulder, left from his many visits to the falls. Mara followed his gaze to them, kicking at one herself. 'You have come here many times, Mr. Venter. You think to end your life, but something stops you each time, yes? Holds you back?'

'And I suppose it's you stopping me?' Eddie asked, rolling his eyes. 'That it's not my time?'

'I have no rule over people who wish to end their own lives, just like I have no control over people who end the life of others. It is not why I am.'

'Then what is it?'

'It is your own sub-consciousness stopping you. Your mind knows where your fate lies. You know you have a job to do. You have a purpose.'

'And what job would that be exactly?' Eddie asked. He lowered his head to rub at the back of his neck.

'To help Ellie find those deserving to be taken,' Mara answered.

Eddie shook his head as he looked to the bottles. A couple still held an inch or two inside he thought of picking up.

Mara continued on. 'Death comes to us all, Mr. Venter. Every living thing born, must die. And for all other species, all animals, no interference is necessary. They acknowledge death simply for what it is.'

'Which is?' Eddie asked.

'The end, Mr. Venter. There is nothing more. It is the essence of peace. Once it is over, you belong back to she who gave it to you. All living things receive time, and when it is up, your body returns to her. Only humans think they are above this, that they deserve more, that they are special. It is only for this reason I exist consciously at all. I have always been, of course. I am the rule. As long as life exists, so does death. Unfortunately, as human populations grew, so did your attitude towards eternity. For a long time, we left you to yourselves. But the thirst for power and control and for taking life that is not yours to take, became too much. Humans believe they are the top of the food chain, but there is one step more. Nature will always be at the top. Nature always finds a way. Nature is the one and only god, and so she gave me the consciousness to decide who, and how many to take. And therefore I am, because of her, my mother.'

'What has Ellie got to do with this? Why involve her at all? She's just a child. Why take her in the first place?'

'As long as they have been able to, humans have spoken of me, Mr. Venter. Through their need for self importance, they fabricated elaborate stories to invoke fear into the young and control their minds. I am given thousands of names from thousands of religions. Older generations tell their made up tales passed down through the ages. They create fables. From the beautiful and macabre, poems and scriptures and paintings depict myths of my work and of me. For a long time, mother allowed them. She would think to herself, they do no harm. Let the simple people have their stories. But then she saw what they did because of them, evil people using their legends for their own profit. Nature, Mr. Venter, always finds a way. She gave me the consciousness to do my bidding, and so I began my work.'

She took another drag of her cigarette. 'Pure people, honest souls, help me rid of the evil. Over time, their own tales have worked into the legends to keep order. We do what we can, but we will never end the evil. I have many helpers in the world, known by many names from their own stories. The three you are aware of, you know as The Morrigan.'

Eddie's eyes danced in their sockets again as he rubbed his fingers through his mess of hair. The Morrigan. Ancient Celts told the story for centuries. Early versions told them as a trio of Irish sisters. Later adaptations saw them as a sister from each nation. One Welsh, one Scottish, one Irish.

'She's the architect,' Eddie said, looking back up to Mara. 'Ellie doesn't draw what people plan to do, she plans it herself. She draws who to take. She finds them, evil people guilty of terrible things, and then designs their own deaths.'

'And she is just getting started, Mr. Venter. She has much to learn, and she will need help. We travelled to the Holy Mountain for her confirmation, and to show her the first ones to be taken.. Then she returned to her family to start her work. She will grow to be my most amazing Escort.'

'Escort?' Eddie asked.

'An Escort to the grave, Mr. Venter. A guide for the damned.'

'If there's nothing after death, then how can they be damned?'

'Mother nature finds a way, Mr. Venter. Those deserving of further torture shall be damned to receive it. At their time of passing, those worthy of peace have their consciousness taken away. They spend eternity resting without even knowing it. The true essence of peace. But the others? Why should they experience such a thing? So I and my Escorts see to it that they suffer.'

'But why use her? She's just an innocent girl. Why would you?'

'It takes a pure soul to show evil the error of its ways. It is vital. I tell you death is the end of everything, and for the honest souls, it is. But evil must be punished, to be made an example of, or it will grow like the virus it is. I take much pleasure in taking those who display it, Mr. Venter. They beg for mercy when others rest for eternity. In their last moments of horror, they tell me their darkest secrets and who they share them with. And then I take them too. It is retribution for their sins. I promise them forgiveness, and I laugh at every one when they realise the truth.'

Eddie shook his head. 'She's just a little girl.'

'Yes, she is, and she needs you, Mr. Venter.'

'What for?'

Mara nodded toward Ronan's limp body. 'There are so many more out there just like him, thinking they can do whatever they want and get away with it. This man was one of many involved in the taking of orphaned children from Latvia. Poor children, desperate for better, and believing of the lies told to them. Promised a future then drugged and killed. It has taken some years to find them all. But we have found them, and shown them what they have done, and they have begged for forgiveness. Yet some things must not be forgiven, only punished. Tell me, Mr. Venter, why do you think I gave you your gift? Witnessing how people have died?'

Eddie opened his mouth to answer, but nothing came out loud enough to be heard over the roar of the water.

She answered for him instead. 'So it would lead you to her. Without it, none of this would have happened. And now it is changing, yes? Your gift will continue to grow, just as you are. It began with you reliving the torment of the dead. Feeling their pain and torture in order to help them. It was important for you to experience what they went through, Mr. Venter, in order for you to respect them, to work for them, to honour them by telling their final story. And you did it well.'

She flicked her cigarette down into the void, then nodded toward Donahue's body again. 'When you touched that murdering bastard, you were able to see what he had done, yes? Not how he died, but why he deserved to. You know why? Because you are ready, Mr. Venter. Ellie will be my Escort, and you will be her Warden. Between you, you will find them, and with a touch of your hand you will see what they have done, even when they are alive, and between you, you shall deliver them to me.'

Eddie shook his head, unable to take it in.

'Do you remember the first time we met?' Mara asked. 'At the hospital, after your wife died? Do you remember why I was there?'

Eddie's mouth hung open, his face blank. 'It was just a dream.'

It was Mara's turn to shake her head.

'You said you were there to welcome someone into the world.'

'To welcome Ellie into the world, Mr. Venter. You didn't know she was born the same night your wife passed away, did you? Like I said, your mind knows where your fate lies. And it drew you to Ellie, just as it drew you to Gwenno before her.'

Reaching into her cloak, Mara dug into an inside pocket, pulling out an item he had seen before. The moonlight licked at the gold metal as she handed it to him. Eddie turned the object over in his palm, coating it in blood from his cloth wrapped hand. The same key as Ellie's, for the case to her scrapbook.

'I will take care of Mr. Donahue,' Mara said as she closed Eddie's palm around the key, coating her own hands with his blood. She paid no concern to it. 'You will take care of Ellie's drawing. Then you must go home, Mr. Venter, to your real home. To find out who she really was.'

## Chapter 51

Trudging back along the high street, Eddie couldn't take his eyes off the key in his hand. It weighed enough to prop open a country house door, and so ornate it could be mistaken for unlocking the vault at the Tower of London. The head of the key held that symbol he had seen so much of in the last two weeks, and was even seeing in his sleep, the infinite design twisting into its three points. He rubbed his thumb across it.

The symbol of the Morrigan. The three sisters. The journey of life, through death, to rebirth.

Reaching the lights of the pub, he stopped as he continued to turn the key over in his rough hands. It was indeed the same as Ellie's, and his natural assumption was it opened another case just like hers. But what did that mean?

His ears pricked at the sound of fast moving footsteps coming toward him from across the road. He lifted his head to see DCI Hibbard approach from the dark of the alley opposite, a pair of cuffs in hand. Eddie's eyes moved left and right, looking for the backup. High up the hill, two hundred yards out, the silhouette of two figures flashed under a street lamp as they ran down towards them.

'Mr. Venter, I'd like to ask you a few questions in relation to an incident that occurred last night.' He looked to the cuffs in his own hand. 'I'd like you to accompany me to the station.'

'Do I have a choice?' Eddie asked. 'Of course,' Hibbard replied. 'The easy way or the hard way.'

Eddie burst out laughing. 'Did you really just say that?'

He held out his wrists, ready for the cuffs, as he took a step toward the officer. Hibbard's eyes fell to the ornate object he clasped in one hand, the key holding his gaze a fraction too long. He failed to register Eddie's free hand whipping up and around, clenched into a tight fist that smashed into his temple, sending him into the depths of sleep and to the cold tarmac road. Grabbing him by the collar, Eddie dragged him to the pavement, flipping his body into the recovery position as Hibbard groaned his way through his vivid nightmare. The two giving chase were still fifty yards out, desperately sprinting in pursuit as one radioed in for backup, giving Eddie the opportunity to dash in through the Miner's Arms entrance.

'Keep um busy,' Eddie shouted at Stretch as he thumbed back over his shoulder toward the front door. He paced around the bar toward the rear of the pub, through the back door and to the alley behind, where his battered Ford Focus lay waiting to carry him to safety. His jog fell to a leisurely pace as the welcoming sound of smashing glass rang out from behind him, and he eased into the driver's seat and fired up the engine. Stretch knew exactly what to do in such a situation. Eddie could see it now. A simple nod to one of the regulars and with some bafta winning acting, the intruders would be walking into a full on fist fight. They would, of course, get caught in the crossfire, treated to a cheap shot each after being mistaken for just another couple of the trouble-makers before getting the chance to introduce themselves.

Stretch was no mug himself, being another early product of the Slaughterhouse gym. As short as he was, everyone assumed his nickname was just some ironic piss-take, but Eddie had seen the real reason many times with his own eyes. Through his teenage years at the gym, he'd witnessed many of his unsuspecting opponents getting 'stretched out' on the canvas. It certainly helped when you were the landlord of one of the roughest pubs in the borough to have hands like cured concrete.

When the men came round, he would simply explain the group that ran off down the road had attacked them, he'd never seen them before, and it was a shame his CCTV cameras were coincidentally out of order.

Pulling from the alley, Eddie's head throbbed as he tried to think of what to do next. Getting far away from Hibbard was the priority. He kept away from the high street, negotiating the side roads to get past the pub to the cemetery and back onto the dark, unlit country lanes where they wouldn't find him so easily. Continuing on through the twisting narrow lanes, seemingly with no destination in mind, he pondered his next move, until an all too familiar sight came ahead.

Slamming his foot on the brakes, his body lurched forward as the car slid to a stop. His heart hammered in his chest at the large iron barriers and black and white chevron markers indicating the sharp turn, erected almost seven years ago, shortly after Jane and Gwen had plunged down into the valley below. They had since given the turning a lone street lamp and signage for added safety, and now Eddie sat stationary at the centre of the road, engine still running as the memory of that fateful night came flooding back. He looked to the key sat next to the scroll on the passenger seat. The artificial glow of the street lamp flickered off it, licking like a candle flame. He picked it up and turned it over in his hands again.

'Go home,' Mara had said. 'See who she really is.'

Eddie pinched his eyes closed as Gwen's face came to him. She smiled the most perfect smile, wide enough for her cheek dimples to crease, something that only ever seemed to happen when he made her laugh. Her soft hands caressed at his cheeks, and those beautiful almond eyes held all her love for the man ahead of her. She kissed him, and he fell completely into it, not wanting her to let go, but let go she did.

'I can't keep going without you,' he said as the first tear fell.

'You have to,' she whispered. 'She needs you. Help her end this.' Her soft lips pursed as they came to his once more. Eddie's eyes closed as he kissed back, his chest heaving in desperation to cling to the moment. Then, as their lips parted once more, and he opened his eyes, she was gone.

Looking down at his hands, where the key had last been, Ellie's rolled up painting now sat in its place. 'Help her end this,' Eddie whispered as he cracked the wax seal holding the scroll. Holding the top with one hand, the subject of the drawing revealed itself as he pulled down with the other. It took a moment for the shock to register. 'Dear God,' he said as he took in the image in front of him, his stomach knotting and forcing him to open the car door. He leaned out and dry-retched, his vision filling with flashing stars. Falling back into his seat, he wiped the spittle from his mouth as he flung the drawing to the passenger side. The thumping in his head screamed as he pulled his phone from his pocket. Seeing the missed calls from Price, he hit the button to return the call. She answered immediately.

'Holy shit, Eddie, where have you been? We got in the safe. We know who the Arch-druid is.'

Eddie looked across to the drawing. 'Yeah, same here,' he said. 'I just found out. Have you called it in? Armed response need to get to the house.'

'I need to run it by Hibbard first,' she replied. 'He's the SIO on this. But I can't get hold of him.'

'He's outside the Miner's. He should be conscious by now,' Eddie said. 'Call him and tell him to get straight over there. I'm a few minutes away.'

# THE ESCORT TO THE GRAVE

'Jesus, I'm afraid to ask. Be careful Eddie,' Price replied. 'Wait for armed response to turn up. Don't go in without them.'

Ending the call, he gave one last look to the steel barriers, the wrenching feeling twisting his stomach once more, as he found first gear and gunned the car around the corner.

## Chapter 52

'Boss? You ok Boss?' DC Hadley said as Hibbard sat slouched on the curb with his legs lying limp in the road, his face scrunched tight from the ringing sound in his ears. His hands went to his head in a futile attempt to draw the pain from there. Hadley dropped to a knee, so he was in eye shot. 'You ok?'

'The bastard sucker punched me,' Hibbard said as he pinched the bridge of his nose. He looked back to the front of the pub as Jones staggered over, nursing a cut on his own forehead. 'Did you get him?'

'It's mental in there, Boss,' Hadley replied. 'We ran into a full fist fight. Chairs and glass flying everywhere. Someone hit Jones with a pool cue. We think Venter ran out back, but he's long gone.'

Struggling to think, Hibbard dug into his trouser pocket for his keys, handing them to Hadley. 'Go get my car, and call for uniform to get vans up here and arrest every last one of them scummy turds, especially the landlord. I'll put money on it he knows where Venter has gone. Jones, check his flat next door to make sure he hasn't doubled-back there.'

The two lumbered off as Hibbard lay back on the pavement, still holding a hand to his temple. Above him, the stars spun in an infinite loop, showing no signs of slowing down. The drumming in his head continued, threatening to split it in two, until a 'tutting' sound dragged his attention away. He turned his head to look further down the pavement, where an elderly couple plodded in his direction, shaking their heads as they approached. The little woman, dolled up like she was ready for the bingo, paused long enough to look down at the mess of the man at her feet, and turned to her husband.

'Look at the state of that, Ivor. They can't handle their drink these days.'

Her husband chuckled as they shuffled off, Hibbard's confused gaze following them as they passed Jones's half-hearted banging on the flat door.

'You'd have been packing your bags and sent to your mother's if you'd ever come home like that, Ivor.'

'Aye, don't I know it Maude,' her husband said with another chuckle.

Jones returned moments later, dragging his feet, still holding a cloth over the gash in his forehead. 'No answer there, Boss, not that he'd open up, anyway.'

A car pulled up in front of Hibbard, narrowly avoiding his legs. Hadley left the engine running as he opened the door and ran round to the curb. He held Hibbard's own phone out, ready for him to take it.

'Boss, Price is on the line. She's been trying to get hold of you for ages, says it's urgent.'

Hibbard held a hand up to take the phone, his head staying firmly on the pavement. 'You better be on your way back here, Price. That slippery boyfriend of yours just assaulted me and made off.'

'Sir, we're on our way,' Price said. 'We've found...'

'Hit me from behind the spineless coward,' Hibbard interrupted. 'I told you he was no good.'

'Sir, listen to me, we've found out who...'

'When I get my hands on him, he's fin...'

'For fuck sake John!' Deborah King screamed down the phone from the driver's seat, loud enough for him to pull the mobile away from his ear. 'Listen to what she has to tell you!'

Hibbard kept quiet and waited.

'Sir, I know where Eddie's heading, because we're heading there too,' Price said. 'We got into the safe. We know who the Arch-druid is. We're heading to the house now.'

Hadley and Jones shared a confused look as Hibbard staggered to his feet, his face turning grey as he listened intently to Price on the other end of the line.

'Jesus wept, Price, are you sure? I mean, it's got to be a mistake?'

'It's him, Sir. What do we do?'

'I'll… I'll call it in quietly, see if I can locate him,' Hibbard stammered.

'Head to the house, but keep your distance, and I want an update as soon as you get there. Don't let Venter get anywhere near. We're ten minutes away and leaving right now.' Hibbard ended the call to find the two detectives staring blankly at him. His head still pounded and his ears continued to ring. The new revelation didn't help, and he was sure if he were alone, he'd be throwing up by now.

'Hadley, you're driving. I need to make some calls en route.'

'En route where Sir?' Hadley asked.

'Head for Pontsticill village,' Hibbard replied.

## Chapter 53

Rolling the car to a stop, Eddie killed the engine and sat pondering what came next. A loud whirring sound came from the engine bay as the radiator fan attempted to cool the old motor down, making it a suitable theme tune for what was going on in his head. Through the windscreen, the cottage looked cold and uninviting, the curtains of each window drawn closed and filled with darkness. A halo like glow emanated from somewhere toward the back garden and he was sure he knew where from. His hands shook uncontrollably as he moved them to the steering wheel, and the knot in his throat tightened with every swallow. Turning to the parchment on the passenger seat that had rolled closed into its relaxed state, a mixture of rage, hurt and grief overwhelmed him. Clamping his eyes and jaw tight, matching the knuckle whitening grip he held the steering wheel, he wished it was all just some sickening joke.

It took an age for him to step from the car, his courage deserting him as fast as it came. He had arrived here with so many questions, but he was unsure if he could handle the answers. Eventually he pulled himself from the safety of the car and lumbered toward the waist-high stone wall surrounding the immaculate front garden, stopping at the front gate, before following the contours of the wall to the driveway gates, left wide open. The concrete pavement underfoot gave way to block paving, and as he rounded the car on the driveway, the security light at the side of the house illuminated, announcing his arrival. Making his way to the back of the house to the annex, a warm glow flickered behind the curtains of the far window, candle light, Eddie realised. The annex door stood wide open, and he took deep breaths to compose himself. His chest heaved with effort, the clean evening air unable to fill his lungs, forcing him to lean on the door frame. Sweat began to build at his forehead and cheeks again, and it took everything he had to stop himself from hyperventilating.

An all too familiar voice came from within, startling him. Oddly, it relieved his breathing, but sent a curdling to his stomach instead. 'Is that you, Eddie?'

He crossed the threshold to the narrow annex hallway. Family photos of good times gone adorned the walls, the smiles on the faces masked in the shadows as if hiding from the guilt. He continued forward. The doors leading to the bathroom and games room were closed tight, so he moved to the last of them, the office door ajar, allowing the light from within to creep through the open edges. The door creaked on its hinges as Eddie eased it wide. Staying at the threshold, he surveyed the room with caution. The swivel chair behind the mahogany desk was empty, but mounted high on the wall above it was a mask, the skull and antlers of a stag rising high toward the ceiling. A mask he had seen before, in his vision at the lake. Leaning against the foot of the desk was a large portrait, the subject staring back with a sinister smile as he sat posing in his white and purple robes. At the centre of the desk sat a large wax candle, the lone light source in the sombre room. It was almost two feet tall, expertly carved spirals weaving in and out to its wicks, where three flames danced against each other in contest. Through the spirals of wax, Eddie could make out the three-pronged Triquetra symbol laced in gold leaf.

'It's called the relief candle,' a voice slurred from the other side of the room. 'It's lit only when the Arch-druid retires his position, ready for the next to begin.'

Peter Enfield sat on the black leather couch at the right side of the office, facing his display of awards on the opposing wall. Across his lap laid one of his many game-bird shotguns. He held a crystal decanter in one hand, half filled with whisky, and a glass tumbler in the other. He emptied the tumbler with one swallow before filling it again, closing his eyes to savour the taste. Then he offered the neck of the decanter out to Eddie. 'Take a drink?'

'Don't think so, Pete,' Eddie replied, his eyes firmly held on the gun.

'Pfft,' Peter replied, followed by a snigger. 'When have you ever turned one down?' He lifted the tumbler and downed the contents again, then pointed the decanter neck towards the corner of the room. 'You'll have some more, right?'

Eddie followed where Peter was pointing, stepping further into the room to peer around the open door. Sat in her wheelchair in the corner, Jane nursed her own glass of whisky. Tears streamed down her face, her cheeks raw and blotchy from wiping them away. Eddie had seen her like this once before, shortly after leaving hospital almost seven years ago. Stealing a glance to him, she sniffed through another series of tears and ran the back of her free hand unlady-like across her nose.

'Hey Ed,' she managed between sniffs.

'Hey Jane,' Eddie replied. 'You ok?'

Jane twirled the glass in her hands, swishing the last finger of whisky around it, then swallowed and held it out for her husband to fill again. He did as asked, stopping just an inch from the top. She looked up to Eddie again, eyes brimming. Through the pain there, Eddie could see truth in them. 'As ridiculous as it might seem, yes, yes I am.'

'You know about last night?' Eddie asked.

Jane gave a slow nod, followed by another sniff and nose wipe. 'About the temple? Yeah, he told me what he did.'

Eddie looked to the man sat beside her, his one-time mentor, confidante and friend. Peter slumped further into the couch, looking close to unconsciousness. He held up his glass as though giving a toast, then knocked it back again.

'The police are on their way, Pete,' Eddie said. 'I got a few minutes head start, just in case you felt like explaining it to me first. You know, being your mate and all.'

'Your mate? That's a joke. What sort of mate tries to get his friend killed, hey? I'm assuming you've already crossed paths with the last of the Donahue lads, and he's a little worse off than you, right?'

Eddie stared back in silence.

'I'm sorry. I had to get you off my back. You were right. I shouldn't have involved you in the Morrison girl's kidnapping. None of this would have happened if I didn't ask you. Somehow you got too close.'

Eddie edged further into the room.

'I bet you're feeling like you don't know me at all,' Peter replied. 'But the fact is, I'd been in the South, Mid and West Grove Druids a long time before I even met you.' He held up his tumbler again. 'The youngest to hold the position of Arch-druid in two hundred years.'

'Why would you ever get involved with it?'

Peter looked to his glass for an answer. 'I was a young man when they approached me to join the temple,' he said. He looked across to his wife as she lowered her head toward her lap.

'I'd just been promoted to Sergeant when Jane fell pregnant for the first time. We moved here and everything began slotting into place. It was the perfect life. And then...'

'And then I lost the baby,' Jane said, holding back more tears.

Eddie turned to her, wanting to comfort her, but stayed put. He needed to hear it all.

Peter picked back up. 'We were both devastated. Jane shut herself off from the world. We hardly spoke a word in the weeks following the miscarriage. I hid away in my work. But it wasn't long before the cracks began to show. I had to take time off. I was sure I'd get demoted again, and positive our marriage wouldn't last.'

Moving to the swivel chair at the near side of the desk, Eddie dropped into it like a dead weight, blowing out a dejected breath.

'We both ended up in therapy,' Peter continued. 'A last attempt to save our marriage. I had to keep it from the force, of course. Back then, if you were seeing a psychiatrist, they automatically labelled you a nut job with a drug problem. It's how people saw it.'

'I never had you down as giving a shit what others think,' Eddie said.

'I was ambitious, climbing the ladder,' Peter replied. 'People couldn't know, so I met with a councillor from out of town twice a week. Right from the off, I knew he was different. The stuff he talked about. I expected him to tell me none of it was my fault, that my conscience should be clear. But he didn't.' He took another gulp of whisky. 'Instead, he told me Death had come for my baby because I didn't serve him. Can you imagine someone telling you that? The rage I felt? I had to do everything I could to stop myself from beating the shit out of him. I walked out of his office and swore I'd never go back.'

'But you did,' Eddie replied.

'I couldn't get what he said out of my mind. Sleep became non-existent, wondering what he'd meant. A week later, I went back to get an explanation. I was vulnerable, in mourning, and found myself completely lured into what he had told me. A week later he introduced me to other members of the Grove Druids and they inducted me into the guild as a Bard.'

Rubbing his rough palm over his face, Eddie struggled to take it in. He looked to Jane sat in her wheelchair; the pain etched onto her face. She looked twenty years older than yesterday. 'And what about Jane?' he said. 'Your wife has a miscarriage, and you're practising secret handshakes and building wicker men.'

Jane's head lifted, her reddened eyes desperate for relief. 'I had him back,' she whispered. 'My doting husband had returned, showering me with love and compassion. We sat and talked for hours about how we were feeling. I thought it was the therapy, and so I made more effort and progress with my own doctor. We were like newlyweds again.'

'But it was all a lie, Jane,' Eddie fired back. 'He was living a secret life.'

'Fulfilling my own and my wife's,' Peter said. 'We were happy again. We talked about trying for another baby. Then we were blessed with the twins, and it was all because of my servitude to the Grove, to the Temple, and to Arawn, the Lord of Death.'

'You're insane,' Eddie said.

'If only you'd seen what I've seen,' Peter said. 'Then you'd think you were, too.'

Eddie sat upright. 'Try me.'

Peter looked across at his wife. Sensing his gaze, Jane clamped her own eyes shut like she was making a wish. A wish the world would open up and take her.

'Grove Druidism pays homage to the otherworld and the afterlife. We offer gifts to Arawn in return for more time for ourselves and our families.'

'Gifts? You mean sacrifices?' Eddie said.

'Long ago, they used precious livestock. Goats and lambs,' Peter replied. 'The Grovers thought the Lord would favour them if they made the offerings, but it did nothing. Members and their families continued to contract disease and die prematurely. There was still so much suffering and pain.'

'So they started killing people instead!' Eddie screamed, jolting in his chair. The candle flame flickered with menace, threatening to extinguish from his outburst. Jane's hands covered her face, the whole top half of her body trembling.

'Not at first,' Peter replied. 'As the organisation spread across Europe, so did the practices. Interpretations transformed through the languages. Very little in the religion is ever written down. The Grove Druids pride themselves on passing the teachings through the generations, but as it grew through the many countries, translations got lost, new ones developed, and the history of the Druids became muddled. Then everything went full circle. In the 14th century, the Black Death raged through the world, Arawn's wrath and anger clear and evident. But word came back he had spared some Eastern Europe temples, entire factions avoiding the plague, their families all safe. It was nothing short of a miracle. Desperate questions were asked, and the answers, though extreme, came funneling back west. Reluctant trials began. Sacrifices were found, mostly vagrants and nomads, homeless people. Men and women with no families, and no purpose in the world. People ready to transition to the afterlife. Some even welcomed it. So the Grove Druids helped them, and in turn kept Arawn satisfied with the offerings. Or so we thought.'

Suddenly, Peter dropped his glass to the floor, spilling the last of the whisky it held over the carpet. He grabbed for the shotgun, holding it out in front of him towards the new arrival at the door. Price stood frozen at the threshold, her face pale and eyes wide with shock at the greeting she received.

Eddie raised a hand in front of him, slowly standing from his seat. 'Easy Pete, it's just DC Price. She's with me. You're alone, right Price?'

'I... I told Deb to stay with the car,' she replied.

'You're a good detective, Lauren.' Peter said. 'You'll do well. Come in and sit down.' He gestured with the pointy end of his shotgun toward the empty settee behind Eddie. Price did as asked, slow and deliberate, keeping an eye on the barrel as it followed her. The weapon returned to its resting place across his lap as she sat.

'What happened last night, Pete?' Eddie asked.

'We were summoned to the temple, the entire guild. They all assumed it was my doing, of course. An emergency meeting called by the Arch-druid is not to be missed. Rumours would have circulated about Malcolm Glover's death, and they would want answers. But I didn't call it.'

'Then who did?' Eddie asked. A sad smile crept onto one side of Peter's face. 'Why Arawn, of course. Death presented itself to me in person, full of anger and rage, waiting for me as I arrived at the temple.'

'Arawn?' Eddie asked. 'You mean Mara?'

Peter's face fell slack. 'She has come to you too? Why?'

'Keep going,' Eddie said.

'I was the first to arrive. And she told me who she was, and what was to be done. I wouldn't believe it, but then she showed me. I saw it for myself. We had failed her, and her anger burned through me. We were no longer alone at the temple. All of them were there, all the sacrifices. All those children we had killed over the years, even from my early days in the Grovers. It was unbelievable. They were all on their knees, hands gripping their own throats, choking, their eyes begging for my help. Arawn gave me the knife, the ceremonial blade we had used so many times before. They needed me, and she showed me what to do, and so I helped them. I opened their airways, ran the knife across their necks until they could breathe once again. They were so happy.'

Peter's face turned sour, sagging from the pain he felt for his fellow Grovers. 'But then she showed me what I had really done. All of my friends, all gone at once.'

Eddie looked to the mask on its mount behind the desk, its long skull and towering antlers glistening in the candlelight. 'So you tried to cover your tracks?'

'I took the mask and removed my portrait from the temple. The only evidence remaining was the accounts book in the secretarial chamber...'

'But you couldn't get in it,' Eddie interrupted. 'Malcolm changed the code to the safe.'

'I'm guessing you have?' Peter said. 'Or you wouldn't be here now.'

Eddie looked over his shoulder. 'Price was the one who cracked it. But it was Ellie Morrison who sent me here,' Eddie said. 'I told you, it's all connected, Pete.'

Peter shook his head. 'What? How?'

'It was Mara who took her in the first place. It was part of her plan all along, leading to bringing down your cult and everyone associated with it. You were never paying homage or serving any god. You were killing innocent children, you sick bastards. The irony of it is she's hunted you all down, *because* of what you've done.'

'And I'm the last one left,' Peter replied, his eyes dropping to the weapon in his lap. His right hand working into its position around the trigger. Price looked to Eddie, her eyes spreading wide, pleading for him to do something. Eddie leaned forward, feet planted and coiled ready, the knuckles on his calloused hands straining from the grip he held on the armrests. He stared into Peter's eyes, the man he had trusted all these years, ready to pounce at the first movement and take him out. With their attention on Peter, they failed to see Jane in time as she reached behind her wheelchair, pulling out a second of her husband's prize shotguns. It trembled and rattled against the metal arm of the chair as she struggled and heaved to point it in their direction. More tears streamed down her cheeks.

Eddie's mouth fell open, and he slumped back once more. He closed his eyes tight as one hand came up to rub at the pain there. 'Jesus,' he said as he looked toward Jane, tears forming in his own eyes. 'How long? How long have you known about what he's been doing?'

'Since I tried to kill myself,' Jane replied. 'The night of the accident.'

Eddie took a moment to realise what she was saying. 'The night with Gwen? You were *trying* to kill yourself?'

'And she saved me,' Jane said between sobs. The barrel of the gun trembled in front of her, something Eddie was all too aware of. 'She was an amazing journalist, Eddie. And a wonderful friend. We'd become so close, so when she told me she'd been investigating some sick secret religion responsible for killing people, children no less, and my husband was a part of it, my world fell apart in seconds. It destroyed me. I could only see one way out, but she got in the car with me and tried to talk me out of it. I was planning on driving straight into the reservoir to end it all. She tried to give me a chance before she took it public. She knew it would ruin me, but she offered to help, to protect me, to do the right thing. We drove on, but my mind was in bits. I raced toward the reservoir, but we didn't get far.'

'You crashed down the valley,' Eddie whispered. 'And she pulled the wheel the last second to take the impact. She saved you, to give you that chance.' His eyes flashed back and fore as he clenched his fists. 'An opportunity to do the right thing, to blow the lid off it all.'

'When I woke up in hospital, Peter admitted it all,' she said. 'He told me everything about the Grove, the Temple and the teachings. Of the monthly sacrifices they made to this god, Arawn. I thought I must still be sleeping, still living my nightmares, but I wasn't. Then the doctors told me I'd never walk again, and Peter told me it was because Arawn had spared me, leaving me as a reminder to the Grove not to fail him again. Before the accident I was determined to end my own life, but afterwards, I suddenly feared for it. So I did the unthinkable. I kept quiet.'

Eddie's teeth clenched as he spoke. 'All those people who died. Did you ever think of them? Did you ever think of Gwen?' He stood from his chair, fiery rage engulfing him, as Peter pulled the barrel of his shotgun around towards him. The threat no longer mattered. Eddie's anger had completely engulfed him, but he knew he was too far away to get there in time, and too close for anything but a direct hit.

But he was ready. Ready to be with her.

He pounced forwards and the shotgun blast lit up the room.

# Chapter 54

DCI Hibbard pointed to the two cars parked outside the Enfield cottage, directing DC Hadley to pull up behind them. The grey Mercedes he had been in many times, and the clapped out Ford Focus in front of it, could only belong to one person. Eddie Venter.

As they killed the engine, the driver door to the Mercedes opened, Deborah King stepping out and racing back towards him in a panic. 'I… I heard a gunshot,' she stammered.

'Where's Price?' Hibbard asked, leaping from the passenger side.

'She went around back,' Deborah said, pointing towards the driveway leading to the rear of the property. 'Eddie's in there too.'

'For Christ's sake, I told her to keep her distance,' Hibbard said. He turned to the two detectives. 'She could be compromised. Armed response is still twenty minutes out. We'll have to move in.' He pointed a finger in Deborah's face. 'You, get back in the car and stay there.'

'Oh John, I love it when you take charge,' she cooed, turning on her heels and marching back to the car.

The three men crouched as they scurried along the stone wall and in through the driveway. Hibbard signalled to Jones to break off and check around the back of the main house. Stopping short of the ramp leading to the open annex door, he listened for any sign of commotion. 'I'm going in,' Hibbard said to Hadley. 'Wait here.'

# THE ESCORT TO THE GRAVE

'Do you think that's wise, Boss?' Hadley whispered. 'Maybe we should wait until armed response is here, especially if shots were fired.'

'Price could be in trouble. I have to go in. If anything else happens, you stay put until backup arrives.'

# Chapter 55

'Is he dead?' Jane Enfield asked. Beside her, her husband's left leg and hands twitched sporadically. He lay on the couch on his right side, the top half of his head spread high on the wall behind like some morbid Tate Modern exhibit. Eddie leaned against the office desk, the bulk of it stopping him from falling flat on his back. The wall and settee had taken the brunt of the mess, but his face and torso came a close second. Blood and blackened chunks of brain tissue soaked through his shirt. Expecting to have been ripped apart as he made his move for the gun, he'd instead taken a front-row seat as Peter's head exploded all over him. He stood in silent shock, resembling some extra from a gory horror movie.

'Yes… he's dead,' Price said, sat frozen to her chair. Small specks of blood coated her cheeks like freckles. 'It's over, Mrs. Enfield.'

Jane turned the gun toward more movement at the door. DCI Hibbard stood, mouth open, eyes wide at the scene in front of him. It took three efforts for the words to come out. 'Dear God.'

Eddie stepped toward Jane. The barrel of the gun turned its attention back in his direction, stopping him in his tracks.

'Please Eddie, no closer,' Jane pleaded.

'It's done, Jane. He was the last one, the final link. Now they're all gone, they can't hurt anyone anymore. It's over.' Eddie glanced toward Hibbard at the door as he edged in slowly.

'Mrs. Enfield, Eddie's right. It's over. But there's a lot of missing pieces we need help with. Your help.'

# THE ESCORT TO THE GRAVE

Jane looked over to Peter's body, sprawled across the couch. Her grip tightened on the gun in her hands. 'The day Gwen came to me with the evidence of their crimes, I wondered how those monsters could sleep at night. How they were capable of doing what they did to those poor people, to those children.' The gun barrel began to shake. Eddie took a step back. 'I wondered if anyone in the world was capable of anything worse,' she said. 'And now I know. There was a bigger monster all along. One with the power to stop it all. One who watched her husband leave at the dead of night every month, and return the following morning with the sickest of smiles on his face. She cooked him breakfast and poured his coffee, imagining what he and his friends had done through the night. She would lie in bed as her husband slept and tell herself her children were alive and safe because of the sacrifices others made, and that it was all worth it. She would fall asleep, and wake up refreshed and ready to start the day ahead, wearing her very own sickening smile.'

Tears streamed down her face again as she looked up to Eddie. 'Is *that* not a more evil monster, Eddie?'

He stared back, unwilling to answer.

'She came to me too, you know,' Jane said. 'Mara. To make sure I knew I'd pay for what I've done, and what I had failed to do. She will punish me until those children's souls lay to rest.'

Flipping the gun 180 degrees, Jane closed her mouth around the barrel of the gun and leaned forward, dropping the butt to the floor. A shrill cry leapt from Price's throat as Hibbard made for the gun. He was too slow, his senses still sluggish from the earlier knockout. Reaching down, Jane pressed her thumb into the trigger and pushed, sending her last thoughts and the contents of her head high onto the wall behind her, matching the mess her husband had left just minutes earlier. Eddie stood motionless, eyes glazed over.

He could have made it in time. If he had reacted, he could have got to her, and pulled the gun away. But she was right. There is always a more evil monster.

The injustice corrected.

## Chapter 56

### Friday

DCI Hibbard's shirt and trousers were so creased it looked as though he'd slept in them, which was rather ironic, as he hadn't slept at all. He'd been too busy working the Enfield house into the early hours, finally getting back to the station at 02.30 to start the enviable task of breaking the news to the Assistant Chief Constable. It was not something that could wait until morning, and certainly not something he had been looking forward to. Being woken at that time of night had set the ACC in a bad mood by default, but was nothing to what came next, when he had informed him of exactly what the Detective Superintendent had been involved in. The manner in which he had screamed down the phone, you'd swear he blamed Hibbard for it all himself.

Enfield had destroyed the South Wales Police reputation, and with that, the name of the ACC and the Chief Constable. Now she would also have to be informed before first light by the ACC, and then take her turn in relaying the information all the way up to the Home Secretary. It was a shit-show of epic proportions travelling all the way up the rungs of the ladder, and they would ensure it rolled straight back down the hill to stick with Hibbard. As the Senior Investigating Officer, they would expect him to have answers, and when they realised they had their scapegoat, they could cook up an elaborate spin, keep him at a distance, then hang him out for the media vultures to pick at.

Ever since he'd joined, he'd wanted to lead the Major Crime Unit, knowing in his heart he could do a better job of it than Enfield ever could. But now? Now he found himself set in a pair of concrete boots standing at the deep end of the pool, waiting for the two handed push to come. And now that shove would likely come from David Morrison himself. No doubt he would be all over this by the morning, eager to sink his teeth in. Without Morrison in the mix, he'd likely get the nod as acting Super of the department, but after telling the man to get stuffed last night, he wasn't holding his breath. Sipping at his lukewarm coffee, he squinted at the clock on the far office wall. 8.15am. He rubbed at his eye with a knuckle to get rid of the burning feeling fizzling there. The words on the screen in front of him, his closing report on the events surrounding the events at the farm, lake, temple and Enfield's house, had long ago blurred into one colossal mess. His body and mind pleaded for sleep, yet he was still unsure if ACC Bentley would show his face at the station today, or wait until he'd taken direction from the Chief Constable on what to tell the press and when.

'Hey boss,' Price said, as she walked in with two fresh cups in hand, placing one in front of him and taking the seat opposite. 'You managed to get your head down at all?'

'No chance,' Hibbard replied. 'You?'

'Think I dropped off about four, but was wide awake and in the shower by six. It helped. Why don't you try that?'

'Don't think a shower's going to help me today, other than the smell, of course.'

'Well, there is that,' Price said with a smirk.

Hibbard let out a muted chuckle, then fell silent again, his eyes dropping to the coffee cup.

'Have you decided what you're going to do with Eddie yet, Boss?' Price asked in between sips of her drink.

Hibbard let out a deep, solemn breath. 'He assaulted a member of public, and a police officer,' he said, as he touched at the tender lump on his temple, still raw and yet to develop any bruising.

'And led us to the ringleader of a murderous cult,' Price whispered, hiding behind her cup.

'We would have got in the safe anyway,' Hibbard said.

'But not in time to get the confessions from Enfield and his wife,' she replied, a little too confidently. She was walking a tightrope now.

'Yeah, I know. Truth is, I don't think I've got the energy to even try to charge him with anything. Right now, I just can't be arsed. He was interviewed earlier this morning and co-operated to an extent, even if it *was* full of smart arse remarks. But I'm pretty sure he's not holding anything back, and I know where to find him if he is. Want to do the honours and let him out?'

Price smiled and continued with her coffee, sharing the silence for a moment, then tossed her empty cup into the bin beside the desk. 'You're a great Chief Inspector, Sir. When you get the big chair, you'll be an even better Super.' Hibbard watched her go, pondering her words. Would she have said it if she knew the truth? If she knew what David Morrison had demanded of him, and how he'd almost been weak enough to give in? The thought was enough to make his coffee taste sour.

Eddie lay on the bench of his holding cell with his back to the door. Sleep had come in short bursts through the night, the harsh fluorescent lighting tormenting him in the early hours, and at one point he'd woken shaking and sweating, he guessed from the lack of alcohol. The desk sergeant on duty had been kind enough to bring him a pillow, and in the early hours provided a microwave meal of cold-in-the-middle cottage pie he demolished anyway. The weak vending machine tea accompanying it washed it down all the same. At more than one point in the night, he'd dropped off and dreamt of Gwen.

In the first dream, Eddie sat in the back of Jane's car as she drove through the winding roads toward the reservoir. Gwen sat in the passenger seat, her body turned toward her friend. Her hand rested on Jane's shoulder in a comforting gesture, but her face told another story. She begged for Jane to pull over so she could explain everything she had found, but she wouldn't. She drove faster, taking each turn wider and wider as she crossed into the opposite lane. The tyres screeched beneath the car, pleading for relief. They narrowly missed an oncoming car that flashed its headlights and blasted its horn as they passed. Then the blind bend came. Looking to the rear-view mirror, Eddie could see Jane's eyes. They looked forward, glassed over and distant, like she wasn't really there, until they flashed to the mirror to stare back at him. Lines creased at the edges, and he could tell she was smiling as she pulled the steering wheel harshly to the right and down into the valley below.

Then he stood in a hallway, outside a door he had seen before, painted in bright butterflies and bumblebees haphazardly flying in all directions. He pushed open the door to be met by Gwen and Ellie lying on her bed, Gwen's back resting against the headboard as Ellie cuddled into her. Her scrapbook lay open over Gwen's propped knees. They both looked up to him, gesturing for him to join them. Walking over, he sat at their feet. Gwen stroked her fingers through Ellie's hair as the young girl rested her head on her chest, both admiring her latest work. Lifting herself upright, a massive grin spread on Ellie's face as she turned the book around for Eddie to see her drawing.

The door to the cell opened, and footsteps clacked their way to the bench closest to his head. He ruffled a hand through his hair before swinging his legs around to sit upright, regretting the sudden movement instantly. His head hurt and his eyes stung, but he was pleased to see Price sitting next to him.

'You look like you've slept as much as the rest of us,' she said with a grin. 'You ok?'

'Felt better,' Eddie replied.

'I've got an hour before we have to head back to Enfield's house,' Price said, getting to her feet. 'Let's go get some breakfast, my treat.'

'Is my car still outside the Enfield's place?' Eddie asked.

'Yes, and you'll be able to collect it when we get there, as long as you take off straight away, and as long as we eat first.'

'I'm guessing even though Hibbard would love to stretch this out and make it as painful as he could for me, he's got bigger problems to deal with and just wants me out of his sight, yeah?'

Price smirked as she shrugged her shoulders. 'Just take it as a lucky break and move on, Eddie. Now, Full English? I could murder some bacon and eggs.'

## Chapter 57

Price pulled up at the brow of the hill leading down to the Enfield property. It was as close as she could get, because of the fleet of police vehicles lining both sides of the road closed off since the early hours. Reversed into the drive, a black private ambulance had the boot open. Opposite the detached cottage, at the turn in to a small cul-de-sac of houses, blue and white tape ran from one side of the entrance to the other. A small gaggle of men and women stood arms crossed at the tape, no doubt concocting their own versions of what had happened overnight at the cottage. One man waved his arms manically at a uniformed officer, pointing at the mass of cars and vans. Whatever had happened, he obviously thought it couldn't be important enough for all those vehicles blocking off the road. Eddie pulled the door handle, ready to step out, stopping when Price's warm hand dropped onto his.

'Are you sure you're ok Eddie?'

'Yes Mam,' Eddie replied. 'For the ninetieth time.'

'Where are you heading now?' she asked.

'Once I've got the car, I'll be heading home,' Eddie said. 'There's something I need to do.'

'Um, Eddie… about Ellie Morrison. The drawing she gave you. Was it… was it Enfield?'

Eddie's head lowered. 'Yeah, and she knew I'd keep her promise. It's like she sent me there at that exact moment on purpose, you know? Like she planned it all.'

'But how could she do that, Eddie? She's just a kid. And why you?'

'I'm about to go find out,' Eddie said.

'Do you need me to be with you? I'll find an excuse to get from here. If you want me to, that is?'

'No, I think I need to do this next bit on my own,' Eddie said. 'But I'll let you know how it goes.'

Two uniform officers guarding the entrance to the Enfield property eyed Eddie suspiciously as he walked towards them, stopping at the rusting Ford littered amongst the police vehicles and jumped in. One appeared ready to challenge him until he saw Price walk down behind and wave him off.

The drive back to Merthyr was a blur, his mind churning over what Ellie had told him yesterday morning and what Mara had told him last night. Every minute or so, his eyes wandered to the key sat on the passenger seat. If it held the answers to the many questions warping his fragile mind, he hoped when he got to the house, it would finally put him out of his misery.

Turning into the estate, Eddie stopped the car in the middle of the road. The house stood facing him at the end of the street, waiting. A group of children were already out playing in the early autumn sun, enjoying the last days of their time off before returning to school next week. On seeing the car approach, one boy grabbed for his football, shouting to his friends a warning, only to scratch his cheek in confusion as the driver continued to stare ahead rather than drive on. It had been a couple of years since Eddie had been here last, when he had turned up a drunken mess in the early hours to fall asleep on the front lawn. Farah, Sam's wife, had found him there in the morning, tried her best to rouse him into coming in for a coffee, only for him to stumble off in the opposite direction to find his next bottle. Little he remembered had changed. The house appeared as immaculate as the last time, maybe a fresh coat of paint, but then he couldn't even recall what colour it had been before. The four bedroom double-fronted house stood out on the estate for all the right reasons. Its grey sash windows and large weeping cherry blossom tree in the front garden completed a stunning look in the months of bloom. Even now, with its lack of foliage, it still looked impressive, the symmetry of the hanging copper colour branches giving the appearance they were melting and dripping to the ground below. To the right of the garden, a driveway leading up to a single garage currently held Farah's white BMW X5.

The children all stared as Eddie finally crept past, allowing them to resume their game. He slowed to a stop in front of the driveway, his hand reaching across to palm the key. He sat for a while until the front door opened, pulling him from his trance. Sam's eldest son Noah ran out, stopping as he spotted Eddie on the drive, then turned back to the open door. 'Mam,' he shouted. 'Uncle Eddie's here.' He gave a little wave before running off in direction of the children in the street.

Eddie stepped from the car, rounding it to the passenger side to lean on the wheel arch. A moment later, Farah appeared, wiping her hands on a dishcloth, her eyebrows raised high with surprise.

'Eddie?' she said, 'Are you ok? I heard about the police at the pub last night.' She stepped out into the garden, catching under his arm. 'They almost kicked the door in at the flat looking for you. Sam raised hell with them in the shop.' She lifted a hand to her mouth as though to catch the giggle as it came out. 'For a quiet man, he can find a nasty streak on times.'

Eddie frowned as he looked up at the house, his lips squeezing together until they disappeared. It had been a long time since he had been inside, but he remembered it like it was yesterday. For several days following the crash, he had tried to stay, only to find himself plagued with bouts of insomnia and heartache. Alcohol helped, allowing him to fall unconscious for longer periods, but then the nightmares would come instead. He would sleep and dream of Gwen in her last moments, drenched in blood and lost in death. Then they would switch to the hospital corridor, and to the woman he now knew as Mara. She sat with him, telling him things about the injustice he had refused to hear, and refused to act on.

Farah eyed him intently, giving his arm a gentle tug. 'Can't remember the last time you came here, Eddie. Are you going to come in this time?'

Eddie looked down at the key in his sweaty, shaking hand. 'Is Gwen's office still... Gwen's office?'

'Of course it is Eddie,' Farah said, rubbing at his arm. 'We told you when we first moved in it would always be waiting for you, whenever you were ready. None of us ever go in there and it's exactly as you last saw it. Come on. I'll make us some tea.'

She pulled Eddie through the front door before he had a chance to lose the courage. The inside of the house looked as well presented as the outside. Family canvasses lined the soft pastel hallway walls. Atop a console table sat a crystal vase filled with blooming white Lillies. Farah led Eddie through to the hustle-bustle of the kitchen, where her two youngest, Laila and Oscar wore mini cooking aprons and chef hats, propped up on footstools. The unmistakable smell of oven baked cookies filled the air as the two argued over whose turn it was to cut the shapes out of the dough. There was flour everywhere; covering the worktops, floor and the children themselves that Farah appeared to have little issue with.

'It's my turn,' Laila shouted into her brother's face.

'You cut out the last ones,' Oscar screamed back. 'Mam, tell her.'

'Laila, give your brother a turn,' Farah said.

'Hey kids,' Eddie said. 'Can you save some for me?'

'Hi Uncle Eddie,' they said in unison.

'We're baking teddy bear cookies,' Laila said, holding out a rolling pin. 'Want to help?'

'Uncle Eddie has something to do right now kiddos,' Farah said as she walked over to a high shelf, pulling a key from a china bowl and handing it over to him. 'We keep it locked, just in case. This pair can be rather nosey at times. You go ahead while I make us a cuppa.'

Eddie left the kitchen and turned toward the stairs, creeping up to a large landing area. The door to Gwen's office was in the far corner. He stared at it for a long time, trying to find the courage to open it. Sweat had formed around his forehead, and he was suddenly very aware of the dryness in his throat. Unlocking and opening the door, a painful cocktail of emotions engulfed him, like he'd travelled back in time to be dumped into his old life. Farah wasn't exaggerating. The room was exactly as Gwen had left it, even down to the mass of paperwork filling the desk. White boards adorning the walls held more, with different coloured magnets keeping them in place and post-it notes littering the borders haphazardly. Eddie ambled in, a knot of guilt twisting in his stomach, as if he were breaking the trust in a relationship that, in truth, had been destroyed nearly seven years before. He rounded the desk and eased into her chair, staring at the blank computer screen with its untouched layer of dust. To the side stood a framed picture of the couple, Eddie in a tuxedo and Gwen in a ball gown, holding her 2010 British Independent Journalist of the Year award. A smile rose on his face. Gwen was adamant she wouldn't win, nervously putting herself down for the entire train journey to London, getting frustrated at her relaxed husband, who was confident of the result. They had made and shook on a wager, and after she had won the award and lost the bet, Eddie had claimed his prize as soon as they had got back to the hotel. They laughed and joked afterwards they really should gamble more often.

It was a strange feeling being in here, like he was snooping at something he shouldn't be. During their time together, they had agreed to keep their personal lives separate from their professional. Eddie was a police officer, and with Gwen a journalist, it was important the line didn't get crossed. Gwen often reminded him he'd lose his job in a heartbeat if found by a disciplinary panel to be handing confidential information to her. It was a practise that happened all the time, the police and media constantly scratching each other's backs, but the fact they lived together meant there was a twenty-four-seven spotlight shining over them. Eddie rolled his eyes often at Gwen keeping a closed office door, but it was something she held strong opinions on, and Eddie had no option but to respect it. Eventually, it was like everything else that took time to get used to, and he kept his distance from his wife's workspace with respect. He had continued the practise the years following her death, and now today, he had broken it for the first time. He couldn't help but feel guilty about it.

Easing back into the chair, his head hit the rest behind it. He swivelled toward the nearest white board, looking up at the vast amount of Gwen's marker pen handwriting and post-it notes and arrows pointing in all directions like it had been through so many tremendous brainstorming sessions. Gwen's handwriting was little better than a doctor's scrawl. Most of it looked gibberish, with surnames and towns and pictures he didn't recognise.

And then he spotted a series of names, Eastern European surnames, and one he'd heard only this week from Price. Azarenka.

Standing from the chair, he walked to the board. Beneath the list of names, a sheet of A4 paper had been stuck to the board, taped at the top edge. Lifting it up revealed another series of names, more common ones. Two stood out that struck him hard in the chest.

Glover. Enfield.

He imagined Gwen writing the names there. She had found all of this, keeping it to herself when it was all so close to home. He imagined the pain she must have felt.

Why didn't she turn to him? Why didn't she share the burden? Her own father and her husband's commanding officer were guilty of such unbelievable, heinous acts, but still, she kept it secret. Unwilling to turn to Eddie, she had instead befriended Enfield's wife, and given her the chance to help bring the monster to justice. She had undoubtedly expected her to find strength in her grief and shock, hoping she would unite with her and find the courage to report her own husband to the force he himself worked for. With that mistake, Gwen had paid the ultimate price.

Eddie dropped back into the chair. He leaned back and closed his eyes. It was surprisingly comfortable, and the tension he felt when he unlocked the door was easing. Using his legs to swivel around, he looked to the beat up filing cabinet tucked neatly under the desk. Pulling open the top drawer, he took out the first brown folder that came to hand, opening it to find a criminal profile, complete with mugshot photo of a man dating back to July 1995. Behind it was a newspaper clipping of the man's arrest and subsequent charge of serial rape of fourteen women, spanning twelve years, through the North Wales counties of Gwynedd and Clwyd. A second article from a newspaper a month later told of how he had taken his own life while working in the prison kitchen, pouring a pan of boiling oil down his own throat. Some way to go.

Eddie pulled a second folder, dated August 1995, with more newspaper articles telling of a woman found sat in her open-top car that had rolled to a stop on a dual carriageway in Swansea, minus her head. Police found it half-a-mile back, close to the hundred metre length of rope she had used to tie around a layby barrier at one end and her neck at the other. A second newspaper from the following day explained police had found her two young children chained to a radiator at their home, completely emaciated and covered in their own faeces, starved close to death and saved just in time.

# THE ESCORT TO THE GRAVE

Folder after folder revealed more of the same. Running a finger over the top of them, there must have been well over a hundred. Each one held articles of the premature deaths of the most wicked of people, criminals guilty of unspeakable crimes. Eddie rubbed at his temple, trying his best to join the dots. Pushing the drawer shut, he opened the middle drawer, finding it rammed tight with even more of the brown folders. He didn't bother to sample any, knowing what was inside. He slid the drawer back home on its runners just as there was a knock at the office door. It opened enough for a hand to slide in, holding a mug of tea, allowing a smile to creep up on Eddie's face.

'Thanks Farah. You're ok to come in. I've got all my clothes on.' She pushed the door open some more and marched toward the desk, leaving the mug on top. She turned without a word, heading back the way she came.

'Haven't you ever been curious, Farah?' Eddie said. 'About this room?'

She stopped and thought for a moment, keeping her back to him. 'I never got to meet your wife Eddie, but I can tell from the years of pain in your eyes she meant everything to you. Whatever is in here is for you, and you alone. It always will be. For as long as you want it to. You're a wonderful man, Eddie, for everything you have done for my family, and I hope whatever you find here brings you one step closer to peace.'

She closed the door behind her, and the room fell silent again. Eddie took a sip of his tea as he opened the bottom drawer of the cabinet. The shock registered too late as the mug fell from his grasp, spilling the hot brown contents over the cream carpet beneath it. He barely registered the mess, his focus purely on the contents of the cabinet drawer. A dark rosewood chest, with gold and black inlays of the Tree of Life and Triquetra symbol, identical to the one Ellie owned.

*Please. No.*

Eddie strained to lift it from the tight metal surrounding, digging his fingers in around the edge to gain purchase. Eventually it gave, and he pulled it out and dropped it onto the desk in front of him. Standing and pushing the chair back, he let out an almighty breath, then ran his fingers over the familiar lock engraved with the even more familiar three pointed symbol. His hand moved to his pocket, coming back out with the key Mara had given him. It found its way straight into the lock, clicking open with a half turn, pushing the lid up an inch. The musky smell of aged paper emanated from it. Flipping the lid back on its hinges, Eddie swallowed hard, sure of what he would find inside. A large book, intricately detailed with carved leather symbols, again, identical to Ellie's, lay facing up, close to the brim of the chest. Beneath it were two more. He lifted them out onto the desk.

Cracking open the book from the bottom, he desperately hoped he wouldn't find what he expected. His head lifted to look at the ceiling, a moment to brace himself, as he turned the cover to reveal the first page. A flawless charcoal drawing, expertly detailed of a grotesque subject. A man he recognised from the folder, dressed in his prison garments, his face contorted in pain and horror as he knelt and poured boiling liquid down his own throat. Wisps of steam rose from his mouth and his skin burned to blisters. At the corner was a date, two days before the newspaper article.

The tears broke through as Eddie collapsed back in his chair a sobbing mess. Ellie Morrison was born the same night his wife, Gwenno Catherine Venter, had died.

Ellie Morrison, the Welsh Morrigan sister. The six-year-old Escort to the Grave, already responsible for punishing a number of monsters. Given the role by the Goddess of Death herself, following the premature end of the previous Escort.

# THE ESCORT TO THE GRAVE

The woman he had loved for fourteen years, and mourned the past seven. Gwen, the Morrigan sister prior to Ellie.

His wife was an Escort to the Grave.

## Chapter 58

Eddie pulled into the layby overlooking the Morrison grounds. David Morrison's black Jag sat outside their garage, exponentially reducing his chances of speaking with Ellie, but he had no option other than to try. He opened the Messenger app and scrolled to Sarah's name, tapped out a text and hit send.

*Outside the gates. Need to speak to Ellie. Urgent.*

He kept the message on screen, waiting for the icon to shift to show she had read it. The phone rang instead.

'How did it go?' Price asked. 'Find anything at your house?'

'Too much to explain over the phone,' Eddie said. 'I'm outside the Morrison's. I need to speak with Ellie again.'

'Is her father there?'

'His car's outside, so I guess so.'

'Then wait until I get there, Eddie. Please don't go in causing a scene.'

A tone pipped in Eddie's ear, indicating he'd received a message. 'I've got to go, Price,' he said.

'Wait, wait,' she said. 'The Agnes Clark reported missing in Scotland. They've identified her as our girl on the mountain. Police searched her house, and you'll never guess what they found?'

'A Rosewood chest, and a bunch of leather scrapbooks, just like Ellie's?' Eddie replied.

'Jesus Eddie? How did you know? There were hundreds and hundreds of morbid drawings. And old newspaper clippings, too.'

'Got to go, Price.'

# THE ESCORT TO THE GRAVE

'I'm en route. Don't go in without me.'

He ended the call and pulled up the messenger app again. Sarah had left a message.

*Not a good time. He's here.*

Leaving the car in the layby, he strolled down the lane towards the house. The road dipped to the bottom of the hill beneath overhanging trees either side of the road, blocking out the late August sun and casting him deep into the shadows. He stopped short of the gates, away from the CCTV cameras monitoring visitors, and tried again.

*Need to speak with Ellie. Just need five minutes.*

After thirty seconds, a text came back.

*Can't do it. David will kill me this time.*

He'd had enough. Walking to the ten-foot gates, he prepared to climb over. He gripped high with both hands, lifting one foot into a gap for purchase, and pushed hard. As he did, the gates jerked and began to open with a whirring sound. He climbed back down, slipped through into the courtyard and marched across the gravel to the front door. The bell made a harsh rasp loud enough to wake the dead. A moment later, David Morrison opened the door, a scowl on his face like he'd smelled something disgusting.

'How the hell did you get in through the gates?' He turned back to look down the hall. 'That bitch. Sarah!' he screamed into the house.

Over David's shoulder, Eddie could see Sarah Morrison standing outside the kitchen door. She wore a thick woollen dressing gown, her arms wrapped tight around herself, and her puffed eyes, raw from the tears, begged for help.

'What did I tell you about letting this piece of shit into my house?'

'It wasn't her,' another voice said from inside. Jenny Morrison came into view from the living room. 'It was me, and the only piece of shit around here is you.'

David Morrison heaved the heavy door shut as he turned toward the women. Eddie instinctively stuck a foot out, taking the full brunt of its momentum. He felt a crack, and a sharp pain stabbed at his ankle as he pushed it back open. David Morrison held his daughter by the throat, the young girl thrashing her legs and letting out a stifled cry in desperation. Her hands gripped around his wrists to prise them away as he squeezed, but he was too strong. Sarah ran from the kitchen and pounced onto his back, wrapping her legs around his waist and, with a sinewy arm around his neck, pulled back as hard as she could manage. It was enough to draw his attention from his daughter, David loosening his grip on the girl who collapsed to the floor, wheezing for air. He peddled backwards to the far wall with force, Sarah's back slamming into it, causing her to release her grip. He bucked her to the floor, sending a kick into her mid-section, but turned too late to react to Eddie's first sledge-hammer blow catching him square on the chin. His legs buckled beneath him, and he hit the floor next to his wife, smacking his head on the bottom step of the stairs. The momentum of the punch, combined with his now broken left foot, saw Eddie follow him down. Through pure rage, he wrestled and powered his way to straddle David, one hand holding his collar while the other rained punch after punch to his face. David clawed at his attacker's face, finding an eye with his thumb, and pushed hard. Eddie continued to hit out hard and fast, putting every ounce he had into the blows. A perfect shot splintered David's nose before his resistance faded, his arms flopping limp at his side. The anger in Eddie continued on, refusing to tire as David's face turned a bloody pulp, even when he felt a knuckle cave in on his eye socket.

It was a soft hand placed on his shoulder that pulled Eddie from his blind fury, his smashed hand poised high, ready to hit again. He looked to the hand on his shoulder, then to the little girl standing beside him. Ellie looked deep into his eyes, telling him no more. He did as she asked, falling off her unconscious father to lie on his back beside him. Sarah grabbed for Ellie first, pulling her in tight before holding out her hand to Jenny, gesturing for her to join them. He heard movement from the front door, but complete exhaustion prevented Eddie from lifting his head from the floor. Eventually, a face came into view as Price stood over him, her face screwed into a pained and disappointing scowl.

'You look like I feel,' Eddie said.

'Jesus, Eddie.' Price said, as she pulled her mobile from her pocket. 'I told you to wait for me.' She looked over at Morrison, then to the three women huddled and sobbing, then back to Morrison.

'He's going to need an ambulance.'

## Chapter 59

### Monday

It was the bottom of his fourth pint and the clock hands were yet to hit midday. The self-destruct button was fully armed and ready. Knocking back the last of it, he raised the empty glass skyward with his good hand, giving it a little shake like some silent servant bell. Stretch gave an exhausted blow of his cheeks, but did as asked, pulling a fresh glass from the shelf to fill. He rounded the counter, made his way to Eddie's table, and set it down.

'I don't do waiter service for any old customer, you know. And I don't offer advice to just anyone either.'

'Then don't offer it now,' Eddie snapped. 'Just let me drink in peace. If I don't do it here, I'll go somewhere else to do it.'

Stretch lifted his hands up in defense, before wandering off to the other side of the bar to continue pretending he was cleaning and not keeping a concerned eye. Slumped in the chair at the table closest to the television, Eddie kept his back to the steady throng of the morning regulars and deadbeats littered amongst the walled pews and tables. It was a captain's style chair, with a round back and high arms that hunched his shoulders up around his neck as he rested in it, and close enough to the table in front of him it took minimal effort to lift his glass to his mouth and back again. The cast on his right hand hung over the end of the armrest, and the ridiculous looking boot protecting his left ankle propped on the bench seat opposite him.

# THE ESCORT TO THE GRAVE

Sitting beneath the television meant no one could make eye contact, attempt a small talk conversation on his injuries, and save him from telling them to do one, to sling their hook and bugger off somewhere else. He was not in the mood. The news reports over the weekend had been full of typical media speculation over the events at the Morrison estate on Friday, each station trying to get one up on their rivals by forming their own opinions and having the 'inside scoop' on the incident.

The heroic David Morrison MP, a front runner to gain a top job in the rumoured upcoming re-shuffle, courageously defended his family fighting off some opportunist thieves at their home. Another reported he'd been involved in a freak accident with some garden equipment. One even concluded there had been an extra-marital affair and an attempted suicide. The gutter press, always willing to slump to new depths to get those viewing or listening numbers up. Better to guess incorrectly in the headlines and risk having to apologise on page eleven afterwards, than to allow a rival paper to get the scoop.

The truth was, he'd spent the weekend in an undisclosed hospital after getting his face smashed in on his hallway floor. He'd undergone emergency operations to reset his nose and cheekbone, and he'd been fortunate with his left eye socket. Following his release yesterday, he'd been taken straight into police custody and interviewed under caution following his wife's statement on the incident. And then this morning, Sarah had messaged Eddie herself, telling him she'd retracted it. It was a blow he hadn't expected, a real kick in the teeth with steel toe cap boots on. Her husband hadn't assaulted her or her daughter after all. It was nothing more than a simple domestic incident and a big misunderstanding. Exactly what a pressured victim would say. He could see it now, David's lawyer sitting her down and explaining unless she changed her story, he would do everything in his power to ensure Eddie spent jail time for trespass and GBH with intent. He was likely used as the bait, and she obviously fell for it. Now she will be told to play happy families again for the dust to settle. Eddie had tried calling her back, only to get her chirpy voiced answerphone instead. He'd gone straight downstairs and next door at that point, and been in the pub ever since.

The front door opened and in walked Price, followed closely by Hibbard, holding a sour look on his face. The smell of stale beer and the great unwashed had him turning his nose like he deserved better. He looked around the bar at the twenty-year-old decor, with its grim threadbare carpets looking as old and worn as the regulars. Price made for the bar, only for Stretch to point a digit towards the television and the figure sat beneath it. She gave an appreciative nod, making her way over with a mortified Hibbard in tow.

'You look like shit,' Price said as she sat across the table from him. 'Hope the other guy looks worse. Mind if we sit?'

'Not if you buy me one of these,' Eddie replied, pointing toward his pint without taking his eyes off the television. 'And a whisky chaser.'

Hibbard slotted into the bench seat next to Price. Eddie looked across at his old colleague. He looked haggard, eyes holding dark shadows beneath them that clearly hadn't seen enough sleep. His skin held a grey hue matching the stubble around his chin, now too long and scruffy to be considered designer. A purple bruise covered his right ear and jaw that crept around the side of his face.

'How's the head?' Eddie asked.

'Tip top,' Hibbard replied. 'No thanks to you and your cheap shots.'

Eddie nodded and pressed his lips tight as he looked back to the television. The BBC presenter in the studio went across to the spritely reporter, camped outside the Morrison gates at that very moment. No new information to report, but plenty to conspire on. The two detectives pivoted to get a view of the screen above them. They sat in silence for a moment, listening.

*The brave MP has apparently sustained multiple injuries fighting off his attackers...*

Eddie struggled from his chair on unsteady legs. 'I'm going for a slash.' He hobbled off toward the back and out of sight, returning moments later to slump back in the same position he'd been in for hours.

Price dropped her elbows onto the table, leaning forward. 'Eddie, Sarah Morrison dropped the charges this morning. Because it was a first complaint, and all the safeguarding procedures had been completed, he was free to go home.'

'I know,' Eddie said.

Hibbard took his turn. 'He's reached out to instruct he's willing to put the whole episode behind him, drop his counter charges against you as long as you agree to stay away from his family. Apparently, he wants to concentrate on being a better father and husband.'

Eddie took a big gulp from his drink. 'Course he does.'

'Please, Eddie,' Hibbard said, rubbing his face. 'Just stay away from them, for everyone's sake.'

Eddie slumped further into the chair, lifting his booted foot up onto the seat again. He drained the last of his pint and held it overhead with a shake, knowing the landlord pretending to clean the bar and not keep a concerned eye was, in fact, watching every move.

'Anything else?'

'Yeah,' Hibbard said. 'Yeah there is.' Colour rose in his cheeks as he rubbed at the nape of his neck. 'With everything that's happened the last couple of weeks, I think it's fair to say we'd still be scratching our arses on a lot of it if you weren't involved. So I guess I should say thanks.' They stared at each other for a long moment until a smirk rose on Eddie's face, setting the two of them chuckling. When it died down, Hibbard slid out from under the table.

'The ACC is releasing a statement on Enfield's involvement in the farm and temple murders tomorrow morning.' He looked at the reporter on the television. 'Always a bigger story round the corner. Stay out of trouble Eddie,' he said, slapping him on the shoulder as he passed. 'Let's go Price.'

'I'll be out in a minute, Boss.'

Hibbard walked to the door, pausing at the counter. 'Thank you for your hospitality bar-keep.' He gazed around the room, feigning awe. 'Charming place you have here.'

'Eat shit, copper,' Stretch replied, as he poured yet another pint.

Hibbard smiled at that, turning on his heels and out the door.

'So, it turns out the house Armed Response raided in Aberystwyth Thursday night was owned by one of the Donahue gang. They didn't find any laptop linked to the events at the farm though, and it wasn't one of the family found dead at the temple either. Ronan Donahue, one of the sons. His mother hasn't seen him since Thursday morning.'

'Is that right?' Eddie said.

'Yeah, funny thing is, she admitted he was heading to Merthyr to deal with the person who'd messed with his family. Wouldn't give police a name.'

'Is that so?' Eddie said.

'Wouldn't know anything about that, would you?' Price asked.

'Why would you think I did?'

'I heard him, you know.'

'Heard who?'

'Enfield. When he said he set you up with the last of the Donahues. To get you out of the way.'

Eddie stared at her for a moment.

'And when you tried to get her to give up the gun, you told Jane that Peter was the last one, that they were all gone. So why would you say that if you weren't sure of it?'

# THE ESCORT TO THE GRAVE

Stretch dropped his new pint in front of him. Eddie took a sip.

She continued on. 'Then there's Ellie's drawing of you and the man at your feet. I haven't checked, but I can't help but wonder if the picture matches the missing Donahue.'

'Why haven't you mentioned it to Hibbard?' Eddie asked.

'He already knows. It was his call to let it go,' she said.

Eddie nodded.

'We haven't had a chance to talk since Friday morning,' Price said. 'About what happened between you leaving the Enfield's house and being at the Morrison's? What happened when you went home? What did you find?'

Eddie looked to his lap as he pondered his answer. Price laid a hand on top of his. 'When you're ready to tell, I'll be ready to listen. Look after yourself, mate.'

As she turned to leave, Eddie leaned back and called out. 'Does this mean you believe it? What Ellie is doing with her drawings?'

Price turned back, her shoulders square and sure. 'You mean do I believe a six-year-old girl is responsible for casting vengeance on sinners? That death itself has taken on human form to grow a legion of workers to do its bidding? Vigilantes being judge, jury and executioner?' She let the questions fester for a moment, as if the answers were difficult to say.

'To be honest, I'm still struggling with it all, Eddie. If you're demanding an answer right now, I'd have to say no. I've always dealt in evidence-based reality, not the supernatural.'

'Then how do you explain the drawings?'

'I can't. She's drawn terrible things. But just as I don't know how magicians or mediums carry out their parlour tricks, I don't just assume they're supernatural, either. Everything has an answer, and they're always simpler than they appear. I don't profess to be all knowing, and I'm no psychologist, but I do know that girl has been through a lot these last few weeks. Who even knows what she's been through altogether? Her mind needs healing, and those pictures are her cry for help.'

Eddie nodded, pressing his lips together. 'And what about me?'

'What about you?' she replied.

'Do you believe me?'

Price stalled. 'I… I want to. It's forced me to do a lot of soul searching these last couple of days. What happens to you, I can't explain either, but it pushes me into a corner. I lost my relationship with my father because I refused to have faith in something I just couldn't believe in. But I do believe science alone can't explain what's happening to you, so I suppose at some point I'll have to concede it requires me to renew that faith. I'm just not sure if I'm ready to do it yet.'

She walked back towards him. 'Let me ask you something, Eddie. If all of it is true, I mean, if Ellie was part of some supernatural vigilante group exacting their revenge throughout the world, would it be ethical? The right thing to do? An eye for an eye? Should we leave the fate of wrongdoers to a six-year-old girl, guilty or not?'

Eddie smiled. 'I'll see you around, Price.' He turned back to his near empty glass, all ready for another.

# Chapter 60

## Friday 6th September 2019

Cracking a sticky eye open, it took Eddie a moment to realise he'd fallen asleep on his settee again. The leather arm peeled from his sweaty face like Velcro as he pushed up into a seating position. The room swam around him, the drum beating inside his head playing an unforgiving tune. He looked to the clock on the mantel. 11.30 am. Sunlight fought its way through the thin curtains, casting weak, dust mote filled spotlights on the mess of empty bottles and cans. A cramp deep in his gut had him doubled over the arm, retching to vomit, but nothing came up. Falling back into the seat, stars pulsed in his vision and his hands shook uncontrollably. He reached for the open whisky bottle on the coffee table, almost knocking it over in the process, then chugged the contents back. The relief was immediate, settling the nausea instantly.

The week had been one long bender, a vicious cycle of drinking and sleeping, supplemented by the odd warmed up pasty or pot noodle. He vaguely remembered eating paper wrapped sausage and chips from the takeaway down the road at some point, but couldn't say how long ago or what day it was. He'd watched the Assistant Chief Constable's press conference on Tuesday from his front-row seat in the pub. Stretch had sat with him, completely mesmerised by the details being relayed to the press.

'Things like this don't happen in Merthyr,' Stretch said.

It was carnage as soon as the ACC finished his opening statement. Reporters clambered over each other to get a question in.

'Following the untimely deaths of Detective Superintendent Peter Enfield and his wife Jane, the Major Crime Investigation team uncovered evidence suggesting their involvement in the deaths at a property across the border in Dyfed Powys last week. Investigations are ongoing, but we are also working to establish the connections to an underage trafficking syndicate running from Eastern Europe into the UK. Further information will be released as and when we receive it.'

The room erupted with a thousand questions asked at once. He couldn't blame them, the statement as vague and open-ended as he could imagine. ACC Bentley had ducked for cover as soon as the last word left his mouth, clearing the podium for the press manager to take over and answer questions from the charged room. Every question received similar answers.

'Investigations are ongoing and we will let you know as soon as the information becomes available.'

They had left the press to interpret the information however they saw fit, and they didn't hold back. They completely ripped apart the South Wales Police's reputation from all angles. Public opinion would fall to an all-time low. Little shock there, considering the officer in charge of their Major Crime team was found to be, himself, a mass murderer. They had issued no official statements since Tuesday afternoon, and no doubt pressure was mounting on the Chief Constable to take a grip of the situation and feed the full story to the media. The problem was, the truth was even worse than the rumours. How could the public trust the police following this? How could their children walk the streets safely when the people charged with the responsibility of looking after them were capable of such atrocities? The outrage would be immeasurable.

# THE ESCORT TO THE GRAVE

Eddie drained the last of the bottle, wiping the spillage from his mouth with his sleeve as he scanned his miserable surroundings. Where did he go from here? The last two weeks, as brutal and testing as they had been, gave a sense of purpose that was now a distant memory. The last few days had gone by in a blur of self-abuse, all building up to this very day.

The anniversary. Seven years since she'd been taken from him. Over the last week, flashes of memory had continued to torture him, playing on a loop in his fragile mind. That sacred last moment wasted saving Jane when he could have tried to help his wife. He should have known. What if she wasn't gone? What if there was a chance, a slim hope he could have brought her back? It was all his fault.

The aftermath: The endless drinking, fighting, arrests. The disciplinary action, the two-finger salute and the 'have a nice life.' The breakdowns and the self-pity. The crying at the Enfield's kitchen table and their patient comfort and understanding and sharing of grief.

The life he and Gwen shared at their home. The days filled with so much love and laughter. The evening meals they cooked together, the film nights, the hours shared at the candlelit dining table over a bottle of wine and the endless small talk. The tough days at work, coming home to a massage so often leading to more. The days she spent working away at her desk, of him rapping a knuckle on the door and leaving cups of coffee outside for her to collect. The separation of professional and private life he'd reluctantly agreed to.

The lies.

His eyes roamed the mess littering the coffee table and floor surrounding it. A patch of smashed glass lay beneath the mantel, another result of a late night outburst he couldn't remember. He scratched at his chin, going over last night's events, the memories coming back in spits and starts. Staggering from the Miners, taking an age to get his key into the lock and open the front door. Dragging himself up the stairs, protective boot catching on every step. Collapsing to the settee and wincing at the stabbing pains in his bandaged hand. Gwen's photo on the mantel, as ever giving her brutal opinion. *Nice one Eddie. What a way to live.* His hand catching around the bottle. The shattering as it hit the wall to join the mixture of glass already there. The fresh tears running down his cheeks. The never-ending cycle of pain and suffering and misery.

---

Sam watched from behind the counter as Eddie stumbled in through the shop door. The customer leaving backed up against the shelving as he passed, her wide eyes watching him as he made for the counter. Slapping a twenty pound note down, Eddie gave a lazy nod toward the shelves behind the shopkeeper. Sam gave a heavy sigh as he reached back for a bottle, opened his mouth to say something, then thought better of it. Turning toward the door, Eddie stopped at the shelving rack near the exit. Masses of multi-coloured cards and envelopes poked from their slots for various celebrations. Birthdays, weddings, anniversaries and condolence. He pulled out a card of some Disney characters holding up a large number seven, returned to the counter and paid a confused-looking Sam for it. His mouth opened again to say something, and for a second time, thought better of it.

The air held a bitter chill, spelling the end of the summer months. Dark clouds formed overhead threatening a downpour any minute. Hobbling through the cemetery gates, Eddie cracked the cap of the whisky bottle and took a long pull, spilling enough down his stubbled chin to reach the neck of his shirt. Wiping it away with the back of his hand, he trudged his way up along the broken concrete path

## THE ESCORT TO THE GRAVE

toward Gwen's resting place. Reaching the grave, Eddie took up his favourite position sat in front of the headstone. Ignoring the damp grass and the cold air, he wrapped his jacket tight into a makeshift pillow, ready to fall back on. Rubbing a finger over the polythene wrapping of the card, he traced the big number seven on the front.

*Seven years. Seven years without you. Any normal person would have moved on or ended it all by now. But here I am, stuck in my very own purgatory.*

He raised his bottle toward the headstone in toast, ready to neck another mouthful. The small cream envelope leaning against the grave stopped him. Written on the front in black ink styled in flowing italics, the capital E and V swirling in fanciful loops was his name. He turned it over, revealing the red clot of wax making the seal. He imagined its owner, heating and dripping it onto the paper, then stamping the pool before it hardened. The indents in the wax formed the three pointed symbol he had seen everywhere the last few weeks, even in his sleep. Sliding a finger into the envelope, the slivers of wax fell to his lap as it broke. The card within was finely made, embossed with gold lettering, matching the font on the envelope.

Cofio y meirw, Dathlu bywyd.

Heno. 7.30pm. St. Michael's Inn.

Pulling his mobile from his pocket, he flicked through the phonebook before lifting it to his ear. 'Hey Joyce,' he said, turning the card over in his hand. 'How's my number one librarian?'

'Eddie? We've been worried about you, my boy. Where have you been?'

'Working a case,' he slurred. 'Need a translation if you don't mind?'

'Betty and I have been glued to the TV this week Eddie, awful goings on.'

'Translate this note for me and I'll take the two of you on a date to a fancy restaurant and tell you all about it.'

'Got the perfect dress ready.'

'Cofio y meirw,' Eddie said.

'That's a sombre message,' Joyce replied. 'It means remembering the dead.'

'Dathlu bywyd?' Eddie asked.

'Celebrating life.'

'Last one,' Eddie said. 'Heno?'

'My dear boy. Tonight, of course.'

'Thanks Joyce. Got to go. Speak to you soon.' He ended the call. For a long time, he stared at the card. Remembering the dead. Celebrating life. Tonight. 7.30pm St, Michael's Inn.

The pub where Ellie was found.

# THE ESCORT TO THE GRAVE

# Epilogue

A car horn sounded outside just as Eddie opened his front door. Following his visit to the cemetery and finding his invite, he'd gone back to the flat to sober up with a shower and a fresh change of clothes. The night was drawing in, the overhead lights switching themselves on sporadically up and down the street. The taxi waited at the curb, and as he walked over, a voice called from further down the road.

'Hey, Eddie.' Price strode toward him, her arm looped into the crook of the man beside her.

'Well, well,' Eddie said. 'Look at you all glammed up.'

'I could say the same to you,' Price replied, gesturing to his smart shirt and trouser combo. 'I didn't think you even owned a proper pair of shoes.'

Eddie looked to her companion, who gave a shy smile back. The man held out his hand. 'Great to meet you, Mr. Venter. I'm Iefan. I've heard a lot about you.'

'Good things I hope, and please, it's Eddie.'

'This is the Iefan I told you about from the digital forensics team,' Price said.

'Ah, the man who took down the traffickers. Looks like I've heard a lot about you too, Iefan.'

Iefan blushed a lovely shade of cherry as he let out a school boy snigger. 'You're too kind, Mr. Venter. I think the real plaudits should go to yourself and this wonderful lady here.' He squeezed Price's arm as she dropped her cheek onto his shoulder. 'You've been quite the partnership, taking down the culprits.'

Eddie held back the frown threatened to break out on his face as he pushed any thought of Peter and Jane to the back of his mind. Looking to Price, the happiness radiating from her, another smile cracked instead. He tried to remember the last time he'd been able to. 'Yeah, I suppose we have,' he said through his widening grin.

'We're heading into town for a drink, but I was hoping to buy you one first, see how you are.' Price said. 'Looks like we only just caught you.'

Eddie scratched at his chin. 'Yeah, I've got somewhere I need to be.'

'Another time then,' Price said.

'I can get the taxi to drop you off first, if you like?'

'No, it's fine,' Price replied. 'I think we'll go in the Miner's for one first, right Iefan?'

'You can't like him much if you're taking him in there,' Eddie said with a smile. 'See you around both. Nice to meet you, Iefan. Look after her.'

'Tell Ellie I was asking about her,' Price said over her shoulder as she walked through the door.

---

The taxi cab turned into the busy car park and Eddie reached over the driver's shoulder, handing him a twenty. Stepping out into the clear night, the bitter air pinched at his cheeks as he shut the door for the car to U-turn and drive away. Checking his watch, he walked back out to the unlit road they had arrived from that ran in front of the pub, splitting the property in two. He checked his phone. 7pm. He was early.

Sounds of music and laughter boomed from the centuries old building, the stone walls and slate roof pleading under the stress of the noise. High above the ground-floor windows, large gold lettering spelling out *The St. Michael's*

# THE ESCORT TO THE GRAVE

*Inn* glistened from the cowl lights illuminating them. Positioned a good five hundred metres from its nearest neighbour along the road, a motor repair garage, the pub sat a lonely beacon in an ocean of black valley surroundings. For a reason he couldn't quite figure out, his gut knotted and hands shook as he crossed the road to the open front door. A pub had been his safe space for years now, even ones he was a stranger at. A place he could go to find his answers at the bottom of a glass. He rarely found any, of course, but more often than not, he was left to his own devices, and the alcohol dulled his senses to a point it took away the punishing guilt racking him.

Tonight was different. He was nervous.

Walking through the frosted glass foyer to the open plan lounge, the familiar smells of flowing beer and aged upholstery filled the air. Raucous laughter, clinking of glass and scraping chairs on flagstone floors accompanied it. Elaborate wall mounted and table top candelabra, along with the homely fireplace, illuminated the large room, casting dancing shadows in every direction. As the door closed behind him, so did the conversation, the patrons turning to eye the new arrival. He quickly scanned the faces he could make out, recognising no-one as they all stared back from the busy tables. There were men, women and children of all ages, sat together, all cloaked in identical red robes. Some faces frowned with puzzlement, others nodded with acknowledgement. To the left, towards the back of the room, one woman with brown curly hair and sharp green eyes raised her wine glass and smiled a welcome. He had seen her face before, when he had climbed the mountain that first time, investigating Ellie's disappearance. The woman he had seen carrying her away. She sat with another lady, a middle-aged woman dressed like she'd come straight from the 1950s. She wore a white sleeveless knee-length dress with black polka dots, tied off at the waist with a huge white bow. A headscarf matching the colour of her dress held her blond curls high on her head. She stood out in the sea of red, looking dainty and elegant and strangely unnerving all at the same time. She eyed Eddie with a raised brow as she sipped at her glass of champagne.

An empty bar stood ahead of him, mahogany paneled with matching decorative beading, finished with brass arm and footrests. More candles stood atop it, and behind, above the displays of many liquor bottles, the bare stone wall held black and white photographs of landscapes and portraits and buildings from the surrounding areas. His eye caught on one he recognised from his research at the library. St. Michael's chapel, or more precisely, the ruin where it once sat, at the summit of the Holy Mountain overlooking this very pub. The chapel Ellie told him they had taken her to.

A portly man dressed in navy trousers and a white shirt was busy adding a small log to the stack in the huge fireplace and stoking the hot ashes beneath it. Satisfied with his work, he returned the grate into position and dusted his hands off as he worked his way through the throngs of bodies back toward the bar. On seeing Eddie, a frown etched on his face.

'Private party tonight I'm afraid, Sir,' the man said, as he made his way behind the counter.

Eddie fished into his pocket, pulling out the now crumpled card left at Gwen's grave earlier that day. 'Um, I received this,' he mumbled, handing it over.

The landlord smiled as he looked down to the card, turning it towards the seated patrons as he nodded his approval. 'What'll it be, Sir?' the man asked, as the chatter and laughter returned amongst the revellers. Eddie scanned the choices of brass tap handles adorned with emblems of locally brewed beers. He pointed at one reading *The Hounds of Annwn*.

'I'll give that a go,' he said.

The barman pulled off a pint with three tugs of the handle, dropping it down onto the counter mat in front of

# THE ESCORT TO THE GRAVE

Eddie, who was busy reaching into his pocket for payment. 'Complimentary tonight Sir, courtesy of the host.'

'And who might that be?' Eddie asked.

'She'll be through shortly. She's just making some final arrangements in the function room with the landlady, ready for the ceremony.'

'The ceremony?'

'Still waiting on the guest of honour, Sir. Expected any moment now.'

'Guest of honour?'

The landlord gave a smirk as he filled a tray with drinks, hoisting it up onto the palm of his hand. He nodded toward an empty table in the corner. 'Make yourself comfortable, Sir. I'll keep an eye out and a glass ready for a refill,' he said, before heading off toward the waiting drinkers.

Eddie looked around the busy room full of people in high spirits. Children chased each other between tables, their red gowns flowing behind them as they ran. Groups of adults continued to laugh and joke noisily in a number of foreign languages he couldn't make out. Some mingled between tables, shaking hands and hugging and introducing others. Drinks were drunk and replacements ordered. It was a proper party in full flow. Through the throng of bodies, at the far end of the room, the lady in the white polka dress continued to stare at Eddie. Moving sheepishly, he sat at the empty table, dragging the closest chair out from under to sit facing the crowd.

The landlord had a knack of turning up at the table with fresh drinks, just as he was needed. With a drink inside him, the knot twisting Eddie's stomach loosened some, but he kept his guard and senses sharp. On the landlord's second visit to the table, Eddie caught his arm and questioned him again, getting a similar response.

'Just waiting on the guest of honour, Sir. Any moment now.'

Eddie checked his watch. 7.45pm. From the other side of the lounge, the woman from the mountain, he now remembered Ellie called Shannon, toasted her glass to him once again. He played with the idea of going over to get some answers, but her companion in the white dress continuing to stare his way, giving him an unnerving sense of inferiority. There was something about her, an air of power she held in the charged room setting the hairs at his neck tingling. Since he'd walked through the door, he hadn't seen her speak, and from the aura emanating around her, he somehow doubted she needed to often. She sat, sipping at her drink, staring him down, as the room bustled around her. He decided to stay put.

A figure sitting down in front of him blocked his view of the woman. Eddie's eyes widened, and he pulled back as Mara, dressed as ever in her favourite colour, joined his table. She wore a stunning black lace cocktail dress that matched her velvet cloak, and as she sat in the empty seat next to Eddie, she flicked her long dark hair over her shoulder. Placing her champagne glass down on the table, she eyed the man next to her.

'Hello, Mr. Venter,' she said with a smirk. 'I see you got your invitation. Thank you for joining our celebration.'

He shook his head as he stared at her. 'My... Gwen...'

'... was so much more than a humble wife and journalist. She was my finest Escort, Mr. Venter. You saw her files, yes? Over the years, she has saved hundreds of lives from the most wicked and devious of people. Vile and immoral individuals, deserving subjects of the highest retribution. I miss her dearly.'

'She died because of all this.' Eddie spat. 'If she wasn't a part of this, she'd still be with me.'

'No. If Gwen wasn't my Escort, you wouldn't have met at all.'

Eddie narrowed his eyes. 'What do you mean?'

# THE ESCORT TO THE GRAVE

'Look around you, Mr. Venter. This room is half filled with my Escorts from all over Europe. They are all here to celebrate and welcome the new member to the family. The other half are their Wardens, tasked with the responsibility of protecting them until they come of age, and to help them find those worthy for me to take.' She took a sip of her drink, staining the glass with her red lipstick. 'Gwen was my Escort, Mr. Venter. And although her own Warden left her before you even met, it was not a coincidence you were drawn to her.'

'What are you saying?' Eddie asked.

'You only met Gwen because she was my Escort, and you are a Warden.'

'That's not true,' Eddie said, shaking his head. 'She was my everything.'

'And you hers, Mr. Venter.' Mara replied. 'This is why she decided not to tell you who she really was. Her love for you was so great she feared it would be compromised when you found the truth. It was her first mistake. I tried to show her that together, you could become my most powerful pair, but she was adamant. Your relationship was to remain as she wanted, innocent and pure and unbreakable. She loved you so much she decided to keep her secret from you, to protect you.'

The room was silent again, all ears and eyes on their conversation.

'Gwenno died making her second mistake. She placed trust in evil, giving her life for a soul not deserving such kindness. Her moment of weakness broke all of our hearts, just as it did yours. In the aftermath, a new Escort was born. Unfortunately, Gwen's work in bringing the murderers to justice had to wait until Ellie came of age to escort them to the grave herself. As is the way, no-one could interfere, not even me, or some of the evil souls responsible would have escaped their fate. It was Gwen's third mistake. Unfortunately, scores of children were lost, but now, because of Ellie and yourself, thousands more will be saved.'

Through the frosted glass of the foyer porch there was movement, as the figures of new arrivals blocked out the light. Several children in the room squealed their delight, only for some elders to shush them back to silence. Everyone poised ready. The door swung open, and the crowd erupted in cheer.

Sarah Morrison walked in with her two daughters, Jenny and Ellie, all three wide eyed and beaming with surprised elation. The room exploded with life, people rising to their feet as they applauded them with glee. Ellie's hands went to her face as she jumped up and down from the excitement. She wore a cute layered dress under her winter coat that flared out at the bottom and little red heeled Wizard of Oz shoes glistening in the candlelight. Her mother and sister, equally made up in their own fancy party outfits, hugged with joy, then pulled Ellie into a joining embrace as the nearest guests welcomed them with hugs and claps of their own. The three of them worked their way through the throng of red cloaks, the older two taking handshakes and cheek kisses and Ellie getting high fives and head rubs as they went. A young party-goer pulled her into a cuddle and Ellie rubbed the girl's own red cloak between her fingers, awe and excitement etched over her face as she spoke to her.

Eddie watched it all from his seat, a flat smile on his face the sadness in his eyes deceived. She was just seven years old, and she had been through so much already. The things she had seen and done. What lay ahead for her? He couldn't help but think her childhood was being stolen. The thought filled his eyes with more tears until the mass of cloaks blurred into one. He tried blinking them away, attempting to clear his vision. Eventually, the definition of the shapes ahead of him returned, details refining into figures.

# THE ESCORT TO THE GRAVE

Then the bodies of two standing guests parted, and he saw her, his Gwenno, in all her beauty. Her eyes found his, and she gave him the warmest of smiles as she raised her glass in toast, her lips puckering as she blew a kiss across her open palm toward him. Closing his eyes, he let the moment take him, knowing it wasn't real, but welcoming it all the same. The grief would never leave him. He didn't want it to, because if it ever did, then she would leave him too.

A hand dropped onto his wrist. Eddie looked down to it, then across to Mara. Looking back to where his wife had been, she was no longer there. The blonde woman in the polka dress sat in her place, staring back. Ellie made her way to join her and sit on her lap, her arms wrapping around the woman's neck. The woman beamed a magnificent smile, matching the one the young girl wore, then began tickling and hugging and laughing with her. Dabbing her finger on Ellie's nose, she pointed toward Eddie. Her eyes lit up as they followed the woman's finger toward him.

'Who is she?' Eddie asked.

'She is the creator,' Mara said, looking back over her shoulder. 'The reason I am, and the reason we are all here. She is Mother.'

Eddie rubbed at his face. 'I don't think I can do this,' he said. He stood from his chair, scraping the legs back on the flagstones. 'I need to get out of here.'

Hands grabbed around his legs and a head buried its way into his belly, knocking him back a step. He let out an 'oof' as he looked down to the young girl that had darted from the other side of the room. 'Hello Ellie,' he said, giving her hair a playful, messy shake. She didn't seem to mind it at all. 'You came, Mr. Eddie, you came,' she replied, giving another squeeze.

'You're all she's talked about on the way here.' Sarah Morrison stepped toward them. 'Will he come Mammy? Will he be there?'

'I knew you would, Mr. Eddie,' Ellie said. 'I just knew it.'

'It's good to see you,' Eddie said to Sarah. 'You look really... happy.'

Sarah looked down at her daughter, then back to Eddie. 'I'm glad you're here, too. I wanted to thank you for everything you've done, for my children, and for me.' Crossing the last couple of steps, she wrapped her arms around him in a warm embrace. Eddie's eyes filled again, and as they parted, Ellie jumped up onto Mara's lap.

Eddie and Sarah walked to the bar. 'No Mr. Morrison tonight?' he whispered.

A confident smile rose on Sarah's face. 'A lot has happened since we last spoke. Any hope of him seeing the error of his ways will disappear with his bruises, but there was one thing he didn't count on, the solidarity of a mother and her daughters.' She looked to Ellie sat on Mara's lap, then to Jenny chatting away like a celebrity in the crowd. Sarah dropped her soft hand, locking her fingers between his. 'You gave me the strength to fight back, Eddie. My husband has manipulated us for the last time. You should have seen his face when I told him I'll be filing for divorce. He tried to laugh it off, threatening to destroy me and take the kids, but I called his bluff, and in the end, he's nothing more than a bullying politician. I stood up to him, gave him an ultimatum. He signs the papers, or I go to the press and tell them everything he's done to our family. He knew it would ruin his reputation, true or not, and if what he says about a cabinet reshuffle coming up is true, then he can't risk losing out.'

'So he's gone?' Eddie asked.

# THE ESCORT TO THE GRAVE

'Staying at his flat in the capital,' she replied. 'I agreed to keep the news private until he finds out if he's got a fancy new job, then we won't see him for dust.'

The barman thrust a tray filled with champagne flutes toward Sarah. She took two off, giving her thanks, and gave one to Eddie.

'Won't he fight for custody of the girls? Once his job is safe.'

Sarah chuckled. 'No chance. The girls hate his guts as much as I do for what he's done. All he's ever worried about is his job, so he won't ruffle any more feathers when he's got it. He'll crawl off and pretend he wants to see them once a week.'

'So what happens now? What will you do?'

Sarah looked to her daughter hugging with Mara. 'I have a feeling things are going to get very busy from now on,' she said.

Eddie looked back to the table. From Mara's lap, Ellie gave him a huge, toothy grin. 'She's just a kid, Sarah. Don't you think she deserves to be just that?'

'She'll still do all the things other kids do, Eddie. She'll start back at school next week and get to see all her friends. She'll go to the park and feed the ducks. She'll help me bake cookies and have horse riding lessons and go to sleepovers...'

'... and draw images of death in her spare time,' Eddie spat.

Sarah sighed. 'Do you remember I told you about when I first received the box, Eddie? The note that came with it, from my late mother? Well, in her last days, when the doctors had told me there would be so much pain and suffering and they would do all they could, there was only peace and comfort and acceptance. They couldn't understand it at all. Even knowing it was the end, my mother seemed so happy. She drifted off to sleep and died peacefully, and while I've mourned her and missed her ever since, I take so much comfort in knowing the truth.'

Eddie shook his head. 'What truth?'

'It was Mara, helping my mother in her last days. She took away the pain so my mother could enjoy those last moments. She told her stories of how she would be a grandmother again and gave her the chance to send a last message to her unborn grandchild. I can see my mother's face now, bursting with pride and aching with love for a baby she was yet to meet. Mara explained everything to her, helped her write her last letter and blessed my little girl with her gift.'

Eddie pulled his hands away. His mind whirred away as a realisation dawned. Sensing his distress, Mara lifted Ellie from her lap and joined him at the bar.

'You knew all along,' Eddie said. 'You prepared Ellie's gift months before she was born. You would only do that if you knew she was taking over as your new Escort. You knew my Gwenno would die.'

Mara nodded toward the barman, who arrived with his tray. She took a glass of champagne. 'I did everything I could to stop her, Mr. Venter. But as I told you before, a mind knows where its fate lies. Gwen chose her path, just as you choose yours.'

Eddie turned to Sarah. 'Don't you get it? The plans she has for your daughter? What she wants her to do?'

'It's ok Eddie,' Sarah said, attempting to take his hand again. 'She chose Ellie for something truly remarkable, a chance to make a difference in the world. And you too.'

Eddie looked to Mara as her lips twisted into a wry smirk. 'Tonight, Ellie will receive her cloak and become one of us, Mr. Venter.' She opened an arm toward the mass of party-goers, all staring back in silence. 'But Ellie has already been confirmed at the Holy Mountain. She is not the guest of honour for tonight's ceremony.'

# THE ESCORT TO THE GRAVE

Eddie frowned as he looked to the young girl smiling back at him. 'What are you saying?'

'You are, Mr. Venter.'

'No,' Eddie replied, shaking his head. He squeezed his eyes shut in defiance. 'I won't.'

'You will guide her on her journey until she is ready to work alone. You will help find them, the mongrels worthy for me to take, and take them I will.' She grabbed Eddie's face with one hand, her nails digging into his cheeks, just like his dream. 'She is the most important of my Escorts, Mr. Venter. When she is of age, she will take on the most important role of all. Until then, she will need your help, and together, you will do wondrous things.'

Eddie pulled away, taking a pained scratch across his face for his troubles. 'I need to go.' He made for the door, swinging it wide as he ran through and out into the bitter night. His heavy breaths turned to clouds above his head as he steadied himself on one of the picnic benches out front. It was too much, what she asked. All this time, he had felt responsible for his wife's death, not knowing the truth. Gwen had kept it from him. If he had known everything, her true purpose, would things have been different? Could he have saved her? Would she still be alive? No. And he couldn't stand by while an innocent, seven-year-old girl took up her mantle. Would her fate be the same?

'Thank you for my birthday card, Mr. Eddie,' a soft voice from the doorway said. Ellie held it between her fingers, clutched close to her chest, the large number seven surrounded by Disney figures twinkled under the signage lights. 'It's my favourite.' She opened it up and read the inscription.

*To my little chum Ellie, I wish you all the joy and happiness in the world, everything you deserve and more. I hope all your dreams and wishes come true, and wherever I am, whenever you need me, I will be with you. Always.*

*Your good friend.*

*Eddie.*

'Did you mean it?' Ellie said. 'The last bit? Whenever I need you?'

Eddie froze, unable to form the words he wanted to say. Ellie walked closer until she was right under him. 'It's not just me who needs you now,' she said. 'My mammy will need you too. There will be a lot of people at our house tomorrow. Lots of police people she doesn't know. The camera people will be outside our gates again and will ask her a lot of questions and she will need you to help her after they have gone.'

'What do you mean, Ellie? What people? Why will they be at your house?'

Ellie opened her coat, stuffing the birthday card into the inside left pocket. Then she opened the other side, pulling a familiar roll of paper out, the red wax seal holding it closed. She looked up at Eddie, handing it into his open palms.

'I'm so excited to get my cloak, Mr. Eddie. They really are quite beautiful, don't you think?' She turned on her heels, skipping back to the door, giving a last glance over her shoulder before disappearing back inside.

His hands shook as he held the scroll, struggling against the non-existent weight of the paper. With a deep breath, he ran a finger across the seam, cracking the wax to release the roll. He pulled his hands apart, revealing Ellie's latest image.

The likeness was perfect, just like all the others. The body contorted and face twisted in death. At the bottom corner, the date read *6th September 2019.*

Tonight.

Another cloud of cold air rose above his head as he exhaled a tired sigh. Relaxing his hands, the scroll closed in on itself, hiding the image once more. He folded it up tight, stuffing it into his own jacket pocket as he looked down at the dark, empty road.

# THE ESCORT TO THE GRAVE

Then he turned and walked back in through the entrance door.

## THE END

## Note from the Author

The idea for this story has picked at my mind for many years. It was only during the lockdown at the start of 2021 did I decide to get it down onto paper. I've had an odd curiosity about death for a long time and always loved the fiction trope that tells it as a conscious human being, so decided to create my version involving it. While this story is an obvious work of fiction, there are elements from my research I found fascinating and well worth including, even if only loosely based. Age old Celtic myths such as the Four Branches of the Mabinogi, tell stories of Arawn, the king of the Otherworld or Annwn. He had his dogs, white wolfhounds with red ears, and he was often depicted with a head of a Monarch stag, complete with huge, twelve pointed antlers.

Later interpretations saw the king of Annwn attributed to Gwyn ap Nudd. He appears prominently in the medieval poem *The Dialogue of Gwyn ap Nudd and Gwyddno Garanhir,* found in the Black Book of Carmarthen, and tells of his role as a psychopomp, a mysterious figure who gathers the souls of fallen British warriors. The poem ends with Gwyn's proclamation found at the start of this story, and inevitably gave the title for the book. In later tradition, he is told as the leader of the Wild Hunt, in which he leads a pack of supernatural hounds known as the Cwm Annwn to harvest human souls.

Researching for this story, I came across a number of other interesting tales from other nations. The Irish myth of the Morrigan, in particular, I found intriguing. Mainly associated with war and fate, especially with foretelling doom, death or victory in battle, the Morrigan is often described as a trio of sisters called 'The three Morrigna.'

There are many other references in the story to age-old traditions in Celtic folklore. If you have an interest in that sort of thing, I encourage you to delve a little deeper, find them in the story and look them up. Some have history, such as the Triquetra symbol and the bronze age cairns, some I have simply fabricated myself, such as the Grove Druids. One thing that has stayed with me, is that through the ages, every myth or tale gets interpreted differently, and this is simply my way of playing with it. Some people take them literally, and I have seen arguments on social media surrounding the roles of psychopomps and deities as sacred, valued and cherished. While I see the honour in that, I also see it as important that myths evolve so they continue to be told to future generations and not lost to the realms of history and lost forever.

One last thing I'd like to touch on, is the continuous reference to alcoholism and suicidal depictions in the story. I appreciate these are tough subjects to include, and understand they can provoke serious emotional issues. I promise I haven't taken the decision to include them lightly. If you have any need to reach out and speak to someone, please do. Even Eddie seeks help from his psychiatrist, Wendy. You can too.

If you enjoyed my story, then I would really appreciate a review on Amazon. This is the first thing I have ever written, and while I'm under no illusion it's anything close to perfect, I've found a passion that I only want to get better at. Your review will help me in my pursuit to improve and continue creating stories worthy of reading. You can also contact me through email or Facebook (contact details at the back), as I'd love to hear your opinions on the moral dilemmas in the book. I'm currently working on book two in the series, and a free prequel novella surrounding Eddie's wife Gwenno, The Diary of Death, you can get from my newsletter. Details are in the contact information section.

# Acknowledgements

It's taken over a year for me to get this story to a place where I believe it is fit for retelling. I have done it for the most part, keeping it to myself. No-one wants to continuously hear about you trying to write a novel, so I kept it quiet. There were some friends who I did happen to pester though.

To Leighton Ross John Hadley and Gareth 'Algie' Jones, thanks for putting up with the questions surrounding police procedures. I'm sure there's plenty in the story you could pick holes in, but as it's a work of fiction, I'll 'cop out' and use that as an excuse for any notable mistakes.

To Stephen 'Stretch' Lewis, thanks for giving me the idea surrounding the Grove Druids, and advice on some of the mythical tales. You have knowledge of some creepy stuff, you weirdo.

To my Beta readers, Clare and Natalie. Thank you for your time and honesty.

To my mother, Catherine, who raised us to work hard in whatever we chose to do.

Finally, to the three people I really couldn't have done this without.

My son, Nathan. The best piece of advice I ever received was when you told me 'it's never too late to do what you love in life, so keep going, Dad.'

My daughter, Gracie. Nothing made me smile wider, than working on this story only for you to sit beside me and start writing one yourself.

And my wife, Clare. For allowing me to spend so much time putting this into words. So many times I felt like giving up, only for you to sort me out and get me back on track.

Maybe one day I'll be able to repay you and put some truth to that nickname, Job-share-Clare.

## Contact Information

Email: gtwalkerbooks@hotmail.com

Facebook: www.facebook.com/gtwalkerbooks/

Instagram: gtwalkerbooks

Newsletter:

https://dashboard.mailerlite.com/forms/26131/52738049431308202/share

Printed in Great Britain
by Amazon